BOOK FOUR IN THE JADED HOLLOW SERIES

PERFECTLY TRAGIC

ALEX

USA TODAY BESTSELLING AUTHOR

GRAYSON

Perfectly Tragic

Jaded Hollow #4

Cover Design by T.E. Black Designs. Editing by Hot Tree Editing.

I dedication this book, the final of the Jaded Series, to all the wonderful readers out there who have taken a chance on me and read my books. It is you all that make this possible for me. Thank you.

one

Nick

"NICK." I HEAR THE soft broken whisper and whip my head around.

The once beautiful eyes I see staring back at me are now dull and almost lifeless. The stark pain radiating from them sends a sharp pain to my chest.

"I'm here, baby," I whisper, my voice no longer sounding like my own.

A whimper leaves Anna's lips when she tries to move. I have to force my body to relax at the sound, when all it wants to do is lock up and seize. I look down at Anna's broken body, covered in a dirty piece of cloth I found on the floor of the house, and every part of me aches with her. Every mark on her body, I feel on mine.

"No, Anna, stay still," I tell her, and take a deep breath before continuing. "The ambulance is on their way, okay?"

She ignores my plea to stay still and lifts an arm that's covered in marks. A flash of rage runs through my blood at the sight, but I push it away. My focus needs to be on her right now, not the fuckers that did this to her.

My gut clenches and my stomach plummets when she winces in pain and drops her arm. I gently grab her wrist and bring her hand to my lips, kissing the back, before placing her hand on my cheek. Her hand is ice cold and fear almost cripples me.

She closes her eyes and takes a few shallow breaths before opening them again.

"I love you, Nick." Her voice is barely audible.

As much as I love hearing her say those words, they scare me. They're too final. I know the broken woman lying in front of me is dying. I know that her condition is dire. But I refuse to think of any other outcome other than her surviving. This is my Anna. She can't leave me.

I bend over and lay a soft kiss on her forehead. "I love you too, Anna Banana," I whisper.

My lips are still at her forehead when I hear her weak voice say, "Be happy for me."

I close my eyes, and pull in air that no longer feels life sustaining. All it does now is remind me that I'm whole and safe, while the woman I love with my entire heart lies broken and bleeding in my arms.

Anger at the injustice of it all has me pulling back and growling, "Don't do this, Anna! Don't you dare die on me! You hang on goddamn it. You can't die on me!"

My voice cracks and rises with every word I say. By the time I'm done, I'm panting. This isn't the way it's supposed to be! She's not supposed to leave me! We're a fucking team!

"It's... too late... for me, Nick. I need... you to promise... you'll be... happy. Promise... me. Please."

My heart cracks wide open at her words. She doesn't realize it, but pieces of my heart lie right beside her, a ruined and bloody mess. She's asking the impossible. There's no way I could ever be happy if she's not with me. She can't expect that of me.

"No!" I tell her angrily, and bring her body closer to mine. "I can't promise that! I can't be happy without you. You're my happy. Please, Anna, just hang on a little bit longer."

"Promise me, Nick," Anna says, her voice weaker than it was before.

"Fuck!" I snarl to the sky.

How can she think that I could ever be happy again? I've loved this woman from the time I was old enough to know what love was. We've made plans together. We were supposed to grow old together. Without her, my life is useless.

As I glance back down Anna, I know I have to give her what she wants, at least in words. Her eyes are begging me. I've never been able to say no to her.

Gathering up every bit of courage I have, and praying to God that he and Anna forgive me, I utter the lie. "I promise."

The smile that graces her face almost has her looking like my Anna again. My heart pounds in my chest, and I freeze when she slumps in my arms, her eyes closing with the smile still on her lips.

Ah, fuck no!

"Anna?" No response. "No, no, no! Jesus Christ! Please, Anna, baby, answer me!"

She still doesn't respond. The breath I'm holding whooshes out, and my lungs won't allow me to bring in more air. A piercing pain shoots daggers in my chest where my heart used to beat. It just feels hollow now.

I can't believe she left me. The reality of it hits me, but I still don't want to accept it.

I gather her in my arms and bring her body up mine. Her limbs hang like dead weights and her head rolls to the side. I bury my face in her hair and breathe in her unique scent. Even through the filthy smell of the bastard, I still smell my Anna.

I gently rock her back and forth, waiting and praying she comes back to me. I know in my head it's in vain, but the place where my heart is supposed to be won't believe it.

"Please come back to me," I murmur in her ear, my tears soaking her hair. "I can't do this without you, Anna. Please, baby." I continue begging her, but she stays quiet in my arms...

I JERK AWAKE AND snap up in bed. My chest heaves up and down from the hard work of trying to pull air into my lungs. My heart's pounding so hard I can hear the *thump-thump* in my ears. Breathing in through my mouth and out through my nose, I try to settle my churning stomach. I release the death grip on the sheets, lean back on my hands, and let my head fall back on my shoulders.

That damn dream is going to be the death of me. I squeeze my eyes closed, trying to push back the images. It doesn't work. They slip through the cracks and crevices I never manage to seal shut when I sleep.

"Fuck!" I snarl to the ceiling.

Frustrated, I yank the damp sheet off my lap, swing my legs over the side of the bed, and plant my feet on the floor. I lean forward and drop my head in my hands, squeezing my hair so tight I feel the strands biting into my knuckles and hear the pop of them coming loose of their follicles. My body is covered in sweat and the cool air in the room sends goose bumps across my skin.

No matter what I do, I can't escape the visions. I've relived Anna's death hundreds of times and each time it feels like the first. I wake up smelling her scent, and I swear I still feel her limp body in my arms. Memories of her still body play out in my head over and over again, bringing the crippling pain of losing her to the forefront.

I lift my head and look around the barren hotel room I'm in. Overall, it's a shitty room with its germ-infested linens, outdated tube TV, stained carpet, and shower and toilet that barely function. I can afford better accommodations, but with what I plan to do in these rooms each time I rent one, this type seems like it fits more.

I look to my right and see the single bullet and 9mm pistol lying on the nightstand. Picking up the gun first, I release the clip and let it slide into my hand. The metal is cool and smooth. I reach over without looking and pick up the silver bullet with a gold tip. I flip it around a few times before I push the bullet in the clip with my thumb. The clip slides smoothly into the gun next with a click.

Memories of Anna sitting on the tire swing I have in my backyard flash through my mind. She always loved that tire swing. She used to say that when we got married our kids would play on the same swing. At the time I could picture Anna pushing a little girl with sandy-blonde pigtails.

Another memory surfaces of Anna and me playing house in the fort we built in her backyard. I built the unsteady frame out of leftover two-by-fours from my house and sheets, and she decorated the inside with unused items her mom let her have. We even had hand-drawn family pictures hanging from the walls. Most boys my age at the time were out playing sports and riding their bikes, and sometimes I was, but I always made time for my Anna.

From the time I reached twelve years old, I knew I was going to love Anna. She was my everything. She was the air I breathed, the reason my heart beat, and everything I saw. She was the first thing I thought of when I woke up and the last thing I saw before I fell asleep. She was my sunshine, my moonlight, and my stars. There was absolutely nothing I wouldn't do for her and nothing I wouldn't give her. She had my heart so tightly wrapped around her that I'm surprised it didn't suffocate her. Anna was my reason for living, and with her gone, I no longer have anything to live for.

Looking down at the gun in my hand, regret and guilt churn in my stomach. I flat-out lied when I made that promise to Anna two years ago. I promised her I'd be happy, knowing that I never would be again. But I had to give her what she needed. Knowing deep down she was saying good-bye and that was the last time I was going to see her beautiful face, I said the only thing that would give her peace.

It's been over two years since my heart turned cold and stopped working properly. Two years since I've seen Anna or held her in my arms. Two fucking years since I've looked into her bright blue eyes. Two years, and it still feels like yesterday. Some people say I should move on and let my grief go. But it's not just the grief I hold on to. It's the guilt of lying to Anna and not keeping my promise. The regret for not being there when she needed me. The rage for not killing the bastards who took her away from me.

Yes, I still grieve for her with my whole being and have not let go of her, but she hasn't let go of me either. It's like there's still a connection between us that can't be severed.

I grip the cool black metal in my hand tightly and bring it closer to my face. I flipped off the safety so the little red dot is visible. Red means fire. With shaky hands, I bring the barrel of the gun up under my chin. My finger slides across the trigger and rests there.

Of their own accord, my eyes flicker over to the picture I have on the nightstand. It's of me and Anna. I have my arm wrapped around her neck. Her head is tilted up, while mine is bent toward her; our foreheads are resting against each others'. I had just pulled away from kissing her.

I squeeze my eyes shut and try to block out the picture, but it's no use.

I take a deep breath and apply light pressure to the trigger. I know at this point asking for forgiveness is useless, but I still send up a silent prayer, asking Anna to forgive this one last sin.

Gathering my courage, I squeeze the trigger the rest of the way...

Click.

All I hear is a fucking click.

I pull the gun away from my chin and look down at it. I didn't chamber the damn bullet.

A big rush of air leaves my lungs, and I glare down at the gun. Knowing that I won't have the courage again tonight, I put the gun back down on the nightstand and pick up the bottle of Jack instead. Uncapping it, I take a big swallow and relish the burn it leaves in my throat.

Anger and disappointment rush through me. With a roar, I rear back and throw the half-empty bottle at the wall. It connects with a loud crash and the amber liquid goes everywhere.

I'm angry because I couldn't follow through. My beautiful Anna is dead, and I'm left here. I was the one that was supposed to protect her. I should be the one in a cold grave. Not her. I'm the one who failed her.

I get up from the bed, ignoring the mess across the room, and walk the short distance to the bathroom. Once I'm in front of the mirror, I grip the edge of the vanity and look at my reflection. I look like shit. My eyes are bloodshot with shadows under them from drinking too much and lack of sleep. My face looks pale and gaunt.

My eyes travel to my naked chest and stomach, and I notice that I've lost weight. The muscles are still there, but not as bulky. My stomach is starting to sink in and my ribs are a little more pronounced.

I release my grip and turn to the shower. Once the water finally turns hot, I pull the curtain back and step inside. The hot water does nothing to settle my nerves or help the never-ending sorrow.

Knowing that I need to present myself halfway decently, I start the task of doing just that. The last thing I need is people knowing just how dark my world has become. I have to mentally prepare myself for what's to come and the pitying looks I know I'll receive.

Because tomorrow I go home.

two

Chris

I PICK UP A BOOK from the shelf that has a black-haired Adonis on the front cover. The guy is standing on the porch of an old farmhouse with his hands resting on the railing, gazing out across the yard. He's in nothing but a pair of faded jeans and a cowboy hat. His dark tan, bulging muscles, and six-pack abs send a tingle to my girly bits.

Shit. I'm pathetic.

I've never understood Bailey's obsession with reading these romance books, but after looking at the guy on the cover and my never-ending dry spell, I can totally see the appeal.

I open the book to the middle, skim over a page, and immediately see the words "yeah, baby, fuck my fingers good." I'm no prude by any means, but that makes me blush. I continue reading and the more I do, the hotter I get. I really need to find some action soon.

"Whatcha looking at?" Bailey whispers in my ear, causing me to jump and drop the book.

I'm sure my cheeks are still pink when I look at her after picking up the book. I'm just glad she didn't catch what part I was reading. Bailey and I are very close, but that doesn't mean I want to read erotica with her.

"Oh, I've read that one. It's a good one. You should get it," Bailey says, eyeing the book in my hand.

I glance down at it and see the cowboy again. "Hmm... maybe I will. The description looks good." I'm lying. I haven't even read what it's about yet. But from the tingles the guy on the front is giving me and the short paragraph I read inside, I think I've finally found something to perk up my libido. Lord knows the only other thing, or rather person, that's gotten my motor running lately wants nothing to do with me.

I wipe the thought from my mind before it takes hold and regret and sadness have a chance to swarm me.

Bailey takes a step closer and lowers her voice even more. "It's definitely something you want to read when you're alone though. There are scenes in there that're very... arousing."

I barely contain myself from laughing at the red that's creeping up Bailey's cheeks. I may be embarrassed to read such explicit material with Bailey hanging over my shoulder, but talking about sex is another thing. Bailey has always been cutely shy and blushes at the smallest mention of anything sexual.

"What do you have?" I ask Bailey.

She looks down at the book with a loving expression, her hands caressing the cover like it's the most precious thing. There's excitement in her eyes when she looks at me. "Just the final book in a series I started a while back. It came out a few days ago. Mrs. Stewart held it for me."

"So, in other words, I won't see you for the next couple of days?" I say with a laugh.

She looks at me sheepishly. "I know it sounds bad, but I'm going ask Jaxon to watch Amari for a bit today. I'm dying to know what happens with the two main characters. I've been waiting months for this."

God bless Bailey and her romance stories. But then again,

according to Bailey, it was the fictional happy endings that helped keep her sane while she was running from her crazy husband. No way could I ever fault her for that.

"You know Jaxon. He takes any and all opportunities to spend as much time with Amari has he can. But let me know if he can't take her. I'd love to spend the evening with beautiful Amari."

She reaches over and squeezes my hand. "Thank you, Chris. I know it sounds ridiculous, but besides you, these books were my only friends for a while."

I smile tenderly at her, understanding her meaning. "I know. And I get it."

After a few more minutes of browsing the shelves, we make our way to the front of the library to check out our books. Mrs. Stewart is behind the counter showing a volunteer how to check books back in. When she sees us, she smiles and walks over.

"Hello, Bailey and Chris. Did you find everything you wanted?" she asks, and grabs our small stack of books.

"We did. I wanted to thank you for holding the book for me."

The older lady smiles kindly at Bailey as she scans our library cards and then taps keys on the keyboard. "You're very welcome, sweetie. I remember how excited you were when you found out we were getting it." She leans closer to Bailey when she continues. "I started the first book a couple days ago."

"That's wonderful!" Bailey says happily. "I should be done with this one before you get through the second one. You won't have to wait like I did."

When Mrs. Stewart picks up the book that I'm checking out, she looks at me and smiles wickedly. "This is a good one too, Chris. Just make sure you read it in private. There's this one scene where they're on a horse..." She wiggles her eye brows suggestively. I catch her meaning and my eyes nearly bug out of my head. Don't get me wrong, to each their own when it comes to reading material. It's just I would have never pegged the sweet grandmotherly looking woman in front of us for reading something so naughty.

I glance at Bailey when I tell Mrs. Stewart, red staining my face again, "So I've been told."

They both share a chuckle, making me even more curious about the book I'm checking out. It also makes me impatient to get home to start it. Luckily, it's the weekend and I don't have to be at Jaxon's until this evening.

"You ready, Freddie?" I ask Bailey once Mrs. Stewart is done with us.

"Yep!"

"Wanna grab some lunch at Maggie's before you pick up Amari from Lilly's?" I suggest once we leave the library. Lilly is Jaxon's mom. She's about the only person Jaxon will let watch Amari without a fight.

She looks down at her watch before replying. "Sure. I've got about an hour before I have to be there."

We walk in silence for a few minutes, enjoying the cool breeze. I have to admit, I'm looking forward to winter. Being a southern girl, I never had much chance to see snow. This will be my second winter here. The first winter was mild and only got a few inches. I'm hoping this year will be different.

"Did you hear Karyn and Ethan's twins are a boy and girl?"

Shocked, I glance at Bailey. "Oh wow! No, I hadn't heard. That's wonderful news. I thought they were going to wait until they were born to find out what sex they are."

"I guess they couldn't wait any longer. They were both tickled pink when they came in to Maggie's yesterday morning and told me and Jaxon. They get both a boy and girl with one go."

We laugh, happy for Karyn and Ethan. They're lucky. It'll be tough on them in the beginning, especially since they are new parents, but I know they'll love it.

On the way to the diner, we're stopped a couple of times by people walking down the street. I love living here. Everyone has been so nice. It's a small community, but it's one that's close and the people are willing to help out their own, even if you didn't grow up here. A lot of small towns like this are reluctant to accept new members, not wanting to share their territory. You don't get that here. You're considered one of them as soon as you drive into town.

We're almost to the diner when Bailey's next words have me tensing. "Looks like Nick is back."

I look up and see Nick's big dark gray truck rolling down the street. A mixture of emotions floods through me, and I'm not sure which is dominant. On one hand, the thought of seeing Nick again has me excited and impatient. On the other hand, I'm nervous. There's no telling of the reception I'll get from him. The last time I saw him was the morning after the night I was almost kidnapped by Damien, my brother Jase's ex-psycho-boyfriend. Memories of that morning bring a flush of embarrassment to my skin and butterflies into my stomach. I close my eyes, trying to push the images away. The first part of that morning I loved. The second part, not so much.

When I open my eyes again, Bailey is watching me sadly. I look away from her, not wanting to see the pity on her face. I'm aware that my friends know of my feelings for Nick. Nick's also made it quite clear to everyone his feelings toward me.

Almost from the moment I met him I've felt a connection to Nick. The pain I saw in his eyes made my chest hurt. No living person should ever look that dead. I tried so hard to be a friend to him, to try to help him through his pain, but he's always pushed me away. At first, it wasn't sexual. Don't get me wrong, Nick is about as hot as hot can get, but it was the deep-seated pain that drew me to him and had me wanting to help. But no matter what I do or what I say, he never lets me in. As a matter of fact, he seems to push me further away than anyone else. I have no idea what I did to make Nick hate me. And he does. You can see it in his eyes when he looks at me. There's so much venom there that I'm surprised I haven't died from the poisonous look. I know I should just give up, but there's something about him that won't let me.

"Chris—" Bailey starts, but I cut her off.

"I'm fine, Bailey." I try to give her a smile, but it's forced, something I'm sure she sees. I've never been good at hiding my feelings. I wear them on my sleeve so everyone can see. I don't do it on purpose; I just could never hide them.

"Let's go get lunch so you can get your baby girl and I can go start my book."

After watching me for a few more seconds, she nods, grabs my hand, and we both walk to the door of the diner. Right before we walk inside, I turn and see Nick's truck stopped in the middle of the street. I would swear his head is turned in our direction, but I know it's wishful thinking. No way could I tell through the tint on his window. Not to mention, Nick has no reason to look this way. He certainly wouldn't be looking at me. He can't stand the sight of me. He's told me so with not just his actions, but his words on more than one occasion.

I turn back to face the door and dip my head, hiding the miserable look on my face, before walking inside.

FOURTY-FIVE MINUTES LATER, Bailey and I are done with lunch. Karyn, with her bump of a stomach, was on shift today. She took every opportunity to come talk with us. The excitement blasting off that woman lifted my mood. It couldn't be helped, and I'm glad for it. Thinking about Nick always dampens my mood.

Karyn went on and on about all the stuff she and Ethan are going to get this weekend for the babies. Now that they know what the twins' sexes are, it'll be easier to pick out the colors. While Karyn was helping other customers, Bailey told me she wants to plan a baby shower for her. I told her I wanted to help. Every woman should have a baby shower.

Bailey and I go our separate ways once we leave Maggie's; she to go get Amari and I over to my apartment above Jaxon's pub. I didn't take my car today because I knew we weren't going far. As I pass the front of the building, I notice Nick's truck out front. I have to force my legs to keep moving around to the back and not go in the front, where I know Nick is. As much as I want to see him, I'm scared. My battered heart can only take so much, and I'm not ready to test Nick to see his reception of me since that morning a month ago.

I pull the keys from my pocket and unlock the door that leads up to my apartment. Just as I'm about to open it, Andrew walks out carrying a bag of trash.

"Hey, girl!" Andrew says, showing off his sexy dimples.

"Hey, Andrew. How're you today?" I smile back at him.

He dumps the trash into the dumpster before replying. "Fabulous. You headed up or down?"

"Up. I'm not due for my shift for another few hours. I have a few things I need to do around the apartment and then I'm starting on a new book."

He looks at me strangely for a minute, like he's trying to decide to say something or not. I start to shift on my feet, becoming uncomfortable. Andrew normally doesn't hold his tongue. For him to do so now doesn't bode well for me. It must be something serious. I have a feeling I know what it is.

"You should come in for a visit. It's not busy inside. We could play pool. I'll even let you pretend to beat me this time," he says with a wink.

I shake my head at his suggestion, not really in the mood for his jokes. "Not right now. I have things to do upstairs."

"Nick's here," he says quietly.

"I know."

He watches me, his eyes drooping with sadness, and my heart clenches. I used to be the type that would never let anyone treat me with anything other than respect. If you couldn't show me respect, then you didn't deserve to know me. Now I'm this person that allows a man to pull me down anytime he's near, when all I want to do is help him. He's broken and I want nothing more than to fix him, even when he's a total jackass. I don't blame Nick for his actions. He's hurting. I may not have known him before Anna passed, but I've heard enough about him from others to know he would never normally treat anyone the way he treats me, especially a woman. I know the old him has still got to be in there somewhere. He's just lost and has no way of finding himself again. He needs people to stick by him, and I'm bound and determined to be one of them, no matter how nasty he is to me. However, I'm not ready to face him right now. I need to prepare myself first.

"I don't think it's a good idea for me to go in there right now," I tell Andrew, shaking my head. "I can't handle it. If he's still there later when my shift starts I'll see him then."

He nods, the look in his eyes shifting to understanding. "Okay. I get it. But please don't give up on him, Chris," he says gently.

"I won't," I tell him, and look down at my keys. Nick may not feel it, but there's a connection between him and me. Something is pulling me toward him for some reason. It's unexplainable and uncontrollable. I don't know, maybe it's my need as a counselor to help him, but it seems so much more than that. It's deep and unbending There's no way I could give up on him. To do that would be like ripping my heart out.

Andrew leans down and lightly places a kiss against my lips, before walking back inside. My brother is lucky to have found him. Andrew is one of the sweetest, most loyal and protective men I know. I've never seen Jase happier than he is when he's with Andrew.

I walk through the door and head straight to the kitchen. Dropping my keys on the counter, my next stop is the coffeemaker. Coffee is my best friend. We get along great. And I need my best friend right now.

After putting on a strong pot, I walk down the skinny hallway to the bathroom. The apartment used to be Bailey's when she first got to Jaded Hollow. She didn't stay here long before Jaxon moved her in with him. It was passed on to me when I got to town. It's tiny, but perfect for me. Not to mention the rent is almost nonexistent, which gives me the opportunity to build my savings account for when I want to buy my own place.

I walk up to the sink and turn the water to warm. It takes a few minutes for the warm water to flow up the pipes to the second story. While I wait, I look in the mirror at my tired face. Working full-time at the school as the guidance counselor and then weekends at Jaxon's is tiring, but I love it. I love helping the kids with their problems and issues. I didn't have the support kids need when I was younger. Being there for them as an adult feels good and right. And working at Jaxon's is great. I get to see my friends and socialize with them. The atmosphere there is calm and relaxed. I can be myself and have fun.

After splashing water on my face and drying it, I look at myself in the mirror. I puff out my cheeks, scrunch up my nose, and cross my eyes. Yes, I'm a little weird and have to make faces at myself anytime I see my reflection. I've done it since I was five years old.

I go back to the kitchen and make myself a cup of coffee. Taking a much-needed sip, I set the cup down and fill the sink with hot soapy water for the few dishes that are in the sink. I don't have the luxury of a dishwasher, but I'm okay with that. It's only me here, so there's hardly ever any dirty dishes.

Thirty minutes later, my kitchen and living room are now clean. The book I borrowed earlier calls my name, so I grab it out of my bag. I look at the cover again and feel the tingle return. I love my life, don't get me wrong, but it's pretty sad when you get turned on by the cover on a book.

Shrugging, I grab my refreshed cup of coffee and take a seat on the old floral couch with my date for the afternoon. I get comfy with my back against the armrest and my feet stretched out in front of me. I crack open the book and get started. I just hope this date doesn't slash my heart to shreds.

three

Nick

I SIT WITH MY ELBOWS on the bar and a beer bottle in one hand. Andrew just left to take the trash out. The bar opened an hour ago and it's early in the afternoon, so I'm the only one here right now. Give it another thirty minutes and I bet more people will start showing up. Yes, I may drink too much, but when the memories invade, my ass is finding the nearest bottle. I used to cherish the memories I have of Anna. Now all I want to do is escape them.

I hear a noise off to my left and glance over to see Jaxon walking out of the hallway. The surprise in his eyes isn't hard to see. I don't blame him. I haven't been back to town for over a month. I have spoken with him a couple of times on the phone though.

He gives me a chin lift and heads my way. After taking the stool beside me, we sit in silence.

After a few minutes, I ask him, "How are things here?"

He knows what I'm after and doesn't hesitate in giving me the answer.

"She's fine. Took a bit to get over what happened, but she's good now."

I look straight ahead, take a swallow of my beer, and think about his answer. A little over a month ago I found out that some whack job was after Chris. I had no idea what was going on until I almost got my head blown off when the guy came after her. I was drunk off my ass and Chris was helping me up the stairs to her apartment to sleep it off, when a guy came in with a gun and made a grab for her. I intercepted him, fell down the stairs in the process, and ended up with a knot the size of a baseball on my head. The next morning when I was somewhat sober, I called her brother to find out what the hell was going on. What he told me had my blood boiling.

That was also the morning I made another colossal mistake. I had just gotten off the phone with Jase and was walking down the hallway at Jaxon's house, when Chris came out in just her robe. Her hair was wet, and I smelt the sweet smell of her body soap and almost lost it. I have no idea what came over me, but before I could stop myself, I had her up against the wall and my face buried in her neck. It only lasted a few seconds, and as soon as I realized what I had done I backed up and got the hell out of Dodge.

I haven't felt any real emotions in over two years, but when Chris came out the way she did, I actually *felt* something. It scared the shit out of me.

"That's good. I'm glad she's better," I tell Jaxon.

He's quiet for a moment, before he says, "Why do you care anyway? She isn't your favorite person by the way you treat her."

I look over and scowl at him. What the fuck is he getting at? Just because she bugs the shit out of me doesn't mean I want her hurt.

"I don't. I was hurt in the process of protecting her. I have a right to know how she's doing," I lie through my teeth. I may wish the girl would leave me alone in my grief instead of always being in my face, but there's something about her that has me intrigued. I don't like it and it pisses me off.

"Yeah. Keep telling yourself that," he mutters, before continuing. "How are you doing? How's work?

Irked at his first comment, but glad for the subject change, I let it go.

"It's fine. I've got a break for a few weeks, unless something comes up. The last job was a bitch. Damn guy kept changing his mind on the design he wanted. I almost told him to forget it and cut my losses."

"You sticking around here for a while then?" he asks, eyebrows raised.

"Yeah."

"That's good. Hasn't been the same without you." He grabs my shoulder, gives it a squeeze, and stands up. Before he leaves, he turns back to me. "You should take it easy on Chris. She cares about you."

I clench my jaw in irritation. I fucking knew he wouldn't drop it.

"Jaxon, don't start. I can't take this shit right now. I've got a lot going on up here." I tap the side of my head. "Everyone needs to back off about it."

His voice is low when he says, "I know what you're saying, Nick, but all that girl wants to do is be there for you. Hell, we all do. I know the pain you're going through. She was my sister. Do you really think Anna would want to see you like this? What she went through hurt us all, not just you. I know you'll never get over it, but you can learn to cope and live again." Before I can tell him to fuck off, he continues. "Don't screw something up you'll regret later."

"What the fuck does that mean?" I snarl at him, anger making my skin hot.

"It means don't do something that's unfixable. We all grieve in our own ways, but we can't push away the people that care about us. You push too far and they're gone forever. There's no getting them back."

With that, he turns and leaves me steaming on my barstool. He has no clue what he's saying. I know he's not talking about him and the rest of the crew. I know they would never give up on me. He's talking about Chris. I don't give a shit if I push her away. I *want* her gone. If she's gone, so will be the feelings she stirs in me. Feelings I have no right to feel. Feelings I want to burn from my soul.

I sit there, hunched over my beer, and stew. I'm pissed that Jaxon feels he needs to say what he said. He has no right to interfere.

Andrew walks back behind the bar a few minutes later. His eyes flicker to me as he grabs a rag and starts wiping down the other end of the counter. They narrow the longer he watches me.

"Who stuck something up your ass?" I growl, and then roll my eyes as soon as the words leave my mouth.

Fucking idiot.

Surprisingly, Andrew doesn't come back with a smart-ass remark. His eyes blaze with anger when he grunts, "You."

"What in the hell did I do?" I ask.

He drops the rag on the bar and then taps his chin, like he's contemplating his answer. He looks back at me and says, "Hmm… I don't know. Maybe the fact that you treat Chris like shit."

"Andrew—" I start, but he talks over me.

"And maybe because you accused Jase of purposely bringing danger to her. That was a dick move, Nick. And poor Chris. All she wants to do is help. And what do you do? Call her nasty names and belittle her. What the fuck is wrong with you?"

I grit my teeth, trying to control my temper. It may make me a selfish bastard, but none of these people know the debilitating pain I go through every single fucking day. Yes, they loved Anna as well, but it's different when you lose someone who was everything to you. Your entire fucking world. Someone who meant so much to you that you know you'll never be the same again without them. My life used to be bright and beautiful. Now it's dull, dark, and gray.

I get up from my stool and turn to face him, my face going hard and my hands clenched at my sides.

"You have no fucking clue, Andrew. No idea of what I'm going through. All of you tell me to be nice to Chris," I sneer. "Chris just wants to help. Why won't you let her? Why are you being such a dick? You all act like I still have a heart left." I thump my chest with my fist and raise my voice. "It's gone! There's nothing there anymore. It died along with Anna and is buried right beside her! I don't give a shit if Chris wants to help! There's nothing anyone can do!"

I stop. My chest heaves from my outburst, adrenaline rushing through me. Andrew's eyes soften and it just pisses me off even more.

"Nick, I may not know the extent of your pain, but don't you think I feel an inkling of it? We all lost Anna. I almost lost Jase. When he was on the ground with blood surrounding him, I thought my world was ending. I couldn't breathe and the pain in my chest was—"

I don't let him finish. Laughing harshly, I pick up my beer and throw it across the room. I turn back to Andrew and roar, "He's still here! You still have him! He's not gone!" I lower my voice. "So no, there's no fucking way you could come even close to feeling what I am. What I go through every night when I close my eyes. What I wake up to when I dream. The pain that's imbedded so deep in my empty heart that it feels like it's literally killing me." I shake my head and take a deep breath. "Until you lose the one person that gives your life meaning, leave me the hell alone. Chris tries so fucking hard, you all do, to do something that's just not possible."

Before he can say another word and set off my ire again, I turn on my heel and stomp to the door. Slamming it open with my fist, I storm outside. I tip my head back, take a lungful of crisp air, and just stand there for a minute with my hands on my hips.

After calming my breathing and my racing heart, I walk over to my truck and climb inside. A thought comes to mind while I drive the short distance to my house. Maybe it's time I move. There's nothing but memories here that constantly plague me. People normally say that the good always outweighs the bad. That remembering the good times is supposed to help with the bad memories. I've tried it. That shit doesn't work. All it does is remind me of what the future could have been like. It reinforces the notion that I wasn't there for Anna when I needed to be. I failed her, and now because of that, she has no future. Neither of us do.

I toss around the idea of moving away from the place I grew up.

Could I really up and move like that? I know I've been a shitty friend lately, but I'll miss the people here, especially my friends. However, I know having me around has been hard on them because of the shit I've pulled. I know they would miss me as well, but I can't help but to think they may be better off if I leave, at least for a while. Will *I* be better off? Would it help me get over losing Anna? It's definitely something to think about, because I know damn good and well one of the times I rent one of those shitty hotel rooms, I'll end up following through.

I JERK AWAKE AND TRY TO clear my mind of visions of Anna once again dying in my arms. The dream started off sweet, with her running toward the lake on Jaxon's property, laughing. I was chasing after her. I dove underneath the surface and pulled her legs out from underneath her. We both surfaced sputtering water, laughing. I caught her in my arms and planted my lips against hers. She tasted so sweet, like cinnamon cookies. We leisurely explored each other's mouths until we were breathless.

Pulling away from her, I rested my forehead against hers and whispered for the first time, "I love you, Anna Banana."

She smiled her beautiful smile and whispered back, "I love you, too."

I was fifteen and she was fourteen. We had been dating for a year. I had known I loved her a long time before then. I had no idea why I waited so long to tell her and make her mine. I knew she loved me too. Maybe I wanted to wait until we were older and really knew what love meant. We were still young, but I knew in that moment I couldn't hold it back anymore.

She wrapped her arms around my shoulders, and I buried my face in her thick blonde hair. When I pulled back, it wasn't the young Anna I had just kissed in the lake. It was the broken Anna outside that cabin. She was bloody, bruised, and lying their dying. It felt like I was dying in that moment along with her.

That's when I woke up. Sometimes the dreams play out to the end and sometimes I can force myself to wake up before she dies.

I run my fingers through my hair and growl in frustration. These dreams are slowly killing me. I don't need to worry about me offing myself; the dreams and memories and broken promises are doing it for me. Some people may say I feel sorry for myself and I need to get over my shit, but getting over this isn't so simple. Not when every piece of yourself feels like it's being ripped from you until there's nothing left. I know I need help, but there's no way I'll talk to anyone about it. If you haven't gone through it, then there's no way you can offer help.

I get up from the bed and walk into the bathroom. After throwing some water on my face, I make my way into the kitchen. I open the cabinet above the coffeemaker and grab the bottle of whiskey. It's about half-empty. I'll need to make a run for more tomorrow. There's no way I'll get any sleep without it. The dreams are always worse when I'm at home. Just another reason I should leave. Maybe one day I'll be able to come back without having my heart ripped out of my chest the moment I stroll into town.

Forgoing a glass, my bottle and I step out onto my wraparound porch. The place is old and needs updating. Anna and I had planned on doing it together after we married. All the magazines and notebooks for our plans for the place are still down in the basement. I had planned on asking Anna to marry me on our anniversary, but she died a couple months before.

Now, I just don't care. Yes, it's my family's home, but it was supposed to be a project for both of us.

I take a seat on the wicker loveseat outside and uncap the bottle. Taking a big swallow, I lean my head back against the back of the seat and close my eyes. I see a flash of red hair and green eyes in my mind and it irritates me. Chris is invading my mind more and more lately. Ever since that day at Jaxon's. The way she smelled that morning had my cock hardening. I haven't gotten hard since the last time I was with Anna. It was like my body shut down and said fuck you. I haven't felt even a lick of desire toward another woman since I knew Anna was it for me. Seeing Chris in her bathrobe with water dripping from her fiery hair had my body reacting. I didn't like it. My body and heart only wanted Anna, and when it showed signs of life for another woman, I almost lost my shit. I don't want to feel anything for her. I don't want my body to tense or my blood to heat when looking at her.

Even if I could get over Anna's death, there's no way I would ever get involved with another woman. Life is full of surprises and unpredictable things. Taking the chance of going through that kind of pain again is not worth it. Who's to say I wouldn't be there for the next girl? Who's to say I wouldn't fail her too? I won't take that chance again.

I take another healthy swig of the bottle and look out over my property. It belonged to my parents. They both died in a car crash when I was seventeen. Luckily, the courts deemed me old enough to care for myself. I have no other family left. If I decide to move, I would have to either sell the place or pay someone to take care of it for me. I don't know if I would be able to sell it. My grandfather built it for my grandmother when they got married.

I chug the rest of the bottle and set it down on the table beside the loveseat. The temperature has dropped and my feet are cold, but I don't feel like going back inside. Sometimes when I first walk in, I swear I smell Anna's perfume. It hits me again in those moments.

I lean my head back again and close my eyes. The alcohol coursing through my body has my eyes dropping closed. Hopefully I'll be able to get some type of sleep, even if I do freeze my ass off in the process.

I WAKE THE NEXT morning with a headache from hell and my balls shriveled up so far they're almost nonexistent. My feet feel numb when I try to wiggle my toes. The sun is barely starting to rise, and I hear a rooster crowing off in the distance somewhere. I turn my neck from side to side to try and loosen the muscles. When I go to stand up, dizziness hits, and I drop back down. Groaning from the impact of my ass hitting the seat and jostling my head, I squeeze my eyes shut.

Too much fucking drink. Too bad it's the only thing that helps.

Gritting my teeth and ignoring the pounding in my head, I grab the empty bottle of whiskey, get up, and walk into the house. My stomach grumbles, making realize I haven't eaten since yesterday morning. Definitely not good when you've been drinking. I walk to the fridge and open it. Nothing edible. Of course there wouldn't be anything; I've been gone a month.

I pop a couple of pain pills for my head and make my way to the bathroom. Shower and a trip to Evelyn's Market for food and whiskey is needed.

Once I'm done, and still feeling like shit, I grab my keys and wallet and head out to my truck. The trip only takes a few minutes. As I pass by a small house, I see a realtor sign out front. I mentally remember the name and number to call them later. I haven't made up my mind, but I'd like to know my options if I decide to move and sell the property.

I snatch one of the small buggies and start loading it up with a few things. Guilt hits me when I walk up to the cooler that houses the beer. I know I'm drinking too much, but I'm at the point where I don't care. I'll do anything to help keep the dreams and memories at bay. They still slip through when I'm in a drunken haze, but not as often. I'll take any relief I can get. It's not that I want to completely forget, I just don't want it to hurt so bad.

I push the guilt aside and stick two twenty-four packs of Sam Adams in the bottom of the buggy. Then I make my way over to the liquor shelf and grab a few bottles of Jack. I have nothing pressing to do, so it doesn't matter if I decide to get hammered.

The cashier looks at me with pity when she rings me up, and I bite back a retort. These people may know what happened, but it doesn't give them the right to judge. Until they feel the pain I live with on a daily basis, they can keep their pity to themselves.

After putting the shit in the back of the truck, I make my way around to the driver side. My eye catches on Maggie's Diner across the street. I think about going in and saying hi to Maggie, but I decide against it. I hate going in there and don't do it very often. It's another place where the memories bombard me.

Another memory surfaces of me driving into town yesterday. Chris and Bailey were walking down the road. Unwillingly, my eyes were drawn to her until I had no choice but to force them back on the road. I ended up on the shoulder with my head turned toward them. I watched as Chris and Bailey made it to Maggie's. Right before they walked inside, Chris turned her head and looked straight at me. I knew she couldn't see me through the tint of the glass, but it *felt* like she was looking all the way into my soul. I hadn't seen her since that morning over a month ago, and I'll never admit it to anyone, but I missed seeing her. However, the look in her eyes had my brows drawing down into a frown. She looked unhappy. A pang hit my chest at the look. Pissed at the emotion, I turned back around and drove away.

I shake my head at the memory and climb into my truck. My phone buzzes in my pocket, and I pull it out. Mia's name is on the screen, and I think about ignoring it, but she knows I'm in town and if I don't answer it now, she'll just keep calling back or come storming to the house.

Pulling in a deep breath, I accept the call.

"Hey, Mia."

"Hey, you," comes Mia's sweet voice. It's a total contrast because the last thing Mia is, is innocent. Her short frame may fool you, but she has a big attitude and isn't afraid to use it. "I heard you were back in town. How have you been?"

"Busy, but I'll be here for a few weeks," I tell her and drape my arm over the steering wheel.

"That's good. Mac and I were wondering if you'd like to come over for dinner on Tuesday."

I roll my eyes at her attempt to see how I'm doing in person. Mia, just like everyone else, knows how precariously close to the edge I am these days. They also know how easy it is to push me over. I appreciate the worry, but I don't want it. I just want to be left alone, which makes me an asshole because they are my friends.

So I don't worry her further and have her banging on my door tonight, I give in.

"Sure. What time do you want me there?" I ask.

"Really? You'll come?" The disbelief in her voice in unmistakable.

"I said I'll come, didn't I?"

It comes off harsher than I intended, and I wait for Mia to bite my head off, but it never comes. Instead she rushes with her reply, like I may change my mind if she doesn't hurry. The thought has occurred to me. I really don't want to be around people, but I hate disappointing her. And maybe if I put on a good front, she'll back off for a while.

"Six. Is that good for you?" she says quickly.

"That's fine," I say, and blow out a breath.

"Great! We'll see you then." In a quieter tone, she says, "I've missed you, Nick."

And now I feel like shit because I know I haven't been the best of friends. These people love me and only want to see me happy again.

"Missed you, too, Mia," I tell her softly.

We hang up, and I start my truck. Checking my side mirrors, I pull out onto the street. My number-one priority when I get back home is to crack open one of the bottles that's now in the back of my truck and get shitfaced.

four

Chris

MIA, MAC, JAXON, BAILEY, and I are all sitting around Jaxon's living room. Andrew and Jase would have been here, but Ally had a checkup today to get the results from her latest tests to see if the bone marrow transplant worked. No way would Andrew miss it and none of us would want or expect him to.

We're gathered today because we're all really worried about Nick. He's been here for over a week and no one's seen or heard from him since his second day back. Everyone's tried calling him, with the exception of me. I'm sure I'm the last person he wants to hear from. He's ignoring everyone. Jaxon and Mac have been over to his house, but Nick never answers the door. The only reason we know he's still alive is because a couple of townspeople have seen his truck around a couple of times.

He was supposed to go to Mia and Mac's for dinner last week, but he never showed. He didn't call either. Mac said Mia was pissed and upset. He had to calm her down before she went over to his house to raise hell. It took some doing, but he finally got her to agree to not go over and with guns blazing.

"I don't know what to do anymore," Mia says, her face riddled with worry lines. "He's drowning in his sorrow and won't take any of the life preservers we throw him. It's like he doesn't care anymore."

"Well, we've got to do something," Jaxon says. "He can't keep on like this."

Bailey sniffles beside her husband and Jaxon wraps his arm around her shoulders, bringing her closer to his chest.

"I'm scared for him," Bailey says tearfully. "I understand grief, but what he's going through is beyond that. It's as though he's dead inside."

I grip my hands together in my lap. From the moment I first saw Nick, his eyes seemed dead to me. There was no life in them at all. Bailey had told me about what had happened to Anna, and before I was even introduced I knew the man I was looking at had to be Nick. My heart squeezed, and I wanted to rush to him and pull him in my arms. I knew then that I had to find a way to help him.

"If he's not willing to accept the help he needs then we can't force him," Mac says, sitting beside Mia on the couch.

Mia turns narrowed eyes to Mac. "Like hell we can't," she says vehemently. "I hate that he's going through this. I hate that he's still hurting so much. But if he's not willing to do anything to help himself, then we're taking the choice from him."

"Mia—"

"No, Mac. I refuse to sit by and watch it anymore. It's gone on too long. Something has to give. He's my friend. Anna was my sister. If something doesn't change soon, we'll lose him for good." She stops and looks around at us all, determination in her eyes. "I'm not willing to take that chance."

We all take in Mia's words for the truth they are. I may not know Nick as well as everyone else in this room, but even I know he's on a destructive path. People become reckless when they give up on life. One of my deepest fears, a fear I haven't voiced, is that Nick may try to do something to end the pain. I can see it in his eyes. The pain is eating his soul.

"You're right, Mia," Jaxon says gruffly, still holding Bailey. "I'll head over to his place once we're finished here. See what type of frame of mind he's in and go from there. If he doesn't answer, I'll bust his damn door down."

"I'd like to go with you," I say quietly. I shift in my seat when everyone looks at me. This is the first time I've spoken since arriving. "If it's okay, I'd like to go with you. I know he doesn't care to see me, but I want to help if I can."

Jaxon watches me for a few seconds before he says, "I think that's a good idea. He may not want to admit it, but I believe he's not as opposed to seeing you as he likes to think. You scare him, Chris. I think having you there will help."

I sit shocked at his words. How in the world could I ever scare Nick?

Jaxon registers my shock and explains. "You make him feel. He watches you when he thinks no one's looking. There's life in his eyes that hasn't been there in a long time. He doesn't like it. In his mind, he's still committed to my sister and probably feels like he's betraying her for feeling something for someone else. I've known it for a while and have been waiting for him to realize it too. But he's obviously still so deep in his grief that he *can't* see it."

Still stunned at his words, I look around the room at the others. They're all watching me expectantly. If only I could believe what Jaxon said. But it's hard when Nick constantly looks down his nose at me.

I glance down at my hands and squeeze them together. When I look back up to Jaxon, he's still watching me. Gathering my courage and hoping Nick won't flip his shit when he sees me, I ask Jaxon, "When do we leave?"

WE PULL UP TO NICK'S house an hour later. He has a large chunk of property that's covered in trees. The woodland is beautiful. With the season changing, most of the leaves' colors are changing to yellows, reds, and oranges.

I've only ever been out here once and that was at night. This is my first real glance at his home. The two-story is in need of a serious paint job and maintenance. The light blue paint is peeling and part of the porch is sagging. However, overlooking that, the house is gorgeous. It's old and has a wraparound porch. I look to the left as we pull to a stop and see a tire swing hanging from an old oak tree.

I reach for the doorknob, but Jaxon stops me before I can open it.

"When we go in, let me talk to him first. He won't be happy to see you, but he needs this, okay?"

I nod. I'm nervous about going into Nick's house. I have no doubt that Nick will be pissed that I'm there, but if what Jaxon says is true, then I'll suck it up. I'll do anything to help Nick, even swallow my pride—what's left of it.

We get out and slowly make our way to the porch. The old wood creaks as we walk up the steps. Jaxon stops abruptly when he reaches the top, and I almost run into his back.

"Son of a bitch," Jaxon mutters.

Worry wiggles its way down my spine at Jaxon's curse, and I quickly step up beside him to see what's wrong.

My hand flies to my mouth and I give a little cry at the sight of Nick slumped over in a wicker love seat with an empty bottle of whiskey perched between his legs. His neck lies at an awkward angle. His face is covered in days-old beard and his dark brown hair looks oily, like he hasn't washed it in days. His cheeks are sunken and he looks pale. He's in a pair of cut-off sweatpants, a dirty light green t-shirt, and nothing else. It's cold outside, so I know he has to be freezing. The table beside the love seat is covered in beer cans and Jack Daniel's bottles.

My heart breaks at the complete mess he's in.

Forcing the tears back, I push past Jaxon and walk to Nick. I take slow measured steps, not wanting to startle him. And if I'm honest, not wanting to bring on his ire. I don't think I could handle him pushing me away at the moment. The need to help him, especially in this instant, is too strong.

The ache in my chest intensifies the closer I get. Even in sleep he has frown lines between his eyes. His chest rises and falls and his hands twitch a little. A soft moan leaves his lips, and I'm nearly brought me to my knees at the pitiful sound.

I hear Jaxon walking up behind me, but I pay him no mind, my attention focused solely on Nick. Praying I don't alarm him, I get down on my knees in front of him. My eye catches on something shiny between him and the arm of the seat. My eyes widen as recognition dawns. Fear slithers through me at the gun lying there.

"Jaxon," I say, my voice wobbly.

When he steps beside me, I point down at the gun. Jaxon curses again and gently pulls it out from beside Nick. He fiddles with it for a moment and then the clip slides out.

"I'll be back," he says in a grave voice.

He walks away, and I turn back to Nick. His brows are still pulled down into a frown and there're shadows underneath his eyes. The scruff on his face is darker than his hair. When I first met Nick, his hair was cut short, but I don't think he's cut it in months. It goes past his shirt neck, but wouldn't be considered long.

"Nick," I say softly, trying to gently coax him awake.

He doesn't respond.

I lay my hand on his knee, give it a little shake, and call his name again.

Again nothing. If it wasn't for his chest moving, I would be really worried.

Jaxon comes back up on the porch, and I turn to see him looking at Nick with a concerned expression.

"I tried waking him, but he's not responding. Do you think he's okay?" I ask, frightened he may have gone too far this time.

"Yeah. He's just drunk off his ass. He'll be hurting tomorrow. The dumb fucker hasn't showered in days. I'm thinking now is a good time for him to have one."

I get up as Jaxon steps up to Nick. Grabbing his arm, he pulls him forward and leans down so his shoulder is in Nick's gut. With a grunt, Jaxon stands with him over his shoulder. Nick moans, but doesn't open his eyes. I rush to open the door.

"Fuck, this bastard is heavy," Jaxon grumbles.

"Do you think it's smart to put him in the shower like this?" I ask Jaxon, following him and Nick down a hallway.

"Don't know, but we're doing it. It'll help sober him up some. The bastard needs a wake-up call, so he's getting it."

I nod. I just hope it helps and he doesn't kick us out immediately.

I move around Jaxon when he stops at a door, and I open it. I flick on the light and brightness fills the room. It's painted in a bright yellow and is very spacious. On one side is a big tub with attached shower, and a toilet. Across from it is a long counter with a sink and a tall cabinet.

Other than a few twitches, Nick still hasn't moved and it's starting to scare the shit out of me. How can someone get so drunk that they have no idea they are being moved around so much?

We stop beside the tub, and I wait for instructions from Jaxon.

"Make sure his head doesn't hit the tub," he grunts.

"Okay."

I do as he says as Jaxon steps in the tub and starts lowering Nick. I grab the back of his head and place it gently on the wall of the shower. Jaxon steps out, and I walk around to stand beside him. We both look down at the still passed-out Nick.

Seeing Nick lying in the tub has my gut clenching. I hate seeing him this broken. What must it be like to love someone so much that you would rather let yourself go than live without them?

"You ready? It's not going to be pretty," Jaxon warns.

Taking a deep breath for courage because I know it's going to be bad, I nod.

Jaxon grabs the handheld showerhead, points it at Nick, and twists both knobs.

It only takes a few seconds for Nick to spring up in the shower with a shouted "What the hell?" He sputters out water and wipes at his face, but it does no good because Jaxon is still spraying him. Trying to get away from the water, Nick huddles in the corner. I step slightly behind Jaxon, to get away from the water that Nick is slinging across the room.

"Fuck!" Nick slurs loudly. "Stop that shit!"

"You awake yet, fucker?" Jaxon retorts.

"Goddamn it, Jaxon, turn the fucking water off," Nick growls.

I stay huddled behind Jaxon, not yet ready to show Nick I'm here. So what, if that makes me a coward. I do peek over his shoulder though. Nick has his head laid back against the wall while Jaxon sprays his chest, water splashing up on his face. His shirt is soaked, and I see his dark ink through the thin fabric on his muscular arms and chest. His gray shorts are soaked through as well, showing off thick thighs. There's a little more color in his cheeks, and I sag in relief.

Jaxon reaches over and turns the knobs until the water shuts off. Nick still has his head back but now his eyes are shut. His chest heaves up and down. Water drips from his hair and beard.

"What the fuck was that for?" Nick asks Jaxon angrily, without opening his eyes.

"I'm done. We're all done. You won't take care of yourself, then we'll do it for you. I get you're hurting. Believe me, I get it, but that doesn't mean you get to give up. Anna would be so ashamed of you right now, Nick. It would break her fucking heart seeing you like this."

Nick cracks his eyes open and glares at Jaxon. "Yeah, well, she's not here, is she? She's not here to see me like this, so I think your point is moot. Fuck off."

"Moot or not, I don't give a fuck. Now get your ass up and put dry clothes on. We'll see you in the living room. Let's go, Chris."

At the mention of my name, Nick lifts his head from the wall. I watch as he slowly brings his eyes over Jaxon's shoulder and meets mine. Something unfamiliar flashes in his eyes before they turn hard.

He opens his mouth, I'm sure to say something cruel, but Jaxon steps in front of me, blocking Nick's view.

"Keep your fucking mouth shut."

Jaxon turns, puts his hands on my shoulders, and ushers me out of the bathroom, but not before I look over and see Nick watching me.

I hear a loud crash come from the bathroom and Nick's muttered curses as we make our way to the living room. It takes everything in me to continue walking. Jaxon must sense my hesitance, because he grabs my elbow. "Leave him. He'll be okay."

I give one last glance at the door, turn, and walk into the living room. Jaxon continues and walks through a doorway across the room.

Before following him, I look around the messy living room. There're even more beer bottles in here and a few microwavable plastic containers with small portions of food still in them on the coffee table. At least he's been eating something. There's a stack of papers, some folders, and a laptop on one of the end tables. Some of the papers have fallen to the floor, and I reach down to pick them up and put them back. Over by the sliding glass door there's a pile of wrinkled clothes.

The dark brown leather couch looks old and worn, but comfortable. Across from it, there's a big-screen TV hanging on the wall. It's got to be the newest thing in the living room. The walls are painted off-white and the floors are hardwood. They are scuffed and look original to the house. With a little bit of cleaning and updating, the place could be gorgeous.

When I walk into the kitchen a few minutes later, Jaxon is making coffee. The kitchen is in no better shape than the living room. The appliances are a bit outdated and the countertops are old. The wood cabinets look worn and dull. The sink is full of dirty dishes and the trash is overflowing. There's a multitude of items all over the counters. This is definitely a place where the occupant doesn't care how messy it gets.

"You want a cup?" Jaxon asks. He's holding up his cup of coffee in question.

"Yes, please. Two sugars and a splash of milk," I tell him.

He turns back and sets to making me a cup. With his back turned to me, he says, "Nick and Anna were planning to redecorate. She passed before they got the chance."

"It's a nice place," I say, and take a seat at the bar. The stool wobbles when I plant my ass on it, so I sit real still. "Do you know why he still hasn't done anything with it?"

Jaxon sets my coffee down in front of me and leans back against the counter opposite me. He shrugs while taking a sip. I pick mine up and breathe in the amazing aroma.

"Not sure, but I'm sure he feels it was supposed to be a project for him and Anna to do together and he's scared of doing it without her. It solidifies the fact even more that she's gone and not coming back."

I nod, understanding his meaning. Losing someone precious is hard enough on its own. When you add in all the reminders from places and things that were important to the both of you, it just magnifies the pain. Continuing on with plans of the house they made together would be a slap in the face.

"I know I've said it before, but I'm sorry for what happened to your sister," I tell Jaxon quietly.

He smiles sadly at me. "I am, too."

He turns, opens the fridge, and starts shoving stuff around inside. He takes a few things out and puts them on the counter. With his back to me, I ask him a question I'm not sure I want the answer to. It's a question that scares me.

"Do you think he would have done it?"

At my question, he straightens and gently closes the fridge door. I don't need to clarify what I'm asking. He knows.

The pain in his eyes slithers through me when he turns around. Without him saying anything, I already have my answer and it nearly breaks me.

"I don't know," he says, but the truth is in his eyes. He's scared of the answer as well. "Grief does a lot of things to people. It makes them do irrational and stupid things. I want to say no, but Nick's never had a gun before. Anna hated them, so he never owned one because of that. For him to have one now, in the state he's in..." He stops, but he doesn't need to finish anyway.

It's true. Grief takes many forms. Sometimes it's so overwhelming that it makes a person think the only way out of the grief is to end it. Tears prick the back of my eyes and a sharp pain shoots through my chest at the thought of Nick hurting himself. I don't know him that well, but I already care for him.

"What did you do with it?" I ask, not really caring as long as it's gone.

"In my truck," he replies. "I'm going to go call Bailey and let her know I'll be here for a while. I want to make sure Nick's in the right state of mind before we leave. I also need to let Mia know I'll need her to open the bar. After, I'll make us some lunch."

I grab his arm when he goes to pass by me.

"No, you go. I'll stay here with Nick."

He's shaking his head before the words even leave my mouth. "I'm not leaving you here alone with him. Not until he's sober."

I squeeze his arm. "It's okay, Jaxon. Like you've told me before, he won't hurt me. He'll try with his words, but I'm tough. I can take it. I want to be here for him. I *need* to. And I want to do it on my own."

His eyes flicker back and forth between mine. I know he's weighing the choice of staying with me or leaving. He's seen how nasty Nick can be toward me, and I'm sure he'll be beyond pissed to see me in his home, especially alone. But as I told him, I can handle it. I can handle just about anything as long as I'm there for Nick and can help him through his pain.

After several seconds, Jaxon comes to a decision. "Alright, but you call me if you need me. I'll be back in the morning to check on him. The keys to his truck are on the table by the door. If you need to leave for some reason, let me know and I'll come back. I don't want him left alone."

"I will," I promise.

Before he leaves, we both walk back to Nick's room to find him passed out on his bed. I blush and feel a tingle between my legs when I see he's only in his boxers. He's on his stomach, lying diagonally across the bed. It's dark in the room because of the curtains, but I can see the dark shapes of his tattoos across his muscular back and biceps. The hand that has the spider web tattoo is up by his face. He finally looks peaceful.

I spy a blanket on the chair by the window. Jaxon watches while I unfold it and place it over Nick's sleeping form. He's been cold enough already. After picking up another collection of empty beer cans and whiskey bottles, Jaxon and I leave the room. We deposit the bottles in the trash and walk out to his truck.

"He's going to try, but don't let him push you away, Chris," Jaxon tells me, while he stands there with his arm slung over the open truck door. "You get in his face and push right back if you have to. He can be a mean sonofabitch, but underneath it all he's a great guy."

"He can try all he wants, but I can be bullheaded just as much as he can." I smile at him, before it turns into a frown. "I hate seeing him like this."

He reaches over and kisses my cheek before saying gruffly, "We all do. It's gonna be hard, but I think you can help pull him out of this. He reacts to you. Shows emotions I haven't seen in a long time."

I sure hope he's right.

After saying good-bye, I walk back to the house. I make myself a ham-and-Swiss sandwich and wash it down with a glass of water. I wash the dishes in the sink, clear the clutter, and disinfect every surface in the kitchen. Next, I move on to the living room. I pick up and throw away the nasty food containers, then gather up the papers and folders, and move down the hallway, opening and closing doors along the way. Halfway down, I find what I'm looking for: an office. This room seems to be the only one that's already been redecorated.

Feeling like I'm trespassing on sacred ground, I slowly make my way inside. The desk in the center of the room is huge and made out of dark wood. There're various papers thrown all over the desk, and a couple bookshelves full of books. There's also a tall filing cabinet. Over in the corner sits a comfortable looking black recliner with a small table beside it. The walls are painted a light brown and there are a couple of framed blueprints hanging from them, along with a few pictures of buildings.

I tiptoe to the desk like I'm scared of making any noises, and put the papers and folders on top. I notice a small frame lying facedown on the desk. I pick it up and flip it over. I never met Anna, but I've seen plenty of pictures of her at Jaxon and Bailey's house, so I know the girl looking back at me is her. It's a close-up. She has sandy-blonde hair that's braided to the side and lying over her shoulder. She has her head bent but she's looking at the camera shyly through her lashes. Her eyes are a beautiful blue. I can see why anyone would fall in love with her. She has such a sweet and wholesome look.

I put the picture back down the way it was and take one last glance around, before making my way to the door. I close it softly behind me. I decide to check on Nick before settling down in the living room.

When I push his bedroom door open, I find he's flipped to his back with the covers pushed down to his waist. Feeling like a pervert but unable to help myself, my eyes drift to his chest and I admire it. He has a tattoo on his left pec of a beating heart. I have to lean down and squint to see the date inside the heart: the day Anna died. He has a few more tattoos on his stomach and sides, but I can't tell what they are in the dark. In the almost two years I've known him, I've never seen him without his shirt. The sight of his naked chest pulls me in and before I know it, I'm leaning closer. His arms bulge with muscles and his stomach is flat with a six-pack. With him lying on his back, his stomach is sunken in a little, showing off his hip bones. The light dusting of hair on his pecs travels down his abs and disappears in the waistband of his boxers.

An image of me running my fingers through the hair comes to mind. I feel heat hit my face and my eyes swing to his. Relief floods me when I see he's still sleeping. Resisting the urge to push away the hair hanging over his face, I turn and walk out of his room.

I don't know what it is about Nick, but something pulls me to him. Yes, in the beginning it was the pain his eyes radiated, but it's something more. I've tried pulling back, tried not caring, but something tells me I should. That I need to be there for him. I'm not under the illusion that he's just going to willingly let me help. Lord knows, he's shown me in enough ways he wants nothing to do with me. But no matter how much of an ass he is, I still come back for more. I'm not the type who gets off on being treated like dirt, or hurt, but coming from Nick and knowing the reason he's doing it makes it not quite so hard to handle.

I grab my purse from the floor where I dropped it and walk over to the couch. I sit and pull my book out. This is a new one I got from the library a couple of days ago. I devoured the one I got when Bailey was with me. I can understand her love of romance books now. Of course, this will only be my second, but I sense a new obsession coming on.

I grab the small throw off the back of the couch and snuggle up against the armrest. After getting comfortable, I crack open the new book and my eyes stay glued to it until they drift closed a couple hours later.

I DON'T KNOW WHAT it is that alarms me, but I jerk to a sitting position. Something from my lap falls to the floor with a thump. I look around and at first I'm confused because I don't know where I am. Memories of coming to Nick's house and finding him on the porch drunk with a gun beside him flash through my mind.

I look down to the floor and see the book I was reading when I fell asleep. I pick it up and put it on the end table. I lean my head back, close my eyes, and try to calm my rapid breathing. Just as my heart starts to beat normally, I hear a noise from the hallway. Pushing the blanket from my lap, I stand up just as the noise happens again. It almost sounds like someone is moaning in pain.

Worried about Nick, I rush down the hallway to his room. I have no idea what time it is but it's dark outside, so I turn the light on in the hallway. Afraid of what I might find, I gingerly push open the door.

In the light from the hallway, I see Nick is still in the bed with the cover kicked to the side. I slowly walk to him and notice his chest pumping rapidly. He's breathing heavily and the frown is back in place. He mumbles something in his sleep, but I can't understand him. He starts thrashing his head in irritation. I want to reach out and soothe him, but I'm worried I'll scare him awake. His moaning is getting louder and his body starts jerking.

Unable to watch him in this state any longer, I step closer to the bed and reach out to place my hand on his bicep. His skin is clammy.

"Nick," I whisper worriedly.

As soon as my fingers brush his arm, he settles down. His head turns my way, and I watch as the frown disappears. I run my fingers up and down his arm. He moans again, but it's not pain filled. It almost sounds like he's enjoying my touch.

Gently, I lower myself to sit on the edge of the bed. His breathing has calmed some, but I still don't want to leave him yet. I like watching him sleep. It gives me the opportunity to look at him without seeing the scowl he so often wears.

His thick lashes lie against his cheeks. He's lost a little weight so his cheeks are thinner than usual, but it makes him no less handsome. And I have to admit the scruff on his face is hot, even though it looks unkempt. There's something extremely sexy about a man with a beard.

Pushing away the desire to run my fingers along his face, I decide to just sit there and watch him for a few minutes. Without realizing it, my hand has moved from his upper arm to his chest. I know I should move it back. I've gone beyond trying to calm him. But I just can't make my fingers leave his warm skin.

I lightly graze along his pec and a slight moan leaves his lips. I jerk my eyes to his face and see him still sleeping. I feel like a pervert sitting here petting him.

Beneath my hand, Nick's heart is pounding in his chest and it makes my own speed up. My breathing has also become heavy and with each breath I take, I smell his unique smell. He starts to shift on the bed, and I know it's time I get up before he wakes. I reluctantly remove my hand and start to stand. But I don't get far.

One minute I'm getting ready to stand and leave Nick, and the next I'm flat on my back with his warm, hard body lying over mine.

five

Nick

I'M DREAMING. I know I'm dreaming, and I don't want it to stop. I want to stay in this fake world forever. In this world all is right. I know once I wake up the pain will be fresh again, but I don't care. It's worth it to have Anna whole and safe back in my arms, even if it isn't real. I'm tired of dealing with the pain. I just want it to go away.

The dream started off bad, with Anna dying in my arms, making me promise things I can't. Once her body went still, I grabbed her tight to my chest and rocked her back and forth, murmuring in her ear, begging her to come back to me.

The dream changed quickly to me and Anna sitting on a grassy hill, watching the sunset. We're both quiet. My arm is slung over her shoulder and she's snuggled up to my chest. This isn't a memory, but my imagination creating visions of us together. Maybe wishes for a future we'll never have? I don't know, but I don't feel pain during the dream, even knowing it's not real and never will be real.

As we sit there watching the golden rays of the sun fade, I breath in

Anna's scent. She's always smelled like cinnamon cookies. She used to make me snickerdoodles because I loved the smell so much.

Once the sun disappears behind the horizon, I tip Anna's face back and gently kiss her lips. She's pliable in my arms and a soft moan slips past her lips. My tongue runs across her bottom lip and she opens her mouth. I slide my tongue inside and taste the peppermint gum she was chewing earlier.

I gently grip her hair and lay her back against the warm grass. She smiles at me and my heart nearly explodes from the love I feel for her.

I settle down between her spread legs and run one hand down her side until I reach her thigh. I grip the back of it and lift it to lie over my hip. She grinds up against me, and I groan in her neck. I lay kisses there, loving the taste of her.

It's quiet all around us; the only sound is our heavy breathing. It's almost as though if we speak, we both know the dream will end, and neither of us wants it to.

I run my nose along the places I just left a wet trail from my mouth and notice her smell has changed. It's no longer cinnamon I smell, but vanilla and sugar. I frown, not liking the change, but not altogether hating it either. It's nice, but not my Anna's scent.

Frowning, I bring my head back and am shocked to find wavy red hair and not straight sandy blonde.

What the fuck?

This isn't right. Anna has sandy hair, not red. Who in the fuck am I lying on top of? It pisses my off that whoever it is has invaded my dream and replaced Anna.

She has her head turned to the side, away from the fading light of the sun so I can't see her face. But I know she's not Anna. I want Anna back. And who in the fuck thinks she can interfere with my *dream?*

I grip the chin of the woman and turn her head to face me. My breath catches as I look into Chris's green eyes, a beautiful smile on her face.

MY EYES SNAP OPEN, and all I see is a curtain of red. Vanilla and sugar still assault my nose. I'm lying on something soft and warm.

My dick's hard and snuggled against something it likes. I'm disoriented because I don't know what the fuck is going on.

I lurch back and meet Chris's heated gaze. I have one hand on her hip with her wrists locked together in my other hand above her head. Her breasts are smashed against my naked chest and I feel the little points of her nipples poking me through the thin material of her shirt. My hips are grinding against her heat, just as I was doing to Anna in my dream.

I pull my hand back from her thigh and rest it beside her head. Instead of yanking back from her like I know I should, I narrow my eyes and growl, "What the fuck are you doing in here?"

She lies still for a moment, her eyes watching me fearfully, but also with desire. She should be afraid. I have no idea why she's in here, but she shouldn't be. My body, however, disagrees. The fucking treacherous appendage between my legs likes where she is right now. It gives a little jerk in my boxers, like it's reminding me it's still alive and in working order. The fucker's been worthless for two years, even though I wouldn't have used it had it been willing to work for me anyway. Since Anna died, Chris has been the only woman to get a reaction out of my body. And I hate it. I don't want to react to any woman.

Chris's throat bobs up and down before she replies. "Y-you sounded like you w-were in pain. I came to check on you," she says quietly, then chews on her bottom lip.

I have no doubt what she's saying is the truth. I've woken myself numerous times by yelling in my dreams.

My grip tightens on her wrists and I watch her flinch. The look bothers me but I push it away. She needs to learn I'm not a nice guy and she shouldn't invest her time in me.

"You still shouldn't have come in here. It's none of your fucking business."

"I'm sorry. I was worried."

"Well, you shouldn't be," I tell her harshly.

She wiggles a little and I bite back a moan, reminded I'm still snuggled between her soft thighs. I release her wrists with a curse and lift my body from hers. I want to hit something when my idiot dick instantly misses her warmth.

My head starts to pound when I swing my legs over the side of the bed, and I grip it in my hands, waiting for the worst of it to go away. Once I'm sure I won't puke all over the floor, I lift my head and stare at the wall across from me. I feel the bed shift behind me.

"Why are you here?" I ask Chris.

She's quiet, but I hear her shuffling feet as she makes her way to the door.

"Jaxon and I came over to check on you. You missed dinner with Mia and Mac a few nights ago and no one could get in touch with you."

"Maybe that's because I didn't want to talk to anyone," I tell her, but keep my eyes on the wall. It really needs to be repainted. Should I do it before I move, if I decide to?

"Everyone's worried about you, Nick. They just want to make sure you're okay," she says gently.

I jump up from the bed, turn to face her, and have to grab the footboard before my ass hits the floor. The world shifts under my feet and my stomach flip-flops. I grit my teeth and take a few deep breaths, pushing the nausea back down again.

"I'm so fucking tired of hearing that," I grit out between clenched teeth. "I'm not a fucking child that can't take care of myself."

"Well, from the way you're acting it sure doesn't seem like it," she says, her voice rising slightly. I look up at her, surprised at her tone. "Jaxon and I found you out on the porch in nothing but a thin shirt and boxers. It's cold outside, Nick. How long were you out there?"

It takes me a minute to answer, not that I really need to, but this shit is getting old and I'm tired.

"It doesn't fuckin' matter how long I was out there. Why in the hell do you care so much? You don't know me. I wish you would all just leave me the hell alone."

"I have no idea why I care, but I do. I can't make it go away. Lord knows I've tried."

I laugh bitterly. It doesn't stop her.

"Do you think I like being treated like less than dirt? Do you think I enjoy the nasty things you say to me? I don't, Nick. It hurts every time, but I'm still here. I don't know why, but something's pulling me toward you. Something that can't be ignored. Get used to it. As far as your friends, they love you. You wouldn't turn your back on them if they needed you, and neither will they."

With that, she turns on her heel and walks away. Before she steps through the doorway, she turns back. Her eyes are downcast, but I still see the pain on her face. I feel like an asshole, but I push that away too.

"I'll be in the living room if you need me. You should get more sleep. You look like shit."

She shuts the door before I can say anything else. Of course, there's really not much I can say. I know I'm an asshole. Not only to my friends, but especially to her. She hasn't done anything a friend wouldn't do. I have no idea why she feels the need to be my friend, but for some reason she does. I don't know much about her, just bits and pieces here and there from hearing the others talk about her. I know she's been here almost two years and she has shitty parents.

I run my hand down my face and feel the short beard I've neglected to shave off. Maybe I'll do it tomorrow. Right now I'm tired as fuck and all I want to do is crawl into bed and sleep for the next century. However, sleeping isn't good for me unless I'm wasted. Looking around, I search for the bottle of Jack I know was there last night. Or maybe I've already finished it off? I have no clue. My days are starting to run together. I know I have a problem, but I don't give a shit. A small part of me wishes I could just drink and drink until I've drunk enough and died of alcohol poisoning, alone in my house. At least that way I wouldn't have to grow the balls to attempt it again myself.

I stumble to the bathroom that's connected to my bedroom and head straight to the sink. Forgoing looking in the mirror because I know I probably look like shit, just as Chris said, I turn on the cold water, cup my hand and drench my face in the cool liquid. It doesn't help the pounding in my head. I grab my toothbrush, drown it in toothpaste, and remove the cotton from my mouth.

I wrench the shower curtain back and turn the water to warm. Stripping out of my boxers, I step inside and immediately relax my shoulders as the water beats down on me. I brace my hands on the wall and bow my head.

An image of Chris beneath me on my bed appears behind my closed eyes and blood rushes to my dick. I fight the urge to grab it and stroke. No way am I doing that shit thinking about Chris. An image of Anna pops in my head next and guilt has my gut clenching. Except for when I lost my virginity at thirteen to a girl who lived in Jaded Hollow for a couple years, and a couple other girls at fourteen, Anna's been the only girl I've ever had sex with. Those other times never felt right because they weren't with Anna. I haven't wanted it or even thought about sex with someone else since she's been gone. Even thinking about sleeping with another woman has me breaking out into a cold sweat and my dick shriveling up.

Until Chris.

The guilt of wanting someone else weighs heavily on my shoulders. I'm not meant to be with anyone else. I was Anna's just as much as she was mine. I don't want to want anyone else. It feels like a betrayal to Anna.

After soaping my body and washing my hair, something I have to admit I haven't done in a few days, I get out of the shower. Still naked, I walk out of the bathroom just as my bedroom door opens and Chris walks in.

She doesn't see me standing there, so she jumps when I ask, "Don't you know how to fucking knock?"

She stops in her tracks and just stares at me, struck dumb I'm sure by my nakedness. Her eyes aren't focused on me, but on my hard cock. The bastard never went down from my shower and has now decided to go to full fucking mast.

"You mind turning around, Sugar, or are you just going to stand there and molest me with your eyes?" I smirk when I see her blush and quickly turn her back to me.

"Sorry," she mutters. "I was just coming to tell you I'm making omelets if you want one."

My stomach rumbles at the mention of food. I try to think back to the last time I ate, but can't remember. Even though my stomach is still queasy and unsure of food at the moment, I know I probably should eat something.

"Sure," I grunt as I walk to my dresser. I pull out a tank top and a pair of sweat pants. After putting them on, I turn to see Chris has already left the room.

I grumble to the quiet room and make my way to the door on bare feet. I hear tinkling in the kitchen when I walk into the living room. It's cleaner than what I remember. It irritates me that she was riffling around in my living space.

I quietly walk to the doorway leading to the kitchen and lean my shoulder against the doorjamb. She's facing the sink, washing something, but the way she's turned, I can still see the side of her face. Of their own accord, my eyes rake down her body. She's wearing a pair of hip-hugging skinny jeans and a dark green short-sleeved shirt. On her feet she has on flat ballet-type shoes with no socks. Her red hair falls to the middle of her back in soft waves. It infuriates me that I find her attractive. Not in just an appreciative way, but in a flat-out carnal way.

While I stand there and watch Chris, she does something that's weird and has me leaning forward for a closer look. From my angle and the small bit I can see reflected by the window in front of her, it looks like she's—I step forward to get a better look—making faces at herself in the window.

What the fuck is she doing?

Before I get a chance to ask her about her silly behavior, her eyes meet mine in the glass and she spins around with a screech, dropping what she was washing back in the sink with a crash. Her hands fly to her chest and her eyes go wide.

"Jesus, Nick, you scared the shit out of me!" she says loudly, causing me to wince as my head throbs from her shout.

"What were you just doing?" I ask.

She looks down at her feet, and I see the blush creep up her cheeks. Instead of answering me, she walks over to the stove, picks up a spatula, and flips over the omelet she's cooking.

"I wasn't sure what you liked in your omelet, so I just put in the basics; cheese, tomato, peppers, and ham. I hope that's okay."

She turns and looks at me over her shoulder. I give her a chin lift, letting her know it's fine.

"There's coffee as well." She gestures to the coffeepot with the spatula.

I don't want coffee. What I want is an ice-cold beer. Or something stronger. I walk to the fridge, open it, and don't see a damn beer in sight.

I slam the fridge shut with a bang and face Chris, who's watching me warily.

"Where's my beer?" I look over to the bar and don't see my Jack either. "And my whiskey?"

Her throat bobs as she takes a swallow. She turns back to the stove. I barely hear her when she murmurs, "Down the drain."

My back stiffens at her words. What gives her the right to pour my shit down the drain?

"Excuse me?" I ask in a deadly calm voice.

She turns at my tone. I can see the fear in her eyes and it sends satisfaction through me.

After a few seconds, I watch with fascination as she straightens her spine and sets her jaw. "I poured it down the drain. You don't need it. You're killing yourself by drinking so much."

"Maybe that's what I want," I tell her quietly. "Maybe I don't want to live anymore with the guilt and pain. Maybe I want it to go away. Maybe, just fucking maybe, I want out." I snarl the last.

There's a sharp ache in my chest when I see the stark pain in Chris's eyes, like it physically hurts her hearing me say that. I still don't get why she cares so much. Yes, I can see it coming from my friends, but not her. She hasn't known me long enough, doesn't know me well enough to feel pain like that for me.

"I don't know what you want from me, Chris, but don't waste

your time. It's not worth it." I take a step toward her, but stop when I realize what I'm doing. I don't want to get near her. "I had my chance, and I blew it. I don't get another one. Even if I did, I don't want it. What I wanted, what I'll always want, I can't have anymore. Anna's gone. I don't know what you hope to gain out of being my... *friend*," I sneer the word, "but nothing will ever come of it. I don't want you, friend or otherwise. So just fucking stop."

She doesn't say anything at first, just stands there with tears glistening in her eyes. I harden my resolve against the look, even though every bone in my body wants to rush to her and gather her in my arms. I'm an ass. I know it and she needs to know it too. As I told her, I don't want another chance. Anna was my chance and now she's gone. No one will ever compare to her.

"I know," she says, and lowers her eyes to her hands. "I just wish..." She doesn't finish. Shaking her head, she looks back up at me and the pain there is ten times worse. My gut tightens, but I hold my place.

She offers me a smile, but it doesn't reach her eyes. "Have a seat. The omelets are almost done," she says, gesturing to the bar.

I stand there for a moment before shaking my head and taking a seat. Of course she's not going to listen. She's stubborn as fuck. She'll learn, though, that what she is doing is futile.

She puts a plate down in front of me and then makes her own. Instead of sitting beside me, she stands at the bar on the other side. I watch as she cuts the edges off her omelet to make it a perfect square, before cutting that piece into small individual squares. When she's finished, she eats the leftover parts first. She spears her first square omelet piece before she realizes I haven't touched mine yet. She looks to my plate and then up to me.

"What?" she asks.

One corner of my lips tilts up into a smirk. I shake my head, pick up my fork, and start eating. It tastes like fucking heaven to my empty stomach. Even though it's a simple omelet, I can't remember the last time someone cooked for me.

We sit and eat in silence; the only sounds are the clinking of our silverware against our plates. When I finish, I grab my plate and rinse it in the sink. The rolling in my stomach has lessened, but the pounding in my head is getting worse. I grab a glass out of the cabinet, fill it with water, and down a couple of pain pills.

"You wouldn't need those if you'd stop drinking so much," Chris says from behind me.

I deposit the glass in the sink, turn, and lean against the counter with my arms folded against my chest.

"I also wouldn't need them if you would all stop nagging me, Sugar," I tell her.

She clenches her jaw, and I can tell she's holding back a retort. Brave little girl is finally trying to grow some balls. This'll be interesting.

I feel a pang of disappointment when she remains quiet and instead takes her plate to the sink. I'm standing right beside it, so she's close enough I can smell sugar and vanilla.

Suddenly angry, I step away from the sink, and her, and walk to the doorway. "I'm tired. I'm going back to bed. Don't," I say, and turn to face her, "come back in my room."

She nods and goes back to what she was doing at the sink. My eyes drift down to her ass in her tight jeans, before I curl my lip at her back. I turn on my heel and walk back to my bedroom, closing the door a little too firmly.

I strip my clothes off and sit on the edge of the bed. I pull the drawer open and take out the picture I have of Anna inside. It's just a simple picture of her smiling big at the camera. We're outside in the snow, so she's bundled up in coat, scarf, and hat. It's one of my favorite pictures of her.

I run my finger down her face and whisper, "I'm sorry, Anna. I miss you."

I bring the picture to my lips and kiss it before replacing it safely back in the drawer. I lie down in bed with my hands behind my head.

I have no idea what Chris hopes to accomplish by being here, but what I told Andrew the other day was true. You can't fix something that's irreparable.

The pain I saw flashing in Chris's eyes when I told her I wanted out appears in my head. As much as the woman bugs me, I have to admit I hated seeing that look on her face. I'm the one who's a fuckup, not her. I'm sure she's a great girl and any man would feel lucky to have her. I'm just not that man. I'm broken and sad and so far down in my black hole there's no way out. There's no safety net, or rope long enough to pull me out. All I would do is pull her down with me.

Chris is the type of woman who deserves roses and romance and sweet talk. Someone who would cherish her and treat her like gold. I did that before. I sure as shit am not doing it again. All my sweet and romance was reserved for one woman, and that one woman is no longer here. The goodness in me died along with Anna. All that's left is a bottomless pit of despair and loneliness.

six

Chris

I DROP THE DISHRAG back in the sink, dry my hands, and wipe the few stray tears that I couldn't stop from falling.

Hearing Nick say there could never be anything between us hurt, even though I knew the possibility of that happening was slim from the start. I have no idea why I have feelings for him. It's not like he's shown me any kindness or caring or acted like there's a possibility he could ever be interested in me. He's never, not once, except for that one time in Jaxon's hallway, given any indication that he could ever be attracted to me. I also have no clue why he feels this hatred toward me. And that's what it is. Hatred. It's in his eyes when he looks at me and it's in his actions. I don't know what I did to garner such behavior.

It doesn't matter though, because no matter how much he may hate me, I don't feel the same for him. I won't stand around and watch him wither away into nothing. He may not care for me, but God knows I care for him.

When he spoke so carelessly about his life, it took every bit of strength in me to hold my legs up. The pain was so debilitating that all I wanted to do was sink to my knees in despair. I swear all the air in the room was sucked out because my chest hurt to breathe. I have no idea how I kept my feelings from showing, but somehow I did. I don't know why I want to hide them from him, but I do. Maybe I just don't want to give him more ammunition to use against me.

I finish cleaning the dinner dishes, turn off the lights, and walk to the bathroom. I plunder the cabinets until I find a toothbrush still in the package. I break it open, scrub my teeth, wash my face, and run my fingers through my hair. I'm going to have to ask Jaxon to bring me some clothes tomorrow. I don't feel comfortable leaving Nick here alone, and I don't want to ask Jaxon to stay with him. I just have this feeling that *I* need to be here.

I suck in my cheeks to look like a fish and open my eyes as far as they will go. When Nick caught me making faces at myself, I was embarrassed, so I avoided his question. What started out as something funny as a kid became an almost OCD quirk as an adult. I can't see my reflection without making a face at myself. Life is always so serious. We all need to stop for a minute, make faces at ourselves, and laugh.

I quietly close the bathroom door behind me. When I glance over at Nick's door, it's closed, just as I figured it would be. If I'm honest with myself, I'm kind of glad. I'm not sure how much more of his black mood I can deal with tonight.

I walk silently down the hallway to the living room. I stop at the coffee table to check the time on my phone. A little past nine. Although I slept several hours earlier, I'm still tired. I'm always exhausted after my encounters with Nick. Probably due to the emotional toll all his negative comments put on my body.

I undo my pants and slip them over my hips. I love my skinny jeans, but they're a bitch to get out of. I end up sitting on the couch so I can peel them down my legs and force them over my heels. No way am I sleeping in them again.

Once my jeans are off, I reach behind me and unclasp my bra, slide the straps down my arms, and then pull it out from underneath my shirt. Wearing a bra to bed is another thing I hate doing. I'm an underwire kind of girl, so my boobs either fall out of my bra when I'm on my side or get poked from the wire. Either way, not fun.

I tuck my bra into my jeans and move them to the chair. There's a throw pillow on the same chair, so I grab it and the blanket off the back of the couch and snuggle down. I blow out a tired sigh once I'm comfortable.

I wonder how long it will take before Nick decides he doesn't want me here anymore and tries to kick me out. I'm actually surprised he hasn't yet. I blame it on him not being quite himself. He was so drunk this morning that he didn't even realize Jaxon and I were moving him. I'm shocked he was moving as well as he was a bit ago. Yes, he still looked groggy and hungover, but he didn't really act like it.

I roll over with my back facing the back of the couch and hug part of the blanket to my chest. My eyes drift closed and a few minutes later I'm out.

I WAKE TO A LOUD banging coming from the kitchen. When I pull my eyes open and sit up, I don't see Nick, but I hear his curses. I also smell fresh-brewed coffee and my mouth waters. Light filters in from the sliding glass door, and I wonder what time it is.

Before I get a chance to check my phone, another loud crash comes. I bolt up off the couch and make my way to the doorway. I come to a halt when I see Nick, his back to me. He's barefoot and is still wearing the sweats from last night. The shirt is gone, leaving his toned torso bare. I almost drool before I stop myself. Seeing even his back in the light of day mesmerizes me.

On his lower right side there is a rainbow that only has the colors black, blue, and green. The blue and green are bright against the black. Across both shoulder blades is a bird of some kind. Its wings expanded. It's mostly black, but there are bright yellows, greens, and reds throughout the entire bird.

I guess he senses me standing there, because as soon as I move to walk in the kitchen, he whirls around and barks, "Stop."

I freeze in my tracks.

"I dropped a coffee mug and there's glass on the floor," he says and walks over to a door, opens it, and pulls out a broom. Looking down, I see blue glass all over the floor. I totally missed it while I was ogling his body.

"I can help." I take a step into the kitchen, but don't get far.

"Fucking stay there, Chris," he says, and pins me with his intense blue eyes. "No sense you cuttin' your feet to help when I can do it myself."

I stay where I'm standing as he sweeps the broken glass into a pile, being careful to get it all. The muscles in his arms flex slightly with every swipe of the broom. Once he's done, he grabs a dustpan from the same closet and deposits the mess in the garbage can.

He turns to me after he puts the broom and dustpan away. His eyes sweep up and down my body, and I swear I see desire in his eyes a split second before they narrow. I watch with trepidation as a tic appears on his scruffy jaw. His hands bunch into fists at his sides. It's not until his eyes linger on my legs that I realize I'm standing there with no pants on.

Crap!

"Where the hell are your pants?" he asks, his lip curling up in disgust.

I wince and shuffle my feet backward through the doorway, keeping my eyes locked on his.

"Sorry," I mumble. "I jumped up when I heard a crash. I forgot to put them back on."

I stand there like an idiot as he continues to watch me.

After a couple of seconds, he lifts his brow. "What are you standing there for?"

I turn on my heel and rush back to the living room.

"Jerk," I mutter to myself.

"What?" he hollers.

I ignore him, grab my pants, and fight to pull them up my legs. I also maneuver my bra back on. My boobs aren't big, but still big enough for a man to tell if I'm not wearing a bra. And I know my nipples are hard.

Shit. I wonder if Nick noticed.

I make a pit stop in the bathroom to brush my teeth, wash my face, and pee. I try to tame my hair, but there's no help for it. After looking in the cabinet, I find a comb and spend several minutes trying to brush out the tangles. Giving up, I take the hair tie I always have on my wrist and pull it back into a loose bun. When I make it back to the kitchen, Nick is standing in front of the stove cooking something.

"What are you making?" I ask and walk over to the coffeemaker to pour myself a cup.

"Pancakes. You're leaving today, right?" he deadpans.

I feel a little pain in my chest. It shouldn't surprise me; I knew he would ask sooner rather than later.

Instead of answering his question, I ask one of my own.

"How are you feeling this morning?"

I don't look at him when I ask, but I feel his gaze on me. He waits a few moments before answering.

"Fine. A bit of a headache," he replies.

I peek at him from under my lashes and see he's back to flipping pancakes. He has one hand on the counter beside the stove, leaning on it. His head is bent, and I can tell he's thinking about something. I wonder if it's Anna.

"Do you need help?" I ask.

"No," he says simply, without looking at me.

I grab my coffee and go sit at the bar. Although I'm glad he's at least being somewhat cordial, it still saddens me that he disregards me without a second thought.

We both stay silent, me with my thoughts on Nick and the devastation that surrounds him, and him with... well, there's no telling.

I watch as he stacks pancake after pancake on a plate. He pushes the pan to the back burner, turns the stove off, and places a few pancakes on a separate plate before setting it in front of me. I'm about to get up and grab the butter and syrup when he appears with both and puts them down as well.

"Thank you," I tell him.

All I get in response is a grunt.

I stay silent after that. No sense trying to start a conversation with him. He obviously doesn't want to talk. Instead, I watch as he prepares his own pancakes with his back to me. The smooth lines of his back grab my attention. He's tanned beneath the tattoos and has a few freckles scattered about. When he moves his arms, the muscles in his back move with him. My eyes drift down to his butt. The sweats he's wearing hang loose on his hips. When he turns around, I know I'll see the sexy V that all girls drool over. I'm no different. It's been complete torture keeping my eyes above his chest since I've been in the kitchen.

And sure enough, as soon as he turns around, my eyes automatically go to the V before I can stop them. They linger there a few seconds before I drag my eyes up his stomach that's covered in a light dusting of hair, over his well-defined pecs, up his stubbled neck and jaw, and then finally to his eyes, which are watching me.

He lifts a brow at my blatant staring, and I drop my eyes to my plate, knowing my face is now bright red. This is the second time he's caught me staring at him.

Out the corner of my eye, I see him walk around the bar and take a seat next to me. After smothering my pancakes in butter and syrup, I cut them into pieces and start eating.

"What time is it?" I ask between bites, trying once again to draw him into a conversation.

"A little after ten," is all he says, before shoveling a bite of food in his mouth.

I take another bite as well.

"How did you sleep last night?" I prod.

"I didn't," he replies with a mouthful of food.

My fork stops midair, and I look over at him. Now that he's mentioned it and he's closer to me, I can see the start of dark circles under his eyes. He looks tired and worn down. Even more so than usual.

My heart breaks for him when I realize why he didn't get any sleep. It's because I downed his alcohol. He drinks himself into such oblivion that his body gives him no choice but to shut down to recuperate. I wonder how often his dreams slip past the fog of drunkenness, as they did last night. I'm not under the illusion the reason he dragged me down on the bed and was practically fucking me through our clothes is because he was dreaming of me. No, the dream had to have been about Anna, and his body automatically reacted to mine, thinking it was Anna.

It doesn't matter either way, because what he's doing is dangerous. If he continues the way he is, there's going to be a time he goes too far. I understand his need to block out memories and dreams, but he needs to find a better way. Some way that won't ultimately harm him, even if that's what he wants. Grief counseling would be ideal, but I don't see Nick willing to go that route.

"I'm going to call Jaxon," he says, pulling me from my thoughts. When I bring my focus back to him, he's not looking at me, but at his now empty plate. "I want you out of my house today. You don't need to be here."

Again, his words hurt, even though they shouldn't. It's no surprise he wants me gone. It doesn't take a genius to figure that out. But I'd started to think that since he wasn't being quite as harsh with me, maybe he is becoming... I don't know... used to me being around?

He doesn't wait for my reply. Just gets up and carries his plate to the sink and dumps it in. He stands there for several moments, hands braced on the counter, looking outside through the trees. I wonder what he's thinking.

I've lost my appetite, so I just set my fork down and sit there and wait. I have no idea what to say to him. I do know that if I can help it, I won't be going anywhere today. He may not like it, but damn it, someone needs to care for him since he's not doing it himself.

I'm just about to break the silence when I hear a car door slamming outside. I jerk at the unexpected noise at the same time Nick turns around with a scowl on his face.

"Now who the fuck is here?" he mutters.

He walks off to see, and I get up to follow. I'm walking through the kitchen doorway when my phone starts ringing. I veer off to answer it, not bothering to look at the screen.

"Hello?"

"Hey, Chris," Bailey says in her sweet voice. "I was calling to let you know Jaxon and Mac are on their way over to check on things. They should be there any minute."

I turn to the door as Bailey speaks, and sure enough, both Jaxon and Mac are standing there with Nick. They both have worried frowns on their faces. I can't see Nick's but I'm sure it carries the same dirty look as before.

"Yeah, they just got here," I tell Bailey distractedly, watching the interaction between the guys.

"Okay, good. I sent a couple changes of clothes with Jaxon, just in case. Just some that you left at the house when you stayed here."

Bailey knows my feelings toward Nick. I haven't outright said anything to her, but she's the one person who knows me the most. She's seen the way I look at him, how my eyes follow him and how they turn sad when he's around and acting his normal assholish self toward me. She knows it's killing me inside watching him self-destruct. And she knows I would do just about anything to make it better for him, to help him in any way I can, or make his life easier.

"Thanks."

I watch as Jaxon looks over at me, his brow creased in concern. I try to give him a reassuring smile, but I'm sure it looks fake. He looks back to Nick, says something quietly, and they all step outside.

I'm pulled back to the conversation when Bailey asks me, "How are things?"

Bailey still carries guilt for what happened to Anna, and therefore feels responsible for Nick's depression. She has nothing to feel guilty for, as so many others have told her. However, I don't know if Nick has ever talked to her about it. I get the feeling he hasn't, which pisses me off. As far as I know, Nick's never blamed Bailey, at least not out loud, but he's got to know she feels responsible. He should have spoken to her and reassured her she was not to blame. Bailey gave herself up to save Anna. Yes, the outcome was horrible and the sacrifice was in vain, but it was no less important. Bailey was devastated afterwards. Nick needs to realize that and make it better for Bailey. I think he's the only one who can, since he was the most affected by Anna's torture and death.

With all this, I'm reluctant to tell Bailey just how bad it is here, but I won't lie either.

"It's not good, Bailey," I tell her somberly. "Nick isn't doing well. I'm going to stay here a couple more days."

I hear a sniff over the line, indicating Bailey is trying to hold back her tears. It hurts to know she's still in so much pain over this. I have to talk to Nick about it, make him understand that he *has* to talk to Bailey.

"How is he treating you?" she asks.

I laugh bitterly. I sink down onto the couch and prop my elbow on my knee with my head in my hand.

"Not as bad as usual, which I'm grateful for, but he still hates me."

"Oh, Chris," Bailey breathes across the line. "He doesn't hate you. I think it's like Jaxon said. You make him feel and he doesn't like it."

"Ha! I make him feel, alright. Disgust and revulsion. It was all over his face today when I walked into the kitchen with just a shirt and panties."

"What?" Bailey yells, forcing me to pull the phone away from my ear. "Why were you in just your shirt and panties? Did something happen?"

"Relax, Bailey. Geesh!" I roll my eyes at her dramatics. Of course she would think something happened. "I took my jeans and bra off before I went to sleep on the couch."

"Oh," she says disappointedly. She's not the only one. I know it's just a pipe dream and Nick is in no way ready for a relationship, but a girl can't help but wish.

"Look, I've got to go. I've got to prepare for my battle with Nick over me not leaving."

"Okay. Call if you need anything," she says.

"I will. Thank you, Bailey. Love you," I tell her.

"Love you too, sweetie."

After we hang up, I release a tired sigh and drop my phone on the coffee table. Nick's going to shit a brick when he finds out I'm not leaving, but he'll have to learn to suck it up.

I slip my shoes on and walk out on the porch. Nick is walking off toward the large shed, his shoulders stiff. Jaxon and Mac are by Jaxon's truck. I walk over to them.

"Hey," I greet them.

"You stayin'?" Jaxon asks.

I nod.

"He's not going to be happy about it," Mac says next.

"I know."

"He's already pissed because I brought you here in the first place."

I give Jaxon a half smile. "I know that, too."

"How are things here?" he asks.

It takes me a few seconds to answer. I turn my head in the direction Nick walked off to. I don't see him anymore. When I turn back to Jaxon and Mac, they are both watching me with troubled eyes.

"He was mad when I told him I poured out all his booze, but it wasn't as bad as it could have been. He's mostly quiet, trying to avoid me."

Jaxon nods, reaches out, and puts his hand on my shoulder.

"I know this is hard for you. I really appreciate you doing this. We all do. I really do think you'll be the one to pull him out, Chris, but if it gets to be too much, let me know. We'll figure something else out. We won't let anything happen to him."

I know what he's referring to, and from the look on Mac's face, he does too. Jaxon must have told him about the gun we found. He obviously didn't tell Bailey, because she would have mentioned it, or at the very least been more upset on the phone. I'm grateful he didn't tell her. She already carries enough guilt.

I don't know if what Jaxon says is true. I don't know if I can help pull Nick out of the misery he's in, but I'll damn sure give it all I've got.

"I'll be fine. He can be an asshole, but I'll bite back if I need to." I give both Jaxon and Mac a smile.

Jaxon reaches in the back of his truck and pulls out a small travel bag.

"Bailey packed you a couple changes of clothes and some essentials," he says, handing me the bag.

"Thank you."

"Call one of us if you need anything, okay?" Mac says, leaning over to give me a hug. At my ear, he whispers, "Watch him for us."

I pull back from him and look into his eyes. He's really worried about his friend. It hurts to see all these people upset over someone they love. I know my parents loved me and Jase, but we've never had the type of love these people feel for Nick. And me and Jase now. One thing I've learned about the people of Jaded Hollow, especially my friends: when they accept you into their fold, they love you fiercely, they consider you theirs, and will do anything for you.

"I will."

I lean up on my toes and give Mac a kiss on the cheek and then do the same to Jaxon.

We say good-bye, and I watch as they get in Jaxon's truck and pull away. I look again over at the barn, but there's still no sign of Nick.

Pulling in a deep breath, I decide to leave him alone for a while and go back into the house.

I put my bag down by the couch and wander around aimlessly. I go to the kitchen to make myself another cup of coffee. Leaning against the counter, I spy another door. I set my coffee down and decide to see what's on the other side. Opening it, I discover a set of stairs leading down to a basement. After flipping the light switch, I take the stairs slowly. The room at the bottom is big and filled with gym equipment.

What's up with men and having a gym in their basement? Jaxon has one as well.

An image pops in my head of Nick lifting weights, sweat pouring down his stomach and his arms bulging with exertion. Him punching the speed bag, the muscles in his back stretching with each swing. His abs hardening each time he lifts weights.

I feel a tremor at the visions and goose bumps appear on my arms.

I see another door off to the left, and I walk over to it. A blast of cold air hits me when I'm standing in front of the door. I look up at the ceiling, expecting to see an air vent, but there isn't one. Tingles go up my neck. I have no idea why, but I get a feeling there is something important behind this door.

I glance over my shoulder because it feels like someone is looking at me. Of course, no one is there. Feeling foolish, I reach out and grab the doorknob. The silver metal is cold. I twist the knob and the door opens soundlessly.

Light filtering from the room behind me shows several boxes stacked on top of each other. I reach my hand out to the wall beside the door without looking until I find the light switch and flip it. There're more boxes along the walls. There has to be at least twenty altogether. Most have "Anna" written on them. Some are taped shut, while others are open with the contents sticking out of the top. One box is turned on its side, books spilling out of it. It looks like it was purposely kicked or pushed over, as there's a dent in the cardboard. Obviously, Nick has been in here recently. Or he comes in here a lot.

Knowing I shouldn't, it's an invasion of privacy, but unable to help myself, I walk over to the nearest open box and look inside. It's full of picture albums. I pull one out and flip through page after page of Nick and Anna, just Anna, Anna with Jaxon and Mia, or Anna with her whole family. Every single picture has Anna in it. Looking at the ones with both her and Nick, it's amazing to see the difference in him. His eyes shine bright, the color on his face is healthy, and he wears a stunning smile as he looks down at the girl in his arms.

I'm not jealous of Anna; how could I be when she brought out pure joy in Nick? But I do wish I could have known him before. Before the sadness hit that constantly leaves a black look on his face. I don't think I've ever seen him smile in the almost two years I've known him.

I slide the album back in the box and move on to the next one. This one is full of clothes. The next box is smaller and has jewelry in it, most of which looks like costume jewelry, but there are a few pieces that seem expensive. A bigger box has a bunch of magazines, color schemes, a couple of notebooks with designs and notes in them, and various other items. I assume these are the ideas and plans that Nick and Anna made for remodeling the house.

I kneel down beside the box that's tipped on its side and right it. When I pick up one of the leather-bound books and flip to the first page, I realize it's Anna's diary. They all must be diaries, because they all look about the same, with the exception of some being older than others.

Curiosity gets the best of me, and I sit beside the box with one of the older books in my lap. I know I shouldn't. I know Nick would kill me if he knew I was reading something as private as Anna's diary, but I feel a need to. A need I can't push away.

Looking over at the door one last time to make sure I'm still alone, I open the book to the first page.

May 19, 1999

Dear Diary,

One of the best things happened today. Finally, after fantasizing for so long, Nick kissed me. It was the single most amazing thing that has ever happened to me and it's something I will never forget for the rest of my life. I was so nervous, but after the first couple of minutes, the nervousness went away and was replaced by a thousand butterflies in my stomach. I swear there were so many butterflies I wouldn't have been surprised if I had floated away from them flying in my stomach. The way his lips felt against mine was both scary and exciting. I hope we do it again soon.

I smile as I read Anna's words. I have no doubt I would have liked her. The way everyone talks about her, I know she was very special.

I skip ahead a few entries.

June 30, 1999

Dear Diary,

There was a boy at school today that was picking on me. His name is Tommy. I was standing by my locker when he came up to me, calling me nasty names and then knocked my books from my arms. His friends were laughing and pointing at me and all I could do was cry. I hate Tommy. All he's ever been is mean to me.

I was sniffling my tears away and bending down to pick up my books when Nick came out of nowhere and punched him in the nose. There was blood everywhere. It was nasty, but I couldn't help but feel good about it because Tommy deserved it. In Nick's deep voice that always send shivers down my spine, he told him the next time he saw him picking on me he would put him in the hospital. When I looked at Nick, I could tell he was telling the truth. He looked very angry.

Then Nick came to me, wiped the tears from my cheeks and kissed me softly on the lips. He told me everything would be okay, and promised he would make sure Tommy didn't bother me anymore. Everything was right in the world again. I knew Nick would do what he said. That's the type of person he is. He always keeps his promises. That's why I love him so much. That's why I'm going to marry him someday.

A tear trails down my cheek at Anna's dream that never came true. Although I want Nick for my own, I still feel sorry that Anna never got her happily ever after.

I read several more entries, some involving Nick and some not, but the one constant is that Anna is a very charming person. I can see why everyone in town loved her. Her personality demanded it, and if you didn't, you were missing out on one of life's precious gifts.

I tuck the diary back in the box and get to my feet. I've been down here long enough. The last thing I need is for Nick to find me down here.

I look around the room one more time before leaving, turning the light off and closing the door behind me. I head back up the stairs and switch that light off as well. Getting a peek into Nick and Anna's life left me feeling hopeless. I know Nick loved Anna, still loves her, but I couldn't help but secretly wish he could maybe one day hold feelings for me. I could never replace Anna, I know that, but I'm coming to wonder if it's even possible for Nick to develop even a smidgeon of what he held for his first and only love. The hold he still hasn't released on Anna makes me think it's impossible. I wouldn't want him to forget their life together or the love they shared, but maybe open more of himself up? It seems so unrealistic now though.

Once in the kitchen, I decide to dig around to see what I can make for dinner. Looking through the freezer, the only thing I find is some hamburger meat. I put it on the counter to defrost. I'm sure I can do something with it. I look through the pantry and find a couple cans of kidney beans and a can of tomatoes on the top shelf. Chili it is, then.

I look out the window over the sink, wondering where Nick is. What he's doing. What he's thinking right now.

I wash the few dishes in the sink. After, I take a seat on the couch and grab the remote to see what's on TV.

Nick needs time to himself. I know when to push and when to withdraw, and the hard set of his shoulders as he walked away from Jaxon and Mac earlier said *do not fuck with me right now.*

I hate feeling helpless like this. I hate not knowing what to do to help him. I would give almost anything to see the Nick I saw in the pictures downstairs.

seven

Nick

I SWING THE AX over my shoulder until it meets wood and relish the burn it leaves behind on my arms. I reach up and swipe the sweat from my forehead with the back of my arm. I took my shirt off an hour ago when it started sticking to me from the sweat. I've been at this for hours. My back is getting stiff, and I know I'll be sore tomorrow, but I can't stop. I need the exertion so my thoughts don't drift off.

I don't know which is worse; thoughts of Anna or remembering what Chris looked like standing in my kitchen in nothing but her shirt and panties. And it wasn't one of those shirts that girls wear that goes down to below their ass. Oh, fuck no, this shirt was the kind that barely covers the stomach, so I got a full-frontal view of her goods, which had my own goods turning hard. Her smooth pale legs taunted me, reminding me I haven't had sex in over two years. Her white panties with a little strip of sexy black lace around the leg holes practically had me drooling.

Then an image of Anna in nothing but her bra and panties,

laughing in the kitchen while we cooked breakfast together, steals through my mind, bringing on a whole slew of emotions. Pain for losing the one woman who was my entire life. Irrational anger for Anna leaving me. Guilt for blaming Anna for leaving me. Remorse for not making it to Anna in time. Rage at Chris for making me want something I have no right wanting.

I hate myself in that moment because it took everything in me to not walk up to Chris, turn her around, bend her over the counter, and force my way into her warm body. I wanted to beat my dick and mind into submission and make them realize the same thing my heart realizes: I don't want Chris.

I throw the two logs off to the side and place another on the thick stump I'm using. I bring the ax over my shoulder and let one hand slide down the handle when I swing it forward again. I hit the log hard and feel the vibrations of the ax going through it until it hits the stump.

I was happy to see Jaxon and Mac when they came by earlier. It meant they could take the redheaded sugar-smelling temptress away and things could go back to normal. Or my kind of normal anyway.

When Mac asked if we could talk outside and then mentioned the gun Jaxon and Chris found me sitting with, I got pissed. He asked me about it, and I told them it was none of their damn business. Neither took kindly to that, and they reminded me that it *was* their business because they cared about me and didn't want to see me hurt. Then Jaxon and his big fucking mouth made me feel like shit when he told me Bailey still blames herself for what happened to Anna and told me it would kill her if something happened to me, especially by my own hands.

After that, I was done. I completely forgot about demanding they take Chris with them and walked off. She already knew I wanted her gone, so I figured it would be a foregone conclusion. I mean, who would want to stay with a total dick anyway?

I straighten up after replacing the two logs with a fresh one. Apparently, Chris does, as she's walking toward me.

I grip the handle of the ax until my knuckles cramp. I clamp my teeth together and try my damndest to hold in the anger I'm feeling. Jaxon's voice from earlier warning me to be nice to Chris rings through my head.

Fuck! Why can't this girl just leave me the fuck alone!

She watches me warily as she stops by the pile of split logs.

"I have chili on the stove. It should be ready in a few minutes," she says in a small voice.

Unclenching my jaw, I tell her in a forced calm voice, "I'll be in later."

I turn my back to her and launch the ax through the wood again. I do this several more times while she stands there, watching me. It's making me feel uncomfortable. I'm just about to turn around and demand she leave, when she speaks.

"Why are you cutting wood? You don't have a fireplace."

I drop the ax on the ground and pull in a lungful of air. I am so fucking tired. I swear, if I could just not have my nightly dreams, I would sleep for a week. Having Chris here isn't helping matters. My body is wound tight around her and that's wearing me down as well.

I grab my shirt out of my back pocket and wipe my face clean. When I pull the material away from my face, Chris is still watching me, except this time there's something else in her eyes. She has them pinned on my chest and there's blatant desire, heat, and want reflecting in them.

She lifts them to my face and she immediately flushes and looks down at her hands, which are twisting together. As with most redheads, her skin is pale, so the red creeping up her face is very noticeable. I don't know if I like the fact that my body makes her react in such a way, or if it pisses me off because she feels she can look. Either way, I watch as she stands there fidgeting with the bottom of her shirt... a different shirt than what she was wearing this morning.

"You weren't wearing that shirt this morning. Where did you get it?" I ask, and hope my suspicions are wrong.

She looks up, her knuckles turning white before she admits, "Umm... Jaxon dropped a bag off for me this morning."

I tip my head up at the sky and grind my teeth together. *Why in the fuck are you making this so difficult? All I want is some peace, but instead you drop this stubborn-ass woman in my lap.*

I try to calm my breathing before I speak again, because I know if I open my mouth, I'll say something harsh and mean.

After several seconds of deep breathing, I bring my head back down.

"Why? I've told you I don't want you here. What the fuck, Sugar?" That's the third time I've called her that. Each time was on impulse. It's that damn sugar smell on her skin that does it. Fuck, it smells good, but giving her pet names is stupid. Why in the fuck does it keep slipping out? It's not like this chick means shit to me.

Her brows are pulled into a straight line, like she's thinking of something to say, but isn't sure if she should. Next, a look of resolve comes across her face. She's like an open book. Almost every emotion that crosses her face, I recognize. She can't hold anything in.

"I decided to stay and keep you company," she says, her voice determined.

Her answer is so fucking ridiculous, a laugh bursts out before I can stop it. It only lasts for a second, but it's enough to feel foreign to me. I can't remember the last time I laughed, or even smiled.

Chris looks mesmerized or some shit, and it irritates the fuck out of me. All humor now gone, I glower at her. The look soon leaves her face and is replaced by apprehension, and fuck it all to hell, I want the awestruck look back.

Son of a bitch! I'm all over the fucking place!

One minute I want her fascinated with me and the next I want nothing to do with her. What the fuck is wrong with me?

"Just stay the hell out of my way," I demand in a harsh voice.

I turn my back to her, stuff the dirty shirt in my back pocket, and pick up my ax once again, rudely dismissing her. It takes a few moments, but then I hear the crackle of leaves, indicating she's walking away. I can't help myself and turn to watch. She has her head down dejectedly and remorse sweeps through me.

I used to never talk to women like I talk to Chris. I don't know what it is about her that brings out the anger. Actually, yes I do; she reminds me of everything I could have had. The life I could have had. A life I wanted with Anna, but I'm now seeing glimpses of Chris in the mix. She's starting to insert herself in little ways, has been for the last several months. I find myself at the oddest times thinking about her. I'm starting to see her in my dreams. The dream I had last night wasn't the first time she's invaded my thoughts while I slept.

I hate this because I don't want her in my life. I don't want her invading my space and thoughts. I don't want her concern or sympathy. I don't want her to take the sadness away that surrounds me. And I certainly don't want my body to react to hers.

But no matter how much I push her away, it seems like it only draws her closer to me, and I don't know what to do. I love Anna with every piece of my heart. I'll always love her. There are no pieces left for anyone else to claim.

Even if I did want to be with someone else or learn to care for another woman, how could I when I know I would be secretly wishing she were someone else? Knowing I could never truly give myself to her fully?

I chop wood for another hour, exhausting myself, hoping I'll get some undisturbed sleep tonight. Sweat dribbles down my back and face. The sun is starting to settle behind the trees and the temperature is dropping fast. I hate the time change this time of year. It takes away so many of the working daylight hours.

Deciding to stop for the evening, I slam the ax down on the stump until it stands on its own. My back aches from all the chopping I did today, and my eyes feel like there're ten-ton weights hanging from them. I walk sluggishly back to the house.

When I walk in the front door, all the lights are off, except for the lamp in the living room. I spy Chris's head over the back of the couch. She lifts herself a little and sees me at the door. I close the door behind me, slip off my boots, and avoid her eyes.

My stomach protests as I walk away from the kitchen and the delicious smells and instead head toward my bedroom and the connecting bathroom. I'm hungry, but I need a shower first. I'm dirty and sticky from sweat, and I'm hoping the warm water will stop the headache I feel starting in my temples.

I've been getting a lot of headaches lately that just won't go away. I know they're from stress. I've been having problems with some of the contractors I hire out for odd jobs that my crew and I can't do. Being home is also stressful. I know my friends mean well, but having them at my back all the time gets to be too much. I see the way they look at me and there are times I want nothing more than to snarl to whip the looks of pity from their faces. I hate myself when I feel that way because they love me and only want me happy again. But they just don't understand that it's not possible for me. It may never be possible for me. I am so far beyond fucked-up in the head that there may never be any going back for me. Losing Anna destroyed a piece of me I don't feel I could ever get back. My life without her in it is bleak and empty. I don't want happiness back if I can't have it with her. She's gone. Why should I be happy while she's rotting away in a grave?

To top it off, I now have to deal with Chris being in my space and all the fucked-up and inconsistent feelings I'm having toward her. One minute I want to demand she stay the hell away from me and the next I want to snatch her to me and take whatever she wants to give. I've also seen the way she looks at me, and I know deep down for some reason she has feelings for me. I have no idea why, but it's there in her eyes. That's why I'm such a dick to her. She needs to learn now that I can't give her anything. It's better for her to know that before she gets too involved. It just seems harsher not to warn her.

I step out of my clothes and into the shower. There is a lot of work that still needs to be done on the house. I know I need to get it done—I own a fucking construction business for Christ's sake—but finding the motivation for doing it without Anna beside me is the problem. I don't *want* to do it without her. It was to be *our* project.

However, I did change the showerhead in my shower. I installed a rain showerhead about a year ago. It may sound girly as shit, but it only sounds that way if you haven't been under one. If you have, then you wouldn't care if it spit out rainbows, as long as it beats down on your shoulders the same as the water does. It's pure fucking heaven.

After ten minutes of the wonder spray, I step out, dry off, and head to my dresser naked. I slip on a pair of old worn jeans and a black thermal shirt and head out of my room on bare feet. Chris is still on the couch reading her book. Neither of us acknowledges the other as I walk by, but I feel her eyes on me as I go into the kitchen.

What does she see that makes her so interested in me? What am I to her?

Ignoring the questions rolling around in my head, I go straight to the pot on the stove. There's a clean bowl on the counter beside it. She finished the chili over an hour ago, but the pot is still hot, indicating she must have kept it warm for me. I feel a pang of guilt in my stomach at the thought. All she's ever done is be nice, and I repay her by being an asshole. It's in her best interests, though.

After scooping a generous amount of food into the bowl, I take a taste and nearly burn my tongue off in the process. It's good. Very good.

I grab a container and pour the rest of the chili into it to store in the fridge for later. It's the least I can do, since she cooked.

I open the fridge to grab a beer and then scowl when I remember Chris poured them all down the drain. It's times like these that I truly hate the damn woman. She has no right making decisions like that for me. If I want to drink myself into a drunken stupor, then I should be allowed to.

See? My emotions are all over the place when it comes to Chris.

Instead of my much-needed beer, I grab a glass and get some water from the sink. I take both my glass of godforsaken water and my chili and walk back into the living room. Chris is still in the same position on the couch; back against the armrest and knees drawn up with a blanket thrown over her legs.

I don't say anything as I sit on the opposite end of the couch. She pauses in her reading and looks at me. I ignore her, pick up the remote, and switch on the TV. I flip it to football. She cranes her head around to look at the TV and then looks back down at her book. I eat and watch TV in silence, while she sits there and reads. I can tell she's distracted though, because I've haven't seen her flip a page once.

After I finish my food, I set my bowl down on the coffee table and kick my feet up beside it with one arm propped up along the back of the couch.

"Chili was good," I say quietly with my eyes still on the TV. "Thank you."

My words surprise her. I can tell because she drops her book in her lap. I can see her shocked expression from the corner of my eye.

It takes her a few seconds, but she eventually responds with "You're welcome."

She doesn't pick her book back up. Instead she sets it down on the couch between us and swings her legs around until they are on the floor. With the blanket still in her lap she turns to watch the game with me.

During a commercial break she faces me again and says, "You need food. I used the last meat in the freezer and all you have in the fridge is limp lettuce and a few condiments. Can we go to Evelyn's for groceries tomorrow? Or take me to my car so I can go?"

I contemplate her question before answering. I know I need food. I've been living off microwavable dinners for too long, and I know I ate the last one the other night. But I really don't want to spend time with her if I don't have to.

Instead of answering, I ask a question of my own.

"How long you plan on staying? Don't you have work?"

As stressful as it is to have her here, I can't help but feel a tiny bit of pleasure. It's fucked-up that I feel that way, but it is what it is. And I have no idea why. It's not like I *want* her here.

"As long as it takes," she says, shrugging. "And no, it's a four-day weekend, and I can take off Wednesday as well if I want."

"Don't," I tell her harshly.

Her body jerks at my hard tone. When I finally look at her, the concern is back in her eyes. Doesn't she realize I don't want or need her concern? Why won't this girl just give up already?

"You've stayed long enough. You can go back and tell everyone I'm fine. Jaxon took my gun, so there's no chance I'll shoot myself."

My words come out deeper than before, and I know my eyes show hatred. I'm a bastard, and I know it. I'm a bastard for feeling resentment toward the people who care about me. It would destroy them if I purposely hurt myself. But I can't help but feel it. I hate living like this. I'm tired and just want the pain to go away. But then again, I deserve to feel it.

Her eyes mist, and I push away the pain in my stomach at the look. I know the reason she's here. I probably could have talked my way out of having a babysitter had they not found the gun. Everyone knows I've never owned one because Anna was terrified of them. I do know how to use one though. Jaxon, Mac, and I used to target practice quite a bit. Anna was fine with that, as long as I didn't have one in the house.

"Nick," she whispers in a broken voice that nearly has me soften toward her. I steel my resolve.

"No, Chris." I silence her protest by dropping my feet back to the floor with a loud thud. "Fuck, woman! Get a damn clue already. I don't want you here. I haven't from the beginning. Stop fucking pushing me."

Her mouth snaps shut, and she fiddles with the blanket on her lap, her head bent. She has a look of defeat on her face, her eyes hurt. My words hurt her. Better to hurt her now, not when the pain will be ten times worse.

Her throat bobs as she nods and turns back to the TV without another word.

We sit in silence again for a while. I try to let the game on the TV distract me from the woman sitting next to me, but my eyes keep flickering to her. Her red hair is pulled into a braid that falls down her back. Strands have fallen from the hair tie and lie around her face. My eyes follow the line of her profile until they land on her full pink lips. They fascinate me. They look soft and glossy, like she just licked them. They tempt me to lean over and lay mine against them to see what they taste like. Would they taste the same as she smells? Vanilla and sugary. She has high cheekbones and her eyelashes are miles long, hiding her tantalizing green eyes.

What is it about this woman that has me so fascinated?

Her hands are still in her lap, twisting and turning the blanket. She's not so distracted either. She's very much aware of me right now, she's just trying to hide it. The way she's holding her body stiff is telltale.

In an attempt to get my mind off the redheaded temptress, I pick up the book beside me. She spies the book in my hand and the look on her face is almost comical. Her eyes grow wide with panic, her brows go up, and she bites her bottom lip. Her hands jerk in her lap, like she wants to snatch it back from me, and her chest rises and falls rapidly with her heavy breathing.

"Give that back!" she says forcefully.

"Why?" I ask.

"Because it's mine." Her cheeks turn pink as she looks at the book and then back at me.

Curious as to why she's acting this way, I flip the book over and see a guy with his shirt off, chest and arms covered in tattoos. His head is bent slightly but you can still see his eyes. They are a bright green and he has fangs with blood dripping out the corner of his mouth.

What the fuck is this shit? Woman and their romance and paranormal fantasy shit. How in the hell can they think getting bitten by a vampire can be sexy? That shit would hurt.

Crazy woman.

I flip to the page she has dog-eared, and I swear I hear a groan from Chris. Ignoring her obvious discomfort, and now even more curious, I read the first few lines and instantly feel my dick grow in my jeans.

She screams my name over and over again as I grip her hair in my fist and hammer my dick into her viselike pussy. I lean down and growl in her ear, "You want it harder, baby? You want me to tear that pussy up?"

"Fuck yes," she yells and bucks her hips against mine.

I lean down and rest my chest against her back. Reaching around with my free hand, I wrap it around her throat and bring her head back, exposing her delicious neck to my hungry gaze. I see the pulse there and my mouth waters.

I lick from her naked shoulder to that tempting life-saving beat, preparing her for my bite. She knows what's coming and really starts to fuck back against me.

"Don't fucking move!" I order her in a harsh tone, and give her neck a squeeze.

She stops, but I know it's killing her.

With her greedy pussy gripping my cock, I sink my teeth into her beautiful neck and start sucking her life force, letting loose the beast inside me and pistoning my hips forward.

Jesus-fuckin'-Christ! This isn't fucking romance. It's fucking porn! And she was reading this sitting right beside me on the couch.

Shit!

The thought of that has me hot as hell and my body reacts accordingly. My dick jumps, and I almost palm it.

What the fuck is wrong with me?

I look up at Chris and see her looking at the ceiling with her eyes closed, as though she's embarrassed and can't bear to look at me. I just bet she's embarrassed, knowing I now know she was reading this crap right beside me.

"You like this shit?" I ask her, just to embarrass her some more. I want to see the red on her face get deeper.

She still doesn't look at me, but she does open her eyes, though she keeps them trained on the ceiling. Heat creeps up her cheeks, giving me what I want.

"I just started reading them," she mutters, so low I almost don't hear her.

"And the thought of being bitten by a vampire turns you on?"

She whips her head around so fast I wouldn't be surprised if she got whiplash.

"What? No!" she says loudly, and then lowers her voice when she continues. "It's just the idea of something forbidden."

"And do you get wet when you read stuff like this? It turns you on?" I ask, and watch her mouth drop open in shock.

I'm kind of shocked myself at my question. What the hell am I doing? This is dangerous shit right here. But I'm genuinely curious.

She squeezes her eyes shut for a few seconds before turning to me. I'm actually surprised she's willing to face me.

Inhaling deeply, she asks, "Do you really want me to answer that?"

I think about her question for a minute. Do I really want to know?

Yes. Yes, I do.

Should I want the answer?

Fuck no! Her answer is the very last thing I need. I don't need the visual in my head of her getting wet while reading her romance books, maybe even getting herself off at night. It's already bad enough knowing her panties are more than likely wet as we sit here and talk.

Shit! That thought punches my gut.

Shaking my head to rid it of visions I definitely do not want in my head, I hand her book back to her and give her a resounding "No."

I get up from the couch and take my plate and glass to the kitchen. The book is out of sight when I walk back to the living room. I'm sure she's hidden it somewhere.

"Get up," I order her when I'm standing beside the couch.

She watches me with a frown before she pulls the cover from her lap. I silently curse when I see she's in a pair of short sleep shorts, her toned legs on display. They look smooth. My hands itch with the need to run my fingers up them.

This woman really needs to leave my house. Like yesterday.

"You can sleep in my bed. I'll take the couch," I tell her and walk to the small linen closet in the hallway to grab a sheet and blanket.

"I can't do that, Nick. There's no way you'll fit on the couch."

"I'll be fine. It's not like I'll be sleeping anyway," I tell her, and throw the linens on the chair. I pull the cushions from the couch and drop them to the floor. Grabbing the metal bar, I give it a yank and pull out the sofa bed.

I ignore her grunt at the sight of the sofa bed. Yeah, I know I'm an ass for making her sleep on the couch last night when I had a workable and quite comfortable sofa bed. I don't want her comfortable in my house, but the good manners my mom taught me are plaguing me. That's why I'm giving up my bed now.

"I don't have a problem sleeping here," she says gently behind me. "I don't want to take your bed."

I whip around to face her. I really need her to leave. I can't be around her right now, especially with what she's wearing and the vision of her and her damn book. Her fucking face and body and my wild imagination are making it very hard to keep my restraint right now.

I take a couple of steps closer to her before I realize what I'm doing. Her breath hitches and her hand travels to her chest with my sudden movement. I'm only a foot away from her. Entirely too close. My nostrils flare when I take in her sugary smell. I see black flecks in her green eyes and watch as her pupils dilate. I want to reach out and tuck the loose hair around her face behind her ear. I clench my fists to keep from doing just that. This woman is hazardous to my sanity.

I lean down a bit and get in her face. "Go. To. Bed." I punctuate each word by leaning down a little more.

Her eyes go wide and her throat bobs as she watches me with fearful eyes. I'd never hurt her, not physically anyway. Emotionally? I'm sure I already have. She just doesn't get it. I'm precariously close to the edge. If I'm pushed over, I have no idea what'll happen, but I'm sure it won't be good for either of us. I don't have soft and gentle in me anymore. That ship sailed right along with Anna.

I've always known if I ever did get to a place where my body and heart allowed me to have sex with another woman again, it would be just that: sex. No emotion, animalistic, rough, and completely uncaring of the person I'm doing it with. My body may want Chris, but my empty hollow heart knows it could break her. I may be a bastard of the top order, but I don't enjoy watching her hurt.

Air shudders out of her mouth. Even her breath smells like sugar cookies. She licks her lips, and I close my eyes to block it out. When I open them again, her eyes are looking at my lips.

I don't realize I'm reaching for her until my fingers skim across her neck. Mesmerized, I watch as they run down the soft column. It's she who closes her eyes now. I can feel the beat in her throat and it only causes mine to pick up as well.

Shit! What am I doing? I ask myself, but I can't make myself stop. The need to touch is too much to ignore.

She leans her head to the side as I glide my fingers down to her collarbone. A slight moan escapes her lips, sending a shiver down my spine.

I grip her hip tightly with my other hand and step closer to her. She draws me like a light draws a moth. It's uncontrollable and there's not a damn thing I can do. It's like if I don't follow through, I'll suffocate.

Drawing her closer, I bend my head to her neck and take in her scent up close, almost becoming delirious. Her body isn't flush against mine, but I still feel it. The tips of her breasts brush against my chest, and I want to puff it out so I'll feel more of her. One of my feet is planted between hers, and if I move just another inch her sweetness will be against my thigh. I can picture it now. Her rubbing her pussy against the hard muscle there.

I breathe in deep and rest my forehead in the crook of her neck and close my eyes tight. I shouldn't be doing this. It's wrong in every way. It's leading her on. I know it is, but I'm doing it anyway. Just for another minute. I'll give myself this one minute, even though I'll probably pay for it later.

I wrap my arm around her back and bring her willing body against mine. We both suck in a sharp breath. She feels so damn good. So warm and sweet and pliable.

And sweet heaven! Her hot pussy meets the hard muscle of my thigh, and I swear I feel wetness there.

I bend my legs slightly and lift her off the floor, keeping my face in her neck, not wanting to look at her, scared of what I will see and what I'll feel.

She wraps her arms around my shoulders and throws her head back, the perfect picture of someone being pleasured. One of her legs goes around my waist and she grinds down on my hip. My hand grabs her ass, helping her.

Having her like this is one of the best things I've felt in a long time.

It's that thought and her moaned "Nick" that bring me back to my senses. My name being moaned in pleasure sounds different. It's not the sweet sound that Anna used to make. This is deeper, huskier; not innocent, like my Anna.

What in the fucking hell am I doing?

Guilt rushes through me, and I drop Chris and stumble backward, almost tripping over the coffee table. Chris staggers too, but catches herself by grabbing the arm of the couch.

Her eyes are wide, desire still there, along with shame. What the hell does she have to feel shame for? It's I who should be ashamed of myself. And I am. I feel shame. And remorse. And anger. There's plenty of anger. For fuck's sake, I told her leave me be, but she didn't listen.

Guilt eats at me. I know Anna is dead and she won't be coming back. It's ridiculous to feel guilt for touching another woman, but I can't help but feel like it's cheating. She's still so much a part of my life. She's still so deeply imbedded in my heart.

And that angers me even more, because it's partially Chris's fault. She won't leave my thoughts and it's starting to take over. Anna used to be all I ever thought about. Now Chris is creeping her way in, pushing Anna aside.

We both stare at each other, breathing heavily. Our encounter only lasted a short couple of minutes, but it was intense. I haven't felt another woman in so long and my body is still feeling the effects, taking its time playing catch-up with my mind.

She takes a step toward me and opens her mouth to say something.

"No," I say fiercely.

She stops, not only because of my harsh command, but also because of the look on my face.

"Don't come near me," I growl. "Just stay the fuck away from me. Stop fucking looking at me. Stop trying to help me." I snarl the word "help." "And for the love of God, stop acting so damn desperate. You want to get your rocks off, find someone else who'll stick his dick in you, because it sure as shit won't be me."

She blanches at my words and throws a hand to her mouth. A small sob escapes before she can stop it. Tears appear in her eyes and my chest tightens.

I almost go to her, but I force my legs to walk toward the front door instead. I slam the door shut behind me and walk off the porch. I grip my hair and scream to the dark sky. It's not lost on me that I did the same thing while Anna was dying in my arms. And just like then, I receive no answer in return.

eight

Chris

I STRETCH MY ARMS over my head and give a big yawn. I don't want to get up, but I know I need to. I roll to my side, open my eyes, and see dark sheets.

Wait.

The cover on Nick's couch is a light color, not the navy blue I'm currently looking at. The pillow feels different too. It's soft, but firm.

Memories of what happened last night come flooding in and my face heats at the reminder. What Nick said last night cut deep and has me clutching my chest from the pain. I had no idea I appeared so desperate to him.

God!

What an idiot I've been. Yes, I care for Nick and want to help him get over his grief. I know I could never replace Anna; that's never been my goal. My goal isn't even to get him to care for me. I just want him to realize there is life after her. That it is still possible to be happy. I would love if I could give him that happiness, but that's not why I feel the need to be there for him. I don't know why I have this strong need, but it's something I can't stop. I don't want to stop it. It's important for some reason.

As soon as he walked out the door last night, I ran to his room. I don't know if he ever came back in, but I didn't want to be present if he did. I couldn't stand to look at him after what he said. He obviously doesn't want me, friend or otherwise. For him to say I was acting desperate made me feel dirty. It didn't feel right to sleep in his bed, but I didn't want to take the chance of him saying something else to me, so I chose the safer route and slept here. I don't even know why he offered his bed. It's not like he cares if I'm comfortable or not.

There're two pillows on his bed. I chose to sleep on the one that looked less used. I now stare at the other one. I hesitantly reach out and lay my hand on it. I know my head is playing tricks on me when I feel warmth coming from it. I curl my fingers and watch my hand fist the pillow. I slowly bring it forward until I have my face buried in it. I instantly smell his woodsy scent, and tears prick my eyes.

I keep my head there for several moments, just breathing in. I wish things could be different between us. It's not that I wish he'd never had Anna. That would be wrong. Obviously, their love was epic. But I can't help but wish we could have met in another lifetime. That way I could have had Nick without all the anguish. I would love to have seen what he was like before Anna died.

I wish I could just keep my face buried in his pillow forever. I love the smell of him. But that would be stupid and is a heartache waiting to happen. Inhaling deep one more time, I release his pillow and flip the covers back. After getting up and using the bathroom, I walk back out, flip the light switch, and look around his room. It was too dark the other day to get a good look.

The walls are a soft white, with light blue trim around the windows. They're clean but it's plain to see the paint is old. In one corner there's a chair with a footstool in front of it. Beside it sits a small round table. The massive bed where I just slept is a four-poster. The head and footboards are made of dark wood, with nightstands on either side. Across from the bed is a tall dark dresser.

There's a closed door to the left that's probably a closet. A desk and chair are in the opposite corner from the ottoman. There are clothes thrown about and the dresser is cluttered with random things. A pair of boots lie beside the desk. Although this room is well lived-in, it still feels empty, plain. It sounds stupid and silly, but there's no emotion in this room.

A few moments later, I walk out to the living room, anxious about the mood he'll be in. I don't have to worry, though, because he's not in there or in the kitchen. He did come in, though, because the couch is folded back and the blanket and sheet are in a mess on it. I walk over and fold them. I hear a creak at the front door and glance over. Through the curtains, I see him sitting on the love seat.

Still not ready to face him, I grab my bag off the floor by the couch and take it with me to the bathroom. I pull clean clothes out, get dressed, and brush my teeth and hair.

I make my customary silly face and then walk back out, dropping my bag in the hallway. A glance to the front window confirms Nick is still outside. Walking past the door, I opt to pour a cup of coffee first from the pot that's already made.

All too soon, my cup is finished. Dread fills my stomach at what I might encounter when I walk outside. Gathering every bit of courage I have, I slowly make my way to the door. I hate this feeling.

The screen door creaks as I open it. Nick is still in the same clothes as last night. His feet are bare and are propped up on the railing in front of him. His sleeves are pushed up to his elbows, showing off muscular forearms crossed over his chest. He doesn't say anything or look my way as I walk to the railing and rest my arms on it.

Deciding to stay silent as well, I look out to the yard. The sun is up, but it's shady outside because of all the trees. A cool breeze whips across my arms, sending a shiver through me. Off to the left is the barn with peeling red paint. I don't think it's a traditional barn that houses farm animals, but just a huge garage. The grass is a lush green and thick. It's beautiful out here. You almost feel like you're in a private world, with the coverage of trees and their stunning colors. It must be a shame when winter hits and all the leaves fall.

"How's your brother?" Nick asks, startling me.

I glance over my shoulder at him to see him still looking out into the yard. He looks relaxed, the constant scowl that's usually on his face absent at the moment.

"He's fine. Healing good." I chuckle. "He's about done with Andrew's hovering though. Says he keeps babying him."

Jase was shot a little over a month ago when I was held hostage by his ex. The dumb ass charged Damien in attempt to get the aim off me and got hurt in the process.

I shudder when I think of how much worse it could have been. The bullet grazed his lung and it collapsed. Surgery was needed to take the bullet out and to make sure nothing else vital was hit. He was very lucky. I thank God every day that he's okay.

Andrew took it really hard. Seeing the love of his life laid out on the ground bleeding almost destroyed him. Now's he's waiting hand and foot on Jase, which is driving Jase bonkers, but I understand the need to feel useful, wanting to take the pain away from the ones we love in any way we can.

"And you?" Nick asks.

Surprised at his question, I turn to face him. He's still not looking at me, but the relaxed expression is gone. His jaw's hard and his eyes are narrowed as he continues to look over the railing.

Why would he care how I am? I wasn't even sure he knew what had happened until he asked me about Jase. But then again, I'm sure Jaxon keeps him in the loop of current events in Jaded Hollow just because he lives here. He has no reason to want to know how I handled the attack. And he doesn't know Jase well enough to really care about what happened to him. I'm not saying he doesn't care, I'm sure he wouldn't want anything to happen to Jase or me, but for him to ask about either of us, especially me, is surprising.

I don't answer right away. Instead I remember his hands on me last night. Having him touch me felt right, perfect. When he buried his face in my neck, I wanted to grab hold of his head and keep it there always. The woodsy scent of him engulfed me and held me hostage as his hands roamed down my back to my ass. Feeling my center meet his hard thigh and then hip nearly had me climaxing. Never have I felt something as good as having him touch me the way he did. It's crazy, but it felt like something clicked into place, like what we were doing was meant to be, like we were meant to be. *That's* what makes it crazy, because we aren't meant to be. I don't know what we are, but Nick was never meant to be mine. He was made for someone else. Me? I have no idea what or who I was made for. Maybe I was made to pine after someone who pines after someone else. Maybe I was never meant to find that one person to fulfill every part of me.

Nick's body may have responded to mine, but that's all it was. Sexual chemistry. Hell, it could have been any woman in that moment, and his body could have reacted. It wasn't because it was *me*. I just happened to be there.

That thought brings an ache to my chest, and I look down, no longer able to look at him at the moment.

Knowing he doesn't really care, I answer him anyway.

"I'm fine, too."

He's quiet, so I look back at him. His eyes are pinned on me, like he's gauging to see if my answer it truthful.

I turn back to the yard and watch as the sun filters through leaves and branches. It shoots beams through to the ground. It really is breathtaking.

"It's beautiful. You must love living here," I tell Nick.

I hear the love seat creak as he shifts positions. "It was my parents' place. It was left to me when they died."

I hear the ache in his voice, and I want to go comfort him. I learned from Bailey that Nick's parents died when he was seventeen. Because he was so close to becoming a legal adult, he was allowed to stay here on his own instead of being made to live with another relative. He has no family left in Jaded Hollow, so he would have been forced to move away. He's lived here all his life, and the judge felt since he was already working and the house was paid for, he would be fine on his own the last few months before he turned eighteen.

"I'm sorry about your parents. It must have been hard to lose them that young. It was a car accident, right?"

He drops his feet from the railing and leans up, placing his elbows on his knees, still gazing forward. He has a sad faraway look in his eyes now, like he's remembering that time.

"Yeah," he says quietly. "My dad had just gotten the brakes done in his car earlier that day. They said it was a faulty brake line. Thousands were recalled after that, but it was only my parents, a mother and child, and an old man who died because of it."

My heart goes out to him. It's hard enough to lose one parent, but to lose both in the same day would be beyond devastating. Especially because of some mistake that could have been prevented. My parents are hard to live with, can sometimes be unreasonable, specifically with Jase, and sometimes I want to strangle them, but I can't imagine losing either of them.

I turn to the side and cock a hip against the railing. The old red barn catches my attention and I remember the question I asked him yesterday while he was chopping wood. It's not really important, but I'm curious. And I'm enjoying the quiet talk between us without the animosity that usually comes from him.

"Why were you chopping wood yesterday?"

He looks at me for a moment and then rises from the love seat. He walks over and mirrors my stance with his hip propped against the railing, facing me. He watches me curiously.

"Every fall I chop wood for Mr. and Mrs. Cooper. They depend solely on their fireplace to keep warm in the winter, and he's too old to do it himself."

"That's very sweet of you," I tell him with a smile.

He shrugs and plays it off. "It's no big deal. I've been doing it for years."

"It is to them," I say gently.

We turn back to the yard and stand in silence for a while, both leaning our elbows on the railing. It's not much, but the easiness between us the last thirty minutes is addicting. I wish it could always be like this, but I'm not under the illusion it'll stay this way. I know it's only a glimpse in time, but I savor it nonetheless.

Hating to break the unspoken truce, but knowing I need to broach the subject, I brace myself for the hateful Nick to come back.

"I know this is hard, and I know you'll hate me for bringing it up, but you need to talk to Bailey." He turns to me, brow arched, waiting for an explanation. I swallow before forcing myself to continue. "She still feels so much guilt, Nick. Have you even spoken to her about it?"

His eyes lose the easy look, just like I knew they would. His teeth grind together, and I see a throb on his temple. I know from watching other encounters that anytime someone brings up what happened, he gets pissy.

"It's none of your business whether I've talked to her or not," he says between clenched teeth. "I don't need you butting in or dictating what I do."

Straightening my spine and squaring my shoulders, I prepare for battle. I'm not backing down from this. It's too important.

"Actually, it is my business," I counter, holding my ground when he squints at me. "Bailey is my friend and she's in pain. You have the power to help lessen it. I know you're hurting too, but you need to think of someone else besides yourself for once."

For a moment I think he's going to lash out, like literally lash out. I've never felt even the smallest amount of fear that Nick would ever put his hands on a woman, but in that moment, it looks like he wants to wrap his hands around my throat and squeeze. It's in his blazing blue eyes and the way he's tightening and loosening his hands into fists. I'm sure he's probably picturing them around my throat.

Although I want to shy away, I stand firm and before I know it, the intense look is gone. I feel foolish for even thinking he would lay a hand on me. I may not know Nick well, but one thing I'm sure of is he would never intentionally hurt a woman. Not physically anyway. Emotionally he's already done quite a bit of damage to me, and I'm sure he knows it.

After several seconds, he drops his gaze to his hands and watches as he unclenches his fingers and stretches them out.

When he looks back at me, I see sorrow and torture in his eyes. He knows what I've said is true. Out of everyone, he and Bailey are the ones who were affected the most by Anna's death. He because of what Anna was to him, and Bailey, because she witnessed the horrible ordeal and feels it's her fault Anna was in that situation.

"I'll talk to her," he states, his voice gravelly and raw.

"Thank you."

Once again, we turn back to the yard. I'm about to leave him be when he says, "Grab your stuff. We'll hit the store and then I'll drop you off at home."

I don't want to leave. He still doesn't need to be here alone, but I have no choice. I know I've pushed him as far as I dare. I don't want to do irreparable damage.

Unless...

Looking contrite, I nod and go back into the house to grab my bag in the hallway. I send a quick text to Jaxon, hoping he'll agree to my plan.

WE'VE JUST LOADED up the few bags of groceries that Nick purchased when I spot Andrew's retreating back as he walks into Maggie's. Trying to stall for time, I turn to Nick.

"I'm hungry. Can we stop over at Maggie's for a bite before you drop me off?"

He glances over at the diner before looking back at me, weighing his answer before giving it.

There's a lot I've learned about Nick through his friends. For instance, I know it was months before he stepped foot into Maggie's after Anna died. I'm sure it's a big reminder every time he goes there. I also know that although he's gotten over that hurdle, he still tries to avoid the place as much as he can. It's baby steps that help us the most. I hope he will continue to take them.

I watch closely as several emotions cross Nick's face. He runs his hands down his face and across his scruffy jaw before closing his door and walking around to my side. A rush of happiness runs through me.

"Come on. We can't stay long or the groceries will sour," he says, and I fall into step beside him. It's cool outside, but not cool enough to hold the groceries long.

I feel his hand at my back for a moment before he drops it, and it sends warmth to my stomach.

We enter the diner a couple minutes later. It's between breakfast and lunch so it's not busy. I spot Andrew and Jase sitting at a booth to the left. Andrew is facing me. He sees us walk in and smirks. Jase must notice because he turns around. His eyes hold worry and a bit of contempt when he looks at Nick. I glare at him to warn him to behave. After a second, the look is gone, and I breathe a sigh of relief.

Crisis diverted.

I feel Nick at my back and turn to see him looking at the long white counter. When I look that way, I see Maggie standing behind it, serving a customer. She briefly glances up at us, just long enough for me to see surprise and pleasure, before she looks back at the customer. Bringing my eyes back to Nick, I see pain etched on his face.

Not caring if it's welcome, I reach for his hand and give it a squeeze. He drags his eyes away from Maggie and looks down at my hand on his. Brows pinched together, he lifts his eyes to me. I don't know what it is, but something passes over his face.

I hold my breath, waiting for him to reprimand me for interfering, but it doesn't come. Instead, he pulls his hand from mine and places it on my back, guiding me over to Andrew and Jase's table.

As we get closer, I notice they have another guest with them. I squeal in delight and run the last few feet to their table to drop down on my knees in front of Ally.

Technically Ally is Andrew's daughter, but she knows him as her uncle. Andrew donated his sperm to her parents, Becky and Brent, when they couldn't get pregnant on their own. She has leukemia and the last several months have been hard on her. Because of the chemo treatments, her bone marrow died. Andrew donated his to help. Last I heard they were waiting to see if it took and if the leukemia was in remission. Of course, even if it is remission, there's always a chance it could come back. I pray that doesn't happen. She's been through enough.

"Hey, Ally!" I tell her, holding out my arms for a hug. She smiles big, making her whole face light up. She climbs out of her seat and throws her arms around my neck.

When she pulls back, she kisses my cheek. My heart melts even more for this little girl.

"Hi, Christabelle," Ally chirps at me in her sweet voice. Besides my parents, she is the only one who calls me by my full name. She claims Chris sounds too close to a boy's name.

"How have you been?" I ask, holding her small hands in mine.

She's nearly bouncing on her feet when she says excitedly, "I'm going to be okay! Just like I knew I would be! The doctors said I'm all better now!"

Moisture pricks my eyes, and I look up to Andrew, hoping what she said is what I think it is. The answer is written all over his face when his lips form a big smile, the stressful look he's carried lately finally wiped clean.

"Really?" I ask, looking back and forth between him and Ally.

"Really," he confirms, looking more relaxed than I've seen him in a while. "The marrow took and her white blood cell count is where it should be. The leukemia is in remission."

"Oh my God! This is wonderful news!"

I hug Ally close to me. Not giving Andrew time to rise from his seat, I lean over Ally to give him a hug as well. Jase gets up, and I throw my arms around him too. This is the best news I've heard in a long time. My heart swells for these three. They deserve some good news.

I squat back down to Ally, grab her cheeks, and kiss her forehead.

"Let me look at you," I tell her when I pull back.

She looks so much better than the last time I saw her. She has on a beanie that hides the fact that all her hair is gone. Her cheeks have more color, her eyes are no longer sunken in, and it looks like she's gained a few pounds, even though it's only been a couple weeks since I saw her at Becky and Brent's house. She looks healthier and happier.

I've always loved kids, and I hope to have some one day. It's been a dream of mine since I was little myself. I can't imagine never having them; it would devastate me.

My mind immediately wanders to the man still standing behind me. I know I shouldn't, but an image of Nick holding a baby pops into my head. I wipe it away, knowing it's ridiculous to even entertain such a thing.

I stand and turn to him. He's been quiet this whole time. When I'm facing him, he's looking at Ally with an expression I've never seen on his face before. His eyes are soft and his lips are tipped up at the corners. He looks absolutely breathtaking like this, no longer appearing the hard-hearted man.

I know I must be staring at him like an idiot, so I pull my eyes away and look back at Ally. She has her head tipped back and is watching Nick with interest.

"Nick," Andrew says, standing. "You haven't met Ally yet. Ally, this is another friend of mine, Nick."

"You're Nick?" Ally breathes, seeming mesmerized by him.

I didn't know it was possible, but Nick's expression softens even more. He gets down on one knee in front of her.

"That's me. It's nice to finally meet you, Ally," his deep voice rumbles.

Still in a daze, Ally takes a step closer to him. She lifts her small palm and lays it on his cheek.

"I've heard about you," she says, so quietly I have to strain to hear.

I look up at Andrew and Jase and see them both watching the exchange. Andrew lifts his eyes to mine, arching a brow. I look back down at Nick and Ally.

"You're Uncle Andy's sad friend," she whispers.

I suck in a breath and my hand flies to my mouth. Tears pool in my eyes at her softly spoken words and the weight behind them.

Nick closes his eyes for a moment. When he opens them, they are still soft, but the grief is back.

"I am, but I'll be okay," he tells her sadly, and gives her a small smile.

She smiles at him in return, leans over and kisses his cheek, and then pulls back.

"You will be. I know you will."

He looks at her a few more seconds and then kisses her forehead before standing back up.

The heart-stopping moment is over. I wonder what Nick thought about in those moments.

Andrew resumes his seat, grabbing Ally's hand and pulling her with him. Instead of sitting across from him like he was, Jase scoots in next to Ally. The seat is cramped, forcing Andrew to put his arm on the back of the booth.

"Join us," Andrew says, gesturing to the seat across from them.

I look at Nick to make sure it's okay. He nods, so I slide in the seat. He sits down beside me, and I immediately feel his warmth.

"You going to be okay there, Skittles, or do you want me to put you in a booster seat at the end of the table?" Andrew asks Ally with mischief.

"Really, Uncle Andy? You know I'm too big for a booster seat," she scolds him with her child's voice.

"Just checking," he says, chuckling and ruffling the top of her head.

I love seeing this side of Andrew. He's a natural when it comes to kids and would make an excellent father if given the chance. Thank goodness Becky and Brent allow him to spend so much time with Ally.

"So, what are you both doing today?" Andrew says, giving us a curious look.

It must be strange to see us together like this. I have to admit; it feels strange. I never thought we would be in a place where we could actually sit down and be civil to each other. I had hoped, but never really thought we would.

I love it.

I feel Nick shift beside me. His leg brushes against mine and stays there. I don't know if it's intentional or not, but I don't move my leg either. Is it pitiful of me to take any type of contact I can from him, even if it's just an innocent brush of his leg against mine?

"We just left Evelyn's after picking up a few things. Nick is taking me home after we leave here."

Unless my plan works, I silently add. I glance down at my phone, which I have placed on the table. I haven't heard back from Jaxon, so I have no idea if he got my message or not.

"How's work?" Andrew asks Nick.

Nick moves again and his arm rubs against mine. My body is hyperaware of him, so I feel even the tiniest of movements. I have to work at not squirming from the butterflies currently zooming around in my stomach.

"It's work. Been having trouble with a couple contractors cutting corners. I had to let one go about a month ago because he fucked up a wiring job." He winces and looks at Ally, who's currently drawing on a white piece of paper, oblivious to us talking. Still, Nick watches his language when he talks next. "Had one of my men not noticed, it could have ended with an electrical fire, and God knows how many people inside. When I went to past jobs the guy worked on for me, I found a few more screwups. I don't need that crap. Luckily, he was new and the jobs he'd done for me so far aren't finished and the buildings aren't occupied yet, but it sets me back."

Wow! I think this is the most I've heard him talk. I sit and listen intently. I love hearing his voice. It's gruff and deep and sends tickles down my spine every time I hear it. It's different now though. The animosity that's usually there isn't present. You can tell he genuinely cares about his job and how his work affects others.

"That's awful. How can people be so selfish and think it's okay to cheat that way, knowing someone could get hurt in the process?" I put in, upset for Nick that he has to deal with this.

"I have no clue, but it doesn't fly with me. I don't operate my business that way," he says passionately.

"Some people are just out for themselves," Andrew says. "You can analyze it all you want, but we'll never know why people do what they do. You just have to learn to avoid them."

Just then Maggie walks up to our table, out of breath, and interrupts our conversation.

"Sorry for the wait. Damn Frank wouldn't shut up," she grumbles, looking at each of us. Her gaze lingers on Nick longer than the rest of us.

"Hey Nick, 'bout time you come in here for a visit." Her voice is kind and affectionate, but there's a hint of deep-seated pain there as well.

He gets up and engulfs her in his big strong arms. She wraps her own arms around his middle, hugging him tight.

"Hey Gram," I hear him say softly. "Sorry for not coming sooner."

She pushes him back and gives him a loud kiss on the cheek. "Oh posh!" she says, patting the cheek she kissed. "You're here now. How long are you in town for?"

"Should be a few weeks at least, if nothing pops up."

"Good. You need a break. I don't want you waiting so long in between visits, you hear?" She points a pen she pulled from her apron at him.

He throws up his hands in mock surrender. "I won't. Promise," he says, chuckling, sending goose bumps down my arms with the sound.

Maggie pulls out a pad of paper while Nick sits back down, his leg once again resting against mine. His hand brushes against my hair when he puts his arm along the back of the seat behind me. If I'm not mistaken, he's sitting closer to me than he was before. With his arm on the back of the seat and his leg against mine, it almost feels like he's caging me in. However, this is a cage I would willingly be captured in.

Too bad it's all an illusion.

"So, what can I get for you all?" Maggie asks, bringing me back from my wishful thinking.

We place our order and of course Maggie doesn't write anything down. I don't even know why she carries around a pen and note-book, because she never uses it. I'm sure it's just out of habit. She's been doing this for years, so she uses her exceptional memory to remember everything anyone orders.

She stays and chats for another minute or two and then walks off to put in our order to Cookie, the cook. The chatter around the table is light and enjoyable. I listen to the men talk about unimportant things, joining in the conversation when I need to, but content to stay silent.

"Wanna see what I drew?" Ally asks, holding her picture to her chest, looking hesitant.

"I would love to see it, honey."

Her eyes light up and she holds the picture out for me to grab. I smooth it out in front of me on the table. For a girl so young, she has an amazing artistic imagination and talent. I've seen some of her drawings and every one was outstanding. I can definitely see her doing something in art when she's older.

What I see when I look at the picture has my throat clogging with emotion. It's a picture of a pond with the sun shining down on it. Beautiful multicolored flowers surround the pond. There's even a mama duck with her baby chicks swimming. On either side of the pond are a man and a woman sitting on docks with their feet in the water as they look up at the sun. They are too far away to draw the faces, but I would bet that if they were drawn, the faces would be sad. You can see it by the way they hold their bodies.

I look up at her, only to see her looking at Nick. When I look at him, he's looking down at the picture with an expression I can't quite decipher. I hadn't realized the table had gone quiet until just now.

Nick removes his arm from the back of the bench and reaches out slowly for the picture. He lifts his eyes to Ally and asks in a soft voice, "This is very beautiful, Ally. Who are these people?"

She drops her eyes to her lap, biting her tiny lip before bringing them back to Nick. I hold my breath, wondering if she's going to say what I think she is.

"That's you," she says, pointing to the man. "And I don't know who the woman is. I just..." She trails off.

"You just what, sugar?" Nick asks gently.

"Sometimes I have dreams," she whispers. "Sometimes they are clear and sometimes they aren't. I dreamed that picture the other night. I knew the man was you, because Uncle Andy has talked about you before and I've seen pictures of you, but I don't know who the woman is. Her face wasn't clear."

We all look back down to the woman in the picture, each knowing who she is. She has long red hair, after all. And I think Ally knows it too, but she's too worried to say it out loud.

The picture depicts my and Nick's precarious relationship to a T. We're on separate sides of the pond, filled with sadness; his grief for losing Anna, mine for feeling helpless at seeing his grief.

"That's not all I dreamed." Ally speaks up again and we all look from the picture back to her, waiting for her to continue. "The man looked down from the sun and smiled. A boat appeared in front of him and he got in it and started rowing toward the girl. That's when I woke up."

I freeze, unable to draw in breath. I have no clue what to say. Is this girl special? Can she see things others can't? Does she somehow dream premonitions? When she was in the hospital she told everyone that an angel visited her in a dream and told her she would be fine. And here she sits, cancer in remission.

None of us say anything. We just stare at either Ally or the picture. I feel Nick move beside me and look over at him. His eyes are still on the picture, his face an unreadable mask. I wish I knew what he is thinking. I know he has to know who the woman is. And I also know he would deny what the picture and Ally's dream represent. I can't help but hope it comes true. Part of it has already come true. We have this huge gulf between us.

Maggie interrupts the solemn moment when she brings our

food. I slide the picture back to my side so Maggie can set the food down and it's not in the way. I don't want anything happening to it.

I crook my finger at Ally and lean over the table. She gets to her knees and leans over as well.

"Can I keep the picture?" I whisper, my voice sounding broken even to my own ears.

She smiles and nods.

"Thank you."

What she doesn't realize is I'm thanking her for more than just giving me the picture. I'm also thanking her for giving me that little bit of hope I feel building in my stomach.

I feel eyes on me and look up at Jase. He gives me a small chin lift, and I immediately know what he's saying. He's telling me he understands and accepts what I'm doing in trying to help Nick. That he no longer resents him and the situation.

I grin at him, only to have him roll his eyes, then grin back.

We eat in silence, the easy atmosphere no longer oozing off Nick. His body is tense beside me. His leg no longer rests against mine, and I miss the touch and warmth. I know he's got to be thinking about the picture and it has him confused.

After several minutes of strained silence, Jase and Ally excuse themselves so he can walk her to the bathroom. As they walk away, the bell over the door tinkles. I glance back to see Jaxon walking our way. He gives me a meaningful look, secretly letting me know he got my message earlier.

"Hey," he rumbles, once he's standing beside our table. "I'm glad I caught you here, Chris. I have bad news. Last night your apartment sprung a leak in the bathroom. It's fixed, but the floors are soaked. I have someone coming in tomorrow to vac dry the carpet. I don't want you staying there until it's dry."

I feign shock with a gasp. "What? How on earth did that happen?"

"I'm not sure. There was a busted pipe under the sink. The building and pipes are old, so I'm sure it was just from use. I've replaced them, so it should be good. I've needed to do that for a while anyway. And your stuff is fine. It's mainly the hallway that got soaked." He turns to Nick. "Can she stay at your place a couple more days until it's taken care of?"

Jaxon shows no shame or remorse in asking Nick if I can stay. I almost laugh at the look Nick throws his way. It'd hurt to see the way "No" practically sits on the edge of his tongue if I didn't know Jaxon and I are playing him. I don't know if Nick believes Jaxon's story or not, and I don't care, as long as it gets me a couple more days with Nick. He still has his shitty moments toward me, but since I've been there he's shown me other sides of himself. I cherish the good ones.

"Why can't she stay with you?" Nick grits out, narrowing his eyes at Jaxon in suspicion.

"Because my cousins are staying at my house for the next couple of nights. They're taking the extra bedroom. And before you ask, Mac and Mia have a full house too. His parents are visiting."

Nick glances at Andrew with panicky eyes, I'm sure hoping he can pawn me off on them.

Okay, there's the pain creeping in. The hidden smirk drops from my face and my mood darkens.

"No can do, my friend, Ally has the spare. Looks like you're stuck with Chris for the next couple days," Andrew says, his shoulders shaking slightly with his laugh.

I hear Nick's muttered "Fuck" beside me and his words from last night come rushing back to mind.

"For the love of God, stop acting so damn desperate."

Pain pierces my heart. I may be desperate, but I hate the thought of him thinking me so pathetic. Why am I so determined to be near someone who would rather cut off both hands than be close to me? When did I become the person who tries to push herself where she's not wanted? And why in the world does it have to be the man sitting beside me who makes me feel like I can't breathe without him?

My palms become sweaty and my heart races in my chest. My temples start to pound, and I feel tingles on the top of my head. Shit. I can't breathe. I need to leave. I need to get out of here and away from Nick. I've never had a panic attack before, but I'd bet this is the start of one.

They must notice my impending attack because through my blurry vision, I see Nick turn to face me, brows drawn down over blue eyes when he sees my sweaty and pale face.

"What the hell—"

I stop him with a shove.

"Move, move, move!" I say hysterically, still trying to push him from his seat. He's not moving fast enough. I can't be here anymore. "I need to leave! Now! Please get up! I've got to go!"

"What the fuck, Chris?" Nick asks with alarm, finally sliding from his seat.

I follow closely behind him and am on my feet a second later. The sudden movement from sitting to standing leaves me dizzy. I grab the back of the booth to steady myself before I fall on my face. I hear Jaxon and Andrew talking, but I don't know what they're saying. A hand grabs my arm.

I snatch it back. "No! Don't touch me!" I spit at Nick.

Suddenly, I'm pissed. The dizzy fades away as all the shit he's put me through boils up and overflows.

He throws his palms out in front of him, but takes a step closer to me. I drop my eyes from his and point them at his chest. I can't look at him right now. The dizziness may have faded, but my head is still pounding like drummers in a parade.

"You need to sit before you fall," he says apprehensively.

"Like you freakin' care," I mutter snidely.

When I go to sidestep him, he gets in my way.

"Chris, I don't know what the fuck your problem is, but sit the fuck down," he growls.

"Fuck you, Nick! I'm leaving. I'm going home."

I try to go around him the other way, but he moves with me.

"Move!"

"No!" he barks.

I snap my eyes to his and shove his chest, hard. He doesn't move an inch. And it just pisses me off more.

"Get the hell out of my way!" I demand.

He captures my hands in one of his and bends his knees so he's in my face. I try to yank them away, but he holds them firmly. Why does the stupid jerk have to be so strong?

"Where are you going to go? You can't stay at your house."

Shit! I forgot in my near panic that Jaxon and I staged a leak.

I look over at Jaxon, who's watching us closely, then at Andrew and Jase, who have a worried Ally behind them. Andrew almost looks amused, while Jase looks livid and ready to pounce. The rest of the diner is quiet, the few customers no doubt watching the show.

"Fine!" I grate between my teeth, trying to calm myself down. "I'll find somewhere else to stay. Now let me go."

"The hell you will," he says, ignoring my demand to let go of my hands. "You're coming home with me," he declares heatedly.

My eyes bug out, and I laugh in his face. The gall of this man.

"Are you listening to yourself right now? First you damn near come unglued at the thought of me being there. You pretty much demand I leave. And now you're saying you *want* me there? Do you see how I'm finding this a little hard to take?"

"I don't care how you take it, Sugar, but the fact remains, you're coming home with me." He's only a hair's breadth away from my face when he finishes. "Whether you like it or not."

Ugh! This man is so damn frustrating! I've put up with so much shit from him. My head is spinning from his constant back-and-forth attitude changes. I don't know who I am anymore around him. How much more can I take before it obliterates me?

"Enough!" Jaxon booms from behind Nick.

We both ignore him. Our chests pump with our breathing as we glare at each other. Nick's pupils eat up the intense blue, just as I'm sure the green in mine has disappeared as well.

"Chris, your ass is staying with Nick. And Nick, you're going to be nice about it. Understood?" Jaxon says, his tone brooking no argument.

I pull on my arm and he finally releases it. Taking a step back, I turn to Jaxon. "Fine," I mutter petulantly.

I get a chin lift in return and he turns his eyes to Nick.

"Nick," he warns, when Nick doesn't answer.

After several seconds, he hisses, "Yes."

"Good. Now pay for your and Chris's lunch and get the fuck home."

Grinding my teeth, I walk away from Nick and over to Andrew, Jase, and Ally. Squatting down, I reach for the little girl still behind their legs. Her worried eyes break my heart. She immediately puts her arms around me.

"I'm sorry you saw that, baby," I murmur in her ear.

"It's okay," she says, her voice small.

I pull back from her, cup her cheeks, and look into her eyes. She appears to be fine, but I still hate that she witnessed what happened.

I bring her forehead to my lips for a kiss. After getting a smile from her, I stand up. I lean up on my toes and kiss Andrew on the cheek. He grins down at me, not fazed by what happened. He's used to the shit that goes on between me and Nick.

"I'm proud of you," he says in a low voice. This is the first time I've stood up to Nick, so I understand what he means. I don't feel particularly good about it though. I never raise my voice like that. I try to stay away from confrontation as much as possible. But a girl can only take so much.

I turn to Jase and see he's shooting daggers at Nick. So much for the truce.

I pinch his scruffy chin and force his face down so he's looking at me.

"Stop," I tell him firmly.

He's about to say something, but I silence him by gripping his chin tighter.

"No. Leave it be. I'm fine, and I'll be fine there."

He scowls at me for a minute before giving me a single nod. I kiss his cheek next and then stomp out of the diner, not waiting for Nick.

The bastard can stay behind for all I care.

nine

Nick

I SWEAR I NEED to be committed or something. What in the fuck possessed me to agree to allow Chris to stay a couple more days? Didn't I just come to the conclusion that she had to go for my sanity's sake?

I slam my truck into drive and skid out onto the road, pissed at myself for getting in this situation. A silent Chris sits beside me, stewing I'm sure, and I'm grateful. I need her to keep her mouth shut right now so I can come up with a way to deal with the fact she'll be in my space for another couple of days.

I think back to the panicked look on her face in the diner. She had gone pale and sweat had popped up on her forehead. When she started struggling to get up, mere concern was replaced with outright fear. I had no idea what brought on the near panic attack, but seeing her like that did something to my stomach. I didn't like it one bit. Then when she threw my hand off when I reached out to her, my anger spiked.

Months and months, hell, for more than a year, she's butted her way into my life and tried inserting herself into my business, and the first time I do it, she turns bitchy. There was one thing she was right about though. One minute I'm practically kicking her out of my house and then the next I'm demanding she stay. I am so fucked-up.

I'm not stupid enough to think the story that Jaxon told us about Chris's pipes was true. One look in his eyes said he was up to something. I not only have Chris trying to push her way into my life, but now I have Jaxon pushing her in as well. I could have forced the issue, but I didn't. And I have no idea why I didn't. All I know is that in the end it was just on principle, to prove Chris wrong, that I agreed to Jaxon.

Now I want to cut out my own tongue for saying yes. This is going to be a long two fucking days. I've got to find something to occupy my time and stay the hell away from her.

My grip on the steering wheel is so tight my knuckles are turning white. I loosen my fingers a fraction. I try to keep my eyes on the road, but they keep stealing sideward glances at her. She's in the same position each time; hands clasped tightly in her lap while she stares out her window. I'd bet my left nut that she's not paying attention to the scenery passing by. Her tense body says she has something on her mind, and I know just what it is.

We pull up to the house a few minutes later. She jumps out of the truck before it's even in park. I uncurl my fingers from the steering wheel, open my door, and get out. By the time I climb the steps with a few bags in hand, she's already waiting for me by the door with her own bags.

Without a word, I unlock the door and she rushes inside with a muttered "Thank you."

I sigh and rub the back of my neck, where tension has caused the muscles to bunch.

Chris drops her overnight bag right inside the door and without a word or backward glance, marches the groceries she's still carrying into the kitchen. Her hips sway ahead of me as I follow her at a slower pace. I scowl at her ass for tempting me to reach out and grab a handful. Luckily, the vision disappears when she enters the kitchen, and the need lessens.

She has one bag unloaded on the bar and is emptying out the last one. I place my bags next to hers and we both finish unloading and putting the items away in silence. Tension fills the space around us in thick waves. Chris's movements are less jerky than when I first walked in, but I can tell she's still agitated about earlier. As much as I don't want to, I know I need to find a way to get along with her, or these next couple of days will be even more miserable. I plan to do everything possible to keep away from her, but we're bound to run into each other.

Gritting my teeth, I play nice and ask a random question to break the irritating silence.

"Why did you decide to be a guidance counselor?"

She drops a can of vegetables on the counter and looks at me with surprised but wary eyes. She has good reason. We went from yelling at each other in Maggie's to me asking her a personal question twenty minutes later.

I hold her stare, amazed that I actually want to know the answer. I shouldn't want to know anything about this woman, especially since she's already taking over my thoughts, but I do.

After a few seconds, she collects herself, picks up the fallen can, and grabs two more. She walks to a cabinet and deposits them inside.

"I've always wanted to be that person in school that kids depend on to help guide them in the right direction. I don't know how much you know, but my parents weren't the best. They didn't abuse Jase and me, but they weren't there when we needed them. It was more a form of emotional neglect." She stops long enough to put the meats and frozen rolls in the freezer. Then she turns and leans against the counter beside the fridge. I cross my arms and my ankles and lean against the bar as I listen.

"In elementary and middle school, the guidance counselors sucked. They had the job but didn't actually do the job. Seemed they were always busy or never had time when I needed someone to talk to or needed help with academics. By the time I reached high school, I had given up on them. I had a couple of friends' parents I could go to if I needed something. Pissed at my parents for always missing my soccer games and school functions, I went through a rebellious phase and started missing school and slacked on work. My grades were dropping fast. The counselor noticed and took an interest in me. She pulled me aside one day and asked what was going on. Said she saw how I always had good grades and never missed school, until that year. I was reluctant to talk with her at first because I was so used to them not caring, but eventually I opened up. She seemed genuinely concerned. We started meeting once a week. It was her that made me realize what I was doing was stupid, and I was the only one that could fix it. That if I didn't, I would end up working at a fast-food joint and would never really have anything. It was up to me to make something of myself, and if my grades were good enough I could get into college and away from my parents. It wasn't until my last year of high school that I realized I wanted to be to other kids what Mrs. Emerson was to me. I don't know if I would have continued with my behavior, but I like to think that she helped me get where I am today. At the time she was my saving grace. My hope is to be someone else's one day. Kids should never go without a friend or someone to guide them when they need it, whether it be emotionally, physically, mentally, or academically."

I watch with fascination as she talks. It's the most I've heard her say at once. I know that's my fault. I don't really encourage her to talk. If anything, I normally do everything possible to keep her quiet. But watching her now, how her eyes light up at the mention of her old guidance counselor, is mesmerizing. When she first started talking her eyes looked sad, like she was remembering all the times her parents let her down. Then came a hint of anger, her hands balling into fists on the counter behind her and her body going rigid. When she spoke of Mrs. Emerson, a smile touched her lips and her green eyes blazed bright. This Emerson woman is someone she really cares about. I'm glad she was there for her, and I hope her parents rot in hell for all the times they weren't.

I clench my hands as a mental image of a smaller red-haired green-eyed Chris left alone with no one to depend on. She had her brother, but he was just a kid himself.

"What about you?" she asks hesitantly, pulling me from my thoughts. I look at her with questioning eyes.

"Why did you decide construction?" she clarifies.

I uncross my arms and legs and walk to the fridge for one of the flavored bottles of water I bought. When I close the fridge, she's still leaning against the counter, watching me. Instead of resuming my place across from her, I lean my shoulder against the fridge and face her, leaving about three feet between us. As much as I hate to admit it, for some reason when she's in a room I want to be closer to her. I don't do it on purpose. Half the time I don't realize I've done it until I'm already there.

She waits for me to answer with curious eyes. I oblige her.

"My granddad was a carpenter. He actually built this house," I say, and look around the kitchen. "It was built for my grandmother. He finished it a week before she had my dad. They originally wanted to have several kids, but my grandmother almost died when she had my dad and it scared my granddad so much he refused to have more. My dad took after him and started his own carpentry business. I remember helping him at an early age. He started out building simple things like bookshelves, cabinets, rocking chairs. Anytime he was out in the barn, I'd be right there beside him with my own little tool kit."

I chuckle at the memory of me standing on a stool beside him hammering away at a nail my dad told me to hit. I had to hit the nail three times as many as my dad, but eventually I got it all the way in.

I fiddle with the bottle cap in my hand as I continue.

"I loved working with wood. As I got older, I realized I wanted to build bigger things. My dad still preferred the smaller stuff. By the time I was in high school, I was working part-time with some of the local construction companies that built houses in the neighboring towns. I loved it and decided that's what I wanted to do. I still do houses, but most of my business nowadays is commercial."

Chris has shifted so she's now facing me. Her expression is one of rapt captivation. She's just as much into what I'm saying as I was into her earlier.

"I wish I could have seen some of your dad's work," she says, a small smile touching her pink lips.

I don't know why, but I tell her, "He has some pieces still out in the barn. Maybe I'll show you sometime."

Her small smile turns so big there're dimples on each of her cheeks. I stare at her. I've never before seen her smile so much. She's absolutely gorgeous. Her luscious red hair falls around her shoulders. My fingers itch to run through the thick tresses. The increasingly familiar punch of desire forms in my belly, and I turn away from her. It's getting harder and harder to resist her. And the more I'm around her, the less I think of Anna. Chris makes me forget and that's something I can't do. Anna can never be replaced. There's no way anyone can compare to her. Chris may tempt me physically, but Anna will always hold my heart and soul. And I know if anything were to happen between me and Chris, I would end up hurting her in the end, because I could never give her what she deserves. I have to remember that.

I walk to the bar, grab the plastic bags that held the groceries, and take them to the trash.

"I'm going outside for a while. Do whatever you want in here. I'll be back in later."

I give her one last glance before walking out the door. Her look of disappointment at my abrupt departure almost has me halting. My back and forth between being cordial and a jerk has to be giving her whiplash. Not to mention the heated glances I'm sure she's noticed. I know I'm giving mixed signals, and I'm an ass for it. That's part of the reason why I don't want her here. When she's close, she brings out more emotions in me than I've felt in years. I have no idea what to do with them. They scare me. Being scared is not something I'm used to feeling. Sometimes when I think about it, it pisses me off. She has no right to make me feel this way. Even if it's not her fault, I still blame her. It's crazy and ridiculous, but I can't help but feel like she's purposely playing with me. It's an emotional struggle I don't want to deal with.

I close the front door behind me and head toward the barn. There's more wood I need to cut for Mr. and Mrs. Cooper, but I'll get to that later. Pulling the large red door open, I reach for the light switch and flip it. The big building lights up to show stacks of finished wood, a multitude of tools, small electrical equipment, wood-cutting materials, and numerous other items. In the far back corner are a few handcrafted pieces my dad built. There's a corner cabinet Anna and I had planned on putting in the living room, along with a few other pieces. There's also the first small bookshelf my dad let me help him make. Normally he would have sold it when he was finished, but he wanted to keep that one because it was my first. Anna and I were going to put that one in our kids' room.

Pain lances my chest, and I kick a two-by-four that's in my way. Ignoring the pain in my toe, I walk to the stack of wood lying off to the side. Setting up the two sawhorses, I place several of the one-by-fours and grab an old paintbrush to brush away any dust or dirt. Next, I grab a can of stain, pop open the lid, snag a brand-new paintbrush, and start brushing on the dark color.

The wood I'm working on now was cut over two years ago when Anna was still alive. It's for the front porch. We bickered over what color to paint the wood. She wanted a stain while I wanted black. Just like every other time Anna wanted something, we finally decided to go with the stain. I could never say no to her for long. She'd give her sad puppy-dog eyes, and I was a goner. Every single time.

I dip the brush in the can of stain, let the excess drip off, and carefully bring the brush to the wood again as I think about all the plans we had for the house. I know I need to get over my hang-ups on not wanting to refurbish. Anna is gone and she's not coming back. But the house still needs a lot of work, whether she's here or not. I haven't made a decision on whether or not to sell, but the more I think about it, the more I don't like the idea. I don't think I can get rid of such a big piece of my history. Anna and I had planned to pass it down to our kids, but that's out now. I'll die in this house and then it'll go up for auction to the highest bidder. I have no plans to have any kids, so the line will die off.

Out of the blue, an image of Chris helping me pick out furniture for the living room and bedroom comes to mind. I see her so clearly, her laughing green eyes looking up at me as we walk around looking at sheets and curtains, hand in hand. The vision shocks me so much I drop the brush on the concrete floor.

What the fuck is wrong with me? I ask myself.

I snatch up the brush, suddenly pissed. Why in the hell won't she leave my thoughts? Who in the fuck does she think she is, inserting herself like that? She has no business interfering. There's no way in hell that vision will ever come true.

I grab a rag off one of the work benches and roughly wipe off the extra stain. I set those boards aside to dry and set up a few more on the sawhorses. The more I stain the wood, the deeper the stain on my heart gets. It festers and builds until I want to crawl out of my skin. I miss Anna so damn much that sometimes I feel like it'll kill me if I draw my next breath. But when I'm with Chris, that debilitating pain isn't so bad. The ache I'm used to feeling in my chest eases and my breaths come easier. And that's what makes me angry. That's why I push her away. I don't want it to ease. If it eases, then that means I'm forgetting, or Anna doesn't mean as much to me as she used to. I refuse to let that happen. It would be a disservice to Anna. She's unforgettable in every way.

I stay out in the barn for several hours, staining wood and adding sealant to protect it from the weather. I've come to the conclusion that while Chris is here, I'll work on the house to stay busy. The less I'm around her, the less she'll occupy my thoughts. And once she's gone, I'll continue with the house. Anna would be sad that I haven't done anything with it since she died.

My hands are brown from the stain by the time I'm done. I start lugging the wood to the house and set it on the side porch. I haven't stained all the wood, but I have enough to get started. The sun is setting, so I won't be able to do much with the porch this evening, but I'm still reluctant to go inside. My emotions are raw at the moment, and I don't want to run into Chris while they are. There's no telling what'll come out of my mouth, and I'm trying my best to not be an ass to her.

I sit in my customary spot on the love seat on the porch and take in the stunning view of the sunset through the low canopy of trees. The temperature has dropped since I first went to the barn, but the cold breeze feels good on my heated skin. I smell something delicious wafting out of the house and wonder what Chris is cooking, then feel bad because I've been ignoring her all day, while she's inside making dinner. It still doesn't make me get up and go inside though. I sit outside until the sun disappears and darkness surrounds me.

With a heavy sigh, I know I have to face the inevitable and go inside. I'm met with silence when I walk through the door. It's dark except for the light above the stove and a sliver of light from the bathroom where the door is cracked open. I walk toward the couch and peek over the back and find a sleeping Chris curled up on her side, her hand clutching her damn smut book. The blanket is tucked beneath her chin.

I briefly wonder what she read about tonight. Was there sex? Did her body react to the words like I think it did? Did she ache with the thought of someone touching her? Did she crave it? Did she think about me while she was reading it?

I shake my head and leave the thoughts and Chris behind as I walk to the kitchen. I find a container of chicken fettuccini on the counter. It's still warm, so I grab a fork, sit at the bar, and eat.

I've got to learn how to turn off my thoughts when it comes to her. Unfortunately, they pop into my head before I get a chance to stop them. The woman is driving me up the damn wall, and I don't know how to make it stop.

Once I'm finished eating, I rinse the bowl and go back out to the living room. When I demanded she take my bed last night, I thought that would be her last night here. Watching her sleep, her hair spread out over the couch pillow, her thick lashes resting on her cheeks, I can't bring myself to leave her there. She looks comfortable, but I know she can't be. I've slept on the couch enough times to know it's killer on the back. I could wake her and send her to my bed, but I'd rather not. I've manage to avoid her most of the day. I prefer to keep it that way for the rest of the night. The only other alternative is to carry her. The thought of having her in my arms has my heart speeding up and my imagination running wild. I allow the feelings to surface in the quiet of night. Just this once, before I lock them away again.

I quietly walk around and stand over her, watching her sleep for several moments. She's one of the most beautiful women I've seen. I may act like I'm impartial to her, but it couldn't be further from the truth. I'll never admit it, but every time she points her green eyes my way, I want to get lost in them. Her pink lips hold me captive, and it takes everything in me to not pull her warm body to mine and claim them. When I hear her laugh, which I don't get a chance to very often, it's one of the sweetest sounds ever.

Chris shifts on the couch and lets out a small sigh. I push away my thoughts, already having let them linger too long. I bend down, carefully place my arms under her knees and upper back, and lift her easily. She mumbles something in her sleep and snuggles her face into my chest. She clutches my shirt in her small fist. Having her in my arms feels right. I shove the thought away in the secret box I have hidden in the back of my mind.

Not wanting to wake her, I take measured steps down the hallway to my room, walking sideways so I don't bump her feet on the wall. I gently place her down and pull the covers from beneath her and then up to her shoulders. She turns my way with a small moan and a smile on her lips. I tuck a piece of hair behind her ear and let my finger linger on her cheek. I don't wish things could be different, because that would mean I wouldn't have had Anna in my life for as long as I did, and there's no way I could ever want that, but I do wish I could be someone different for Chris. I hate the guilt that eats at me every day. I hate that I can't move passed it. I hate that I want to be someone different. Someone who can let go of a person that's no longer here and be someone who can love another just as deeply. And when those feelings emerge, I feel disgust toward myself, because I have no right to want those things. Anna was my one and only. I shouldn't even consider wanting something even remotely close to what we had with someone else. It's a never ending vicious cycle that won't give me peace. Guilt, wishful thinking, disgust, and then back to guilt.

Taking once last lingering glance at Chris, I once again push the thoughts away, and leave her sleeping in my bed, a place I know I will forever see her now that she's been there. The first thing I'll be doing once she leaves is throwing away the sheets and comforter. No way could I sleep under the same ones she has. Not because she disgusts me, but because they will forever remind me of her, which is one less thing I need.

I pull the door closed behind me and walk back down the hallway. I go to the kitchen and head straight for the basement door. The light floods the dark room, showing the gym equipment I have down there. That's not what I'm down here for though. I walk across the concrete and stand in front of the white door, both dreading and needing what's on the other side. I hate going in there because my dreams are worse on those nights and the pain of them is debilitating. But I also feel the closest to Anna when I'm with all her things. I need that feeling right now. I need to be reminded of what I had and lost. Of what could possibly happen again if I open myself up. While I'm in this room, I swear I feel her in there with me. Her scent surrounds me, and I bask in it. As much as I dread being in there, I also love it.

I swing the door open and step inside. The door clicks closed softly behind me. I smell her immediately and my thoughts instantly calm. I breathe in deep and release it, feeling more like myself than I have in a long time. Anna had the ability to bring out the best in people. No matter the circumstances, if Anna was around she could always bring a smile to a person's face.

A smile touches my lips now as I spy a big framed picture against the far wall. It's facing away from me, but I know what's on the other side. Anna went through a painting phase. She really did try her hardest, but she definitely wasn't artistically inclined.

I came home one day after a short trip to a job site to find Anna covered in paint. She looked so cute in her paint-covered overalls. There were streaks on her arms, face, and even specks in her hair. She didn't hear me come in, so I was able to sneak up on her. When I circled my arms around her waist, she jumped ten feet and completely screwed up the picture in front of her. I joked and told her the new jagged line made the picture look better. She playfully pouted, her face scrunching with fake hurt, but the twinkle in her eye told me it was all for show. To pay me back, she painted a line down my face, starting at my forehead and ending it at my Adam's apple. We both ended up with more paint on both of us than the painting itself. She begged me not to, but I hung the painting of our house with the purple jagged line on the wall in the living room. I told her it was my favorite.

I sit down, lean back against the wall, close my eyes, and tip my head back. I allow all the memories I normally try to push back to flood to the forefront. Reliving every moment I've had with Anna, except for the most painful one. That's a memory I have all too often. I don't need to bring that one to mind. It comes and goes when it pleases, often leaving me desperate to make the pain of it go away.

ten

Chris

I ONCE AGAIN WAKE to a loud hammering noise. I'm so comfortable where I am that I don't want to open my eyes. I know I'm back in Nick's bed. I felt him carrying me last night. I didn't want him to know I was awake, so I kept my breathing as even as I could. In my guise of sleeping I shamelessly snuggled into his warmth. I was damn near delirious with the feel of his arms and scent wrapped around me. And he was so gentle while carrying me down the hallway. When he pulled the blanket over me, and I felt him shift my hair, letting his finger linger on my cheek, it took a lot of effort to continue the ruse. Just that small amount of affection from him had goose bumps popping up on my arms. Thank God it was dark in the room and he put the covers over me. No way he would have missed them otherwise.

I was hurt yesterday when he left after our semi-normal talk. He was the one to initiate it and crumble some of the wall I put up once we left Maggie's. I don't know what triggered it, but one minute we were fine and the next he was closing himself off again. Then he was gone for hours. I know he didn't go far, but it felt like he was miles away. He always seemed like he's too far to reach, just like in the picture Ally drew.

I crack open my eyes and see the room is still mostly dark. It must be pretty early. It doesn't look like the sun has risen all the way yet. I flip the covers off me, pull myself from the bed, take care of my morning business, and get dressed.

The hammering sounds again. It's coming from the front porch, so I head that way. I'm surprised when I open the door to find a pile of old wood on the ground at the end of the steps. I look to the left and part of the porch is ripped up. Nick is bent over hammering in new planks.

I don't want to interrupt him, so I wait until he's finished with the board he's currently working on before I talk.

"Wow! It's going to look good once you're finished," I tell him. The new wood is a darker color. I've always liked the dark wood look. I'm glad he decided to use it for the porch.

"Thanks," he says, not looking at me. He reaches over and grabs another board.

Before he can start hammering once more, I try again. "Are you planning to repaint the house?"

After lining up the board, he sets the hammer down on top of it and sits back on his knees. He runs his fingers through his hair, leaving it a disheveled mess. It's chilly outside, but his shirt still has sweat spots, causing it to cling to his chest.

I see the internal struggle in his eyes as he stares out at the trees. I almost give up and go back inside, but he says, "Yes. I don't know when, but I do plan on it eventually."

"What color are you thinking?" I ask, pleased and encouraged he's trying.

"Anna..." He stops to clear his throat and looks down. "Anna wanted it white." He shrugs before continuing. "Seems like it would be a good color."

I'm a bit taken off guard by his response. He's never openly brought Anna up before. I know it hurts him to, so I've never brought her up either. I'd like to hear more about her, but I've never pushed the issue. I approach it carefully, just in case he wants to shut it down.

"I think it'll look good with the dark wood. Did she help you pick the color for the porch?"

It takes him a few seconds, but he answers.

"Yeah. We disagreed with the color to begin with. Same with the color for the wood on the porch. I wanted to repaint the house with the same light blue and have black for the porch. That sounds odd, but I've always liked dark against light. She wanted the dark wood for the porch and the house painted white. I could never say no to her for long."

He lifts his head and his lips are curved slightly in a small smile. His hands fumble with a nail as he once again looks out across the yard.

"She sounds like she had good taste. I would have picked the same colors."

I hope like hell I'm not overstepping my boundaries and making him angry with me. That's the last thing I want. But I can't help but be curious about the woman who captured and held his attention for so long, even after she's been gone for over two years. What makes her so special that he's closed himself off from the possibility of forming an attachment to another woman?

"That's just it. She normally had terrible taste." He chuckles for a moment, looking lost in a memory, before shaking his head. "But I think with this, she was right. The dark wood will look great against the white."

"Will you tell me more about Anna?" I ask softly, and edge closer to him.

His body jerks, and I know I've gone too far. The look in his eyes when he swings them my way says I've managed to anger him again. I want to bang my head against the damn railing. I should have known better.

"I'd prefer not to talk about her with you. Why don't you go back in the house and let me do my work."

His words are harsh and my stomach twists in knots.

"I'm sorry. I didn't mean—"

He slices his hand through the air.

"Please just go, Chris. I'm trying my hardest here to be as nice as possible. I didn't sleep last night, so I'm not in the best of moods. You bringing up something that's painful is just going to bring out the asshole in me. I'm trying to avoid that. Go inside before my best intentions fly out the window."

"I'm sorry," I say again and rush inside.

I thought being around him might help. Thought that if he had someone around constantly that cared, it would make him see there're people out there who still need him. Who want to see him happy and would like to help him reach that happy place again. And sometimes I think it does help. But other times I wonder if it's useless. Am I wasting my time here? You have to want the help for it to actually work. He doesn't seem to want to get better. It's almost as if he wants to stay in his dark place. But who would want that? Who would choose that over living in the light?

Feeling sadder and more defeated than I ever have before, I walk with slumped shoulders to the kitchen. The coffeepot is half-full and still warm, so I make myself a cup and sit at the bar while I drink it. Maybe I'll call Jaxon today and tell him it's over. I've tried and tried and I don't know what else I can do. He offered to bring my car over a couple days ago, but I told him no. Having it here would make it easier for Nick to send me away. I know that's drastic, but I did what I thought was best. Now I'm not so sure.

My phone rings in the living room, so I get up to answer it. Looking at the screen, I roll my eyes. It's my mom. As much as I don't want to talk to her, I know I have to. She's relentless and will continue to call if I don't answer.

Sitting on the edge of the couch, I bring the phone to my ear, gripping it tightly in my hand.

"Hey, Mom."

"Christabelle. How are you?" I grit my teeth, her voice grating on my nerves. I love my mom, but I still can't stand her. After all the shit she's put Jase through recently, she and dad aren't my favorite people right now. My mom isn't as bad as my dad, but she hasn't done anything to put a stop to his behavior toward Jase.

"I'm fine, Mom. How are you and Dad?"

I look down at my hand in my lap when I feel a dull pain. It's no surprise when I find my hand clenched tightly into a fist. I straighten my fingers and see half-moon impressions in my palm.

"We're both good. The church is finally getting the upgrade they need, so we've been busy with that." She turns quiet for a minute. I stay silent, waiting for her to continue. "I was actually calling to see when you were coming for a visit. Your dad and I miss you."

Her question just pisses me off even more. There's no mention of Jase coming to visit. Instead of answering, I ask one of my own, already knowing the answer.

"Have you talked to Jase?" My tone is harder than I intended. I can't help it. It seems the more I talk to either my mom or dad, the angrier I get at them.

I hear a sigh across the line. I've asked this question every time I've talk to her since Jase came to town. And the answer is always the same.

"No, I haven't," she says, resignation in her voice. "Please don't start on me, Christabelle. You know your dad's still upset over Jase's... recent news."

"Well he needs to fucking get over it. And that's bullshit and you know it, Mom," I tell her sharply. "Dad's had it out for Jase for years. His revealing his sexual preference is just the icing on the cake. Why can't you both just accept him the way he is? Why does it have to be your way?"

"First, watch your language, young lady," my mother scolds me, making me grit my teeth even harder. "And you know that's not true, honey. We love Jase. It's just hard on your dad. He had such high expectations for him, and then Jase ended up so different than he expected. Your dad feels like he let him down somehow. That he failed as a father."

I laugh at her, but there's no humor in the sound. She actually has the nerve to turn the tables around and make this about our dad.

Unbelievable.

"And how do you think Jase feels? He's the one who has had to put up with Dad looking down his nose at him for years. And you, you don't do a damn thing to make it better. You don't stand up for him. No, you're not as condescending as Dad, but you're still just as bad because you let him treat Jase like shit. People don't just all of a sudden wake up one day and say 'oh, I think I'll be gay.' People are born that way. They can't help the way their hearts and minds work, Mom. He's kept that from you for years and now he's being punished for following his heart. What would you and Dad have done if Pops said y'all couldn't be together when you were younger? Would you have listened? No, you wouldn't have, because your love was uncontrollable. The same applies to Jase's situation. You haven't even called him to see if he's okay after he was shot! What kind of parents are y'all to not want to know if he's okay? He almost died and neither of you seem to care. And you claim to love him?"

I'm breathing hard by the time I'm done. I'm so upset tears gather in my eyes. I normally don't raise my voice to my parents. I've always been the quiet daughter. But there are times I can't hold it in. I've witnessed the shit Jase has put up with for too long. The straw that broke the camel's back is them not calling to inquire about Jase's health.

My mom sobs across the line, and I know I've upset her, but I don't feel any remorse at my outburst. Something's got to change or they'll end up losing both their kids.

"I'm so sorry," she whispers tearfully. "You're right. I've been a terrible mother."

"Don't apologize to me. Jase is the one that needs to hear it."

"I will. And I'll talk to your dad." She sniffs before she asks tentatively, "How is he?"

"He's good, Mom. The wounds healed. But you should call and ask *him* that. He's happy here. The guy he's with is wonderful. His name is Andrew. I think you'd like him if you give him a chance."

"That's good," she breathes. "I hope I get to meet him one day."

"That's up to you and Dad. You need to call him. Before it's too late. A person can only take so much rejection before they give up. Please don't let that happen."

It's not lost on me that my words apply to my own situation. There's no doubt I care for Nick, but a heart can only handle so much pain before it's broken beyond repair.

My mom's voice cracks when she speaks again. I hope my words have given her the reality check she and my dad both need.

"I won't. I'll make your dad see reason. Maybe we can take a trip up there."

"I hope so, Mom. Something's got to give," I tell her honestly.

"I know it does. I'll make things right. I promise."

I hope she does, and I pray it's not too late.

We talk for a few more minutes. Our conversation is easier than it has been for a while. My mom's assurance she'll talk to my dad helps alleviate some of my hostility toward them. I have no idea if it'll work or not, but I'm glad she's going to try. I tell my mom about my job at the school here. She seems genuinely happy for me.

I get up from the couch when we get off the phone. Movement out the corner of my eye catches my attention. When I turn, Nick is standing on the other side of the window, looking in at me. His expression is hard, and I wonder how much he's heard. My raised voice must have alerted him.

I turn my back to him and walk to the kitchen to straighten up the small mess from last night's dinner.

It only takes me a few minutes until I'm done. I decide to wash the few dirty clothes I've accumulated since being here. There's not enough to make a full load. Remembering the clothes on Nick's bedroom floor, I decide to grab those and throw them in with mine.

I only waver a second before pushing the door open and grabbing them. It's only clothes. I'm sure he wouldn't mind if I washed them. Everyone needs their clothes cleaned, don't they?

Once that's done, I have nothing to do. I'm hesitant to do much else, worried he won't like me going through his house. I take a seat and decide to watch some TV while the clothes wash.

The banging from Nick working makes it hard to keep my mind off him. On the one hand, I'm glad he's finally taking on the task of repairing the house. On the other hand, I wish he was inside with me. My time here is almost over, and as much as I know I haven't really helped him like I hope, I'd still like to spend as much time with him as possible. He's been decent to me part of the time, something I'm not used to. I'm worried things will go back to the way they were before I got here.

I find a movie on the Lifetime channel about a woman who has breast cancer. It's about her life and all the complications the illness causes for her and her family. The movie ends well, but still has me crying by the time it's over.

I go to the bathroom to wash my face before making something for lunch. Leaving the door open, I turn the cold water on and cup some in my hand. After drying my face, I look in the mirror, scrunch up my nose, and push my lips out in the awful duck face.

"Why do you do that?" comes Nick's voice, scaring the shit out of me.

I jump and whirl around to face him. Clutching my heaving chest, I tell him, "You've got to stop sneaking up on me like that."

He's in the doorway with his arms raised, his hands latched to the top of the doorframe. He's looking at me with raised brows, waiting on my answer.

"That's the second time I've seen you making faces at yourself. Why do you do it?"

I shrug and turn from him to hang the towel back on the ring beside the sink. Him catching me at my silly habit is embarrassing.

"I don't know. I just do. Life can be so serious. We all need to be silly sometimes to break up the solemnity of it. That's my way of doing that. I've done it since I was a kid."

When I face him again, he's dropped his arms and is now leaning against the frame.

"You look like a little kid when you do it," he says.

For a moment I think I'm seeing things, but the longer I look at him, the more I realize I'm not. There's a twinkle in his eyes and his lips look like they're twitching. It causes my own lips to curl up slightly. It's moments like these that make me not want to give up on him. It may be wishful thinking on my part, but I can't help but hope anyway.

"Come try it," I suggest, motioning my hand to the mirror.

He looks momentarily surprised, before responding, "Uh, no thanks."

"Oh, come on." I pout at him.

His lips tip up at the corners more, revealing a gorgeous smile as he shakes his head. In a bold move, I reach over and grab his shirt and give it a pull. He lets me tug him in front of the mirror. I turn so we're shoulder to shoulder. We both look at each other in the mirror.

I stick out my tongue at him. He chuckles, making flutters form in my stomach.

"Okay. Your turn," I say expectantly.

He looks at himself, then at me again. At first I don't think he'll do it, but then he surprises me when he crosses his eyes and sucks his cheeks in. He looks utterly ridiculous and cute at the same time. I can't help but burst out laughing at the silly look.

"I look fucking stupid," he grumbles, once I calm my laughing. His lips are still quirked up, still watching me in the mirror. I love that look on his face. It almost makes him look boyish.

"No, you don't. You look cute," I tease playfully.

All too soon, the look fades from his face when he says, "I heard you on the phone earlier. Everything okay?"

My smile disappears. Even though I already knew he'd heard, I hate that he did. I'm surprised he's standing here asking me about it. After the way he acted today, I figured he'd be a grouch for the rest of the day. But then again, I'm constantly being surprised by him.

"Yeah. It was just my mom. We've not seen eye to eye lately. But hopefully that's going to change."

He nods and leans back against the doorframe with his arms crossed over his chest. "It's good that you stood up to her like that."

I shrug. "It doesn't happen often, but if pushed enough I've been known to voice my opinion. What they've done to Jase has gone on long enough."

"And what about you? What about all the neglect over the years toward you?"

I shrug and play with the hem of my shirt. I'm not really concerned about myself.

"I'm used to it. It's no big deal now. It's Jase I'm worried about. It was he who took the brunt of my dad's anger. They neglected us both, but it was worse for him because when he did show us attention it was to put Jase down for something or other."

His forehead crinkles with his frown. "Don't do that. Don't discount your own pain. Jase may have had it worse than you, but it doesn't make your own situation any less important."

I don't know what to say to him. What he says is true. Jase did take on more shit from our parents, but the pain of neglect from the two people who were supposed to be there more than anyone else, hurt. But I still feel like the rift between him and our parents is bigger and needs more work than my own issues.

"How's the porch coming along?" I ask, changing the subject.

He twists his head back and forth, rubbing his hand along the back of his neck, like he has a crick there. I want to offer to massage the knot out, but I know that wouldn't go over well.

"It's going. I've got about half the front done. I'm hoping to finish up there and start on one of the sides before it gets too late. I was just taking a break to grab something to drink."

He leans up from his perch and walks out of the bathroom. I follow him down the hallway and into the kitchen, where he grabs a bottle of juice out of the fridge.

"I was just getting ready to make sandwiches for lunch. Would you like one?"

Before answering, and instead of using a glass, he uncaps the bottle and tips it to his lips. I watch, spellbound, as his Adam's apple bobs with each swallow. Because he hasn't shaved in several days, his cheeks and neck are covered in rough hair. It's not long, but I can imagine how good it would feel against my skin.

After drinking a quarter of the bottle, he twists the cap back on and sets it on the counter, before turning to face me.

"Sure. I've got a couple phone calls to make first to some of my crew."

Glad to have a few minutes with him, I nod and move to the fridge, asking over my shoulder, "What do you like on yours?"

He lists off items he wants on his sandwich, and I pull them from the fridge. While I make our lunch, he leaves the kitchen to go his office to make his calls. I grab a bag of chips out of the cabinet, pour some in a bowl, and set it on the bar beside our plates.

I'm opening a bottle of water when he walks back into the kitchen. Seeing the food at the bar, he takes a seat. I walk around and sit beside him.

It feels strange sitting here with him like this. I know we've done it a couple times before, but it feels different this time. Despite the rough start this morning, he seems more relaxed, which puts me more at ease. Too bad it can't be this easy all the time. I push the thought away so it doesn't spoil the moment.

"Things okay with work?" I ask, then take a bite of my sandwich.

"Not sure yet. Kevin, one of my foremen, is waiting on a call back from the sheriff there. They found some bones on one of the sites. We're waiting on word to see if it's human or animal."

"Oh, wow!" I exclaim. "That's awful. Has that ever happened before?"

Washing down the food in his mouth with juice, he says, "We've found dog and deer bones before, but luckily no human ones. There's been other strange stuff we've discovered though."

"Like what?" I ask, and take a bite of my sandwich, enjoying the easiness of our conversation.

"We found a ritual circle once. It had everything, down to the candles, blood-drawn symbols, which happened to be pigs' blood, wooden bowls with dowels and some type of leaves or herbs in them. There was even a Ouija board. It was a group of young girls thinking they wanted to do voodoo or some shit. They got spooked and left everything behind when they heard a noise. One of my men left something and came back for it. We found everything the next day."

I can't help the laugh that slips out.

"Sorry," I say, trying to hold back my smile when he looks at me strangely. "I can just imagine what the girls thought when they heard the noise. Obviously they were trying to talk to ghosts, and I'm sure they probably thought they found one. I remember playing with a Ouija board with Jase once. The little lever thingy moved, and I freaked out. Found out later that Jase moved it. My parents had a fit when they found the board. Grounded us for a month. For a minute I thought they were going to bring a priest in and bless the house. They're God-fearing folk and are firmly against anything like that, even if it is just a childish game."

I can't help but stare at Nick's lips when they tip up in a smile. I've always found him gorgeous, but when he smiles, which I've only ever seen him do a couple times, his whole face changes. The sadness and worry disappears, leaving behind a look of contentment. It never lasts though.

"We took on a charity case to build a church once," he continues with another story. "We had the frames of all the walls up when we came across used condoms." I almost choke on my food. After watching me take a swallow of my water to clear my throat, he smirks at me and continues. "It wasn't just one or two either. We found seventeen used condoms throughout the entire building. We figured it was a group of people who got off on desecrating a place that's meant to be pure."

I put my half-eaten sandwich down, no longer hungry at the thought of used condoms lying around from an orgy, and push my plate away.

"That's awful. And very disturbing and gross. I feel for the person who had to clean that up." I shudder for effect, because really, the thought of cleaning up someone else's used condoms gives me the heebie-jeebies.

He takes another bite and washes it down with his water. Just like a man to not be affected by something like that.

"We also found some pretty cool Native American pottery down in Texas."

"That's so neat. I've always been fascinated by the Native American culture. History wasn't my favorite subject in school, but when it came to Indians, I was all ears."

I remember seeing a necklace once that Nick used to wear. I had forgotten about it until just now. I haven't seen him wear it in a long time.

"The necklace you used to wear, that was Native American wasn't it?"

He has his sandwich halfway to his mouth when I ask. His stops and drops it back to his plate. The shutters come back over his eyes, and I wonder what I said. The necklace is obviously a sore subject. Realization dawns, and I want to slap myself for once again messing up our easy conversation.

"Yeah," he says, and gets up from his stool. He carries his plate to the sink and dumps it inside with a loud bang. I jump at the noise.

He rests his hands on the sink and drops his head. All I can do is sit there helplessly and watch him as he struggles through his pain. It's apparent the necklace has something to do with Anna. Once again, I wish I could go to him and offer comfort, but I know it would be unwanted.

He stands there several seconds with his head bent, before he lifts it and turns around. The stark pain in his eyes has my own eyes glistening.

"Anna...," he says hoarsely, before taking a deep breath and letting it out slowly. Once he composes himself, he continues. "Anna had it made for me because my great-great-grandmother was full-blooded Indian."

He doesn't look at me as he talks, but stares off into space. I noticed he does that a lot. It's like he gets caught up in his thoughts over and over again. I don't say anything back to him, hoping he'll continue on his own. Unfortunately, he doesn't.

"I'm gonna head back outside before it gets too late," he mutters.

He grabs the bottle of juice off the bar beside me, and without another word leaves the kitchen. A few seconds later, I hear the front door close. I hunch in my seat, my shoulders falling forward.

I decide to give Jaxon a call. My time here is up. Nothing I'm doing is really helping him. Yes, he's not as harsh toward me as he used to be, but that doesn't indicate he's getting any better. All I seem to do is say the wrong thing. Makes me wonder if I'm doing more harm than good.

Not to mention, I really need to get back to work. I was hoping to make headway in the four days the school was closed, but that ended a day ago. I called yesterday before we left to go to Evelyn's and took off Tuesday and Wednesday. Today is Tuesday. I don't want to take advantage of the school's relaxed policy on taking days off if need be. There are kids at school that could need me. Yes, Nick needs someone too, but he's a grown man and can ultimately take care of himself, even if he chooses not to sometimes. Besides, it's obvious it's not *me* that he needs.

Our conversation is short, with me explaining that I feel my being here isn't helping the matter.

I hear his deep breath over the line, before he replies, "Okay. We'll try something else. The man can be stubborn as shit. You okay until morning? I'm stuck at work for inventory, but I can get Mac or Mia to come get you."

I can tell he's getting frustrated with the situation, everyone is. Nick doesn't make it easy on the people who care about him. Grief can not only be harsh on the person grieving, but also the people surrounding that person. I can also tell that he doesn't agree with me, but isn't willing to push the issue. He knows the shit I've put up with from Nick and won't ask me to put up with more. It makes me sad knowing Nick will be out here in his wooded wonderland alone, but knowing that I could be making the situation worse has me holding firm in my belief that I need to leave.

"I'll be fine until then," I tell Jaxon.

We make plans for him to come get me in the morning and then hang up.

With a defeated sigh, I get up from my stool, toss the remainder of my sandwich in the trash, and move to the laundry room to put the clothes in the dryer. Once that's done, I pull a roast from the freezer, peel and chop potatoes, carrots, and onions, and throw them in the oven for dinner.

I move aimlessly around the house. I stop and look at all the DVDs and CDs Nick has. I pick out a Johnny Depp movie to watch later. Then I move to the couch to read for a while.

It's not long before I set the book aside, it not able to keep my attention. I check the clothes and see they are still drying and move to the back door. Flipping the switch to unlock it, I step outside onto the back porch. I have on a zip-up hoodie, so I close it when the cool air hits me. The backyard is just as gorgeous as the front.

I hear Nick hammering at the front of the house. I want to sit outside and take in the fresh air, but I don't want to take the chance of disturbing him. With that thought in mind, I sit on one of the lawn chairs next to me and watch the beautiful leaves drift down from the trees. It's quiet out here, except for the inconsistent hammering. In any other situation, the tranquility of sitting out here with the colorful leavings dropping, the beauty of the waning sun peeking through the canopy of trees, the quiet, and the peacefulness would be soothing, but the magnificence of it all is overshadowed by the ugliness of the circumstances. I hope one day Nick can overcome the ghosts of his past, but I'll not be the one to help him get there.

I sit outside until the sun sets. The hammering stopped about thirty minutes ago, but I don't see Nick when I go inside. I fold the laundry, check the roast, and then decide to take a quick shower.

After lotioning up and pulling my wet hair into a messy bun at the top of my head, I leave the bathroom. Still no Nick. The roast is done, so I pull it from the oven. I make myself a bowl and sit at the bar to eat it.

I'm almost done when Nick comes up from the basement. My eyes are immediately drawn to his naked and sweaty chest. He's wearing a pair of loose gym shorts and tennis shoes. He hasn't noticed me sitting there because he's using the towel wrapped around his neck to wipe his face. The thought of him down in the basement working out, his muscles straining and sweat dripping from his skin, has an ache forming between my legs. I squeeze my thighs together to try to relieve some of the pressure.

He freezes for a split second when he sees me with a potato halfway to my mouth. I hadn't even realized I'd stilled until he looked at me. I probably look like an idiot, so I shovel the food in and drop my eyes to my plate. When I sense his movement, I peek up and see him grab a glass and fill it with water. He downs it and puts the glass on the counter. Not sure of his mood, I don't say anything to him. He pulls the towel from his neck and mutters "Shower" before stalking out of the kitchen. My eyes follow him as he leaves the room.

He doesn't seem like he's in the best of moods, so I quickly finish my dinner, wash my bowl and fork, and leave the kitchen as well. I plop the DVD I picked out earlier and sit down to watch it.

Twenty minutes later, Nick strolls out of the hallway wearing a pair of dark gray sweats that hang from his hips and a black Nirvana t-shirt. His hair is wet and looks unbrushed. The scruff on his face is still in place. It's getting thicker and darker the longer he lets it grow.

He barely glances my way as he passes by me and that feeling of defeat takes hold again. I thought we were at least making progress, in the sense we were somewhat talking. His constant mood swings are irritating and giving me a headache. I want to march in the kitchen and demand he talk to me, even if it's over stupid shit or him bitching at me. But I don't want to piss him off my last night here. I was hoping to spend a little time with him before I left, but his attitude tells me that probably won't happen.

With a sigh, I lean my head back against the couch and watch more Johnny Depp as his consciousness travels through different realities. I normally love anything with him in it, but for once he's not able to keep my attention. Instead it keeps flickering back to the man in the kitchen.

Nick stays in the kitchen for a while and then silently slips out the back door. By the time my movie is finished, he still hasn't come back inside. He's obviously back to ignoring me. He'll be glad to know I'm leaving tomorrow. I'm not up to hunting him down to tell him, so I elect to wait until the morning.

I get up and fold the throw I used to keep my feet warm. I decide to go to bed, since he's been working all day and he's using the couch. I change my clothes, brush my teeth and hair, and throw on some moisturizer before crawling under the warm comforter. I immediately grab Nick's pillow and stuff my face against it.

It hurts a place deep inside, knowing that I'm leaving tomorrow. Nick hasn't given me any reason to develop feelings for him, but I have. Over the two years of living here I've silently watched him. In the beginning he was silent and completely withdrawn from everyone. He rarely participated in any social gatherings and when he did, he was always in the background. As time went on, I could tell he was trying, but I think it was more for his friends rather than himself. Or maybe he was forcing himself to try harder to get out of the depressed rut he was in. I thought he was getting better. I was always there watching, hoping I got my chance to become his friend, but eventually he went back to his solitary life, forcing everyone else away.

I don't know what's in store for Nick; I don't know what his future holds or if he'll ever get over his guilt and sorrow. But I do know I can't sit back and watch any longer. It's breaking something inside me I fear can't be mended if I let it continue. My feelings for Nick run deep. I don't know if they are real or if seeing him so sad clicked something in me and made me want to change it. I've tried my best and nothing has worked so far. I'm sad and heartbroken to realize I'm not the person he needs.

A tear leaks out onto Nick's pillow at the thought of stepping back. I've prayed so hard for him, especially over the last several months when I realized he was getting worse again. The thought of not seeing him anymore causes my heart to constrict in my chest. I know I'll see him around town from time to time, but I'll try my best to stay away. Having me around isn't something he wants, so I'll give him that.

I clutch his pillow tighter to my face and chest and let a few more tears fall. Nick still grieves over losing his Anna. And I'll start grieving over giving Nick up. Having never had him in the first place, I would think it would be easy, that I would simply grieve and then move on. But for some unknown reason I don't think it will be. Nick is special. I know he is. Anyone who knows him knows he is. Anna was very lucky to have him and if he ever decides he wants a relationship with another woman, that woman will be lucky as well.

I take a deep breath and pull my face back from the pillow, but I don't release it. I still hug it, needing the comfort it gives me. It's just a pillow, but it's his pillow and it has his scent.

That's how I fall asleep: his pillow, with his scent, clutched to my chest like a lifeline.

I WAKE THE NEXT morning to a quiet house. I release the death grip I have on Nick's pillow and reach over to grab my phone from the nightstand to check the time. I scramble out of bed when I see it's already ten o'clock. I set my alarm for seven, but I guess I was so tired I slept through it. I have a missed message from Jaxon telling me to be ready at ten thirty. That leaves me thirty minutes. I don't have much here, so that won't be a problem. I send him a short message telling him I'll be ready.

Done with the bathroom, I slip on a pair of jeans and a plaid button-up shirt with the sleeves rolled to the elbows. All I have here is my ballet flats, so I slide my feet into those next.

I'm gathering the rest of my stuff when I realize I don't hear Nick working out front. I quickly stuff the rest of my things in my bag and carry it to the living room. Throwing it on the couch, I walk to the door and open it, fully expecting to see Nick on the porch taking a break or something. What I don't expect is to not see his truck in the driveway. My breath catches in my throat and I have to force the tears back. I've prepared myself for finally giving in and letting Nick go, but I thought I still had this morning. I wanted to talk to him one more time, wanted to look into his eyes one last time, just to see if anything at all was there. But he's not here. Did he know I was leaving and decided to not be here when I left?

My stomach twists in knots with that thought. I wrap my arms around my middle and take a few deep breaths to stop the sick feeling there. He could have simply left for something in town, maybe supplies or food, but I doubt it. We bought food the other day, and I still see plenty of wood and nails on the porch.

I quietly close the door and wipe away the few tears that managed to slip free. I walk to the couch, take a seat, and clutch my hands in my lap. I didn't realize how much I needed it, but I *did* need those few minutes I thought I would have with him before I left. I won't have that now. He's gone, and I know he won't be back until after I've left. I know deep down he's not here on purpose. That he somehow figured out I was leaving this morning.

I sit there and stare off into space until I hear crunching on the driveway. I get up and dash to the door, my heart pounding, hoping it's Nick. When I see Jaxon getting out of his truck, my hope dies a quick death.

I leave the door open and walk listlessly back to the couch for my bag. I leave Nick a short note, thanking him for letting me stay, even knowing he'll be happy that I'm gone.

Jaxon's waiting on the porch, looking at all the progress Nick's made, when I make it back to the door. I lock it from the inside and pull it closed.

"Where's Nick?" he asks and grabs my bag from me.

"I don't know," I tell him with a shrug.

His jaw hardens when he sees the hurt in my eyes I know I'm not able to hide.

I drop my gaze and walk off the porch toward his truck. He doesn't say anything as we both climb inside. I take one last look at Nick's house as we pull away, knowing that it'll be the last time I see it. Also knowing I'm leaving a vital part of myself behind.

eleven

Nick

I PUT THE CAN OF kerosene in the back of my truck and make my way around to the driver side. I have the door halfway open when I hear laughter coming from across the street. I look across the hood and see Ethan and a pregnant Karyn walking up the steps of Jaxon's. The music from the jukebox filters out as they make their way inside. I hesitate getting in my truck. Not because of the pull of alcohol; I don't drink because I crave the taste, I drink to help numb my nightmares. Nightmares that went silent when Chris was in the house, except that first night. Nightmares that came back full force the day she left.

Before she came to my house they were always bad and started and ended the same: A memory of Anna and me happy together and then her dying in my arms. Once Chris left, they changed. It scared the shit out of me the first night I had one.

It started the same as normal. Anna and I were lounging on the couch talking about baby names. We had a game where we would each throw first names into one bowl and the middle name into another bowl. We'd each pick one from each and tell the other what we came up with. I got Declan Adele and she got Greta James. The combinations were so ridiculous, so we switched them around to Declan James and Greta Adele, the last still sounding silly to me, but Anna loved it. The dream changed, but instead of Anna lying bloody and bruised in my arms, it was Chris. She stared up at me with lifeless eyes, her body limp and cold.

I woke up yelling Chris's name. I must have been yelling for a while, because my throat was raw afterwards. My stomach was cramping, my palms were sweaty, my breaths were heavy, and my whole body shook.

I didn't try to go back to sleep after that. I was too freaked and wired to attempt it. Instead, I got up and went to the room in the basement. Chris has been gone four days and every dream I've had since then always ends with her being the one in my arms as she dies.

The temptation to drink is there, but that's not why I close my truck door and walk toward Jaxon's. I head that way in hopes of a distraction. Something to keep my mind off my damn dreams and what they mean.

It's Friday night, so when I pull open the door, I'm met with raucous laughter. I walk toward the bar and take one of the remaining two seats available. Jaxon and Mia are behind the counter serving patrons. When Jaxon sees me sitting there, he narrows his eyes at me. I ignore his disdainful look and turn in my seat. I may be here looking for a distraction, but that doesn't mean I want to put up with Jaxon's constant lectures on my life.

Looking out across the room, I spy Jesse, Ethan, Karyn, and Jase over by the pool tables. Each has a beer in hand, except Karyn, who looks to be drinking water. Over in one corner sits Nitra, two of her friends, and a couple of guys I don't recognize. Several people are out on the dance floor, gyrating their hips to the music, and most of the tables are filled.

I used to enjoy coming here to hang out with my friends, but lately I've felt like an outsider looking in. Everyone else has moved on, but I'm still stuck in place, never moving forward. I know everyone was hurt when we lost Anna, but I'm the only one who can't get over it.

I feel movement at my side and turn to see Andrew sit beside me.

"Hey, handsome," he says, and rests his elbows back on the bar. "What brings you to our neck of the woods? Thought you forgot about us."

I grit my teeth and hold back my retort, knowing it's my own fault he feels that way.

"Just thought I'd come sit for a bit. It's been a while."

"It has. As hot and moody as your ass is, we've missed it."

I look over at him and see he has his eyes trained on Jase, who is currently lining up his shot. Jase must feel his gaze because he lifts his head and gives him a wink. When he sees me, his eyes grow hard for a second before he gives me a chin lift.

"Your man doesn't like me much," I inform Andrew.

He laughs and leans toward me. "Can't say I blame him. It's not like you're treating his sister like the precious gem she is."

"No. Guess not," I mutter.

Andrew's silent beside me for several beats, before he asks quietly, "You good?"

It takes me a minute to answer him, and I don't know if my answer is honest or not, but I tell him, "Yeah."

"Good. Keep it that way." He slaps me on the back and gets up from his stool. "Now, I've got a man over there who needs my attention. Talk later."

He takes off toward the pool tables, his eyes focused solely on the man now leaning against the wall watching him with blatant heat. I have nothing against Andrew and his sexual preferences, never have, but I don't need to see them eye fucking each other either.

I turn back in my seat to face the bar again just as Mia walks up.

"You're not here for a drink, right? Because you should know, we're not serving to you," she says, looking right at me without blinking.

Shit. The woman can be harsh sometimes, but I guess that's my fault too. It's fuzzy, but one of the last times I was here, I know I was an ass.

"No drink, Mia. Just water, please," I rumble across the bar at her.

With relief on her face, she nods, grabs a glass, and fills it with water.

Setting it down in front of me, she leans her short frame on the bar and gives me a smile.

"Missed you. It's good to see you out and about."

I reach over, tug a piece of her hair, and tip my lips up at her. "Missed you, too." And I have. As much as I like being alone these days, I also miss my friends. I didn't realize how much until I walked in here tonight. Guilt eats at me with the thought of pushing these people away. I never realized how much doing that would hurt them.

Jaxon walks up to us and Mia straightens.

"What's up?" he asks, eyeing the glass on the bar in front of me. When he sees what's inside, some of the tension on his face relaxes, but not completely.

"Just water, Jaxon." I still feel the need to reassure him. I know it's only out of concern that he's worried what I'm drinking. I did this to everyone. I made everyone doubt me.

"That's good." He nods and walks off.

I watch him, brows pulled low, until Mia speaks again and brings my attention back to her.

"So, I've heard you started on your porch. How is it looking?"

I clear my throat and look down at the bar. Everyone knows why I haven't done anything with the house yet. I'm not completely comfortable talking about it, but I know they'll be curious. The house was to be a big part of Anna's and my life.

"It's finished and looking good. I'm gonna start painting tomorrow."

"That's great. Let me know if you need any help. I'm sure Mac wouldn't mind if we came over to lend a hand. Might do Trent some good. Keep his mind off things."

I watch as a cloud of anger washes over Mia's face. I reach across the bar and grab her hand.

"Hey, how's he doing?" I ask.

It wasn't too long ago that we found out that Trent isn't biologically Mac's son, that he's actually Mac's long-lost fucker of brother's son. They also found out that Trent's mom, Tessa, someone who'd been obsessed with Mac for years, raped Mac when they were younger by doping him up with Rohypnol. It turned out Shady, Mac's brother, and Tessa were in cahoots to break Mac and Mia up from the beginning. When Mac finally told Mia the truth of what happened all those years ago, Tessa found out and she and Shady both tried again to keep them apart, going so far as threatening Trent if he didn't help. Tessa and Shady kidnapped Mac and Mia, drugged Mac with Rohypnol again, and they were going to rape them both. Luckily Jaxon and I got there before it could happen.

Trent doesn't know Mac isn't his father. He just knows his mom is screwed in the head and he was only ever just a ploy to try to get Mac back with her. Last I heard he was coping, but I know it still has to hurt his little eleven-year-old heart, knowing his mom never cared for him.

Mia relaxes her clenched fists on the counter and pulls in a deep breath before looking at me. The anger is still there, but it's under control.

"He's doing better. I can tell it still hurts him, but having his dad and me there helps."

I squeeze her hand, offering the little bit of comfort I can in a situation like that. No child should ever have to go through what he did. And no woman should ever have to go through what Mia went through. When Jaxon and I busted through the door and found Mia almost naked with a half-naked Shady looming over her, I saw red. My eyesight went blurry and visions of Anna naked lying on a table while some sick fuck raped her filtered through my mind. Had Jaxon not stormed forward and taken down Shady, there's no telling what I would have done.

Someone bumps my shoulder, and I look over to see Mac

standing there. His eyes are focused on my hand, still holding Mia's. After a second, he takes a seat next to me and says to Mia, "Beer stat, Pix." And turns to me. "How's it going?"

"You get your beer when I get a kiss, Sheriff." Mia says, pulling her hand from mine and planting it on her cocked hip, brow raised.

He turns back to her and grins cheekily. "Sure thing, baby, coming right up." He gets up from his stool, leans way over the bar, grabs the back of her head with one hand, and pulls her forward.

I can't hide the smile that pops up. If anyone deserves to be happy, it's these two.

I've missed this. The easiness that exists between everyone here. Well, the easiness wasn't there between Mac and Mia until recently, but for everyone else it was. I hate I've become so absorbed in my own pain that I've let everything slip through my fingers. They act as though I've been here all along, when in truth, I've been off in my own little hole, nursing my grief and not letting anyone in. I'm glad they aren't hounding me with questions and are acting normal. Explaining my erratic behavior isn't something I want to do.

When Mac pulls back from Mia, her face is flushed. She licks her lips and turns to get Mac his beer.

"Got an interesting call this morning," Mac says, not taking his eyes off Mia's ass as she bends to get a bottle of beer from one of the small fridges.

"Yeah?" I prompt him to continue.

"A Detective Vines called to request a character check on you. Said it was just procedure. He needed it because of some bones that were found on one of your sites in Kentucky." He turns in his seat until he's facing me.

I turn in my seat as well and give him what I know.

"A couple of my guys found bones when they were digging for the foundation. Didn't find out until yesterday they were human. I was hoping they were animal."

He nods and grabs the beer Mia hands him. She immediately walks off when a customer calls her name.

"I figured that was it. I told him he had nothing to worry about, but still gave him some references he could use. He said he'd be in touch as soon as he had something."

"Yeah, he told me the same thing. I had to close down the site until they do a sweep for evidence. They don't have a timeline yet, but they're working on it. I'm thinking I may need to make a trip there when things are settled."

That phone call happened yesterday morning as I was working on the porch. My crew was already on standby and holding off on moving forward with the job. As soon as I got off the phone with the detective, I called my foreman, Kevin, and told him the job was on hold. With no telling how long the investigation would last, I told him I'd find other sites his crew could work until the job was a go again. I also had contractors I had to call. When I spoke with my client, he was agitated the project was put on hold, but knew there was nothing that could be done.

"Keep me updated," Mac says.

I nod and turn to face the floor again when the door opens. I stop mid-motion when Chris walks in. Jaxon texted me the night before she left to inform me he was coming to get her the next day. I know he was hoping I'd tell him not to, and the words so desperately wanted to leave my lips, but I held them back. I made sure I was gone the next morning. I'm not completely sure I would have let her leave had I been there. It's been four days since I've seen her, but for reasons I'm not willing to entertain, it feels more like four years.

She's wearing a white flowing skirt that's so long it almost drags the floor, with a dark denim buttoned-up jacket. Her luscious red hair is swept up into a loose bun at her nape.

Before I can stop them, my eyes eat up the sight of her. I'll never admit it out loud, and I'm kicking myself internally for even thinking it, but seeing her again fires my blood like nothing has before, even Anna. A bout of self-hatred and guilt enters with the thought. In the short time she was in my house, I got used to seeing her. It just about killed me to leave the house the morning she left, not knowing the next time I would see her.

It's hard, but I yank my eyes from her and continue to swivel my chair until I'm facing the crowd. Out the corner of my eye, I see Mac watching me, and I'm sure the reaction I just had when Chris walked in. I ignore him and try my best to ignore the fact that Chris is walking our way. However, I still notice she stops midstride when she sees me sitting beside Mac.

She continues her trek across the floor and stops on the other side of Mac. I can't see her unless I crane my neck around. I don't know if that's a good or bad thing. It should be a bad thing, but by body's reaction to her says otherwise.

Her voice is low, and I can barely hear her when she says, "Hey, Mac."

I wait, but get no greeting, which is strange. She always says something to me. It's usually soft and hesitant, but it's still there. In turn, I always shut her down or ignore her. I don't like that she's now doing the same to me, which is fucked because I used to hate it when she was in my face. Now that she's removed herself, I find I miss it and want it back.

Mac looks from me to her, also noticing the difference in Chris, and I'm sure feeling the tension. I continue looking out at the dance floor, trying to disregard the dull ache in my chest. Andrew and Jase are grinding their hips together. Ethan, Karyn, and Jesse are still at the pool tables shooting the shit. Karyn looks our way and yells Chris's name.

"I'm coming!" Chris hollers back.

A minute later, with beer in hand, Chris walks off without so much as a glance in my direction. I watch the sway of her ass and the swish of her skirt and feel it in my dick. I sit uncomfortably in my seat because I don't want Mac to notice me adjusting myself.

Once Chris reaches the pool table, she and Karyn hug, she kisses Ethan's cheek, and does the same to Jesse. Jesse's eyes linger on her a bit too long, and it makes me want to tear them out and shove them up his ass.

Chris places her beer on the high-top table and shrugs off her jacket. What she reveals underneath the jacket has my balls drawing up tight and my dick so hard I wouldn't be surprised if it punched through my jeans. Shit's so tight down there now I have no choice but to have my dick snap off or adjust myself. Mac's still looking at me as I adjust myself, but I'm past caring now.

She has on a light green tube top that showcases her breasts perfectly. Breasts that are currently drawing the attention of Jesse. He's trying, but his eyes keep dropping. And the more they drop, the harder my grip on the bar gets. With her hair pulled up in a bun, it leaves her creamy pale neck and shoulders bare. What I would give to have my lips against that soft skin right now.

Chris laughs at something Jesse says and leans in against his arm. He dips his head low, and I damn near jump from my chair when it looks like he's going to kiss her. The bastard is saved when he simply whispers something in her ear. But just barely.

I don't like how they seem to be so cozy with each other. Jesse is an all-around good guy, but at the moment he's pissing me off. Never mind the fact I should want Chris's interest to be focused on someone else. Why I care what she's doing and who she's doing it with is beyond me. What I do know is I don't like seeing her openly flirt with another man and watching him drool over her. I have no right to feel this way and the feeling is foreign to me, but it's there, and the longer I watch, the stronger it gets.

I hear my name being called, but I disregard it. It could be Mac, but I'm too absorbed in watching Chris bend over the pool table to take her shot and seeing Jesse's eyes trained on her ass. They are both courting a death wish and they don't even know it.

What the fuck is she doing? Because I won't give in and give it to her she has to find it somewhere else? Is she so hard up, that she's willing to look elsewhere? She stays in my house for four days, is in my space and my business for over a year and now she all of a sudden stops her persistent interference and ignores me? What the fuck kind of shit is that?

My bloods pumps double time when Jesse tucks a piece of hair that's fallen from her bun. She smiles shyly up at him and the dick-head grins back at her. I shouldn't be pissed at him for getting attention from her. He's done nothing to earn my hatred, and Chris deserves to be treated better than I've been treating her. Jesse is the kind of guy who could give it to her. But damn it, now that she's no longer showing interest in me, I want it back. Do I want her for my own? No. But do I want to see her with someone else? *Fuck no!* I am so screwed in the head and should be kicked in the balls for thinking this way, but at the moment I don't care.

For the first time tonight, her eyes meet mine. She's standing against the wall with her pool stick in both hands when her bright green eyes catch mine. I hold her stare, curling my lip up in distaste. I know she sees it, and for a minute I see confusion and hurt in hers, before she casts her eyes down.

I sit there on my stool, barely holding my shit together, when Jesse takes her hand and leads her to the dance floor. The music, talking, and laughter fade around me as Jesse wraps his arms around Chris's waist and she places hers on his chest. All my muscles tense when he pulls her so close their chests touch.

When he puts his head in the crook of her neck, I can't handle it anymore. I'm off my seat and already moving in their direction before I realize it. A hand on my bicep stops me before I get further.

"Nick, don't," Jaxon says.

I turned to see him, Mac, and Mia watching me. I snatch my arm back from him and growl, "Stay out of it."

He takes a step closer to me and gets in my face. His odd violet-and-cornflower-blue eyes are hard and would scare any other man. They say don't fuck with me. But I'm in no mood to be reasonable. If Chris wants to fuck around, then I'll give her someone she can fuck around with.

"You didn't see the hurt I saw the other day when I picked her up," Jaxon growls. "You fuckin' left, knowing she was leaving that morning. Either let her go or take what you damn well want. Stop with the mind games already. She doesn't deserve that shit," Jaxon warns, and it just pisses me off more.

I glare at him and give my own warning. "Stay the fuck out of my business, Jaxon." I turn my glare on Mac and then Mia. "All of you." I turn on my heel and continue toward Chris and Jesse.

Jaxon's right. I need to get my shit together. I know I'm giving Chris mixed signals. But seeing her out on the dance floor with Jesse is something I can't handle. Something snapped inside me.

She sees me approaching, her eyes going wide. Dropping her hands from Jesse's chest, she takes a step back, breaking the hold he has on her waist.

Smart girl.

I'm looking at her, but my growled words are aimed at Jesse. "Leave."

He has bigger balls than I thought. He shifts on his feet, but doesn't step back. Instead he says, "Hey, Nick. How—"

I don't let him finish before I swing my fierce gaze his way. He hesitates with indecision written on his face and looks at Chris, opening his mouth to say something to her, but she stops him before he gets a chance.

"It's okay, Jesse. I'll be okay," she says, and places her hand on his arm. I want to snatch it off.

He looks from Chris to me and back again. "You sure?"

She gives him a small smile. "I'm sure."

Looking at me one more time, he walks off. Chris turns her body to face mine as I glare at Jesse's retreating back.

"What the hell was that about, Nick?"

Her question has me bringing my eyes back to her. Hers are narrowed into a glare.

"I could ask you the same thing," I reply darkly.

"I wasn't doing anything, except dancing with Jesse," she says tartly, and then drops her eyes.

"Look at me!"

Her head whips up at my harsh tone. I take a step closer to her. Her sugary-sweet scent assails me, and I ball my hands into fists to keep them from yanking her to me.

"That's bullshit and you know it, Sugar," I grind out between clenched teeth. "You're so desperate to get laid that, knowing I won't give it to you, you start looking for it somewhere else."

She sucks in a hard breath and hurt washes over her face. It only lasts a second before rage takes over. I know what's coming before she even has a chance to pull back her hand and swing it toward my face. I reach out and grab her wrist before she makes contact. We've been in this situation before. A couple months ago, I watched her, Andrew, and Mia grind against each other on the dance floor until I couldn't watch anymore. Yes, Andrew's gay and I knew he wasn't getting off on having Chris rub against him, but I still didn't like it. Only difference is, her slap caught me by surprise. Not this time.

"That shit isn't happening a second time," I tell her and give her wrist a squeeze. Not enough to hurt, but enough for her to know I'm serious.

"Let me go," she demands in a low voice.

"No."

"Let me go now, Nick." Her voice is louder, but still low enough to not draw attention to us.

"No." I bend to bring my face closer to hers so she can hear me clearly. "You want someone to fuck you? Is that what you want, Chris? You've been aiming to get at my dick for months now." Not caring that we're in a bar full of people, I grab her hand and place it over my hard cock. Her eyes go wide, and satisfaction hits me. "You want it so bad, you can taste it, can't you? Even knowing I don't want you, but want someone else."

She closes her eyes, but before she does, I see pain in them. I hesitate for a second, but push the guilt of me being a total dick aside. She wants to play this game; I'll show her exactly what she's in store for.

I release her hand, but it lingers for a couple beats before she pulls it back. I wrap my arm around her waist and yank her to me. She falls into my chest with a muffled cry. At her ear, I whisper, "You want it, Sugar, you can have it, but you better be prepared for what you're asking for."

Before she has time to respond, I remove my arm from around her waist and grab her hand. Pulling her behind me, I head straight for the door. I don't look at anyone as I stomp across the floor, but I feel eyes on us.

"Nick." She pulls at my arm, but I pay it no mind, grabbing her hand tighter and moving us out the door of Jaxon's.

"Nick." She tries again, louder this time. Again, I don't say anything.

We walk across the street until we reach my truck. Yanking the door open, I grab her by the hips and lift her inside. She opens her mouth to say something, but I point my finger at her and snarl, "Don't fucking move," before closing the door in her face. Her jaw drops. With grunt, I turn and make my way around my truck.

My mind's made up and nothing she has to say will calm the raging storm brewing in my head. She'll learn once in for all that she doesn't want to get involved with me. I don't know if what she was doing in the bar with Jesse was a last-ditch effort to make me want her by making me jealous, but after tonight she'll not only leave me alone, but she'll be running away from me. I have to make sure of that because my defenses against her are deteriorating, and I can't let that happen.

My name is shouted from across the street. I stop at the hood of my truck to look back at Jaxon's. Jase is standing on the porch, his body tense, with Andrew's arm around his waist holding him back. Jaxon and Mia are standing behind them. Jaxon looks ticked but is physically holding himself back, while Mia has her fists on her hips, looking irritated and a little worried. Both know I would never physically harm her, but both are also unsure if I would emotionally.

"You hurt her and no force on earth will stop me from getting to you," Jase shouts at me, pure rage blazing in his eyes.

I take several steps toward him, so I don't have to yell across the street. He has no fucking clue everything I've held back in regard to Chris. No one does. They think I'm a dick to her because I want to be. It's the last thing I want, but she's leaving me no damn choice. I'm not the man for her. I'll never be able to give to her what she deserves. That part of me no longer exists. The only thing left is darkness and anger. She doesn't need that in her life. No, she didn't instigate my behavior tonight, but watching her and Jesse grind on each other pushed me over the edge. I can't stand the thought of her with anyone else, but I also don't want her for myself. I don't want her, but I can't help but want her when I see her. My thoughts are crazy; I know they are. She's not asking for what I have planned, but I'm tired of holding back something I so desperately need. And I know she wants it too. It's insane, but I'm going to give us what we both want tonight, and also give her what she needs by pushing her away in the process. I'm out of options. It's the only way I know how to make her see what I am and to get her out of my head.

"That's what I've been trying to avoid this whole time, but she won't let it be. She won't leave *me* be. She's always right here," I thump the side of my head. "I need her gone. I need her to realize I can't be what she wants me to be. It's time I show her that."

Jase struggles in Andrew's arms, trying to get at me. I'm sure my words make him want to rip my head off, this is his sister, after all, that I'm talking about. They all need to learn though. Jaxon, Bailey, Andrew, and Mia all need to know that part of me, the good part, is no longer there. Or if it is, it's hidden so deep, there's no way it could find its way out.

Andrew whispers something in Jase's ear that has him calming. I'm surprised there wasn't more of a fight from him or that the others are letting me leave with her. I'm sure I don't appear right in my mind at the moment, I certainly don't feel it, but they also know I would never physically harm her or force her to do something she didn't want. I'd rather stick my dick in a grinder than force her.

I turn on my heel before any of them has a chance to say anything else. My eyes slide to Chris through the windshield as I walk in front of my truck. Her jacket was left inside Jaxon's and it's chilly outside, so I yank off the button-up shirt I have on, leaving me in just my black tee, and throw it to her when I climb inside.

"Put that on," I grunt and turn the key. The truck is no longer warm. She takes the shirt and slips her arms inside. Looking in my side mirrors and seeing no one coming, I pull out onto the road and head toward home. Chris sits in her seat with her hands in her lap, twisting the material of the shirtsleeves.

After several seconds of silence, she asks cautiously, "What are you doing, Nick?"

I keep my eyes on the road when I answer grimly, "What we should have done a long time ago."

It takes her a minute, but then, "And wh-what's that?"

I grip the wheel and dig deep so I don't completely lose it. The roads are empty, and I only live a couple miles from the center of town, but her smell is filling my truck and my willpower to keep my hands off her is waning. Watching her snuggled up with Jesse tonight damn near had me losing my mind. I've always found Chris beautiful and if I didn't have a screw loose from what happened to Anna, I may have enjoyed spending time with her, getting to know her, having her body slide against mine as I took her. But the fact remains, I am fucked in the head. My body may enjoy her tonight, but that'll be it. There won't be any sweet words or soft kisses. No cuddling afterwards or easy pillow talk. What will happen tonight will be raw and for the sole purpose of satisfying the ache in both our bodies and proving to Chris once and for all that she doesn't want my brand of fucked-up in her life.

"I'm giving you what you've been aching to have, and in the process, showing you it's a mistake you'll wish you never made."

twelve

Nick

I PULL UP TO MY HOUSE. The only light that can be seen is the single bulb by the front door. I throw the truck in park, yank open my door, and stalk around to Chris's side. She has the door open and is sliding out when I make it to her. I grab her hand, pull her the rest of the way out, and slam the door. She doesn't say a word as I walk us up the stairs, unlock my door, drag her inside, and carelessly throw my keys on the small table.

It's not until we're walking down the hallway that she digs in her heels and tries to stop me.

"Nick," she says, with a tremor in her voice. "I don't think this is a good idea."

I spin around and back her up against the wall and fit my body against hers.

"Why? After all this time you've been trying to get me between your legs. Now you don't think it's a good idea? Why let me bring you here when you knew this is what we were leading to? Your feeble protests at stopping me weren't worth shit. You could have stopped me had you wanted to." She winces, but I ignore it in my pursuit. "Do you want me?"

She hesitates for only a second and then whispers, "Yes. But this way doesn't feel right."

I rock my hard cock into her center. Her eyes go wide and her breath hitches. "This is the only I can give it, Sugar. You can take it or leave it. Now chose."

I already see the answer in her eyes and feel it in her body. It's the only reason I'm pushing this. There's blatant desire flaring in their depths and her body grinds against me. I don't think she realizes either of these things.

She chews her bottom lip and grips my shirt at my waist. I know I'm on the edge of taking this too far. On the edge of being just an asshole to being too forceful. She only has to say no, and I'll back off and take her home. I silently pray she doesn't though. I fucking *hate* that I want this so badly.

I'm just about to back off and take her home, when her words stop me. "Yes. I want you."

A flood of relief rushes through me. The words barely leave her lips when I grab her hand and drag her the rest of the way to my bedroom.

I don't stop when I come to my half-closed bedroom door. I just use my foot to kick it the rest of the way open. It slams against the wall, causing Chris to jump.

My body is primed and ready. Now that I've made the decision to take Chris and she's given me her consent, I'm impatient. There's not a damn thing that will stop me from having her now, except her telling me to stop. But there's one thing I have to make clear first.

I turn to her, drag my shirt down her arms, and let it fall to the floor. She looks up at me, the green in her eyes swallowed up by the pupils. Her breathing is heavy, causing her generous tits to rise and fall rapidly. She licks her lips, and I swear I feel it on the tip of my dick.

I swing her around and bring her back against my front. Her ass meets my hard cock and it feels like fucking heaven. She sucks in a sharp breath. I wrap one arm around her middle and let the other grip the material of her skirt.

I run my nose along her neck, her scent intoxicating my senses. I stop when I reach her ear.

"You want me?" I ask again, needing her to be sure.

She shivers, and I look over her shoulder to see her hands clenched into fists at her sides.

"Yes," she whispers.

She tips her head to the side when I nip her ear. I kiss and lick a trail from one side to the other. Her taste, vanilla and sugar, is something I could get used to if I let myself. Her head moves forward, giving me access to the back of her neck.

Once I reach her other ear, I whisper, "You want me, even knowing I'll be thinking about another woman while I'm fucking you? Imagining it's her cunt taking my cock instead of yours?"

It's a question that'll start to show her just what she's getting when it comes to me, but it's a bald-faced lie. Anna is the furthest thing from my mind right now. The only thing I'm thinking about is what Chris will feel like once I have her beneath me, the taste of her of her cunt on my lips, the smell of her, and how tight she'll grip my cock.

I squeeze my eyes shut at the realization and block out the fact that it's Chris in the room with me and not Anna. It's Chris's body that I'm getting ready to touch and it's not Anna that's occupying my mind. Guilt churns, and I want to snatch my hands off Chris, but also know that I won't. I want her too badly and I hate myself for it.

Her breath hitches, her body tightens, and I think if I've finally gotten to her. I want to scream at the thought of not finishing this. But a small part of me wishes she will stop it. I hate treating her like this. Someone should cut off my dick with a dull blade. But she needs to know that this is what I am now. I can never be what she so wholeheartedly deserves. I'll never be able to get over Anna's death. Or rid myself of the guilt. I'll never be able to give myself to someone like Chris. And the thought of even trying scares me too much. My dead and cold heart may still be in my chest, but it's a useless organ now that's incapable of feeling.

I'm surprised when she pulls in a deep breath, lets it out slowly, and says in a voice with so much sorrow I almost pull back from her, "Yes."

I squeeze my eyes shut with her softly spoken word. I have to harden my heart against the onslaught of emotions that one word causes. I desperately want to know why she's allowing me to do this. Why let me use her body like I am. However, I don't dwell on it long. This is something I have to do. She needs to move on and forget I ever existed. Because all I would ever be able to give her is heartache. Who wants to be with someone when you know they're pining for someone else and can't get over the fact they're gone?

Knowing I'm going to hell for what I'm about to do, I grip Chris's hips and curl my fingers under her shirt. Her skin feels silky and warm. Goose bumps appear on her sides when I slide my hands up, taking her shirt with me. A little moan comes from her lips, and I hum my approval against her neck.

Her head drops forward again when I trail kisses from one shoulder to the other. My hands stop just below her breasts, and I give her one more chance to stop this.

"You need to stop me now, Sugar, before it gets too late."

She reaches back and grabs my ass, pulling me more into her. "Please don't stop. I want this, Nick," she moans. I drop my hands to hers and pull them away.

"No touching unless I say you can. Understand?" I tell her sternly.

She gasps, but gives me a nod. I move my hands back to where they were and pull her shirt up, exposing her breasts. From over her shoulder, I see she has small rosy pink nipples. They look just like cherries, and I want to lick, suck, and devour them. I pinch and twist them until they turn to hard little nubs. She picks her head up, only to lay it back against my shoulder.

I grab a handful of her hair that's still at the nap of her neck in a bun and twist her head to the side so I can nip and lick her neck. I can't get enough of her taste. She tastes just as she smells. I grip both her tits in my hands and squeeze. She shoves her chest out and digs her ass back into my groin, nearly destroying my control.

I take a step back from her and say gruffly, "Take your skirt and panties off. Then get on the end of the bed on your hands and knees, ass in the air."

She turns and looks up with uncertain eyes. I hold my ground when all I want to do is fall to my knees in front of her and worship every single inch of her body. Her breasts jiggle with her movement and my hungry eyes drop to them. Her body is glorious, and I haven't even seen all of it.

"Nick, I don't want—"

"You're getting what we both want. You're just not getting it the way you want it. We do this my way or no way at all."

I wait for her response. If she tells me she wants to stop, we will. I'll have blue balls from hell, but we'll go no further. But if she wants to continue, this is the only way I'll give it.

She nods and both relief and disappointment flood through me. She slowly lifts her hands to her skirt and hesitantly slides it over her hips. I watch with interest, still expecting her to put a stop to this. Her hands move down, taking her panties along with the skirt and exposing inch by torturous inch of smooth pale skin. My eyes hold for a second on the neatly trimmed red curly hair that lies above her pussy, before following her hands as they continue their downward movement.

Once she has her skirt and panties at her ankles, she stands back up and steps out of them. I trail my eyes up her shapely legs, linger once more at the apex of her thighs, up over her stomach and tits, her neck, before meeting her gaze. She's so fucking beautiful.

She's not looking directly at me, but instead just over my shoulder. Her fingers wiggle, and I know she's fighting the urge to cover herself from my probing gaze. I reach back between my shoulder blades, grip my shirt, and bring it over my head. I lose sight of her for only a second, but when I have it back, her eyes are focused on my chest. Heat flares in their depths and she shudders out a breath.

Fuck, but I want this woman something fierce!

"Release your hair."

Her eyes snap back to mine. Her hands reach back and she pulls a clip from the back. Her thick red hair comes tumbling down her shoulders in soft waves. Some of it falls over her breasts, leaving them partly hidden, peeking through a red curtain. She looks like an innocent maiden from the old days, trying to cover her breasts from prying eyes.

"Bed, Sugar," I remind her.

She licks her lips, but moves to the bed. Her ass twitches as she walks, and I can't wait to get my hands on it. She looks over her shoulder at me when she's standing in front of the bed. I raise a brow in question, but she just turns and climbs up. She stays on her knees, her hair trailing down her back, for several seconds, before she lowers her body until she's on her hands as well.

The sight before me damn near has me drooling. My dick turns to stone as her cunt glistens, spread open for me. Her lips are small and are a darker pink. The puckered hole of her ass tempts me. I want to dive in and devour her and never come up for air. She's fucking driving me insane.

It also pisses me off that she's so willing to allow me to treat her like a whore with no feelings involved. Does she think so little of herself, or is she doing this for another reason? Does she think this is what I truly want and is willing to give it to me? This is the last thing I want, but it's the only choice I'm left with to get through to her.

My eyes stay locked on her pussy and ass as I walk toward her. When I'm standing with only a few inches separating my jean-covered dick and her slickness, I place one of my hands on the small of her back and run it up her spine. She's on her hands and knees, but I want her chest to the bed. Her breath hitches at my first touch.

I reach the base of her neck and apply pressure. She understands what I want and lowers herself until she's on her elbows with her cheek to the comforter.

"Spread your legs more," I tell her and push down on her lower back. She does as she's told, but not enough. "More." I grunt at her, and apply more pressure.

She spreads her legs even wider. I stop her when she's at the perfect level to take my cock.

With both hands now, I start at her ass and move them up her sides until I reach her breasts that are smashed to the bed. I reach beneath, tweak her nipples, and then bring them back down her sides. Her skin is so smooth and feels fantastic beneath my palms. She moans into the comforter and arches her back. When I reach the crease of her legs and hips, I change directions and slide them down her thighs. On my way back up, I wrap my hands around her thighs so my fingertips are right at her pussy. I pull her back against my dick and her warmth hits me, intoxicating me. I tip my head back and release a groan at the same time she moans. When I bring my head back down, she's gripping the sheets tightly in her fists. I pull her back again, grind her wet pussy against me, and have to fight the urge to yank open my zipper and shove my dick in her tight cunt.

I shift back and bring my hands over her ass again until my thumbs are poised right at her wetness. I look down when I pull her lips apart and watch as her juice slides down her thighs. She's fucking soaked and my mouth waters to lap up every single drop.

I run both thumbs up and down her slit a few times, before I slip one inside.

"*Fuck*!" I hiss when her walls clench around my thumb, gripping it tight, and she whimpers, causing me to push in further.

Not able to stand it a moment longer, I take my hands away and take a step back.

Her protest is instant. She looks over her shoulder and says, "What are you—" She stops short when she sees my hands at the waist of my jeans. She breathes an "oh" and her eyes flare wide with desire.

I keep my eyes on her as she watches me slide my pants down my hips. My dick jumps with her stare and a pearly drop of precum appears at the tip.

"Cheek back to the bed," I order harshly.

She bites her lip and looks disappointed, but does as she's told. It's not that I don't want to see her appreciation of me, but this is already hard as it is. If I have to look in her eyes, I may not be able to go through with it. Eventually the heated look she's giving me will give way to hurt. I can't bear to see it.

I bend to untie my boots and then toe them off. Once I step out of my jeans, I grip my cock and give it a few pulls. Stepping back up to Chris, I lay a hand on her left hip and feel a shiver race over her. I can only see one side of her face, but the side I do see shows her eyes clenched tightly shut.

Still holding my dick with one hand, I take the tip and rub it along her opening. Instead of slipping it inside, I grab the base and angle it down until it meets her clit.

Her panted "Nick" against the comforter and her backward push with her hips says it won't take long to send her over the edge.

Thank fucking Christ for that, because I sure as shit won't last either.

I bring the head of my dick back up, trail it past her slit again, and rest it at her back entrance. I want to see how far she'll let me go. She stiffens for a minute, her head jerking up with the slight pressure I put on her asshole, but she doesn't stop me. Although I can tell she's hesitant for me to take her there, she's still willing to allow it. I can't tell if that turns me on more or ignites my fury further. Regardless, I have no plans to take her ass tonight.

My grip on her hip tightens as I bring my hardness back to her pussy. Before I slide inside, I ask her one more time.

"Are you sure you want this, Chris? Once I start, I won't stop until it's done." My voice is tight and guttural. I'm close to my breaking point, but I need her permission one last time.

The words have barely left my mouth before she's saying breathlessly, "Yes, Nick. Please."

"You protected?"

"Yes," she whimpers, impatiently rocking her hips.

I glance down to where my dick is poised at her entrance and watch as I slide every single inch in with one smooth slow motion.

"Jesus fucking Christ!" I groan deeply, as she cries out into the comforter.

She grips me so goddamn tight it's a wonder I don't come as soon as I'm inside. The feeling of her wrapped around me, warm and soft, is like heaven and hell. It's one of the sweetest things I've ever felt, and I know this will be the only time I'll ever feel it.

I pull my hips back until just the tip is left inside. Seeing her wetness glistening on my cock has me biting back a groan and fighting the impulse to pound the fuck out of her. Slowly, I slide back inside and hold myself still, letting her adjust to my size. Once I feel her relax, I grab her hips and slam forward at the same time I pull her back to me. She's whimpering and crying and clutching the comforter in a death grip.

On my next inward movement, I keep her hips against mine and grind my pelvis in her ass, hitting something inside her that has her shouting, "Nick!"

Hearing her cry my name has me wanting to pound my chest like a caveman.

When I pull from her again, I don't stop until I pull all the way out. Immediately, I push her ass until she has no choice but to move up the bed. I climb up behind her and bring her hips back, fitting my cock back inside her sweet warm pussy.

"Make sure you stay on your knees," I grate at her. She holds still as I bend over her back with one arm braced beside her head and one planted diagonally across her back, my hand grabbing her shoulder. I use her shoulder as leverage to push myself forward at the same time making sure she stays in place to take my thrusts. I surge forward and feel my balls slapping her clit. Pulling back, I slam forward again. And again. She holds her position on the bed but with my thrusts she's forced to inch forward. I grit my teeth to keep from spilling inside her.

Her walls tighten around me, and I know she's close. I also know what I need to do next. Something that no woman, or man for that matter, should ever have to go through, but it's something that needs to be done to ensure she gives up this ridiculous ploy to garner my attention. Even if it does make me the biggest bastard in the world.

I wait just long enough to feel her reach her peak. She cries out my name and starts bucking her ass against me. I have to force my own orgasm back when her tightness clenches around me in a vise grip.

I bend more at the waist until my chest is curled against her back. I take my hand from her shoulder, grab a handful of hair, and yank her head back. Once my lips are at her ear, I take the lobe between my teeth and nip sharply, before condemning myself to hell by saying, "How does it feel to be fucked by a man who wished you were someone else? Who would do anything to replace you with the one woman he wants most in the world." With that, before she even has a chance to respond to my blatant lie, I rear back, force my hips forward and unleash my own climax inside her, shouting, "Anna!" to the ceiling.

IT'S NOT UNTIL AFTER MY racing heart settles to a slower rhythm and my body loses its tension from my release that I realize I'm lying full body on top of Chris. My face is buried in her mass of red hair and I'm breathing in her delicious scent. My half-hard cock is still buried inside her, and I don't think it's going to deflate anytime soon.

A noise interrupts my euphoria. I hear a sniffle and realize Chris is crying. I close my eyes tightly, knowing I did this to her, brought her to tears. When I open my eyes and pull back, I see through her curtain of hair that she has hers clenched shut tightly as tears leak from them onto my pillow. I want to pound my head against the wall to block out the tortured whimpers leaving Chris's lips.

My dick slips from her body when I pull back. She flinches and with it my heart cracks wide open. When I climb from the bed, she rolls to her side, drawing her knees up to her chest. A pain so sharp that it steals my breath hits my chest. She has her eyes open now, but doesn't seem to be focusing on anything. A look of loss and utter torment is written all over her face. I want to drop to my knees and beg her to forgive me. To tell her it was all a lie, that she was the only one consuming my thoughts as I took her. But that would defeat the whole purpose of what I did.

When I started this, I knew I would end up hurting her, but I never realized the pain it would cause me would be so deep and profound. I hate myself for what I just did. I want to rip out my heart and lay it at her feet, because I know I just destroyed hers.

With a lump in my throat and an ache in my stomach, I force myself to leave Chris on the bed and go to the bathroom. The last thing I want to do it leave her like this, but I have to keep the charade up. I have to make her believe I don't care, when in reality I want to cocoon her into my arms, weep into her neck, and promise with everything I am that I'll never hurt her again.

Once I hit the bathroom, guilt assails me. Guilt for what I did to Chris and guilt for what I did *with* Chris. Anna isn't here to know what I did, but she's still a part of my soul. She still owns me. She would hate me and be disgusted for what I did to Chris. I never thought I would touch another woman; never thought I would want to. Now that I have, I don't wish I could take it back, but wish I could do it again. And again and again, except with a different ending. With me screaming out Chris's name. The way it should have been. I don't regret being with Chris; I just regret how it ended. I should regret it. I should wish to take every second back because she isn't Anna, but I can't. And that's what eats at me. I love Anna with every fiber of my being, but being with Chris made me feel more alive than I've felt in two years.

I forgo looking in the mirror, not able to face my reflection. I walk to the shower, turn the cold on full blast, and step inside. For once, the calming spray of the rain shower head doesn't smooth the tension from my shoulders. I decide to stay in the shower long enough to give Chris time to collect herself, before taking her home. Through all the heartache I've caused, I hope Chris finally realizes the mistake she made by putting her efforts into me. Hopefully she'll be able to move on.

After ten minutes of soaking in the shower, I turn it off, grab a towel, and get out. I didn't bring any clothes with me, so I slip on yesterday's sweats that are sitting in the corner. No way am I going out there in just a towel. It would only embarrass Chris and make me want to whip it off and take her again. I'm discovering my willpower is nonexistent when it comes to her.

When I walk back into the bedroom, I find it empty. Figuring she's probably in the living room waiting on me, I grab a shirt, pull my socks and boots on, and head out of my bedroom and down the hall. The living room is empty and so is the kitchen. Going from room to room, I don't find her anywhere. Outside, both front and back, proves no different.

A sinking suspicion that she may be walking home enters my mind, and I hope I'm wrong. But I don't see any other alternative. She'd be too embarrassed to call anyone to come get her, and besides, there wasn't enough time for that.

I grab my keys from the table by the door, snag a black zip-up hoodie from the coat closet, and stomp out to my truck. I know she's upset and I'm sure a little pissed, but she should know better than to just leave like that and walk home. Yes, we live in a safe town, it's small and not much crime goes on, but shit still happens. She should know that after what Bailey, Anna, Mia, and Jase went through. Nowhere is 100 percent safe. Not to mention the fact that it's cold outside and she's in just a sleeveless top and flimsy skirt.

The more I think of her out there by herself, not thinking clearly, the more pissed and worried I get. I understand her not wanting to be around me after what I did, but her ass should have stayed until I was out of the shower and could take her home.

I slam my door shut, start my truck, and go after the woman who's been a pain in my ass for way too long.

thirteen

Chris

I'M CURLED INTO A BALL with tears leaking onto Nick's pillow, the same pillow I used several times to cuddle up to, and watch as he walks into the bathroom, silently closing the door behind him. I've managed to only let a few tears fall, but as soon at that door closes, the dam breaks lose. I bury my head into the pillow to drown out my sobs.

I only allow myself to pour out my agony and humiliation against his pillow for a couple of minutes before I uncurl myself and robotically get out of bed. I wince from the soreness between my legs.

I'm such an idiot to think Nick could ever look at me with more than disgust, or at the very least without hatred in his eyes. When he whispered those words, asking me if I would let a man fuck me when he would be thinking about someone else, I wanted to scream no. I had hoped he was just trying to scare me away. I didn't really think he would be actually thinking about Anna. Who does that? How can you have sex with one person and be thinking about another? Obviously Nick can. It was stupid and naive of me to think what he said wasn't true. When he shouted her name, I swear I heard my heart shatter into a million tiny pieces. Never have I felt a pain so deep and piercing as I did in that moment. It left me paralyzed, with no hope of pulling air into my lungs.

Even so, while he was resting his weight on my back, I waited for him to take me in his arms and tell me he was lying. To confess it was *me* he was thinking about. When he pulled away and left me there a broken mess on his bed, the miniscule piece that was left of my heart disintegrated. I've never felt so empty and alone in my life.

With the shower running, I find my clothes and slip them back on. It's past ten o'clock and it's cold outside, but there's no way I want to be here when Nick gets done with his shower. My car is still at home, and my purse, which has my phone in it, is at Jaxon's. Even if I did have my phone, there's no way I would call anyone to witness my walk of shame and utter mortification. I'll just walk home. It'll be a cold day in hell before I ask Nick to take me.

Once my clothes are back on, I quickly walk down the hall, thankful that I'm wearing my ballet flats. I wipe the tears still trailing down my face as I make it to the door. Without looking back, I slip out and walk down the steps, vaguely noticing Nick finished the porch.

As I walk down the driveway and out onto the dark deserted street, I realize that I never really had a chance with Nick. He doesn't want to get over his grief and there's nothing anyone can say or do to make him change his mind. He wants to stay wrapped up in his life with Anna and what the future could have held from him. He's not willing to think of an alternate future. It's a sad realization, one that makes me want to scream at God for letting it happen.

I wrap my arms around my stomach as a cold breeze washes over me. My feet are already numb from the frozen street beneath them, but I still march on. I only live a couple miles away so it's not too much of a walk. I may be frozen by then, but I'll take that over facing Nick.

I jerk my head to the side when I hear a crackle in the woods. I peer into the darkness, but don't see anything. It's really dark out tonight. I look up and see no moon in sight. It's just my luck that the one night I have to walk home there's no moon.

I hear an engine and turn to see headlights approaching. I move off the road onto the grass. The road I'm on is the main highway through town, but normally this late at night it's not busy. I hope the person behind the wheel keeps going and doesn't stop to investigate why a woman is walking down the road alone.

My hope is dashed when they slow down. The lights are blinding so I can't get a good look at the vehicle until it pulls up beside me. I release a tired breath when Nick's truck comes into view. I don't acknowledge him.

"Get in, Chris," he says, leaning over the passenger seat and peering out the window.

I wrap my arms tighter around myself and keep walking without looking at him.

He pulls the truck ahead of me and stops, puts it in park, and jumps out. I walk further in the grass to go around. I don't know how much longer I can hold it in. Being around him hurts too much. I made a fool of myself back at his house. I can only imagine what I looked like to him.

I'm rounding the hood of his truck when he comes around on the other side. He stops right in front of me so I have no choice but to stop as well. I step to my right, only to have him grab my arm. I flinch and pull back but he doesn't let me. I look at his chest as I say quietly, "Let go of my arm."

He ignores me. "Get in the truck, Sugar."

I yank at my arm, but he still doesn't let me go.

"Please let me go," I whisper to his chest.

"Why?"

I snap my head up with his ridiculous question and narrow my eyes. I can't believe he has the gall to ask me that. What in the hell is wrong with him? Do I mean so little to him that he doesn't realize the damage he's done?

"Why?" I grind out between clenched teeth. I lean up on my toes and get in his face. "You're really asking me that? You expect me to want a man to touch me who called out someone else's name while he fucked me?"

He holds my stare, his eyes going hard.

"I warned you," he whispers harshly. "I asked you several times, but you were greedy and took it anyway. You *knew* what you were getting."

I rock back on my heels, hurt beyond belief. He's right. I did know, and he did warn me, and I disregarded his warning. But it still makes me feel dirty and used.

"Who does that?" I ask, my voice hoarse from the emotions I'm trying to hold in. "Who sleeps with someone, knowing they'll be thinking about someone else? No one has ever made me feel so low in my life as you did in that moment, Nick." My voice gets louder the more I talk. "And you know what? You're right. I let it happen. It's my own fault. You did warn me, and I didn't listen. Now I have to live with that regret."

I drop my eyes from his, no longer able to hold his stare. My eyes tear up again, but I blink them away. I don't want to cry in front of him again. It's already bad enough he thinks I'm pathetic; I don't want to give him more ammo against me.

"Can you just take me home now?"

I'm done. I'm done fighting him. I'm done feeling worthless when it comes to him. I'm done feeling like I'm nothing. I'm done trying to be something he clearly doesn't want. I just want to go home, crawl in my bed, and lick my wounds in private. Only then will I allow myself to cry out all my pain.

He releases my arm, but doesn't step away. I feel his finger at my chin when he lifts it. I close my eyes so I don't have to see his.

"Look at me, Chris,"

His demand is spoken softly, and against my will, I find myself doing what he said. I'm surprised at what I see there when I do. It's not the ugliness I saw just seconds ago, but remorse and shame.

"For what it's worth, I'm sorry," he says quietly, rubbing his finger along my cheek.

I close my eyes and bask in the feeling of his finger. It's stupid, and I know I shouldn't, but it feels nice. His words sound sincere, and I want to believe him, but it's hard with the pain still raw and his voice calling out Anna's name still fresh in my head.

I take a step back from him and he drops his hand. Resignation crosses his face.

"Let's go."

He walks me to the passenger side of the truck and opens the door. Before I climb inside, he reaches in and pulls out a hoodie and wraps it around my shoulders. "Arms," he says. I slide my arms inside and he zips it up. His scent surrounds me and another pinch of pain surfaces. I keep my eyes downcast, not able to face his gaze.

He steps back, and I get in the truck. He closes the door and walks around to the other side. Once he's behind the wheel, he turns the heater on full blast. I feel the warmth from it on my face, but I'm still cold on the inside. I don't know if I'll ever be warm again.

We sit in silence and it's not long before he's pulling in behind Jaxon's Pub. I grab the handle, but before I can open the door, his gently spoken words stop me.

"I really am sorry, Chris. I never wanted to hurt you. I'm sorry I can't be what you want. I'm sorry I'm stuck in this place I'm in. You deserve so much more than I can give you. I just don't have in me what you need from a man. That part of me died two years ago."

I grab the handle tighter, his words bringing tears to my eyes again. One slides down my cheek, and I wipe it away. I look over at him and see his hands tight around the steering wheel. He's looking out into the darkness.

"I'm sorry too, Nick. I wanted so much to give you wanted you needed, but I know now I can't. I wish you all the happiness in the world, even if you think you don't deserve it. You do. You deserve it more than anyone. And I know you don't want to hear this, but Anna would want that for you, too." I pull in a lungful of air and open the door. Before I close it, I look back at him. "I won't bother you again."

Even though it was him that came to me tonight and not the other way around, I think deep down I was hoping he would. I never really had any interest in Jesse. I think the only reason I agreed to dance with him is because I knew Nick was watching, and I had hoped him seeing me with someone else would make him finally see me as more than a pain in the ass.

I would have never guessed that it would backfire on me as it did.

I close the door behind me and walk to the small fake potted plant beside the steps. Grabbing the hide-a-key, because mine is still in my purse in the bar, I pull open the outside door. Without looking back at Nick still sitting in his idling truck, I close the door and walk to my apartment door. I unlock it, step inside, and close the door. Leaning back against is, I slide down the wall until my ass hits the floor. There, I draw my knees to my chest, wrap my arms around them, let my head fall forward, and let lose all the heartache of losing someone I never had in the first place.

I WAKE THE NEXT MORNING to a pounding in my temples. At first, I think I'm still at Nick's because the rhythm is the same, but when I open my eyes, the blinding light from the window lets me know it's just a headache. I gingerly roll to my side to look at the clock and see it's 8:30. I'm glad it's Sunday and don't work today at the school. I do have to be at Jaxon's at four, but that's only for a few hours. It still gives me enough time to prepare for all the questions I'm sure will be asked.

I roll my body so my feet are planted on the floor and lift myself up. The pounding in my head gets worse, so I just sit there a minute. The memory of why I have a splitting head comes to mind, and I wince. I'm an idiot. I don't know if I'll ever be able to face Nick again. Good thing he doesn't like being around me. It shouldn't be too hard to avoid him.

After crying in front of the door for thirty minutes last night, I dragged myself up and got in the shower. Another wave of grief hit me while I was washing because I was washing his scent off my body. A scent I'll never smell again. Once I was clean, I put on an old t-shirt and crawled into bed, where I cried more until I fell asleep. I swore to myself last night that that was it. I wasn't crying for him anymore.

I get up, get dressed, down a Tylenol with water, do my bathroom business, and walk out to the kitchen. Caffeine is in order.

I'm pouring coffee in my mug when there's a knock at the door. I grab a spoon and stir it quickly before heading over to answer it. I only get halfway there when the knocking turns to pounding.

"Hold your horses, geesh," I yell.

Seeing who's on the other side through the peephole, I roll my eyes. I do not want to deal with this right now.

"Open the fucking door, Chris," comes Jase's irate tone.

Knowing he won't leave unless I let him in, I unlock and pull the door open. He shoves his way inside before I'm even finished.

"Hey, watch my damn toes!" I bark at him.

He grabs both my arms and pulls me around to face him.

"Are you okay?" My anger dissipates some with his apparent worry for me. His eyes travel all over my face, before settling on my eyes. His brows pull down into a frown and his eyes flare with ire. I'm sure I don't look the best this morning. I avoided the mirror when getting dressed, so I don't know what the damage is, but I'm sure I have red splotches on my face and my eyes still feel puffy. I've always been an ugly crier.

Before I get a chance to answer his question, he releases me and spins on his heel.

"I'm gonna fucking kill that bastard," he growls, yanking open the door.

I reach out and grab the back of his shirt, digging my heels in to stop him. "Jase! Stop it!" I yell at his back. He twists, trying to dislodge my hands. "Goddamn it, Jase, I said stop! You're not going to do anything to him!"

There's no way I can let Jase get to Nick. I know he wouldn't literally kill him, but I'm sure there would be some heated words and then a few punches thrown, from both sides. I can't let either of the two most important men in my life get hurt on my behalf.

He turns to me so fast, yanking his shirt free, that I almost stumble. The rage glinting in his eyes would scare any other person, but this is my brother. I've seen it before, so I'm immune. Still doesn't make it any less fierce and domineering though.

"I told him, Chris," he replies, voice low but determined. "I told him if he hurt you, I was coming after him. I've watched him hurt you time after time. He needs to learn that it's not okay. I can't stand by and watch it anymore."

I walk up to him and lay my hand on his chest, touched he wants to protect me. I love that I have my brother here and that he's finally happy with his life, but he needs to learn he can't protect me from everything. He almost died doing it before, and while this case isn't near as dire, he has to know he can't always be there. I'm a grown woman and can take care of myself. He shouldn't throw himself in front of me every time I'm hurt.

"I love you, big brother, but you need to step back with this one. Yes, Nick hurt me, but only in my heart. You know life isn't always easy. You can't always be there to protect me. I have to protect myself, and I'm doing that. I'm done with Nick, okay? It'll take some time to get over it, but he won't hurt me anymore."

He watches me for several seconds, gaze sliding between my eyes, like he's looking for the truth of my words. I hold his stare, so he knows I meant what I said. And as much as it hurts, I do have to let Nick go.

Abruptly, Jase pulls me into his arms, wrapping them tightly around me. I bring mine around his waist and hold on tight as well. He rests his head on top of mine and we just stand there for a couple of minutes. I soak up the warmth of Jase's arms. I needed this. I needed to just be held by someone who cares for me.

"I hate that you're going through this," he murmurs. "You *shouldn't* be going through this. You deserve to be happy, Chris."

"I do, and one day I will be."

"I know you will. And the guy you find will be one lucky bastard."

I really love my big brother.

I give him one more squeeze before I pull back, blinking back the tears trying to find their way to the surface. I don't want Jase to see them. It'll only bring back the anger.

He kisses my forehead and releases me. It's not until then I see him clutching my purse. He shoves it forward, saying, "You left this at Jaxon's. Don't do that shit anymore. I didn't like not having a way of contacting you. And I had no way of knowing if you were okay."

I grab my purse and nod. I can understand his worry. I'm sure it didn't look good last night with Nick pulling me from the bar, but I know Andrew assured him Nick wouldn't harm me.

"You want coffee?" I ask over my shoulder as I walk to the kitchen.

"Sure," he replies and follows me.

I grab my cup, down a couple mouthfuls, and grab a clean one for Jase. I hand him his, along with the sugar and creamer. While he dumps in spoonfuls of sugar, I ask him where Andrew is.

"At home, still in bed. He worked the late shift. I snuck out because I know he would have tried to stop me from coming over." His eyes twinkle when he lifts them to me.

I laugh, a vision of Jase sneaking out of his and Andrew's house playing in my mind.

"You two are nuts. A grown man sneaking out of his own house. You know that's ridiculous, right?"

He shrugs and takes a swallow of his coffee. "Had to make sure my baby sister was okay. I don't know why he thinks you being with Nick is such a good idea. If he had a sister and saw him treating her like that, I bet he wouldn't think it was a great idea then."

"That's because he knows what you see of Nick isn't the real Nick. He watched the love of his life die in his arms, Jase. It's bound to fuck with anyone's head."

"Still doesn't give him the right to hurt my sister," he mutters against the rim of his cup.

I decide to change the subject before he gets pissed again. Although the subject I'm about to bring up won't be much better, I still need to know.

"Have you talked to Mom?" I hedge carefully, leaning against the counter and holding my warm cup between my cold hands. I don't want him to think anything is up if he hasn't. We don't talk much about our family, but I do bring them up now and then.

It takes him a minute to answer and when he does, the look in his eyes isn't good.

"She called day the before yesterday. She was beside herself apologizing for being a shitty mom. Doesn't matter. Shit's already done."

My heart hurts with his words. For years he's felt like he wasn't good enough. I don't know if things will change between my mom and him, but I hope for his sake, they will. And I hope he gives her the chance for that change.

"You should give her a chance, Jase. I know it was hard on you growing up. And yes, she was a crappy mom, but the last time I talked to her she seemed really upset. Maybe she's realizing her mistake and wants to change."

"You know better than that. Dad won't let her change."

He's probably right. I think most of the time Mom only acted the way she did because she followed my dad's lead. Which doesn't look good for her. She should have loved her kids just as much as she loves her husband. But still, if there's some chance things can be patched up between Jase and our mom, I think he should take it. It would be worth it in the end.

"Maybe Dad will change too," I tell him quietly.

He laughs humorlessly and sets his cup on the counter with a bang. "Now I know you're joking. This is the same man that kicked me out of the house for four days when I was sixteen because I got a small star tattoo on my chest. I had to sleep in the damn shed, Chris. In the winter time. I know you remember that. The only reason he let me back in was because he was worried someone from the church would find out."

I do remember. There was a huge blowup between Jase and our dad. He literally threw him out of the house, locked the door, and told me and my mom to not let him back in. It was in the thirties at night. I brought him blankets and food and stayed with him as long as I could. Eventually, he made me go back in the house each evening. I cried and begged him to let me stay, but he wouldn't. I hated knowing he was out there all alone. I threatened to go to some friends' parents to tell them what was going on, but he made me promise not to. Said he was fine and he didn't want anyone knowing.

"I remember," I reply softly.

"And anyway. Doesn't matter if he changes. The man's done too much shit. Shit that can't be undone and I'll never forgive him for. As for Mom, we'll see."

I'll give him that. If he ever only has a relationship with our mom, I'll be happy. At least it's something.

"Now, come give your big brother a hug so he can sneak back in before Andrew wakes up and has a fit."

I laugh and walk to him. He snags me around my waist and pulls me forward. I squeeze him tight before pulling back and looking up at him.

"Love you, Jase. I'm glad you found your happy."

He smiles a sad smile. "Me too. You'll get yours."

I lean up on my toes and kiss his cheek. After walking him to the door and saying good-bye, I close the door and release a tired breath. The headache I had earlier is almost gone, but I feel it lingering in the background.

I go about the rest of my day doing some cleaning, catching up on a few odds and ends for work, reading for a bit, and putting a pork loin in the crock pot to simmer. Before I know it, it's time for me to get ready for work. I've managed to keep Nick off my mind for most of the day, but when I get in the shower the memory of him taking me comes to mind.

I push the thoughts away, not willing to let it take me under again. I've hurt too much because of him. I refuse to allow it to hurt me anymore.

I get dressed, check the crock pot, grab my purse, and head down to the bar. Sundays are normally slow and this one proves no different. Mia is behind the bar, with only a couple people sitting on stools and a couple playing pool. She looks my way when I lift the partition to go behind the bar with her. I ignore her questioning look and stash my purse beside hers in a cubby hole.

I smile and greet her, and she does the same. I get straight to my normal duties. When I was hired I was originally supposed to be just a bartender, but I've since moved to working the floor as well. Mia and I make idle chitchat, and although she doesn't bring up the subject of Nick, I know it's on her mind. She keeps sending me concerned looks, but she doesn't say anything. That's one thing I like about Mia. She can be persistent and demanding when she feels strongly about something, but she knows when to keep quiet. She's giving me that now, and I'm grateful. However, I know it won't last long, especially if she suspects bad shit went down. I try my best to keep a jovial attitude. The less she sees my pain, the longer a reprieve I'll have from her. Obviously, I do a crappy job because she only lasts for a few hours.

I find things to do until the Sunday rush, which really isn't a rush because Sunday is the last day before the work week begins and people need that day to recuperate from the weekend, comes trickling in. Right on time after five, a small group of people walk through the door.

Between keeping myself busy and the evening crowd filtering in, I've managed to keep Nick off my mind. It's getting harder and harder though and the ache in my chest intensifies. It seems like all I do lately is think about that man and hurt over him.

"Are you okay?" Mia says, sidling up beside me.

I wipe the frown from my face I didn't realize I had and drop my hands that are drying a beer mug to the counter. I turn give her a small smile.

Shrugging, I reply quietly, "Yeah."

"Want to talk about it?" she asks. I look over and see she's picked up her own rag and is drying a glass. She's not making a big deal out of the elephant in the room, but she's letting me know she's there. That's what I need right now. Knowing I have people if I need them, but not have them push me.

"Not really," I say as nicely as I can. I'm not ready to talk about it.

Putting it out there for Jase this morning was enough; even if I didn't really give him the story, he knows the outcome.

She drops the rag and glass on the counter and faces me.

"I learned not too long ago that sometimes it helps to talk about things. It's hard at first, but once you do, you feel better."

I take her words to heart. I know she's right, but I'm just not there yet. It only happened yesterday, and I'm still coming to grips with what Nick did and how it made me feel. How having him inside me made me feel. Up to the point of him asking me that question and then him calling out Anna's name, feeling him inside me, over me, surrounding me, was one of the best things in the world. How could something that felt so right, so perfect, end so badly?

I clutch the rag in my hand until my knuckles hurt.

"Thank you, Mia. I'm sure one day I can talk about it, but I can't yet. It's over between me and Nick." I laugh at that. "Actually, it never really started, but whatever, it's done."

She listens, but I see the wheels turning in her head. It looks like she's going to say something, and I brace for it. Mia can be tenacious, so I worry she's going to continue with trying to get me to talk. She must see something in my eyes that tells her it'll be a wasted effort because she stops herself. Instead, she puts an arm around my waist and gives me a squeeze before pulling back.

"I'm here if you need an ear, okay?"

"Thanks, Mia," I tell her sincerely.

We separate and go about our night. Thoughts of Nick plague me. Of what he's doing. If he feels even a little bit guilty. If he truly feels nothing for me. Of what could have been between us if he would only let it. At the last thought, I shake my head, knowing it's crazy to even think about things like that.

Andrew comes in a little while later to replace Mia, who is picked up by Mac. Neither Mac nor Andrew brings up Nick, although I catch Andrew watching me several times. I'm sure Jase told him he stopped by my place this morning and what was said. He also seems to know I won't talk about it.

The later the night gets, the more people show up, and the busier

I get. Andrew is more than his jovial self, and I know he's trying to cheer me up. I smile and laugh at his silly antics with the customers, but I know it's forced, and so does he. Even so, he doesn't push.

By the time my shift is over at eleven, I'm exhausted. I want to crawl up to my apartment, eat, shower, and drop into bed. I do my end-of-shift duties, grab my purse, and walk to Andrew, who's handing over a bottle of beer to a regular.

His eyes twinkle when I walk up to him. Before I get a chance to let him know I'm leaving, he puts one arm around my waist, the other around my shoulder, dips me backwards with his head shoved into my neck, and blows a loud raspberry on my neck. It tickles and the scruff on his face scratches. I immediately start laughing and clutch his back.

When he pulls me upright, he has a big smile on his face.

"That's the real laugh I've been looking for all night," he says, his finger stroking my cheek.

"Thanks, Andrew. I needed that."

He smiles his megawatt smile, and says, "That's what I'm here for, sister-from-another-mister."

I scrunch my nose up at him. "Uh... that would be sister from another mister *and* mother, because anything different would be gross."

He tilts his head back, like he's contemplating whether my words are true. A moment later, he lowers his head and scrunches his own nose. "Yeah, guess it would."

We both laugh, then I lean up and kiss his cheek.

"I'm dead on my feet. I'm heading out. You got things here?"

"Yep, I'm good." He throws his arm around my shoulders and walks me to the bar partition. Once there, he stops. When I look up at him, his face is serious.

"Things will get easier, you know. Life sucks when we don't get the things we want, but we get over it and move on. Nick is a dick for the hurt he's caused you. You push that shit aside and don't let it eat at you. Nick may come around and he may not, but don't let him keep you from being happy. If that happiness is with Nick, then you and he both deserve each other. If it doesn't, then he doesn't deserve you. He's still a good guy, he's just may not be one capable of giving himself anymore. The closest anyone has a clue as to what he's going through is Jaxon because Anna was his sister, but even so, Jaxon doesn't know the extent of it. He loved his sister to pieces, but the love you have for the person you were meant to spend your life with is more than that. Nick has to let go of his grief and guilt before he can move on. It's up to him whether or not he can do that. Either way, you stay strong and believe that no matter what happens, you'll get your happiness."

It's no wonder Jase fell in love with this man. Andrew is one of the smartest men I know. He always knows just what to say. Yes, he jokes around and doesn't take stuff seriously half the time, but when it counts, he does. He's always there when you need him, even if it's just a simple laugh.

"Thanks, Andrew," I choke out past the tears clogging my throat.

After another hug, I leave him and head down the hall to the back door. I'm glad I live right above Jaxon's. I don't think I'd have the energy to get in my car and drive tonight.

Once I'm tucked inside my small apartment, I do just what I wanted to do a few minutes earlier: I grab a bowl of food, scarf it down with some water, take a nice warm shower, and drop into bed. It doesn't take me long before I drift off into dreamland. A dreamland filled with unrealistic dreams and hopes of Nick.

fourteen

Nick

I GET OUT OF MY TRUCK and head toward the small trailer off to the side of the construction site. I just left the sheriff's office with his permission to go forward with the job. As soon as I got in my truck, I called the client and let him know we were a go. To say he was happy is an understatement.

I walk up the two steps and open the door. My foreman Kevin looks up from his paperwork. He gets up from his seat behind his desk, rounds it, and perches his ass on the corner.

"How did it go? Are we good?" he asks. He's just as anxious to get the job started as the client. But there's a difference between the client and him. The client wants it done because he's greedy and doesn't like not having his way. Fucking rich people. Kevin gets stir-crazy just standing around. I told him I wanted him to stay on site, just in case something came up I needed him for. He's been here for a little over three weeks. I'm sure he's jumping out of his skin for something to do.

I cross my arms over my chest and lean back against the flimsy wall of the trailer.

"We're good. I'll call the crew and have them back here tomorrow."

Relief hits his face immediately. "Thank fuck for that," he mumbles, and then says more loudly, "I gotta tell you, man, I was going to give it another couple of days and then request to be put somewhere else. Close by so I could be back here if you needed me, but somewhere where I wasn't sitting on my ass doing paperwork."

Kevin's been with me for six years. He's a hard worker, loyal, and dependable. I trust his judgment and his skill for getting the job done. That's something you don't find every day. I feel bad for leaving him here, but he's the one I depend on the most out of all my foremen.

"I hear you. If I hadn't heard from the detective running the case soon, I would have moved you myself. I appreciate you staying behind."

"So, what's the news?"

Standing up from the wall, I walk to one of the two chairs in the room and fold my body into one.

"Guy was a cop. He got whacked ten years ago by some gang member whose brother he put away for rape. The cop went missing and they had no clue what happened to him. Until now. Unfortunately, the gang member that killed him was killed a couple years ago. He should still be here to get punished for that shit. The cop left behind a two-year-old little girl and wife."

"Damn," he mutters.

"Yeah. That's fucked-up shit right there. But they released the site. Said they got all they could."

"Doesn't feel right working here now. Not that I'm saying we should pull out, just saying it a shame we'll be working on top of a place where someone was killed."

"I hear you there, too."

I lean an elbow on the arm of the chair and run my hand down my face, suddenly exhausted. Now that this shit is over, my body is shutting down. I haven't gotten more than a couple hours of sleep a night for the past three weeks. If it's not the same recurring dream of Chris dying in my arms, then it's Anna. The dream doesn't happen every night, but damn near. I've stayed away from alcohol because I know if I don't it will eventually become a problem, and that's the last thing I need in my life. So I haven't had the numbness to help with the dreams. Just as before, when I have them of Chris staring up at me with lifeless eyes, I wake up screaming her name.

And as much as it scares me to admit, I miss Chris. The first thing I want to do when I wake from those dreams is to rush to make sure she's alive and well. To look into her beautiful green eyes and see life in them. I know that would be a mistake. The minute I would see her, I know I would take her in my arms and never let her leave them again. She's the reason why I left in the first place. The need to go to her was becoming too strong. I've been here in Kentucky for twenty days. I wasn't needed here yet, but I knew if I didn't leave town I would have gone to her. And the last thing she needs is me in her life. I would only destroy it and make her world just as dark as mine.

Being away from her has been torture, but I think I've managed to put my walls back up. At least enough for me to be around her without hauling her away and handcuffing her to my wrist. I called Jaxon before I left and told him I was leaving and wasn't sure when I would be back. I've avoided his calls since then, worried I'll give myself away and ask about Chris. Mia on the other hand has been hounding me since the day I left. She hasn't brought up Chris, but I know she wants to. I stay on the line just long enough for her to not think I'm dismissing her and then get off. The temptation is too great when I know she sees Chris on a daily basis.

With all this, I know it's time I go home. I just have to keep my willpower and not go looking for her. It'll only hurt both her and me.

"You look like shit, man," Kevin says, bringing me back to the room.

He's still sitting on the corner of his desk, his hands resting on the edge with his ankles crossed, watching me.

"Yeah, not sleeping good." I wipe my hand down my face and sit up with my elbows on my knees. "Look, I'm gonna stay a couple more days just to make sure everything is smooth sailing, and then I'll head home. You call if something else comes up. Work quick to make up time, but do it efficiently. Obviously, we're behind schedule and if we can, I'd like to make that time up, but I don't want corners cut. I may call a couple other sites and get you a couple extra guys if they can spare them."

"Got it," Kevin says, standing. I stand as well and clasp his hand in a shake. "Now go get some shut-eye. I've got it here for the rest of the day."

"Headed back to the hotel now. Holler if you need me."

I walk out the trailer and to my truck. I look over at the mound of dirt and construction equipment about a hundred yards away. It's a shame what happened to the cop that was murdered. Out of curiosity, I asked the detective overseeing the case how the wife and daughter were doing. I was going to open up a charity fund for them if they needed help. He told me they were happy and being taken care of. Apparently, the widow remarried a year ago to a friend of her dead husband. Another cop. I wondered briefly how she could do it. How she could take another chance on someone else who could possibly end up like her dead husband.

I climb in my truck and pull out of the gravel drive to head to the hotel I'm staying at. This one isn't like the dingy one I stayed at the last time I was out of town. I passed by a couple different gun shops on my way to Kentucky. The thought to stop and pick up another revolver crossed my mind only seconds before I pushed it away. My dreams may still plague me, my pain may still be very real, my guilt may still be strong, and I may still want all of that to go away, but ending it myself is no longer an option. I realize that now. It's the coward's way out.

I pull up to a spot in the hotel garage and get out of my truck. Pocketing my keys, I walk to the bank of elevators that will take me to my room on the sixth floor. There, I'll have a flat-screen TV, fluffy pillows and a soft comforter, nice stain-free carpets, and a shower with a hot tub. Yes, this place is a lot different than the roach-ridden motel I was at before.

I slide my key card into the slot and when the light turns green, I push open the door. I drop the key card and my wallet on the desk across from the bed. It's only five after five, but I'm drained from lack of sleep. I decide on a shower before I attempt to sleep, hoping I'll do it without the horrors that wait for me as soon as I close my eyes.

A COUPLE OF DAYS LATER, I'm unlocking the door to my house. It's late, so the place is dark. I find the light switch just past the small table by the door. When I flip it and the room comes into view, I'm immediately swept with a feeling of being home. I *am* home, but it hasn't *felt* like home in a long time. The place doesn't feel the same anymore. The feeling of dread I usually get when I step through the door is unexpectedly absent. I have a feeling it's because Chris invaded my space and new memories are present. Not all good, but not all bad either.

I move around the house, flipping a few lights on. Even though it's past midnight, I feel too restless to sleep. Surprisingly enough, the past two nights I've slept well, with no dreams.

Instead of going to bed like I know I should, I take my bag of stuff to the closet in my room and head back out to the front door. I walk to the barn, grab a can of light gray paint, some rollers, a roller pan, and a few other things I'll need and bring them back to my bedroom. The need to paint and really start working on the house hits me, and I know I won't be able to sleep tonight because of it. I don't know why I have this sudden need, especially when just a few weeks ago the thought of doing anything with the house terrified me, but I know I can't ignore it.

I strip naked and slip on a pair of old jeans, forgoing a shirt. I start with one wall, moving everything around on that side, taping off the areas that I don't want paint to touch, and removing any electrical plates. After putting down a piece of old plastic, I use a screwdriver to pry the lid off the paint can and pour some into the roller tray.

It doesn't take long before that wall is finished, and I move on to another. Three hours later, all four walls have two coats of paint and the trim is done. I turn and look around the room. It looks strange seeing a different color on the walls. They've been the white they were before since I could remember. But it looks good. A pang of sadness washes over me at the thought of Anna not being here to help. I shove the thought aside and put the lid back on the paint can and clean up my mess. I won't be able to move the furniture back against the walls until the paint dries. With the room filled with paint fumes, I make the decision to sleep out on the sleeper sofa instead of risking waking up with a paint high.

I take a shower and scrub the paint splatters off me, get dressed, pull out the sofa bed, and flop down on it. Exhaustion hits, and I'm out within five minutes of my head hitting the pillow, once more having a dreamless sleep.

THE NEXT DAY, I DECIDED to do something I should have done two years ago. I've avoided it because I hate talking about Anna. It's a hard subject for me, and I'm already in a constant reminder of it, so to openly bring it up myself is something I don't do. Chris was right though. Bailey already has enough guilt and pain. If I can relieve her of some of it, I need to.

I'm a dick for not doing it sooner. I've seen the way Bailey's eyes glaze over anytime Anna is brought up, like she's reliving what she and Anna went through. I've seen the guilt on her face sometimes when she looks at me. She feels responsible for Anna's death, and in turn, my grief and pain. She shouldn't. I've never blamed her for what happened. She tried saving Anna the only way she knew how. I saw the pain she was going through when Jaxon and I walked through that door to old man Pepper's cabin. I saw how she tried comforting Anna. I can't let her feel guilty anymore.

I'm standing outside Jaxon and Bailey's house with my palms sweaty and my heart pounding. Coming to the decision to talk to Bailey and actually doing it are two different things. My stomach cramps with the thought of dredging up the one night that has haunted me for so long, the night that changed my life forever by taking the one thing I would give anything to have back.

Before I get a chance to change my mind, Jaxon opens the door. I'm sure he saw me pull up and has been waiting for me to knock. I called earlier and told him I was coming over, but not the reason. I don't know how he'll feel about me being here to talk to Bailey about a subject that's hard on us both. It's Sunday, so I knew he would be here instead of at the bar. Sundays are his only days off. I wanted him here when I talked to Bailey, to offer comfort to her if needed. Besides, he'd have my ass if I upset his girl, and while I know that's what'll happen during this talk, he and I both know this conversation is well overdue. I'm surprised he hasn't demanded it of me himself. Only reason I can figure why he hasn't is because he knows it damn near kills me every time Anna is brought up. Even so, I should have grown some balls before now and come to Bailey.

"You ever gonna knock?" Jaxon asks, standing in the doorway watching me.

I don't say anything at first, just stand there like a damn pussy. *Fuck!* I didn't realize this would be so hard.

I stuff my hands in my pockets and look to my left. I randomly notice way off in the distance some ducks wading in Jaxon's pond at the back of his property. I have to squint to see them. Jaxon's always had ducks in his pond, even during the months they're supposed to fly south for a warmer climate. It's a strange thing to notice in light of the importance of me being here.

"What the fuck, man? What's going on?" Jaxon demands. I bring my eyes back to him and force myself to do what I came here for.

"Hey, Jax. I came to talk to Bailey. She here?"

Several different emotions cross Jaxon's face before compassion and understanding are the only ones left. He takes a step back and opens the door wide for me to enter.

"Yeah, come on in," he says quietly, his voice slightly tense.

"Thanks," I mumble and follow him into the house.

I smell something delicious coming from the kitchen. There's tinkling coming from that way, so I guess Bailey is cooking dinner.

I stop on the threshold that leads to the living room. Jaxon steps past me.

"Take a seat. I'll see how much longer Bailey will be with dinner. You want something to drink?"

"No thanks," I tell him, and watch as he nods and walks away.

I step further into the room. It's been a while since I've been here. Not much has changed, except for a few things here and there. Nostalgia hits me. Anna and I used to come here at least once a week. Almost every night, we were either at home with family over, here at Jaxon's, at her mom's, at Mia's, or at Andrew's. We were constantly around our family and friends. Since Anna died, I've pulled away.

I round the couch and see a playpen with a sleeping Amari inside. I walk over and gaze down at the beautiful black-haired little girl. She's on her stomach with her little butt sticking up in the air. A pink blanket is lying on her from the waist down. Bailey and Jaxon are lucky. With everything Bailey went through and the prognosis from Bailey's old doctor, they shouldn't have been able to have a child. Jaxon claims it was a miracle sent down from someone above. When they told me they chose Anna as her middle name, it damn near brought me to tears. I've only held her once and that was for only a minute right after she was born. It was just too painful.

As I look down at Amari, I realize she very well could be a miracle. A miracle Anna made sure Jaxon and Bailey could have. It would be just like her to make sure the people she left behind ended up blissfully happy. I know she would be devastated that I wasn't. But there's no way for that to happen. She left and took that away with her.

Maybe it doesn't have to be that way, my mind whispers. I force the stupid thought away. It's ridiculous to even think it.

"You can hold her if you want," Bailey says, coming to stand beside me, a smile playing on her beautiful face.

Although the jagged scar that runs from her eye to her ear is pronounced, it only makes her look more stunning. She didn't let what happen to her define her. Instead it made her stronger. She's one of the strongest people I know and it's because she fought with everything she had to get where she is today. She's an amazing woman and Jaxon is very lucky to have her.

I look back down at Amari, and I'm suddenly hit with a fierce need to hold her in my arms, to cuddle her against my big chest, to breath in her sweet baby scent. But I can't do it yet. I need to talk to Bailey first.

When I face her again, Jaxon is behind her with his hands on her shoulders. I look at him and silently ask for help. I don't know if I can do this on my own.

He understands my silent plea and steers Bailey to one of the two couches.

"He can hold her later, Angel. There's something he wants to talk to you about first."

He pulls her down to sit beside him. I walk over and sit on her other side and face her.

She looks at me with a fearful but confused face. I glance down at her lap and see her twisting her hands. I grab one and look back at Jaxon to make sure this is okay. He nods, so I start.

"Bailey." My voice is hoarse, so I stop for a moment to clear my suddenly dry throat. I should have asked for some water when Jaxon offered.

I gather my courage and continue.

"I should have done this a long time ago. I've known how you felt, but it hurts too much to talk about Anna." Her hand jerks in mine when I say Anna's name, and a hurt so deep it's a wonder Jaxon and I don't both feel the pain from it crosses her face.

I squeeze her hand and push forward, needing to do this for both of us.

"I need you to know that I don't blame you for what happened. I've never blamed you. There is nothing you did that caused it. And there was nothing you could have done that would have prevented it. I want you to let the guilt go."

I stop when she throws her hand up to cover her mouth as a sob escapes her lips. Tears start pooling in her eyes and it breaks my heart. One of the worse things a man can witness is a woman falling apart. Especially a woman who's as special as Bailey. She should never feel anything but joy in her life.

Watching her break down because I made it so, makes a heavy weight settle in my stomach. I never should have let it go this long.

Jaxon wraps one arm around the top of her chest and pulls her back against him as she weeps. I sit helpless because there's not a damn thing I can do.

After several seconds, she drops her hand. She closes her eyes a second before she opens them again, water still glistening in their depths. Her lips tremble when she says tearfully, "I'm so sorry, Nick." When I move to say something, she stops me by squeezing my hand. "No, please, just listen. I know none of you blame me, but what happened to Anna wouldn't have happened had I not left and come here. She was taken because he wanted me. She was beaten and raped to punish me. I came here and led him straight to Anna's doorstep. No, I didn't do it on purpose, but it's still because of me that she's no longer here. It should have been me that went through what she did. It should have been me that died," she finishes on a sob.

"Bailey," Jaxon chokes out, tightening his arm around her chest.

Her words pierce my chest, and I can't take them anymore. I drop to my knees in front of her. I look at Jaxon and see torment and devastation in his eyes. If I know Jaxon, I know he's had this conversation with Bailey many times. I'm sure everyone who was close to Anna has. And I'm sure it tears him apart every time Bailey refuses to believe she had no part in Anna's death. I'm the loose end. It's up to me to make her believe.

I grip Bailey's hand and bring it to my unshaven cheek. Her eyes are clenched tightly shut, but when I touch her hand, she opens them. My throat closes at the anguish I see there.

"Listen to me very carefully, Bailey. Okay?" She pulls in a deep breath and nods. "You are in no way responsible for what happened. That's solely on that sick bastard's shoulders. You left him because you were trying to survive. He would have killed you otherwise. You didn't tell him to follow you. You didn't ask him to take Anna and do what he did. You bravely, but stupidly, went out and tried to save her yourself. You sacrificed yourself for her. It hurts knowing you would have knowingly taken her place and endured the torture she did. And you *were* tortured yourself. Maybe not as extensively as Anna, but it was no less important what happened to you. Do you think Anna blamed you in the end?" I wait for her answer. She shakes her head, tears still leaking down her cheeks. "No, she wouldn't have. Would you have blamed her if the situation was reversed?" Again, she shakes her head. "That's right. You wouldn't have. You've got to stop torturing yourself with this. There is nothing that you or anyone else could have done to stop him."

"I don't—" Bailey starts, but it's Jaxon's turn to step in.

"No, Angel. You listen to Nick's words and you believe them," he says in her ear. "This has got to stop, baby. *You did nothing wrong,*" he says vehemently. "It was only Steven. Please, Bailey. Stop doing this to yourself. It's killing me."

More pain flashes in her eyes with Jaxon's words. She sits quietly in his arms, her hand still on my cheek. Her sad eyes flicker back and forth between mine. After several seconds, she nods slowly. She pulls her hand from my cheek and launches herself into my arms. I look over her head at Jaxon. There's still pain on his face, but it's not as deep as before. He mouths "Thank you" and I jerk my chin up slightly in acknowledgement. I pray my words help and Bailey learns to let go.

I hold her in my arms until she's ready to pull back. When she does, she doesn't go far. She brings her mouth to my ear and whispers, "You need to let go too, Nick. You need to release yourself from her ghost and learn to be happy again. She would want that for you."

She finishes pulling back from me and looks up. I drop my eyes to hers and see compassion. I know she's trying to help. Just like I was doing for her. Maybe one day I'll be able to do what she says, but not yet.

Still, I give her what she needs to hear. "I'll try."

"Okay," she says, smiling slightly.

I lean down and kiss her on top of her head before Jaxon helps her up. He engulfs her in his arms. They murmur words to each other, then pull back for a brief kiss.

We all turn toward the playpen when we hear a shuffling sound. Amari lifts her tiny head and looks around.

"You." Bailey points to me. "Are staying for dinner and are holding Amari while I finish." She turns toward Jaxon. "And you can come help me."

"Yes ma'am," Jaxon says, saluting her. She laughs and rolls her eyes as she walks over to pick Amari up. She brings her over to me. The need to hold her is so strong that I barely hold back from snatching her from Bailey's arms.

I gaze down at her and fall head over heels. She's the most precious thing I've ever seen. Her curious eyes watch me. She has her dad's odd multicolored eyes and black hair, but has Bailey's small pert nose and rosy lips. I see some Anna in her as well. It clogs my throat knowing that a small part of Anna will go on. Amari is part of her aunt.

I take a seat and cradle Amari in my arms. Taking one hand, I run my finger down her small nose. She graces me with a big smile and starts wiggling her tiny legs. Something catches my attention, and I look down at Amari's legs. She's still wiggling, and I can't get a good view, so I lay her down on my legs. Her arms flail around as she tries to garner my attention, but my focus is on her right leg. With my heart in my throat, I lift that leg up and look at the back of her knee.

My breath freezes in my lungs when I see the red half heart birthmark. Anna had the same birthmark, except hers was on the back of her left knee. I let Amari's leg go when she starts whimpering. I gather her back in my arms and hug her to my chest. Her head bobs back and forth, so I put my hand on it to hold it steady.

Seeing that birthmark solidifies my belief that Anna sent Amari down here for Jaxon and Bailey and that maybe she sent a little part of herself as well. Tears prick the back of my eyes.

Amari and I sit on the couch until Jaxon comes back a few minutes later. He takes a seat beside me.

"Want me to take her?" he asks.

I don't answer him. Instead I ask my own question.

"Why didn't you tell me about her birthmark?"

He looks from me to Amari, his eyes going soft when they land on his daughter, before coming back to me.

"Because you already have a hard enough time. I didn't want to add more to it, and I know you knowing would have. You have enough reminding you of what you lost. I know a lot of people think it's crazy, and maybe it is, but I truly believe Anna sent down a miracle to help us all heal. That's what Amari has done, except for you. And you need it the most."

I don't say anything in return. There's nothing I can say. Up until a few weeks ago, Jaxon would have been right. Knowing Amari carries Anna's mark would have torn me up. Now though, it doesn't hurt as bad. Yes, there's still an ache in my chest, but it doesn't feel as deep as it would have been. Actually, knowing that Amari is here, and she carries part of Anna, brings on an unfamiliar emotion. Happiness. Something I haven't felt in a long time.

The same little voice in my head that I want to ignore, but can't, says it's because of Chris that it doesn't hurt as much. Chris makes things seem not so harsh. She doesn't take away the grief, just dampens it and makes me feel other things.

Bailey leans her head around the corner of the kitchen to let us know dinner will be ready in a few minutes. Jaxon gets up and takes Amari from me. I want to protest and demand he give her back, but I stop myself. I get up and we both make our way to the table. There's a small reclining bouncy chair sitting on the table, along with several serving dishes filled with delicious-looking food. Jaxon lays Amari in the seat and sits down in the chair closest to it. Bailey comes back out with a basket holding rolls. She takes her seat after putting them on the table.

"Bailey's birthday is next weekend," Jaxon says, scooping some carrots onto his plate. "I'm closing down the bar on Sunday to throw a party here at the house. I'd like all our friends to be there. Including you."

I nod. "I'll be there."

We load up our plates and make small talk, but nothing heavy is brought up again. I'm glad I came here tonight. A heaviness I didn't realize was there is lifted from my chest.

I watch Jaxon and Bailey interact with each other. They both coo over Amari and we all laugh when she makes funny faces or noises. I always thought I would have this one day. Anna and I were supposed to have our own family. Hell, we could have already started one by now. I used to picture us having nights like this, gathering around the table as a family. Those dreams are gone now. My stomach plummets, thinking about never having a family of my own.

My mind wanders to the possibility of still having a family, but with someone else. A little girl with red hair pops in my mind, almost knocking me out of my chair.

I must have made a noise because Jaxon and Bailey look at me strangely. I take a swallow of my water, trying to push the images away. That won't ever happen. My chance at a family died two years ago. It would be one thing moving on with another woman, but a totally different thing having a family with her. There's no way I would allow that to happen. That was mine and Anna's. The role of mother of my child was Anna's. No one, including Chris, could ever take that place.

fifteen

Chris

I'M STANDING AT THE island in Jaxon and Bailey's kitchen putting candles on Bailey's red velvet and vanilla crème birthday cake with trembling hands. I'm a nervous wreck. Nick arrived about five minutes ago. I haven't seen him yet, but I heard Andrew call his name. My eyes keep wandering to the glass door that leads to the back porch, but so far I haven't seen him.

He's been gone for a little over three weeks but it's been only two hours since I've thought about him. It's seems like all I do is think about him. I try to push him from my mind, but he keeps slipping back in. I know he got back a week ago, but I haven't seen him since the night I've dubbed the Beautiful Tragedy. Beautiful, because although I know he was trying to push me away with his words, it still made my body feel beautiful. And tragedy, well I'm sure you can guess. It would be a tragedy for any woman having the man they are with call out another woman's name.

Pain almost cripples me from the memory. It's stupid of me to even think about him, let alone secretly wish to see him again. What kind of person does that make me? The type that still has feelings for someone who broke my heart and left me in tatters. I hate myself for it. I should never want to see him, but I can't help the deep ache I have for just a glimpse.

I finally get the candles on the cake and pull out some matches from the junk drawer. Everybody is outside. It's sunny, but it's November so there's a chill in the air. I'm sure everyone will be moving inside soon.

After lighting the candles, I carefully pick up the cake dish and walk to the door. I tap my foot against the bottom to get someone's attention so they'll open it. It's hard, but I manage to keep my eyes forward and not look for Nick. The last thing I want to do is ruin Bailey's cake by tripping because my eyes couldn't stay focused in front of me.

Bailey's standing by the railing with a table next to her. Jaxon has his arm casually thrown over her shoulder, with Mac and Mia standing by them talking. There are a bunch of other people milling about on the deck and yard. Kids are running around screaming and the grill is going.

I walk toward the small group and a big grin creeps up on my face when Bailey sees me coming their way. When others start to notice me, I start singing "Happy Birthday" and they join me. By the time we're done singing, I've set the cake down on the table. Bailey has a beautiful smile on her face with tears in her eyes.

"Make a wish, Angel," Jaxon says, looking down lovingly at Bailey.

She smiles back and gets on her toes to kiss him softly. After she pulls back, she says, "There's nothing I could wish for that I don't already have."

"Why don't you try." Jaxon leans down and kisses the tip of her nose.

Although I love watching these two, a pang of jealousy hits me square in the chest. I am so happy Bailey has found her happily ever after. Lord knows she deserves it after everything she's gone through, but I wish I could have even half of what she and Jaxon share.

After Bailey blows out her candles, I walk around the table and pull her from Jaxon's arms to give her a hug. She's the sister I never had, and I love her just as if she were my sister.

I pull back and place both my hands on her cheeks. "Love you, Bailey. Happy Birthday."

"Love you, too, Chris. And thank you. For everything."

"You know I'd do anything for you." I kiss her cheek and let her go. As soon as I do, Jaxon's arm goes around her waist. He looks at me with a tender expression. He's thanked me multiple times in the past for helping Bailey. They don't realize that Bailey's helped me too. She was the best friend I needed when I was younger. She was there for me when I didn't get the attention a child should get from their parents. I didn't go to her house and it wasn't often she was allowed at mine, but I cherished beyond anything seeing her during school and the times she was allowed over.

People gather around us, wishing Bailey a happy birthday and kissing her cheek. I step back to give them room.

My eyes drift past Bailey and my breath catches. Nick is leaning against a big tree with a red Solo cup in his hand. I'm not worried it's alcohol. Jaxon made sure everyone knew there was to be no alcohol today because of the kids.

Ethan and Hunter, Jaxon's uncle, are talking to him, but he seems to be not paying attention to them. His eyes are on me and the expression on his face is unreadable, but it's fierce. He lifts his cup to his lips and takes a sip, his eyes never leaving mine. I want to look away, I don't want him to affect me so much, but I'm helpless. I want to know what his expression means. I want to know if he thought about me as much as I thought about him while he was gone. I didn't realize how much I missed him until just now, which is completely wrong because of how he treated me the last time we were together.

"He came by last week to talk to me," Bailey says quietly, breaking my stare at Nick and bringing it back to her.

"Yeah?" My voice sounds casual, but I'm anything but. My body is buzzing with my first sight of Nick in almost a month.

"Yeah. He wanted to talk to me about Anna."

My eyes go wide with her words. Even though I told Nick he needed to speak with Bailey, I figured it would be a while before he did. I think it's wonderful he came forward. Bailey needed that last bit of reassurance that Nick didn't blame her. Hopefully with that, she'll be able to let it go. I can't imagine the pain he went through, though. He never brings Anna up, and for him to openly do it is a big step. I also can't imagine it was easy for Bailey either.

"Oh, sweetie. How did it go?" I ask with understanding lacing my voice.

She tilts her head to the side, contemplating.

"I broke down into a slobbering mess, but I felt good afterward. I still feel guilt, I probably always will, but I'm learning to let some of it go."

Jaxon squeezes her waist and kisses the top of her head in comfort. I reach over and grab her hand.

"That's great. You don't need that on your shoulders."

We're interrupted when a small whimpering sound comes from the baby monitor on the table. Bailey leans up to kiss Jaxon, but I stop her before she leaves.

"You stay and eat some of your cake. I'll go get Amari."

She nods and says thank you. I take one last glance at Nick, whose attention is now on something Hunter is saying, turn, and make my way to the little bundle of joy currently starting to fuss.

When I walk up to the crib, Amari spots me immediately and graces me with a big beautiful smile and an excited kick.

"Hey, precious," I coo down at her. "Come see your aunt Chris."

When I pick her up she latches on to my hair with her tiny fists and a dribble of slobber falls from her mouth. I laugh at her and gently pull my hair from her tight grip.

"You poor baby. Your hair will grow out soon enough," I tell her in a baby voice and run my fingers over her short black hair.

I hold her against my chest and pat her bottom. Noticing she has a full diaper, I take her to the change table to take care of it. Once I'm finished, I decide to take a few minutes before bringing her outside to her mom and dad. I sit in the rocking chair in the corner and bring her back to my chest. She looks up at me with fascination, and I do the same.

This little girl has brought joy to so many people's lives. Bailey had told me previously that she couldn't have kids. When she told me she was pregnant, I swear I almost cried more than her. Jaxon and Bailey are the best parents I've known. There're no two people who deserved a miracle such as Amari more than them.

I've always known I wanted kids. Playing with my dolls and being their momma was a big thing for me when I was little. I would feed them, bath them, tuck them in bed, and read them stories. I never went through the phase of being scared to have babies because I heard having them would be painful. I always knew it would be worth it. I would love and cherish them and always be there when they needed me, no matter what.

I didn't want to be one of those parents who waited until they were in their thirties or forties. I wanted to have them young so I could be youthful with them and enjoy all the activities kids did. I didn't want to have to sit activities out because my body was too old to participate.

A wave of sadness hits me. I'm twenty-seven. I had hoped I would have already had at least one child by now. I kiss the tip of Amari's nose and laugh when she smacks my cheek with one of her little hands.

"She's a strong little bugger, isn't she?" a voice that send shivers down my spine says from the doorway.

Steeling myself, I look over and see Nick just inside Amari's bedroom door. He looks good in a pair of dark-wash jeans and a gray thermal. He has on a hat flipped backwards, and I can see that his dark brown hair is a bit longer than the last time I saw him. I've always loved a man in a hat. It looks like he's shaved recently, but not within the last few days.

My starving eyes are on his hard chest, currently covered by his bulging arms. I can't help but stare at him. When he clears his throat, I snap my eyes back to his to see a smirk on his lips. I look back at Amari as heat creeps up my face.

Why can't I hate him? Especially after what happened that night? I can't place all the blame on him. He warned me, and I stupidly ignored it. Why can't I let him go? What keeps drawing me back to him? These are questions I desperately want answers to, but know I may never have them.

"Uh... yeah, she is strong," I mutter, embarrassed he caught me staring at him again.

I hear a shuffling sound and a second later see his feet coming closer. My heart rate picks up. He's always had this effect on me when he's close. It's hard to catch my breath, especially when the subtle hint of his cologne hits me. I actually came across his cologne the other day while out with Bailey shopping. Bailey doesn't know I secretly bought a bottle so I could spray a mist on my pillow when I'm feeling lonely. It's so pathetic, and I would die if he ever found out.

He stops when he's beside the rocking chair. I hold myself still, not sure what he's going to do next. I'm surprised when he drops to his knees beside us.

I look up and find him looking at me. He has a slight frown on his face, like he's not sure why he's down on his knees either. His eyes drop to my lips, and I unconsciously lick them. Something flares in the depths of his eyes, causing my breath to hitch. Butterflies start to flutter around in my stomach and the muscles tighten. He has me utterly captured with his intense blue gaze and there's not a damn thing I can do about it.

Fortunately, Amari comes to the rescue, grabbing a chunk of my hair and giving an almighty tug. She pulls so hard my head tips sideways from the force.

"Whoa!" I bring my head down further to try and ease some of the pull on my hair. Amari squeals in delight, and I grab her hand to try and loosen the grip.

I hear a chuckle and tip my head awkwardly to glare at Nick. "You could help, you know."

"Guess I could, but I'm enjoying this too much. She's got you good, doesn't she?" the smart-ass says.

"Just you wait until you're holding her. I'm stealing your hat so she can get a hold of you."

He chuckles, and although a second later it dies down, the smile stays in place. It's so weird seeing his eyes smiling. I want to bring my head back up so I can see it properly, but Amari's not letting me.

I feel Nick's big warm hands on mine, bringing goose bumps to my arms. A tingle forms in my belly and slowly makes its way to my legs and chest.

I drop my hand as Nick untangles Amari's fingers. My eyes land on his thick thighs. Thighs that were pounding against the back of mine just a few weeks ago. I wiggle in my seat and clench my eyes closed as a mental image of him behind me, touching me, forms in my head. Now's not the time to be thinking things like that.

A minute later, my hair is free. When I bring my head up, Nick's lips are still tipped up at the corners. I could look at him all day and never get tired. There's something about him that's different. He looks less stressed. The sadness still lurks in his eyes, but it's not quite as pronounced. I can't help the flare of hope I feel. Even so, I'm not sure I trust it. There have been other times Nick has acted nice, even somewhat sweet, and then the next minute he goes off like a loose cannon.

My eyes widen in shock when he tucks a piece of hair behind my ear. His fingers are warm against my skin. I want to savor the feeling and never let it go.

I close my eyes, and without meaning to, lean my head closer to his hand. I've never felt anything like what I get from this simple touch, and I know deep down in my gut I won't ever feel it again with anyone else. Nick may not have been made for me, but I have no doubt my mind, heart, body, and soul were made for him.

Amari kicks her legs, reminding me that it's not just the two of us in the room. There's a precious little girl between us. I open my eyes to find Nick watching me with an expression I've only ever dreamed of seeing. There's longing in his gaze and it makes my heart soar.

"It's good to see you again, Sugar," he says, his deep voice soft. Looking at him, I see sincerity.

I have no idea what's going on with Nick, why he's being so nice, but it's dangerous. Dangerous for my heart and dangerous for my mind. I would give almost anything for things to always be like this between us, but I'm terrified it's only temporary.

Enjoying the reprieve while it lasts, I smile shyly up at him. "It's good seeing you too, Nick. How have you been?"

He moves his finger from my ear and settles his hand against my neck. He swipes his finger over my cheek. Shivers start at the top of my neck and make their way down my spine.

His eyes roam all over my face, and I wonder what he sees, what he's thinking.

"I'm better now," he replies huskily, shocking me even more. His implication that he missed me is more than I ever hoped. I want to respond to him, to say I've missed him too, but I don't, not willing to break the enchantment. And if I'm honest, I'm worried my admission will make my feelings for him stronger. As though, if I admit it out loud, they will become more real. I'm still hurting over what he did the last time we were together. I can't, or rather shouldn't, just overlook that.

His head inches closer to mine. I pull in a deep breath and take in his intoxicating scent. It's a heady smell that leaves me feeling dizzy. His breath washes over my lips, and I lick them in anticipation. I want the taste of his lips on mine more than anything, even when it could be a massive mistake. He didn't kiss me that night and it was one of the things I regret. But then again, what if once I taste him, it'll be the only taste I'll ever want again?

Still in the rocking chair with Amari in my lap, I feel a slight tug on my neck as he brings my lips closer to his. His other hand is on the arm of the chair and he's leaning over it. We both keep our eyes open, watching each other. He has black specks in his eyes and they capture my attention. I swear I could get lost in his blue eyes.

I hold my breath when our lips come within an inch of touching. My heart's pounding so hard in my chest that I worry he'll hear the loud rhythm. Our lips barely graze each other, just a whisper...

"Uncle Nick, why are you kissing Chris?" comes an innocent little voice from behind Nick.

I pull my head back quickly and my eyes immediately land on Amari. Shame slams into me for being so stuck in the moment that I forgot I was holding her. A quick glance to my left shows Nick has his head bent, muttering cuss words under his breath.

"Those are bad words, Uncle Nick. You shouldn't say them," says the voice again, reminding us both of the other presence in the room.

He brings his head up to look at me, and I barely suppress the need to laugh at his expression. He looks pained, but not the normal grief kind of pain. It's more like a pain you get when you want something really bad but you can't have it. Like a little kid wanting an ice cream, but his parents refusing because it'll spoil dinner. I try, I really do, but the longer I look at the sad puppy-dog look, I just can't hold it in. I sputter out a laugh. Luckily, the look in his eyes disappears and is a replaced by a chuckle.

We both look over and see Little Maddie, Jaxon and Mia's cousin, standing a couple feet behind Nick. Her brows are pulled down into a frown, as if she's trying to figure out what's going on. I'd like to know the answer to that myself.

Nick reaches out and snags her around the waist to pull her forward. She giggles and squirms, but she's no match for Nick. He tips her sideways and plants his face in her stomach, making chomping sounds, like he's eating her. She squeals in delight and wiggles around. I laugh at the two of them. I'm utterly transfixed by the sight. I've never seen Nick act so free before. It's something everyone should witness.

"And what are you doing in here, you little munchkin?" he asks her once he sets her on her feet.

"Uncle Jaxon told me to come see what was taking Bailey so long." She narrows her brown eyes at Nick accusingly. "Why were you kissing Chris?" she asks again.

I turn my face away to avoid the question. After all, she wasn't asking me. I'll leave Nick to come up with an answer, as I have no clue what to say.

"If you must know, busybody, I wasn't kissing Chris. She had something in her eye and I was looking at it."

I snort at his ridiculous excuse and he shoots me a playful grin over his shoulder. Even a five-year-old will know that's a load of crock. And a second later, I'm proved right.

Maddie sticks out her hip and plants a tiny fist on it in true irritated-girl fashion. I have to hold in my laugh.

"I'm five, Uncle Nick, not dumb. You weren't even looking at her eye; you were looking at her lips." She finishes with an eye roll.

"Oh yeah? Well how was I looking at her lips if I was kissing them?" Nick asks, arching a brow. Is he seriously challenging a five-year-old? Doesn't he know that all kids at that age know everything and can find their way around anything?

"Don't know. Maybe you did it like this." Maddie, bless her little heart, then proceeds to stick out her lips like she's kissing someone and focuses her eyes down to the tip of her nose, as if she's looking at the person's lips she's kissing. She looks so cute and ridiculous, there's no way I can hold it in. I bend over and stuff my face in Amari's chest and burst out laughing. Amari screeches and knocks my head a few times with her fist. I hear Nick laughing as well.

Desperate to see what his laugh looks like, I pull my face away and see him with his head thrown back.

Wow!

I've never seen anything more beautiful than watching Nick full belly laugh. It's captivating. He's sitting back on his legs with his hands on his thighs. The deep rumble from his chest and the crinkles I see beside his eyes have my breath hitching. My lady bits may have tingled a bit too. I shift in my chair, not liking the thought of getting turned on while holding a baby. Now is *definitely not* the time for that.

When Nick brings his head back down, he's still chuckling. Getting up from his kneeling position, he plucks Maddie from the floor and throws her over his shoulder. With her squirming around, he turns to me and holds out his hand. I don't grab it right away. I'm scared to. Seeing this side of Nick is a dream come true. I'm worried something will shatter the spell and he'll go back to the way he was before. Nothing this good lasts long, and I'm worried how much it'll break me when he does go back to the angry dark person he's been for so long. Because it's bound to happen.

I look from his hand to his eyes. He's watching me expectantly, and I don't know what to do. Do I take his proffered hand and take the chance of him hurting me again? Or do I ignore it and save myself the inevitable heartache? It's such a simple thing, me taking his hand, but it feels significant. Like it'll be life changing if I do.

"It's okay, Chris," he says gently. I look up at him and see understanding. He knows what I'm thinking and gets my reluctance.

Coming to a decision, I tentatively reach out with one hand while holding Amari with the other, and place it in his large callused one. It's feels warm and oddly comforting. There's no way I can not take the chance. I'd regret it later and wonder for the rest of my life.

Once I'm standing, he lets go, and I feel the loss. I want to snatch it back and superglue our hands together so he won't ever let go.

"Uncle Nick, put me down!" Maddie hollers and starts smacking his back. "You're gonna drop me!"

"I'm not gonna drop you, squirt," he says, lightly swatting her butt. "Now behave or you won't get the surprise I got for you and your brother and sister."

"For real?" she yells excitedly, bouncing around on his shoulder even more. "You got us something? What is it?"

I follow them with a huge smile on my face and a giggling Amari. I could get used to seeing this.

"Yeah, I got you something. But you're not going to get it if you keep squirming around up there."

We both laugh again when she drops her arms and sags against his back.

"Okay, I won't move anymore," she promises.

Nick opens the back door and as soon as we walk outside,

Maddie negates her words by making her body stiff as she lifts her head and yells to everyone in listening distance, "Uncle Nick was kissing Chris! He says he wasn't, but I know he was! I saw it!"

Everything goes quiet; even the birds have stopped chirping. My face turns ten shades of red and Amari starts wiggling in my arms because my hold on her tightens. I drop my eyes to her and loosen my grip, not able to look at anyone. Embarrassment doesn't even cover what I'm feeling. I feel tension in the air, and I look over at Nick, who still has Maddie over his shoulder. I watch his stiff form. I can't see his face, and I'm worried about his reaction to Maddie's outburst.

I risk a glance at Bailey and Jaxon, who *can* see his face. Bailey looks shocked, while Jaxon, who currently has Sarah in his lap, has his lips tipped up into a half smirk. A ball of relief starts to form in my stomach. Maybe it won't be as bad as I feared.

"Alright, that's it," Nick says, twisting to the side a bit so I can finally see his face, which doesn't look upset. He pulls her from his shoulder and holds her up underneath the arms so they are face-to-face. "No surprise for you, you little snitch."

He tries to look serious, but fails when his lips quirk up at the corners.

"But Uncle Nick, you didn't say I couldn't tell." She sticks out her bottom lip in a pout, looking sad and pathetic.

I've been mostly quiet since Nick came into Amari's room, shocked speechless by his strange behavior. I decide now is the time to step in and help save Maddie from her crazy uncle.

With everyone still watching us, I tuck Amari closer to my chest and sidle up next to Nick and Amari. They both turn to me. My eyes meet Nick's with mirth.

"She's right, you know, you said she had to be still, not that she couldn't open her mouth."

Out the corner of my eye, I see Maddie's head bobbing up and down dramatically. Nick's eyes turn thoughtful as he thinks about his response.

"Hmm… I guess you're right," he says, and shifts his eyes back to the little girl dangling from his hands. Her eyes go wide with excitement. "Go get your brother and sister and see what's on that picnic table over there." He tips his chin up at the picnic table across the yard.

She reaches out for his ears, brings his head closer, and gives his cheek a loud kiss. He chuckles and when he sets her down, she scampers off for first Sarah in Jaxon's lap, and then down the stairs to find her brother.

"Hey!" Tricia, their mother, calls from the other side of the porch. "Don't you dare forget to thank your Uncle Nick!"

Both girls throw over their shoulders a "thank you" without stopping their mad dash to reach their destination.

Nick shakes his head with a smile as he watches them run off. Jaxon and Bailey walk over. Jaxon takes Amari from me with a meaningful look, while Bailey comes to stand beside me with questioning eyes. I can't help the small smile that pops up on my face.

Nick pulls out an envelope and hands it to Bailey. "Happy Birthday."

She looks at him quizzically and then runs her nail along the edge to open it. I gave her my gift earlier. I went to Jaxon a couple weeks ago asking him for all their family photos. I made copies of the ones I wanted and made a family collage with them. Bailey was ecstatic and tearful when she opened it. It wasn't much but I knew it would mean a lot to her. She finally has the family she's deserved for so long.

Bailey pulls out what looks like two tickets. After reading what's in her hands, she squeals and launches herself into Nick's arms. He laughs as he hugs her back.

"Look, honey!" she says, pulling away from Nick and shoving the tickets in Jaxon's face. "We're going on a seven-day cruise! Can you believe it?"

"I'd see better if they weren't in my face." Jaxon removes the tickets from his face and smiles down indulgently at his excited wife.

"Oh my God! This is amazing! I've always wanted to go on a cruise," she gushes on, making us laugh at her craziness.

"Thanks, Nick," Jaxon says, slapping his friend on the back.

"You bet. The tickets are for both of you, but if y'all decide to take Amari as well, she doesn't need a ticket."

"She'll be with us," Jaxon says, something we all already know. No way would he or Bailey leave Amari for that long.

Bailey leans in to whisper in my ear, "We heard what happened in Amari's room." I look at her questionably, wondering how she could have possibly heard. "The baby monitor," she says with a shrug. "Sounds like Nick may be coming around."

She smiles, and I try to smile back at her, but I know I only manage a half-assed one. I don't say anything back to her, too scared to get my hopes up.

"I'm gonna go grab a piece of that yummy cake. Anyone want a piece?" I ask the others.

I've been dying to dig into the thing since I picked it up for Jaxon in town. It's both my and Bailey's favorite. When we were living together in college, each week we would take turns buying a red velvet cake with vanilla crème frosting. Money was tight, but we always found enough to buy our cake. That was our treat to ourselves each week.

"I'll come with you." Nick says, surprising me once again.

This new and improved Nick is getting to me. I don't know if I should jump for joy or feel his forehead for a fever. As much as I enjoy this change and hope that it's here to stay, the flip-flop back and forth grates on my nerves. He has no right to treat me like a piece of shit, then come back after being gone and act like nothing ever happened. I'm being pulled in different directions. I want to love him, but he makes me despise him sometimes, then he'll be nice, and I'll like him again, only to have the rug pulled out from under me. And each time that happens, the impact of the fall hurts worse and worse.

I love seeing him again, but it's also painful because I'm waiting for the shoe to drop. Not knowing when that will happen kills me. I'm at the end of my rope. One of these days it'll happen, and I'll have enough and lose it. I feel the threads unraveling. The possible results terrify me.

I lead the way to the table and grab a plate. After cutting a slice, I silently offer it to Nick. I feel his eyes on me the entire time. I want to demand he tell me why he's acting this way.

I slice my own piece and lean against the railing. I don't look at him as I eat, but I know his eyes are still on me. I feel the heat of them boring into my skin.

"What's wrong?" Nick asks a few minutes later.

Setting my empty plate and fork on the table, I decide to be honest. I turn to face him.

"You're what's wrong. Why are you being so nice to me?" It comes out accusingly, but that's exactly what it is.

He's silent as looks down at his half-eaten cake for several seconds, before putting it down on the table beside my empty plate. He shifts closer to me. I want to step back, but I hold my ground.

As he talks, his eyes stay focused on mine.

"I'm sorry about what happened," he says quietly. "I was a complete dick for what I did; I regretted it the second it left my mouth. And it was a lie. You may not believe that, but Anna was the last thing on my mind that night. It was only you, and I didn't like it. It scared the shit out of me. And I'm sorry for every time I've been an asshole to you. You don't deserve that. I know you've only been trying to help, just like everyone else." I hold my breath as he stops and looks off into space for a moment, before looking back at me and continuing. "The last thing I want to do is hurt you, Chris, but I'll never be the man you need. I can only ever give you the physical side of me, and even that hurts. Anna may not be here physically, and I know it's irrational, but she's still in here." He taps his chest. "And it feels like a betrayal of her." My heart thumps heavily in my chest. I know this is painful for him, and I want to reach out and put my hand over his. I lose his eyes again when he glances down. When he brings them back up, the pain is back. I want to tell him to stop, but I hold my tongue, needing to hear what he has to say.

"I can never give you anything emotional and you deserve so

much more than that. That part of me no longer exists. It's dead and gone. I've tried pushing you away by being a bastard and hurting you. I called Anna's name out that night because I knew it would hurt you. I had hoped it would push you away enough that you would leave me be, but it's all I've thought about. I hate remembering the look on your face and knowing I put it there. My body is desperate for yours, but my heart and soul will always belong to someone else. You should never settle for something like that."

He finishes, and all I can do is stare at him. My lips feel like they're sealed shut. I feel a lump in my throat, and I try to swallow it down, but it stays in place. I have no idea what to do with his words or what to say back to him. For him to admit he was thinking about me rather than Anna that night stuns me, and I want to believe it so much.

The world around us fades. It's just the two of us. I don't know if others can hear our conversation, but it doesn't matter. I'm so consumed by Nick that the earth could open up and swallow everything and I wouldn't even notice or give a damn.

Taking a deep breath, I say my piece.

"You don't have the right to tell me what I should settle for. That decision is mine. If I want to go out and sleep with an entire football team worth of guys, that's my right." His eyes darken at that. "If I want to sleep with you, that's my decision to make as well." Now his eyes flare with desire and my thighs clench in reaction. I shift closer to him. "I know you can't give me the hearts and roses, Nick. I know that part of you was reserved for someone else. It may be something I would like to have, but it's not something I expect or need from you. I know your pain consumes you. I know you wish every day that you could have your Anna back. I can't imagine what the pain of losing someone like that does to a person, but I'm sure it's damn near debilitating. I'm not trying to replace her." I put my hand where I wanted it earlier; right on top of his heart. "I'd just like a small portion of you, even if it is only physical and temporary."

The last part is a lie. There's nothing I want more than to be his everything. To be what he needs and for him to give me everything in return. I don't say this because I don't want to scare him. Being in Nick's life, even just a small part of it, I'll take. The cruel Nick from before crushes me, but this Nick, the one that's looking at me with want in his eyes, is the Nick I need so desperately. I know I'll never measure up to Anna, but maybe, even if it does just start out sexually, it could build into something more.

sixteen

Nick

I'M STANDING IN FRONT of Chris's door, and I have no idea what the hell I'm doing. I shouldn't be here. I should stay far, far away from her. But when choosing between staying and seeing her again and walking away, the hounds of hell couldn't keep me from being here. It's stupid and reckless. I know I'll only end up hurting her again, but I can't force myself to leave. The need to see her is too alluring.

I was a fool to think while I was away I had built my walls strong enough to withstand the pull she has over me. The only thing that kept me from going to her after talking to Bailey was knowing I'd see her that following week. As soon as I stepped foot into Jaxon's backyard, my eyes scanned the area for her. And when I didn't find her, a huge wave of disappointment filled my stomach. I knew she was there. She would never miss Bailey's birthday if she could help it, but I wanted to see her right then. It had been four long weeks and I was growing impatient. Andrew called out my name, while Hunter and

Ethan walked over to greet me. They were talking, but I wasn't paying them any mind.

When she walked out carrying Bailey's cake, I swear I was sucker punched in the gut. She looked so beautiful in her tight leggings, sweater with one shoulder exposed, and her wavy red hair spilling down her back. I barely resisted the urge to rush over and snatch her to me. I didn't realize I missed her so much until then. I tried push the need away, but I was weak when it came to her.

When she went inside, I couldn't hold back anymore. I followed her and found her in Amari's room. I stood for several seconds, just watching her with Amari. They both looked so cute sitting in the rocking chair. A pang of longing pinched my stomach. I pushed it aside, too scared to even analyze it.

When we spoke on Jaxon's deck and she told me it was up to her whether we had a purely sexual relationship, I wanted to tell her she was wrong. I know she wants something more, every girl wants something more, even if they won't admit it. Eventually she'll get to a point where she can't handle it anymore. She'll get too attached, if she's not already, and I won't have any choice but to end it. I should have told her she was wrong, but I didn't. I was too selfish because I wanted her too. I may not want something more, but fuck if I don't crave her body.

The more I think about Chris, the harder the guilt eats at me. But the need is stronger than the guilt. That's why I'm standing here. The need to just be near her overrides my guilt at needing it. For once, I want something more than I want to rid myself of self-hatred for what happened to Anna. Anna is on the back burner, while Chris takes center stage. And that brings on more shame and pain, but I push that away too.

Taking in a lungful of air and letting it out slowly, I knock on Chris's door with both anticipation and dread. I drop my hand to my side and curl them both into fists.

It takes several moments for her to answer, and I worry she won't. I spotted her car, so I know she's here. Unless she walked somewhere, which is a big possibility. Frustration slowly edges in the longer I stand here. I'm just about to turn and walk away when I hear a clicking noise on the other side of the door.

My body tightens with eagerness as the door cracks open slowly. Chris's head peeks around the corner of the door first and then her entire body.

My limbs lock up and my lungs seize at the sight of her. My cock, which was already twitching in my jeans, turns solid. There she is, standing in front of me with messy wet hair piled on top of her head, a yellow tank top, and lounge pants. I salivate with the need to lick away the drops of water resting on her collarbone. She looks flushed and damp.

"Nick? What are you doing here?" she says on a squeak, clutching the door with one hand, while the other lies right below her breasts. Breasts that at closer inspection show little hard tips pushing against her shirt.

Fuck! She's not wearing a bra!

She gasps, and I yank my eyes away from the tempting sight and back to her face. She crosses her arms over her chest and her eyes are now wide, watching me with a mixture of shock and desire.

"Shit," I mutter. "I said that out loud, didn't I?"

Heat fills her cheeks when she says breathlessly, "Yes."

I'm such an ass.

"Sorry," I mumble. I open my mouth again, hoping nothing else stupid falls out. "I came by to see if you wanted to have dinner." My voice is huskier than I meant it to be, but fuck, she can't expect anything less with the way she's looking at the moment.

"Oh, uh... sure," she says. The red in her cheeks grows deeper when she glances down at her clothes. "I just got out of the shower. There was an accident today at school. Let me go put some clothes on."

I nod, only just restraining myself from getting in her space and pulling her body to mine. My jaw clenches, and I dig my fingernails in my palms.

Fuck, but I want to feel her, touch her, and taste her. I want to have her run her hands down my stomach. I want to wrap my hands in her hair and take her mouth in a punishing kiss. I want to lie face-to-face and rut between her legs. I want to feel her pussy strangling my cock.

Fuck!

"Good idea," I barely get out through my suddenly dry throat.

Instead of walking away, she tilts her head to the side and asks, "You okay?"

Am I okay? I want to laugh. Fuck no, I'm not okay. It's taking every bit of control I have to not storm to her, back her against a wall, and fuck her with both my mouth and dick. She stands there so innocent looking while I'm stuck here watching her in her cute little tank, sleep pants, and mound of hair on top of her head, raging a war with myself.

I take a step toward her. Then another and another, until I'm only a couple inches from her. Her eyes go wider with every step I take, and her chest pumps rapidly with the short breaths she's taking. My own breathing isn't much better, and when I smell her sweet sugary smell, it only makes my need worse. I grab a lock of hair that's fallen from her sexy updo and rub it between my fingers.

"No, Sugar, I'm not okay. It's really hard standing here with your nipples peeking out at me and that cute little glimpse of your stomach. I came here to ask you to dinner, but what I really want right now is to shove you against this wall, wrap your legs around my waist, and drive my cock inside you until we both can't stand." I dip my head and rest my lips against her cheek by her ear. "Now, I want you to turn around and go get dressed before I do the asshole thing and do exactly what I just said."

I pull back from her and see her flushed face. It satisfies me, seeing that look and knowing I put it there.

"Okay," she says breathlessly.

"Okay," I whisper back, and tuck an errant hair behind her ear.

She stays there for a few seconds before she starts walking backward, neither of us dropping our eyes from the other. She makes it to the mouth of her hallway and then turns and walks away. I watch the jiggle of her ass in her tight yoga pants. My cock gives a jerk in my jeans. I remember seeing that ass the night I took her. I want to see it again. I want to grab handfuls of it while I pound into her. And watch it turn red from the slap of my palm.

I take a deep breath and run my fingers through my hair. Glancing around Chris's apartment, I see it hasn't really changed since Bailey lived here. There's not much to it, just a tiny kitchen, a small living room, and the hallway that leads to a linen closet, a bathroom, and the bedroom. All can be seen from where I'm standing. But I guess if you're by yourself, it would be enough. I can't imagine being closed up in such a small space.

Chris walks out a few minutes later in black skinny jeans that mold to her ass and legs, a light blue shirt, and a pair of low black heels. Her hair is still damp and pulled into a loose bun. Her makeup is minimal. I like that she didn't dress up real classy in a dress and high heels.

She grabs her purse and walks to me. Instead of leading her to the door, I put a hand on her waist to halt her.

"Before we leave, there's something I want," I tell her.

"What's that?" she asks.

"This."

I dip my head and put my lips to hers. I haven't kissed her yet and it's something I've thought about since that night in my room. My lips barely skimmed hers at Jaxon's and it's only amped up my need to taste her.

I run my tongue along the seam of her lips and she opens immediately. I slip inside and meet her tongue with mine. Her taste hits me like a ton of bricks. Everything about her tastes like sugar and vanilla. It's quickly becoming my favorite thing. I even bought some sugar cookies from a deli other day because they reminded me of her. It's fucking lame, but I ate every single one in one sitting and thought about her.

I don't pull her to me, instead just keeping one hand on her waist. If I feel her against me right now, there's no way I'll be able to hold myself back. We would never make it to dinner.

Her hands are on my chest, her tiny fists gathering the material there. Our kiss isn't rushed. It's soft, languid, and slow.

I know I shouldn't allow this. The kind of kiss we're sharing is for people who care for each other. And while I care enough for Chris to not want to hurt her, what we're starting doesn't deserve this type of kiss.

I pull away from her before I let it get too far. I need to make sure I keep things platonic. Giving her the wrong idea is the last thing I want to do.

She looks dazed and breathless when I place my hand on her back and lead her to the door.

"Come on," I say huskily. "We're going to that new Mexican place in the next town over."

It takes about thirty minutes to get to the restaurant. Our ride into town is made mostly with small talk about unimportant stuff. We're seated, and the waitress takes our order.

"You said there was an accident at school. Is everything okay?" I ask, curious about what she does at work.

She puts her glass back down and places her hands in her lap.

"Yeah. One of the troubled kids started a food fight during lunch. I was one of the ones who waded in to stop it. Let's just say, I didn't come out the way I went in." She wrinkles her nose, causing a laugh to escape me.

"Do you have a lot of trouble with him?"

"Yeah, but I think something may be going on at home. He used to be a good kid, never caused problems, made good grades, but this year he's changed. I've tried talking to him, but he won't say anything. Just sits there with his head down. I've called his mom a couple times but she never answers. If I can't get in touch with her soon, I'm going to make a trip to his house."

Worry slithers through me with the thought of her going into an uncertain situation like that. I don't like it.

"Are you sure that's smart? Going to someone's house you don't know without any knowledge of the situation?"

She shrugs, like it's not a big deal. I grit my teeth. She has no idea what she could be walking into.

"I can't *not* do anything. There's obviously something going on. He needs help but is too scared to say something, or thinks no one can help. I refuse to sit back and watch him fall, especially because I know the type of kid he was before. That's what I'm there for; to make sure they become the best they can be. I won't be like the guidance counselors in my old school. It took years for someone to notice shit was going on at home and decide to step in and help. He reminds me of me at that age and I have to do something."

I get what she's saying, but that doesn't mean she should put herself in potential danger.

I lean forward in my seat.

"I don't want you going by yourself." I hold my hand up when she tries to speak. "Let me know when you go, and I'll come with you."

She shakes her head like she's going to disagree, but I don't give her the chance. "I'm asking you to do this for me, Sugar. To give me peace of mind."

She considers her answer for several seconds, biting her lip, before she nods. "Okay."

I lean back in my chair, feeling much better. I've seen my fair share of women getting hurt. No way will I let her take a chance with her safety. I'm sure it'll be okay, but just in case... I want to be there if it gets out of hand.

"Thank you."

The waiter brings our food a few minutes later and we both dig in. Talk is limited with us eating, but we still manage light conversation. I tell her about the repairs I've done to the house and she tells me the conversation she had with her mom the other day. Apparently, her mom is trying really hard to make up for all the years she was a shitty mother. She and Jase are talking now, but they've got a long way to go.

"Did you ever find out if those bones your crew found were

human or animal?" Chris asks, setting her fork down and wiping her mouth with her napkin.

I nod. "We did. Unfortunately, they were human. They belonged to a cop who had put away a gang member. The guy's brother killed him in retaliation. It happened ten years ago."

"Oh wow! That's awful. Did they find the guy who did it?"

"No, he was killed a couple years ago. It was gang related."

"Good riddance to him," she mutters, almost making me laugh, surprised she can be so bloodthirsty.

I grab my water and take a swallow to hide my smile. It's not a laughing matter, but the disgust in her eyes for someone she's never met is so different from her normal hesitant sweet self.

Replacing my glass on the table, I ask, "Are you ready?"

Her eyes widen with excitement and nerves as her hands curl into balls on the table. My own body tenses, ready and fucking willing to get back to her place and finally take her the way I should have taken her the first time.

"Yes," she says, her voice unsteady.

I get up, grab her hand, and go pay our bill. We don't say anything on the way to the truck, but the tension is thick in the air. We both know what's going to happen once I get her home. My heart picks up speed and all the blood in my body rushes south, making sitting down very uncomfortable.

The truck is quiet as we drive the dark roads back to Jaded Hollow. I have to force my foot to not slam down on the gas pedal. I'm impatient to get her home and have her underneath me, above me, in front of me. There're so many things I want to do to her that I didn't do the other night. Now that I've given in to this need, my body demands I follow through.

My palms itch to peel down her tight jeans and strip off her shirt. My tongue aches to slide across her delicious skin and taste her dripping cunt. My cock throbs with the need to plunge inside her willing body. I grip the steering wheel to keep for reaching for her, which would be suicide since I need both my hands to drive.

I pull up behind Jaxon's Pub and throw my truck in park. I almost rip the handle off the door in my rush to get it open. I round the hood. Chris has her door open when by the time I make it to her. I don't give her the chance to step down to the ground. Her butt is still in the truck, so I walk between her legs. She wraps them around my waist, and I lift her and slam the door shut. She grips two handfuls of hair when I slant my mouth over hers.

I walk blindly toward the stairs. Both our breaths are coming ragged when I make it to the outside door. Keeping one hand on her ass, I open it with the other one. Chris trails her lips down my neck, taking little bites along the way, as I take us up the stairs. I can't keep the deep groan from leaving my lips.

"Keys," I grunt at her.

She either doesn't hear me or she's too into what she's doing to care. I don't want her to stop, but I need to get her inside.

I pull my head back, so her lips leave my neck.

"Keys, Sugar. Now."

She looks dazed for a moment before she realizes what I said.

"Purse," she rasps out and pulls the strap from her arm so she can dig inside for the keys.

It feels like she takes forever before she dangles them in front of my face. I snatch them from her hand and unlock her door. I kick the door closed behind us and head straight for her room. I hear a thump and know she dropped her purse.

When my knees bump the bed, I drop her onto it. She gives a small squeal and gets up on her elbows.

"Get undressed," I tell her as I strip my own shirt over my head.

She hesitates, and a worried look crosses her face. I know immediately what she's thinking. I grit my teeth, knowing it's me and my stupid behavior the last time we were in this situation that put that look there. It's me that has made her doubt herself.

I bent, place my hands on either side of her head, and look deep into her eyes. "I'm sorry," I tell her and place a soft kiss against her lips. "I'm sorry," I tell her again and kiss down her neck. I pull back and look at her again. "I'm so damn sorry, Chris. I know I'm a bastard for what I did. And for what I'm doing now, knowing I can't give you what you deserve, but I swear you were the only one on my mind that night. And you're the only one I'm thinking about now."

I push away the guilt I feel at that.

She watches me for a few seconds before she nods. I nearly groan with the relief.

I kiss her one more time before I stand back up and watch as she crosses her arms over her chest, grips the edge of her shirt, and pulls it over head. My eyes go to the white lacy bra she's wearing. It's not what I expected. The cups are almost see-through and they only barely cover her nipples. My eyes fly to her to see she's watching me with uncertainty.

"Did you wear that for me?" I ask her hoarsely, praying like fuck she says yes.

She nods and says timidly, "Yes."

Son of a bitch!

This woman is going to kill me. Knowing she wore something as sexy as this while we ate does something to me. And knowing she wore it specifically for me damn near has me shredding both our jeans and plundering her pussy.

"Pants," I growl.

I go for my belt and yank it from the loops. Keeping my eyes locked on hers as she pulls her jeans down her legs, I let mine drop to the floor. She leaves her panties on. If you could even call them that. They are white like her bra and covered in lace. And just like the bra, I can see through them. A dark shadow that I know is the thin layer of hair above her pussy makes my mouth water.

"You're so fucking beautiful," I tell her and watch as a stunning blush forms over her cheeks.

My dick bounces as I stalk toward her. She licks her lips when her eyes drop down between my legs. My cock jumps in response, like she just touched it with her lips. We'll get to that later. There's something else I want more.

I grab her legs and pull until her ass is at the end of the bed. Her arms stay above her head.

"Keep your legs bent," I tell her huskily.

My eyes are intense as I bend over her with my arms on either side of her head. She looks absolutely beautiful below me with her green eyes watching me and her thick luscious hair fanned out around her. Her pale skin glows in the low light of the room. I don't think I've ever seen anything so breathtaking before.

The tip of my dick brushes against her lace-covered pussy, and we both groan. I take a nip at her lips and then soothe my tongue over them. She meets me with hers and we tangle them together. Again, this kiss is soft and sweet, so I don't let it last long.

Chris rakes her nails down my back. I hiss and arch, fucking loving the bite of her nails.

"I want to touch you, Nick," she whispers.

I fight back the urge to let her, but I know if I do, it'll be over before it even begins. And there's no way I'm coming outside her body.

"Later, baby. There's something else I need to do first."

Leaving her delicious lips behind, I trail mine down her neck and across her collar bone. Using one hand, I unclasp her bra and watch as her generous tits spill free. I plump one up and take a stiff nipple in my mouth, twirling the hard numb with my tongue and giving it a little bite.

She moans, and I feel the vibration in her chest, causing my need to ramp up. I switch to the other tit and pay it the same attention. Once they are rock-hard peaks, I kiss my way down the center of her chest, my destination her dripping wet center. I've dreamed about tasting her, and now that it's right there, there's not a force on earth that'll stop me from taking what I want.

"Nick," she moans when I make it to my mark.

I pull her skimpy panties aside and take a moment to look at her pretty pussy. The folds are pink and slick with dampness. I run my finger down the center. She cries out and bucks her hips, making me feel like I'm the king of the fucking world. I yank her panties down her legs and out of my way.

Using my thumb, I spread her wide. Unable to hold back any longer, I take my first swipe and taste fucking heaven. There's never been a better taste than having Chris in my mouth. I swear my eyes roll back in my head. I moan into her mound, not capable of holding it back.

Her hands fly to my hair and grip it tight. I welcome the burn of her tugging and pulling. I wrap my lips around the little bundle of nerves and suck hard while flicking my tongue. She comes unglued on the bed, bucking her hips and thrashing her head.

“Goddamn, woman, you’re fucking killing me with your taste,” I growl against her pussy.

My dick is hard as steel, and I feel it jump with each beat of my heart. The memory of how tight she felt flashes in my mind and my hands tighten on her legs. The need to get inside her heightens to a point where I can’t ignore it.

I get up from my knees, grab her around the waist to put her further up the bed, and crawl above her. Her hands immediately grab my shoulders, digging her nails in.

“Gonna fuck you now, Sugar. You ready for me?” I ask, my voice unrecognizable to my ears. If she says no, I have no clue what I’m going to do. Actually yes, I do. I’ll weep like a damn baby.

She tries pulling me down to her by my shoulders. “Yes, please, Nick,” she moans. And it’s music to my ears. “I need to feel you.” She emphasizes this by shifting her legs and bringing her hips up to meet mine.

I give her a cocky grin. “You got it, baby.”

I put one hand underneath her ass, angle the tip of my dick at her entrance, and with a shove of my hips and a pull on her ass, I impale her. I groan deep in my throat, while Chris’s eyes roll back in her head and she lets out a loud cry.

“Shit, you feel so fucking good,” I groan, and rest my forehead in the crook of her neck.

She feels so fucking incredibly tight around my dick. I have to hold still for a moment or I’ll explode, and it’ll end. Chris obviously has other ideas. She wraps her legs around my waist and digs her heels in my ass, trying to get me deeper.

“More,” she breathes. “Oh, God, Nick. I need more.”

I lift my head, grab a handful of her hair, and bring her face to mine. I nip her bottom lip. "Give me a fucking minute here. Your cunt's too damn tight. It'll end right now if I move."

Her eyes widen, and the pupils swallow up the green. Knowing she's almost beyond control nearly has me losing mine.

I shift one of her legs so it's over my arm and lean the elbow of the other one by her head. Looking down at her, I bring my hips back and push forward again. I do this slowly a couple times. She watches me, her green eyes sparkling up at me and her mouth open on a silent cry. We both stare at each other. My movements aren't hard and fast, but instead slow and steady. Something passes between us. Something I know shouldn't. It makes me feel uncomfortable, and I have to shift my eyes away from her.

Her body clamps down on my cock. I release her leg and get up on my knees. I want to watch as I slide in and out of her. Maybe that will remind me that this is all we'll ever have. Just two bodies trying to satisfy the others. Even if that makes me a bastard, I can't give her more than that.

Up on my knees, I look down to where our bodies connect. I plunge my hips forward and watch as my cock disappears into her warm cunt. The sight has my chest rising and falling swiftly. I wish I could stay in this warm haven forever.

I grip her hips and bring them up my thighs. I pull her toward me as I ram forward. Her panting turns to whimpers, then to loud moans. Her tits jiggle with each push forward.

"Play with your nipples, Sugar. I want to see you pinching them for me."

She complies immediately, squeezing and pinching the tips. When she plumps them together, the temptation before me is too great and I bend down and take one nipple in my mouth while she holds it, before moving on to the next one. They glisten from my mouth when I pull back. I continue to pump into her. Chris cries out and her walls tighten around me, letting me know she's close. I'm on the edge, feeling my balls drawing up, ready to explode inside her.

I drop back down to my elbows, needing the leverage to fuck her like I want to. I power forward, each of my thrusts stronger than the last. I grit my teeth, not willing to let go until she's reached her peak.

I lean down and take her lips in a brutal kiss, crushing our lips and teeth together. Her moans leave her mouth and enter mine. I reach down and place a finger on her pulsing clit, applying pressure. Satisfaction storms through me when she rips her lips from mine to release a loud cry.

"Nick!"

"Oh yeah, baby," I growl down at her and pump my hips harder, my hip bone clashing against the softness of the back of her thighs. "Give it to me. Let me feel you squeeze down on my cock."

My words and relentless fucking push her over the edge. She screams my name, sending fireworks through my blood, and squeezes my dick so hard I'm surprised it's still attached to my body.

My balls seize up impossibly tight, and I feel my orgasm rushing down my dick. I throw my head back and groan deep as I release all the pent-up sexual frustration this woman has caused me. I've never come so hard in my life. It leaves me feeling dizzy, sated, but wanting, no, *needing* more all at the same time.

I rest my forehead in the crook of her neck as she runs her hands up and down my sweaty back. Both of our breathing is rough.

A crushing weight forms on my chest when I realize what I've just done. I knew the moment I got in my truck to come over here, we would end up like this. I knew I was going into this to satisfy both of our sexual needs. I knew I'd be letting part of myself go and displacing the image of Anna in my head. Anna was the only woman I've been with in fifteen years. I barely remember the three girls before her. I thought she would always hold the place in my head of being the last woman I had sex with. I no longer have that. The image is now replaced with Chris. If I were to die tomorrow, it would be Chris that is that last memory. I knew all this when I made the trip here, but now that I've done it, shame slams into me, almost stealing my breath. I can't for the life of me regret taking Chris again. I want to regret it. I know I should *want* to take it back, but I can't find it in me. It felt too good. Too right.

Waging a war with my inner self, I pull my face out of Chris's neck, lift my body from hers, and sit on the side of the bed with my head in my hands. I grip my hair tight, wanting the biting pain. I hate myself for both polluting Anna's memory and for treating Chris like a piece of willing meat, using her to appease a deep carnal need. I want to slam my head against a wall. I've never treated women with anything but respect. And I've done anything *but* that with Chris. She should hate me too. She should run the other way when I enter a room. She shouldn't want anything to do with me. But for some reason she does.

I feel the bed shift behind me. I brace for what I know is coming. The touch on my back is barely there, but it still burns like lava. I only just stop myself from flinching. I want to recoil and fling myself away from her, but that's the asshole thing to do, and I'm trying to refrain from that.

"You okay?" comes her hesitant voice.

I release my hair and wipe my palms down my face. Breathing in deep through my nose, I turn to face her.

"Yeah, I'm fine," I tell her quietly.

She watches me with uncertain eyes, like she's not sure she believes me. That's okay, because I'm not sure I believe it either.

"Just give me a few minutes, okay? I'll be back."

She nods, but her eyes turn sad. And the asshole feeling comes back.

Despising myself for leaving her, but needing a few minutes alone, I head to the bathroom and quietly close the door behind me. I walk to the sink, put my hands on the basin, and hang my head. I never expected it could be this good with Chris. She makes me feel things I've never felt before. Things that scare me and make me want to shut them away so I never feel them again. I felt it the first time, but I put it off as a result of not feeling a warm woman wrapped around me for over two years. I know now that's not true. It's all Chris.

Lifting my head, I look at myself in the mirror. I don't like what I see. My hair is sweaty, my cheeks are red from exertion, my eyes are blazing hot, and my cock still glistens with Chris's essence. I look like I just had a round of hot and heavy sex. Another round of guilt churns in my stomach. I want to smash the mirror with my fists so I don't have to look at myself anymore. I need to stop this. Anna is no longer here. I know she would want me to move on; even if it's only sexually, at least it's something. I just can't get the feeling of betrayal out of my head.

Turning away from the sickening sight in the mirror, I grab a washcloth from the cabinet and wet it with warm water. No matter my inner turmoil, it's not Chris's fault. I may be loaded with guilt, but I still need to care for Chris.

I walk out the bathroom to find Chris sitting on the side of the bed with her bra and shirt on. She's bending over to slip her panties up her legs.

"What are you doing?" I ask, stopping for a second when I realize she's getting dressed. I already miss the sight of her gloriously naked body. I want to rip the clothes from her body and chain her to the bed so I can look anytime I want.

She looks over at me with a sad little smile, and then continues getting dressed.

"I figured you'd be leaving," she says quietly.

A muscle ticks in my jaw as I clench my teeth, irritated that she would think that. But then I remember it's my own fault. I should go home. It would reiterate to her that this is all there will ever be between us. But the thought of leaving her has a pain shooting in my chest. I'm not ready leave. I don't know if I'll ever be ready to leave.

"Well, I'm not," I snap, more harshly than I intended. I wipe the scowl from my face and finish walking to her. "Take your clothes back off and let me tend you."

She looks at me with confusion for a moment, then her eyes drop to the hand holding the washcloth. A cute blush forms on her face.

"You don't have to do that. I can do it myself."

She reaches for the rag, but I snap it out of her reach.

"I want to do it," I tell her truthfully. Now that the idea is in my head, I can't get it out.

"Nick, seriously, you don't—"

I don't let her finish before I bend down and get in her face. Her eyes widen and she leans back to avoid us bumping noses.

"Sugar, take your clothes off and let me clean my come that's running out of you. Please. I want to do this."

Red creeps up her cheeks again. She drops her eyes to her lap before bringing then back up to me. She doesn't react right away, just watches me with eyes that flicker back and forth. After several seconds, she nods, says "Okay" and lets her panties fall back to the floor.

Once she's naked again, she scoots back up the bed, and I follow her. Taking her knees in my hands, I pry them apart. Seeing her laid bare to me has my dick hardening again. Looking at my come weeping from her cunt jacks up my heart rate. Fuck, what I wouldn't give to take her again, but I'm still recovering from the emotional havoc I felt earlier.

I take the cloth and gently lay it over her sensitive spot. I don't analyze why the thought of wiping away my come from her bothers me. I want it to stay inside her. I ignore it and continue.

When the rag touches her, she sucks in a breath. My eyes fly to hers to see her biting her lip. I hold her gaze as I finish. By the time I'm done, we're both a little breathless. I want her again, but I'll wait. I'm not even sure if she's ready to go again.

I drop the washcloth in the laundry basket and walk back to the bed. Chris is on her side watching me. Her gaze drops down to my dick as it sways between my legs.

"Lift up," I grunt at her.

She does as she's told, and I drag the covers back. Sliding underneath them and pulling them over us both, I turn on my side to face her. We stay like that for a while, both just looking at the other. It should be uncomfortable, but surprisingly it's not.

Chris is the one to break the silence.

"I know you travel a lot. Tell me some of the places you've been." Her voice is timid, like she's unsure if I'll be willing to answer. I hate that she's distrustful of me. But again, I remind myself that it's my fault. I've put this girl through the wringer and back. I'm still amazed she wants anything to do with me.

I adjust my pillow so it's folded in half. "Most of the jobs I've contracted are north and southeast. Anywhere from Maine down to Florida and over to Iowa. But I had a few in the Western part of the US and a couple in Canada."

"What was your favorite place to visit?"

One of her hands is underneath her cheek while the other rests on the bed between us. We're about a foot apart. I want to reach out and trail my fingers over hers. I stop myself because that would be too intimate.

I think back to all the places I've been. Each is unique. It's hard to choose just one.

"If I had to choose, I'd have to say Connecticut. The mountains there are gorgeous and it still has that old England feel. The architecture is stunning. It's a very clean state. There's not too many states you can go through that don't have litter on the side of the road. You don't find that in Connecticut. They keep the landscape very fresh looking. I've only been there a few times, but each time I do, I always spend an extra day or two."

"It sounds beautiful," she says quietly, turning her head and looking off into space. "You're very lucky. I've only been to Georgia, the Carolinas, Virginia, and West Virginia. I want to travel."

She turns quiet and pensive, a small frown line forming between her eyes. I fight the need to reach over and run my finger across it to make it disappear. Fuck. I just want to touch her any way I can. I don't know why or how, but this woman is slowly taking over my thoughts. When I'm not with her, I'm thinking about her. When I *am* with her, my eyes always want to travel to where she is. My body craves hers. Even now my cock is straining toward her.

"Maybe one day you'll get to," I tell her.

She turns back to face me.

"Not with my current salary." She chuckles. "I make decent tips at Jaxon's, but even with that, it would take me many years. As it is, I'm already saving up for a house. And that'll take a while in itself. I'll be old and gray, not able to do much by the time I save enough money to travel like I want to."

An irrational and ridiculous thought pops in my head. One that spooks the shit out of me, but at the same time sends a thrill racing down my spine. She could go on trips with me. I travel a lot, see many places. Besides working at Jaxon's, her summers are free, and I'm sure Jaxon wouldn't have a problem finding a replacement for her during those months.

Wait! What the fuck am I doing?

The last thing I need to be doing is making plans to see her more. I already know I'm going to need those trips away from her to strengthen my walls again. This girl gets to me on a nuclear level. I need all the strength I can get when it comes to her.

"Is there any place you want to go but haven't yet?" she asks, pulling me away from dangerous thoughts.

"Colorado. To the mountains," I say, without having to think about it first.

"I want to go to Ireland," she sighs, a small smile tipping up her lips. "From all the stories I've heard from my grandparents and the pictures they've shown me, it's the one place I've always wanted to visit. It seems so beautiful over there." A frown pulls the smile away, and I want to cry for her to bring it back. "That's something that'll never happen. But a girl can dream, right?"

The smile is back in place when she looks at me and the tightness in my chest eases. She moves on the bed and the blanket shifts down a couple inches, exposing a glimpse of her breasts. She's on her side, so they mush together. My already hard dick jerks with the thought of fucking between their lush softness.

Giving in to the need raging inside me and pushing the never-ending guilt away, I reach over, snag her waist, and bring her beneath me. I loom over her. Her gorgeous green eyes flare with desire as her chest pumps with excitement. My chest flattens against hers, and I feel her stiff nipples poking me. She runs her hands up my back, and a growl breaks free from the back of my throat. I grip her hair, tilt her head to the side roughly, and bend to plunder her mouth.

I know over time I'll regret getting involved with this woman. I also know that one day, I'll hurt her. I just hope it's not beyond repair. I don't let either of these stop me though. The thought of ending what we've just started is too incapacitating. I just hope that when the day to end it comes, it doesn't end me as well.

seventeen

Chris

I SMILE AT THE cute Asian woman sitting across from me. She smiles back, but then totally screws up the sweetness of her demeanor by jabbing my cuticle back. I wince and try to hold my smile. *That shit hurt!* For such small women, Asian chicks sure are strong. I glance over at Bailey and see she's wincing as well. Karyn, who's on the other side of Bailey, doesn't look to be in any pain. She's jabbering away at the woman across from her.

Karyn announced yesterday at the bar that she and Ethan decided to go ahead and get married. They were originally going to wait until after the twins were born, but Ethan all of a sudden decided he didn't want to wait. He's grown impatient. We're out today looking for a dress for Karyn and getting pampered in the process. Our feet are done, so now it's the nails. Karyn looks like she swallowed a watermelon at seven months pregnant. Luckily, we located a shop that has dresses for pregnant women. We're headed there next.

I suck in a breath when my torturer clips my cuticle a little too close.

"Sorry," she mutters in her Asian accent.

"Do you know what style dress you want, Karyn?" I ask, trying to take my mind off the crucifixion of my fingers.

Her smile becomes so big it takes up half her face. "Yes!" she says animatedly. "I want a white strapless with a sweetheart neckline. Preferably with a lace bodice and satin skirt. I know it may be hard to pull off with me being pregnant, but it's what I've always wanted. Hopefully we'll be able to find something like that, or maybe something close."

"It sounds stunning," Bailey says, and I agree by nodding and smiling.

She's right though. She's very specific with what she wants, and her options are limited with her being pregnant. But her eyes shone so brightly when she was describing her perfect dress, I really hope we're able to find it. With her being so close to her due date, she and Ethan are getting married in three weeks. It doesn't leave much time to prepare, but with the help of me, Bailey, and Mia (who couldn't be here today because she was working) we'll get it done.

"We won't leave town until we find exactly what you want," I tell her and watch her beam with happiness.

"How are things between you and Nick?" Bailey asks, watching me closely.

I shrug. There's not much to tell. We've been having sex for three weeks now. It's great, freaking fantastic even, but I can tell Nick is holding back. I shouldn't let it hurt me. He told me from the beginning that that's the only thing we'll ever have, and I agreed to it, but I didn't realize it would hurt so much. I couldn't help but hope he would open himself up a bit more. We talk, we eat, and we hang out, but it's very dispassionate, except when we have sex. That's the only time he shows real emotion. He never delves into anything important when we talk. Never talks about the future. And he's never brought Anna up again. Sometimes I'll catch him staring at me, and I wonder what he's thinking. I keep telling myself I'm biding my time, that eventually he'll come around, but I'm starting to wonder. It's only been three weeks, but nothing has changed since that first night at my apartment.

Almost every night since that first night he took me out to dinner, he's been at my place. And every night he's there we have sex. Afterwards we talk about unimportant stuff. Sometimes he'll stay overnight and sometimes he doesn't. There've been a couple times I've woken up to find him sitting on the side of the bed with his head in his hands, drenched in sweat. The first time it happened I was scared to touch him, but I found the courage anyway. As soon as my fingers grazed his back, he stiffened. Then seconds later, he was above me, sliding inside my body and bucking his hips fiercely. His arms are always tight around me, like he can't get close enough. I always welcome him, but my heart aches knowing he's still hurting. And it aches even more knowing he's taking that hurt out on me. I often wonder if he's thinking about Anna in those moments he sits on the side of the bed.

After those times, I lie awake and hold my tears at bay until he falls asleep, then they silently slip free. Every night he stays with me, we fall asleep with me in his arms, but wake up with our backs to each other. It's like during the night we both try to reserve ourselves by putting distance between us. I hate it. I want to wake up with his arms wrapped me. I want to feel his breath on the back of my neck in the morning. I want to open my eyes and have his eyes be the first thing I see. I need to let Nick go, but I can't. Not yet at least. I know eventually I'll have to, or it'll end up destroying me.

"It's the same. He comes over, we have sex, sometimes he sleeps at my place and sometimes he goes home." Bailey and Karyn look at me with sympathy. I've spoken with them before about what's going on between us.

A headache starts to form in the back of my head, and I rub the tender spot. I feel Bailey's hand touch my arm, and I look over at her.

"He'll come around," she says somberly. "He just needs more time. Once he gets to know you and realizes it's okay to move on, he'll do just that."

"I don't know, Bailey. He's grieved for so long that it's all he's used to. I don't know if he'll ever be capable of moving on. For some reason he feels like he's betraying Anna by being with me. How is he supposed to move past that?"

"I'm not sure, sweetie, but he will. I know he will. Just watch and see."

"She's right, Chris," Karyn pipes in, leaning over, like getting closer to me will make the words more true. "The idea of moving forward with his life with someone else is terrifying to him. They were together for years, thought they would grow old together. He needs to get used to the idea and come to terms with it."

I want to believe them with all my heart, but I fear they are wrong. The attachment he had with Anna is unbelievably strong and seemingly unbreakable. Not that I want him to break all ties with her, but maybe loosen them a bit so I can fit in the picture as well.

Thirty minutes later we're walking out of the nail salon with our finger and toenails buffed, shined, and painted pretty colors. My head is really starting to pound, but I push the pain away as much as I can. I don't want to ruin this day for Karyn.

We came into town in Karyn's car, so we load up and head over to the bridal shop. It's a cute place that looks like it used to be someone's house. It's two stories with an old feel to it. We walk in the door and are immediately greeted by a lady who looks to be in her fifties.

"Hello ladies, welcome to Belle's Bridal!" she gushes, waving us through the door. "I'm Margie. Which of you beautiful ladies is the bride-to-be?"

"That would be me," Karyn says, stepping forward and gently taking the woman's hand with one of hers and rubbing the other along her stomach. "I called earlier about needing a dress fit for a pregnant woman."

She drops her eyes to Karyn's big baby bump, then looks back up at her and smiles kindly. "Yes, yes, I remember. I've set aside several dresses according to what you described to me over the phone. I'll also need to take some measurements. Would you like some tea or water while you wait?"

"Yes, please. Tea for me. Thank you." She turns to us and we both tell her tea as well.

Karyn turns and grins big when Margie walks off. "I love it here! It's so cute and charming," she says excitedly. Bailey and I laugh as she walks off to look at all the different wedding gowns and accessories.

I sift through a rack and come across a gorgeous floor-length strapless A-line. It's white silk with no lace or beading. If I were to ever get married, this would be my perfect dress. It's simple but elegant. I never wanted a big glitzy wedding. Just something intimate outside with all my family and friends. A pang of wistfulness hits my stomach when I realize that may never happen. I know I'm still young and have plenty of years left to find the perfect man, but no has even come close, and I refuse to settle for anything less.

You've already found your perfect man, my mind whispers.

Yeah, I have, but that doesn't mean I'm the perfect woman for him, I remind myself.

A tinkling sound comes from behind me, and I turn to see Margie carrying a tray with cups of tea. She sets them down on a small table in a seating area.

"Enjoy your tea, ladies. I'll be back in just a moment with the gowns I selected."

We say our thank-yous and she walks off.

"I found some cute ballet flats you might like, Chris," Karyn says, picking up her cup of tea and taking a sip. She looks silly with the small cup in her hand. It's like something out of an old Victorian movie. All she needs now is to lift her pinkie and wear a dress with a parasol to match.

"She doesn't need any more ballet flats. Her closet's already full of them," Bailey puts in with s snicker.

I have an obsession with ballet flats. I don't know why; I just find them very comfortable. I'd wear them all the time if I could get away with it. Unfortunately, they aren't very warm during the winter months here in Ohio.

"Hey! You can never have enough ballet flats," I grumble.

I reach forward to grab my tea and suck in a sharp breath when a blazing-hot pain shoots through my head. I wince and clutch it with one hand. Damn migraine. I had hoped the headache would go away. I've gotten several the past few weeks. I used to get them when I was younger, but they've tapered off the older I got. I'm sure they are stress related.

"Are you okay, Chris?" Bailey asks.

I look up at her and try to give her a smile, but I'm sure my face must look warped.

"Yeah, just another damn headache."

"We could go home and do this another day," Karyn offers with a concerned frown.

"No!" I say loudly and then regret it when another sharp pain hits. "No," I say more quietly. "This is your day and we need to find you a dress. It's only three weeks before you get married."

"Are you sure?"

"Yes. I'll be okay. I've got some pain pills in my purse I can take."

I dig in my purse that's in my lap and hold up the bottle. I pour a couple in my hand and down them with my tea. The scent and taste of the tea turns my stomach. Unfortunately, another symptom of my migraines is nausea. I just hope I can hold it off until we get back home.

"You're getting them a lot lately," Bailey states quietly.

I shrug. "Yeah. I've just been under a lot of stress lately. I'm sure they'll fade again soon."

"You sure that's it?" she asks.

I look over at her and see her watching me thoughtfully.

"Yes, I'm sure. What else would it be?" I reply, confused by her question.

She's quiet for several seconds, but I see ideas flipping around in her head.

"Your hormones being out of whack could cause migraines, too," she says thoughtfully. "I've also noticed you've been eating a lot more lately. And didn't you say you've been feeling sick lately?" It takes me a minute to understand what she's saying and when I do, my whole world spins on its axis, not helping the nausea at all.

"What?" I yell, then squeeze my eyes shut from the pain of the loud noise.

Her words send panic spiking through me, causing my head to pound harder. There's no fucking way that could be possible. My blood freezes, completely stops moving. A shiver wracks me as I think back to my last period. Two weeks before Nick and I had sex for the first time. I've been on birth control since I turned sixteen. I've never missed a pill. It's just not possible. No, it isn't 100 percent effective, but the chances of it not working are so slim that it's almost impossible.

But it is *possible,* my damn mind whispers again. I want to bang my head on the small table in front of me.

Tears prick the back of my eyes. This isn't good. It isn't good at all. If I'm pregnant, Nick is going to flip out. I know it. There's no way he'll be okay with this. We've never talked about kids. Our relationship doesn't warrant such conversations. But I know the thought of someone who isn't Anna having his child will scare him shitless. I know this won't be something he'll want.

My wide, spooked eyes meet Bailey's and Karyn's. Both are watching me with worry.

"Oh my God," I whisper.

Bailey is the first to get up. She comes to sit by my feet and grabs my hand. Karyn boosts her pregnant self up and waddles her way to my side. I look at both of them, begging them with my eyes for it not to be true. As amazing as the thought of having Nick's baby is, I know that it'll destroy what we have. I'm not ready to lose Nick.

"Don't freak out, Chris," Bailey says, squeezing my hand, trying to offer me comfort. It doesn't work. Nothing will work. There is no comfort to be had with this situation. "You don't even know if you're pregnant yet."

"This could be a good thing," Karyn says from above me. "This could be the wake-up call Nick needs. It may take him time to get used to the idea, but once he gets over his initial reaction, I'm sure he'll be happy."

I laugh bitterly. "That'll never happen. The only person he'll ever want to have children with is the only person he can't have them with because she's gone. He's gonna hate me," I finish on a whisper. "Our relationship doesn't involve a future. He doesn't want a future with me, and if I'm pregnant, he'll have no choice. That's if he even wants the baby."

"Oh, Chris." My eyes swing back to Bailey. Her eyes are sad. "Everything will be okay. Nick may be rough around the edges because of what's happened to him, but he's not heartless."

I wish that were true, but according to him, he has no heart. And I've witnessed the way he can be sometimes. Downright mean. And the way he's closed himself off from anything that's not purely sexual, proves that he's not interested in anything other than that.

We're interrupted when Margie comes back out carrying several long white dresses. She senses the tension in the air and sees the intense looks on our faces. "Is everything okay?" she asks with a puckered brow. "Do I need to give you three a few minutes?"

Karyn turns to me. "We can come back tomorrow."

"No," I say with a forced smile. "We're here and this needs to be done. We can worry about my problems later." I turn to Margie. "Show us what you've got."

MY PALMS SWEAT AND my heart races, making the pounding in my head worse, as I look at the all the different kinds of pregnancy tests. We stopped by Rite Aid on our way back to Jaded Hollow. I don't want to be here. Actually, this aisle is the last place on earth I want to be.

Bailey reaches for a pink box, and I want to snatch it from her hand, grab her and Karyn both, and run like the hounds of hell are after us. I can't though. I've got to know. I'm scared out of my mind to know, but I still need to know if it's true.

"Take this one," Karyn says, shoving a purple box in my face.

"And this one." Another box is shoved my way, this one from Bailey.

"Do you think I should get more than one of each?" I ask them both.

They both have more experience than I do at this. Of course, Bailey found out she was pregnant from her doctor, but Karyn found out through a pregnancy test, probably just like the one I'm getting ready to use. I'm completely lost here.

The longer I stand there, the more nauseous I get. I wonder now if it's from my migraine or because I'm pregnant.

Pregnant.

Even using that word in my head makes me want to hurl.

"Wouldn't hurt," Karyn says with a shrug.

I grab one more box of each.

I need to get home and get this over with. And then crawl in my bed, away from any noises and light, preferably with a rag over my forehead and a bucket beside my bed. I don't know which is worse; the thought of being pregnant or my migraine.

I'm on autopilot as I make my way to the register. All parts of me, except for my raging head, feel numb. My legs work, I know they do because I'm getting closer to the register, but I don't feel them. I clutch the boxes in hands that I barely register are there. I don't remember paying, I don't remember walking to Karyn's car or climbing inside. I don't remember parking and getting out at my apartment.

The next thing I'm really aware of is standing at the bathroom counter with my eyes closed, terrified to open them and see the results that will change my life forever. I don't really need the tests to tell me I'm pregnant. I already know. I've never missed a period in my life. I'm like clockwork. There've been other symptoms as well, like weight loss, tender breasts, and feeling tired all the time. Not to mention the migraines. I didn't think anything of it. I just thought the sore boobs and tiredness were from all the sex Nick and I have been having. Being pregnant never crossed my mind.

I open my eyes, but I don't look down. Instead I look at myself in the mirror. I look just how I feel. Exhausted. There are dark circles under my eyes and my skin sags a little. My shoulders are slumped, like the weight of the world is settled on them. That's how I feel.

A soft knock on the door startles me, making me jerk and then moan from the sudden movement. I really need my bed and a cool cloth.

"Chris, are you okay in there?" comes Bailey's soft voice.

I can't do this. I can't force myself to look, even already knowing the answer deep in my gut. A lump forms in my throat; I try to swallow it, but it sticks there.

I don't even attempt to do my usual funny face. There's nothing that could lift my spirits. Nothing that can take away the seriousness of this mess.

I swing around and open the door to find both Bailey and Karyn on the other side.

"I can't." I choke out on a sob. "I can't look."

Bailey wraps her arms around me and I sag into her. I hear Karyn enter the bathroom.

"Shh... everything will be fine." Bailey rubs my back soothingly.

I clutch her to me, as if she's my lifeline. Tears fall freely from my eyes, and I don't try to stop them. The turmoil swirling through me is just too much to bear. She walks me to the bed and sits down beside me. My face is buried in her throat when I hear Karyn come back into the room.

Gathering every bit of courage I have, I pull my face from Bailey and look up at Karyn to see her holding two pregnancy tests. Yes, I peed on one of each kind. The expression on her face confirms what I already know.

I'm pregnant.

That thought sits like a heavy weight on my chest, robbing me of all my breath. If only things were different. If only Nick could get over his broken heart and be willing to try for something new. It'll never happen though. I'm going to lose him forever once he finds out.

I place my hand on my flat stomach. It'll start growing round soon. I now it's only fanciful thinking, but I swear I feel a flutter beneath my hand. I have a tiny little being growing in there. Someone part of both me and Nick. As hurt as I am, knowing Nick will soon hate me, I can't help but be glad I'll at least have part of him. A part of him no one else has.

Bailey pulls my shoulders toward her and kisses the side of my head.

"It's gonna be okay. We're all going to be here for you, including Nick," she says against my hair.

Karyn comes to sit beside me and grabs my hand. "You let us know if we can do anything. You're not alone in this."

I nod at both of them, not really knowing what to say. These are my friends. I know they'll be there for me and the baby. And I'm so grateful for that, because I know this is going to be one life experience that I'm going to need the most help with.

"Thanks," I say tearfully. I can't help the yawn that follows.

"Okay, lady, off to bed with you. Does your head still hurt?" Bailey gets up from the bed, tugging me up with her, making my stomach flip upside down.

"Yeah, but I'll be okay once I lie down," I tell her tiredly. "I need to get a cool rag for my head."

Karyn points at me and then to the bed. "You lie down. I'll get it. Is there anything else you need?"

"Can you get rid of the tests, please?" She nods, and I turn to Bailey. "I'm supposed to be on shift for a few hours tonight at the bar. Can you let Jaxon know I won't be able to make it? And tell him I'm sorry?"

"Sure, sweetie."

I shed my pants and slip my bra off from underneath my t-shirt and crawl into bed. I feel like a child when Bailey pulls the covers up over me, but I'm beyond caring at the moment. The pounding in my head is getting worse.

Karyn comes back with the rag, and I take it from her. I sigh in relief when the cool terrycloth touches my forehead. I close my eyes. I hear shuffling around and the room dims behind my closed eyelids. A minute later, I feel a touch on my arm.

"Are you going to be okay here, Chris? Do you need one of us to stay?"

I crack open my eyes. Bailey is looming over me with worry written on her face.

"No, you both can go home. I'll be fine in a few hours."

She bends to kiss my cheek. Karyn does the same. "Call one of us if you need anything."

At my nod, she stands back up to leave, but I stop her.

"Hey." When they turn back around, I tell them, "Please don't say anything yet about... you know."

"Chris—" Bailey starts what looks like a protest.

"I'm going to tell him. I just need some time first. Please," I plead.

Karyn nods, and after several seconds, so does Bailey.

"Thank you," I whisper.

They leave on silent feet. I close my eyes and try to drift off, but the image of an enraged Nick won't let me.

eighteen

Nick

I SLIP THE KEY JAXON gave me earlier into the lock and give the knob a twist. Quietly opening the door, I step across the threshold to Chris's apartment and close it behind me. It's dark and quiet, just like I figured it would be.

After locking the door, I flip the light on in the living room and make my way down the narrow hall to Chris's room.

Fifteen minutes ago, I was sitting in Jaxon's Pub waiting for Chris to start her shift. When she was ten minutes late, I asked Jaxon if he knew why Chris wasn't there yet. He told me she wouldn't be in because she was stuck in bed with a migraine. I got a key to her apartment and immediately decided to check on her.

When I pull open the door, the light from the hallway shines in. My brows pull down into a frown when I see the bed is empty. A moan from the other side of the bed has me quickly moving that way. My heart drops into my stomach when I see Chris huddled on the floor, rocking.

I rush to her side and get down on my haunches.

"Sugar, what are you doing down there?" I ask, and gather her sweaty body in my arms.

Instead of answering, she moans, "Bathroom," and puts her hand to her mouth.

"Okay, baby. We're going."

She clutches my shirt as I lift her easily and walk briskly to the bathroom. I know what she needs. From the light in the living room I can practically see the green on her face.

I set her down in from of the toilet and she immediately bends over the basin and releases the contents of her stomach. I gather her hair in my hand to make sure she doesn't get any in it. Each retching sound she makes knots my stomach. Not because of the sounds or smell, but because I know she's in pain. Seeing her like this tears me up inside.

Once she's finished, she lays her arms across the toilet and rests her head on top of them. I find a washcloth in the linen closet in the hallway, wet it, and place it across her neck. Next, I go to the kitchen for a cup of water. When I make it back to the bathroom, she has her back resting against wall, her knees drawn up to her chest, with her head resting against them.

I squat down in front of her. "Chris, baby, I've got you some water."

At first I don't think she hears me, but after several seconds, she lifts her head and peers at me through tiny slits. I blanch at the color of her face. She's as pale as a fucking ghost. Her face is also drenched in sweat and she has dark rings around her eyes.

"Lights," she whispers.

I stretch back and flip the switch.

Once the bathroom is mostly in darkness, she reaches out with shaky hands for the cup of water. I help bring it to her lips and she swallows several mouthfuls.

"Thanks," she croaks, I'm sure with a sore throat.

"Do you need more pain pills?" At her nod, I open the medicine cabinet and pull out a bottle and shake two in my palm. She downs them with the glass of water. "Are you good or do you think you'll have to go again?"

It takes her a moment before she mutters, "Mouthwash."

I nod and help her up. She leans against the counter and grabs the bottle of mouthwash on the small shelf by the sink. I take it from her and pour a small amount in the cap, before handing it to her. She tips it back and swirls it around her mouth for a good thirty seconds, then spits it out and rises with water.

When she's done, I bend and pick her up. She settles her head against my neck and releases a sigh. I place her on the bed and go back for the rag. I rewet it with cold water before walking back to Chris's room. She's on her side with her eyes closed. When I place it on her forehead, her eyes crack open.

"Thank you," she whispers, barely loud enough for me to hear.

I sit on the bed beside her. "How often do you get these?"

"Up until recently, very rarely."

"Do you know what's causing them now?" I ask.

She shifts her eyes away from mine and to the wall across from her. The move shouldn't have looked anything but innocent, but I saw the flash of apprehension in her eyes before she could hide it.

"What? What is it?" I reach out and push away the sticky hair on her neck.

"Nothing," she mumbles, still not meeting my eyes. "It's probably just stress from work."

For some reason I don't think that's it, but I leave it for now. I'll ask her about it once she's feeling better.

"Do you need anything?"

"Yes," she answers, bringing her pain-filled gaze back to mine. "Will you lie with me?"

It never even crosses my mind to deny her. I'd do anything to bring her comfort. Watching her suffer does something to my insides. If lying with her helps ease the pain, nothing would keep me away.

I bend and remove my boots and socks. Next, I stand and take my jacket and shirt off, then my jeans, leaving me in just my boxers. She watches through slit eyes while I undress. I walk around to the other side of the bed and gently climb in behind her, so as not to jar her. I wrap my arms around her waist and flatten my body against her warm one. She releases a sigh and relaxes against me.

We lie in the dark without speaking for a while. I think she's fallen asleep, until she speaks.

"How did you know?" she asks the room.

"Jaxon." I use my bristled chin to move some of her hair away from the crook of her neck and plant my face there. "I was in the bar waiting on you to start your shift. When you didn't show, I asked Jaxon. He said you called off."

"Hmm." she hums. "How did you get in?"

"He gave me a key." I tell her cautiously, not sure how she'll take me having a key to her place.

I get another hum in reply. She either doesn't care or is in too much pain to care at the moment.

"Are the headaches why you didn't want me coming over those couple days last week?"

"Yeah."

"Have you talked with your doctor about them?" I flatten my palm against her stomach and rub soft circles there.

She stiffens in my arms for a moment, but then relaxes again. Before I get a chance to ask her if she's going to be sick again, she answers my question.

"No. I used to get them a lot as a kid, but the older I got, the farther apart they came. As an adult I only got them maybe once or twice a year. I used to get prescriptions for them but didn't see the point anymore, because the chance of it expiring was more likely than me actually needing it."

"Well, you're getting them more now. I think you should make an appointment. There's no sense suffering like this if you don't have to."

"Yeah."

She's quiet for a few minutes, then asks, "Why do you call me Sugar?"

With my nose in her neck, I pull in a deep lungful of air. Even now, all sweaty, she smells like sugar cookies, with a hint of vanilla.

"Did you just smell me?" she asks, yawning. I can hear the smile in her voice.

"Mmmhmm… You smell like sugar cookies. I like the smell."

"There is no way I smell like sugar cookies right now," she says with a chuckle. "I'm icky."

"But you do." I kiss the back of her neck. It's nothing sexual. I'm just glad she seems to be feeling better. Seeing her on the floor when I first walked in is something I don't ever want to experience again.

"Whatever," she mumbles tiredly and digs deeper into the bed.

"Go to sleep, Sugar." I smile into her neck.

"Hmm."

I feel her relax even more against me. I tighten my arms around her and bury my face back in her neck. It's not long before I hear her breaths even out. A few minutes later, I drift off as well.

THE NEXT MORNING, I'm in the kitchen finishing up frying bacon and eggs when I hear a noise behind me. I look over my shoulder and see Chris standing in the doorway. She looks better than she did last night, but she still has rings around her eyes. I heard her go into the bathroom about fifteen minutes ago. She must have gotten in the shower because her hair is wet and she has on fresh clothes.

"How are you feeling?" I turn back to take the finished bacon and eggs off the burners before placing the tongs on the counter.

"Much better," she says, her voice low.

When I walk over to her and put my arms around her waist, I feel her tense. Pulling back, I look down at her. Her eyes are downcast, avoiding mine.

I tip her face up with a knuckle. "What's wrong?"

Reluctantly she brings her eyes to mine. Something's off. She seems troubled and withdrawn. She has her hands on my waist, but any other time she would have them wrapped around me. She's leaning against me, but she's stiff and there's still distance between us. Normally she would be flush against me, like she can't get close enough.

"Nothing's wrong. I just still have a bit of a headache, that's all."

I can tell she's not telling the truth by the way her eyes shift from mine when she talks.

What the hell?

"You're lying," I state. I see the grimace before she can wipe it away.

"I promise, Nick. My head still hurts a bit and my stomach hasn't quite settled yet. And I'm worried about Noah from school."

I'm still not sure if I believe her. I know she's got to still be feeling the effects of her migraine and the green hasn't completely left her face, but she hasn't held my gaze for more than a couple seconds since she's walked into the kitchen. However, this is the second time she's brought up the kid from school. Maybe she's telling the truth, but I think there's more to it.

"You still haven't been able to get in touch with the mom?"

"No," she says with a sigh and fiddles with the shirt over my abs. "I've tried a couple more times with no luck. I was going to ask you if you could go with me next week sometime to his house."

She peeks up at me through her lashes. I still see something hidden in their depths, but again I don't call her out on it. If she has something going on and she wants me to know about it, she'll tell me. Our relationship doesn't really scream "tell me all your secrets." Although, at this moment, I want to demand just that. It both irritates and scares me that I feel that way. I'm not supposed to have those types of feelings toward her.

"I told you I would," I tell her, my voice harsher than I wanted. Her eyes flash with hurt, and I want to knock myself upside the head. My attitude is the last thing she needs right now. I can't help but feel slighted by the way she's acting though. "Just tell me the day and time."

I let her go and walk over to the cabinet with the plates and get a couple out. Her rigid voice stops me.

"I told you, you don't have to go with me. I can go by myself or find someone else."

I whip around to face her, not hiding the scowl on my face. Her eyes are narrowed as she rests one hand on the counter and the other on her hip.

"And I told you I would. I wouldn't have offered if I didn't want to go." I turn back around, ending the discussion there.

"Could have fooled me," she mutters irritably.

I throw some bacon and eggs on a plate and drop it in front of her. I plant my hands on the counter and lean toward her. "Want to tell me what your problem is? And don't give me the same bullshit about not feeling well and that kid at school. I know it's something more."

All of a sudden, her face goes ghostly white. Her eyes widen and sweat pops up on her forehead. She throws a hand to her mouth and dashes off toward the bathroom. I race after her and make it to the bathroom just as she starts puking her brains out again. Gathering her hair in one hand, I use the other to rub her back. My gut twists right along with hers.

Once she's finished, she wipes her mouth with the back of her hand and leans back against the wall with a moan. I refill the glass from last night and give it to her.

"Guess breakfast is out," I say with a quirk of my lips and squat down in front of her.

"Sorry." She tries for a smile but doesn't quite make it.

"'S alright. You okay now?" I tuck a piece of hair behind her ear and swipe my thumb across her cheek.

She nods. I help her up and again she washes her mouth with mouthwash.

"Promise you'll make an appointment tomorrow?" I ask, but it comes out more a demand.

She nods. "I will." I step back when pushes away from the sink.

"I'm going to lie back down for a bit and hope the rest of this goes away."

I walk with her back to the bedroom and pull the covers over her.

She must have changed the sheets when she got up because there's a fresh set on the bed. I get down on the floor by her head.

"I've got to head out. There are a few things I have to take care of at home. I'll be back in a bit."

She's back to avoiding my eyes when hers move to my throat. Even so, they look sad. "You don't have to. Bailey's supposed to be coming over for a while."

I have no fucking clue what's going on, why she's all of a sudden withdrawing. Maybe she's had enough of our arrangement. Maybe she feels she can't do it anymore. The thought of that, of never touching her again, almost cripples me. It's only been a short three weeks. I'm not ready to let her go, but I can't demand we continue this toxic relationship either. I don't let that emotion show though. I'll be damned if I show her how her aloofness hurts. Instead, I get up from the floor and grab my boots. With my back to her, I sit on the bed to put them on.

"Do you need anything before I leave?" I ask stiffly, without looking at her.

"No, but thank you," she says quietly.

"Call me if you do. And call me when you decide to go over to the kid's house."

I'm grabbing my wallet and phone off the nightstand when I hear her soft "Okay."

Without another word, I leave her. I'm at the door when she calls my name.

"Nick?"

Gritting my teeth, I force myself to turn around and face her. Seeing her huddled in that bed makes me want to rush back, crawl in bed behind her, and never let her go.

"I'm sorry," she says, her voice low.

It takes me a minute, but then I say to her, "Yeah. Me too. More than you know."

And then I turn around, walk out the door, and leave her apartment, feeling like my heart just cracked right down the center. I try to rub the ache away, but it doesn't help. When I get in my truck and drive away, I feel like I'm not only leaving her behind, but also a piece of myself.

I HANG UP MY PHONE and drop it on the desk in front of me with a tired sigh. Twisting my neck from left to right, I try to work out the kinks that are forming there. Once again, I'm not sleeping worth shit and it's starting to wear on me. Unsurprisingly, it started three days ago, the day I left Chris in her bed. I haven't heard a word from her since. I've tried calling her a couple times, but receive no answer. The day I left, I called Bailey that evening to check up on her. Her answer was evasive, only telling me Chris was better, up and moving around. Relief swept through me knowing she was over her migraine, but then suspicion took over. Something was definitely going on and Bailey knew about it too. It hurt knowing that Chris didn't come to me with whatever it was, but then again, I haven't been very forthcoming with my own feelings, so I can't really blame her. But it still hurt nonetheless. Then anger took hold because she wasn't big enough to tell me we're over. Instead, she's taking the coward's way out by ignoring me.

Since Chris and I started our arrangement, my dreams have lessened. I still have them, but while I was with Chris, not very often; only a couple, I believe. They were the ones of Chris dying in my arms instead of Anna. Each one terrified me. My only saving grace was I didn't wake up screaming her name. Instead, I'd just jolt awake and sit on the side of the bed to try to catch my bearings. But as soon as I felt Chris's innocent touch, I'd lose it. Nothing and no one could stop me from taking her. I *needed* to feel her body against mine. It was the only way for me to know she was truly okay.

Since the day I left though, my dreams have changed once again. I'm always standing in front of Anna. She's wearing a white flowing dress and her hair blows in the wind. Her beauty takes my breath away. However, she looks worried. Her lips move silently, trying to tell me something, but she never makes a sound. When I try to go to her, the closer I'd get, the farther away she is. Then the dream shifts and I'm in front of Chris. She's also in a dress, except hers is black. She's not facing me, instead looking off in the distance with a sad expression. I call out to her, but she doesn't hear me, just stands there unmoving. And just like with Anna, I can never reach her. I don't know what either dream means, but they scare me shitless.

I shake my head to rid myself of my thoughts and get up from behind my desk. Tiredly, I make my way to the bathroom and a much-needed shower. It's still early, but I've been up since dawn doing last-minute improvements to the house. Other than a few things here and there, it's complete. It feels good to be done with it, but a part of me still grieves that Anna wasn't here to help.

Stripping down, I walk into my shower and stand with my head bowed to let the water rain down on me. I miss Chris more than I thought possible. These last few days have been torture. There've been so many times I've had to restrain myself from going to her. I tried taking my mind off her by finishing the house, but it hasn't worked. Every move or change I make to the place, I wonder if she would approve. The only thing that kept me from going after her is the knowledge that she's better off. I won't force her to continue what we had. It would be selfish of me, because I know it's bound to end eventually. It's better to end it now before she gets hurt.

I soap and rinse, then turn off the water. Grabbing a towel, I wrap it around my waist and find myself standing in front of the mirror. My eyes fall to the heart tattoo on my chest, right over my own heart. Looking at the date, I wait for the heavy debilitating pain to form underneath the tattoo. I'm surprised to find it's there, but it doesn't take my breath away like it normally does.

Bringing my eyes back to my face, I cross my eyes and blow out my cheeks, and then drop the expression when I feel like a complete idiot. I have no idea how Chris can do that every time she sees her reflection, but I miss seeing her do it. I frown when I realize she didn't do it when I was in the bathroom with her the last time I was there. It could be because she was sick, but for some reason I don't think that's it. I don't see sickness stopping her from doing something she's done since she was a child. Whatever the reason is, I don't like that it took something so important away from her.

Flipping the light off, I go to my room, shed my towel, and climb into bed. I think back to my phone call from earlier. A potential client wants me to fly to West Virginia to talk over plans for a hotel he wants built in the mountains. I leave in a week. Even though I haven't seen Chris in three days, I still don't like the thought of leaving, especially with things the way they are. But then again, it may be good to get away and clear my head a bit. Something has to change, because it seems like all I can do is think about her. It's driving me insane, not being near her. But it's also making me crazy, because I want those thoughts to go away. She's dug her way into my life when I didn't want her to.

Yes, what I need is a few days and hundreds of miles away from Chris, and once I come back, things will go back to normal.

Or as normal as I'll ever have.

nineteen

Chris

"WHAT IN THE HELL do you mean, you're pregnant?" Jase yells, jumping up from the couch and causing me to wince. "How in the fuck did this happen?"

I tip my lips up into a smirk and reply, "Well, you see, when two people—"

He doesn't let me finish. "I know how it fucking happened, Chris. This isn't a laughing matter. I want to know *how* it fucking happened. Aren't you on birth control or some shit? Didn't he use a condom?"

Well, at least he didn't question me on who the father was.

"Calm down, Jase," I tell him. "Yes, I was on birth control. That's why we didn't use a condom. We didn't think we needed to. Obviously we were in the one percentile."

"Jesus! Fuck!" he says, pacing back and forth and running his fingers through his hair in frustration. He whips back around to face me. "Does he know?" he demands.

I twist my hands in my lap and look down at them, surely looking guilty. "No," I mutter.

"What?" he yells again.

I look back up at him, getting pissed at his high-handedness.

"No!" I yell back. "I haven't told him yet! But I plan to! Now back off!"

He scowls at me for a moment before he takes a deep breath. The scowl is gone when he releases it. Walking over to me, he sits down on the couch.

"I'm sorry, Chris. It just took me by surprise. I'm shocked." He grabs me by the shoulders and pulls me forward until my face lands in his chest. I wrap my arms around his back. We sit this way for several minutes.

It feels good to be able to tell Jase. It's been almost a week since I found out I was pregnant. The initial shock and worry have worn off and the idea of having Nick's baby has taken root. I know the chances of me losing Nick are great, but the thought of having his baby has helped. The pure joy of knowing I will always have a part of him overrides the pain of losing him. But I still can't help but wish and hope that I'm wrong and Nick will welcome us both.

"I know," I say against Jase's chest. "Believe me, I was shocked too. Still am. It's not like it was planned or anything. But things happen sometimes. I'm happy though, and that's all that should matter."

He pulls back from me but places both of his palms again my cheeks, holding my eyes with his.

"You being happy *is* all that matters. I'm just worried about you. Why haven't you told Nick?"

I swallow the fear his question provokes. There's no telling how Nick will react. And not knowing what he'll say or do scares the bejesus out of me.

"I'm scared," I whisper brokenly, tears forming in my eyes. "I know I'm not what he wants. I just don't know how he'll take it."

"If he knows what's good for him he'll take it how any man should take it and step up to do his duty," he asserts in a hard voice.

"Stop it, Jase." My eyes turn watery. "I don't want me or my baby to be a duty. I want him to want us both for ourselves, not because he's obligated to."

Tears start rolling down my cheeks. I try to wipe them away but they're coming too fast. My emotions are all over the place lately. Which is to be expected, because I'm pregnant.

I'm pregnant.

It's still so weird to think about it.

"Hey." Jase draws my attention back to him. "We'll get through this. If that asshole doesn't want you and that baby, then he doesn't deserve you. You still have me, Andrew, and everyone else."

I don't agree with him. Yes, I deserve a man who would love me and my baby wholeheartedly, but it's not Nick's fault he is the way he is. Grief comes in many forms; sometimes that grief keeps you from allowing others to get close to you. I have no doubt that if Nick and I were in a different situation, he would give everything for me and the baby.

I don't say any of this to Jase, though. He's my brother and automatically thinks any man should love me, no matter the circumstances.

I give him a watery smile. "Thanks, Jase."

"When are you going to tell him?"

I shrug, not sure of my answer. I'm still building up the courage.

"I don't know. Soon."

"I want to be there when you do. I don't want you alone with him," he states.

I shake my head immediately. "No. I need to do this on my own. He deserves to be told in private." When he tries to object, I lay a hand on his cheek. "I'll be fine, Jase. Really. No matter what he says. But I need to do this my way."

He doesn't look happy, but he reluctantly agrees with a nod.

"Now, feed me," I demand and get up from the couch. "Me and the little bean are hungry."

Still sitting, he wrinkles his nose and looks at my stomach. "Really? You nicknamed him bean?" He leans in close to my stomach and whispers, as if I won't hear him. "Don't worry, kid. We'll come up with something better, like Nugget. Or Monster! Yes, I like Monster!"

I laugh at his goofiness. "You are not calling my baby monster. She's going to be a sweet little angel."

He grins and gets to his feet. "Who says it's going to be a girl?"

"I do," I tell him confidently with a smile.

Shaking his head, he grabs my hand and drags me to the kitchen. I dig out the makings for a salad, as he puts together a quick meal of chicken alfredo with broccoli. For once, the smell of food doesn't bother me. I haven't had a good meal in days.

As I stand at the bar chopping veggies, I think back to the last time I saw Nick and the pain I felt as he walked away. I knew I was being cranky. It was done on purpose to push him away. I needed a few days to myself to wrap my mind around being pregnant and to find a way to tell him. I was also preparing myself for the inevitable of him walking away. As soon as he left the room, the tears started flowing. I wanted to call him back, to beg him to never leave, but I had already acted pathetic enough in front of him. Like I told Jase earlier: I don't want him to stay unless he wants to.

These last few days have been bittersweet. I miss Nick like crazy. Sometimes I feel like I can't breathe with missing him so much. The couple times he's called I've literally had to sit on my hands to keep from answering. Tears gather in my eyes as I listen to my phone ring. He never leaves a message, even though I desperately wish he would so I could hear his voice.

But it's also given me the opportunity to come to terms with the situation. I often find myself touching my belly, anxiously awaiting the day I'll feel the flutters in my stomach. The baby will come with sadness, but overriding that sadness is utter joy. I can't wait to hold my baby in my arms.

I dump the fixings in the bowl with the lettuce and place it on the bar with dressing and a pair of tongs. Going to the fridge, I get out a can of soda for Jase and a bottle of water for myself and set them on the bar as well. I turn and jump up on the counter close to Jase as he finishes the fettuccine.

"How's work going?" I ask, swinging my legs.

He looks at me and rolls his eyes at my childish behavior.

"It's good. Joe finally decided to go into semi-retirement. He's giving me a trial run to see if I want to take on the shop full-time. If it goes well, we'll set up a payment plan for me to buy the place from him."

"That's great, Jase! I know you've wanted your own shop for years now."

I lean over to kiss his cheek, and dip my finger in the yummy-smelling sauce as I lean back.

"Hey!" he scowls and slaps my hand before I can bring my finger to my mouth. "No dipping in the goods until I'm finished."

"Screw that." I moan in delight when the delicious taste touches my tongue. I slip my finger back in the sauce for a second time before he can stop me. "You have no clue what it's been like for me, Jase. I miss food so much. This is the first time in days it hasn't turned my stomach. Now hurry up before I eat it before it's done."

"Aww, you poor baby," he says with a pout. "Five minutes. Can you last five more minutes?"

"I guess," I grumble, making him laugh.

My phone rings in the living room, and I jump down from the counter to go answer it. My heart drops to my throat when I see who's calling. I think about answering it, desperately wanting to hear his voice, but then decide against it. I need a couple more days. Then I'll seek him out to tell him about the baby.

I hit the Ignore button just as Jase comes to stand behind me, putting his chin on shoulder and looking down at the phone in my hand.

"Even though I don't care for the guy at the moment, you need to give him a chance, Chris. He may not act like you fear he will."

"Yeah," I say softly, still looking down at the now black screen.

"Come on. Let's go feed you and the Monster."

He grabs my waist and turns me back toward the kitchen. We

make small talk while we sit and eat. Because I'm starving, and I haven't eaten a good meal in what feels like weeks, I have two servings. I get updates on how Ally is doing, and I tell him about the boy at school. Once we're finished, I do the dishes while he finds a movie for us to watch. Telling him about the baby wasn't the only reason I came over. I also wanted to spend some time with him. It's been so long since it's just been me and him.

We're halfway through *What's Eating Gilbert Grape*, one of our favorites, when we hear the front door open. Jase pauses the movie and gets up from the couch when Andrew walks in. The first thing he does, even before putting down his keys, is pull Jase into his arms for a kiss. I can't help but smile at them.

When they pull apart you'd have to be blind to not see the desire in both their eyes. I hear Jase tell Andrew, "My sister's here." Andrew looks over his shoulder and sees me sitting there. A smile forms on his face.

"Hey, you. Get your ass over here and give me my Chris lovin'."

I roll my eyes, but laugh and get up from the couch. Andrew drops his keys on a small table as I make my way over to him. He pulls me in his arms and I hug him back. Before I can pull away, he plants a light kiss on my lips. Some people may find this weird, especially since he just kissed my brother, but that's Andrew for you. He's always been very affectionate.

"How ya been? Seems like forever since I've seen you."

It's only been about a week, but when you're used to seeing someone almost every day, a week seems like a long time.

"I've been good. Darn headache had me out last weekend. But I'm better now."

My gaze flickers to Jase to see him watching me with questioning eyes. I barely shake my head. I hope he gets my meaning that I don't want to tell Andrew yet about the baby. It's not that I don't trust him. I trust him as much as I trust Jase, but the more people who know, the higher the chance of Nick finding out before I can tell him. So far, Bailey, Karyn, and Jase are the only ones who know. I want to keep it that way until I've told Nick myself.

Jase's brows pull down into a frown. I hate asking him to keep something from Andrew, but it's only for a couple more days.

Andrew grabs Jase by the ass, pulls him close for another kiss, and murmurs against his lips, "I'm gonna grab a quick shower. I'll be back out in a few."

Jase watches Andrew walk away longingly. I snicker and slap his stomach with the back of my hand. "That's sad, Jase. You'll see him again in a few minutes."

"Whatever," he mutters with a sheepish grin.

We go back to watching our movie. Andrew joins us on the couch a little while later. I'm on one end with Jase in the middle and Andrew at the other end. They're holding hands, and few minutes, I hear them murmur something to each other. I know I should leave to give them privacy, but I'm enjoying cramping their style too much. I swear these two would stay in bed all day if they could. It's actually quite gross to think about it; Jase is my brother after all, and I in no way want to picture him in a situation like that, but they leave no choice for anyone in their vicinity. If they are close to each other, chances are they're touching or eye fucking each other. The thought makes me shiver in disgust.

By the time the movie is over, I swear the heat in the room has risen ten degrees. Just to mess with them a little bit more, I fake a yawn and ask, "I'm exhausted. Do y'all mind if I stay over for the night?"

Both are quiet for several seconds, before Jase says with poorly hidden reluctance, "Uh... sure. You can take Ally's room."

I look over at them both and see Jase with a look of dejection and Andrew grinding his molars together. I laugh at their miserable expressions. "Geesh, guys. I'm only kidding. Give me two minutes to use the bathroom before I go, then you can jump each other's bones. I promise not to keep you from each other any longer."

Jase gives me the evil eye while Andrew grins cockily. "Oh, you staying here wouldn't have cramped our style, honey. I would have just had to hold my hand over—"

I put my hands to my ears, effectively blotting out the rest of his words, and yell, "Nope! Don't need to hear that!"

Getting up from the couch to go to the bathroom, I hear Andrew laughing behind me.

Well, crap. That backfired on me.

I wash my hands when I'm done with the bathroom and walk out to find Jase and Andrew in the kitchen. Andrew has a plate of leftover dinner, scarfing it down. I hug and kiss them both. At my ear, Jase whispers, "Don't wait too long. And let me know how it goes."

I pull back and give him a slight nod.

Waving at them, I leave and head home to my lonely and cold bed.

I GATHER THE FEW THINGS I need to take home with me and head out of my office. Apprehension and anxiety make me jittery. Nick is supposed to come over tonight. I called him last night and asked him to, so we can talk. It took every bit of courage I possessed to make that phone call. I have to admit though, I'm dying to see him again. It's been almost a week.

"I'm heading out, Mary. I'll see you tomorrow." I wave at the school's receptionist.

"See you tomorrow, Chris," she chirps with a wave.

"Have fun on your date tonight." I wink and smile before walking out the door.

I get in my car and make the less than a mile trip to Evelyn's to pick something up for dinner. I have no idea how tonight is going to go, but I'm hoping for the best. I'm sure it'll be a shock to him. I just hope once the impact of the news wears off, he'll be more accepting. Neither of us planned this, but it happened, so we just have to learn how to work together for the best interests of the baby.

Once home, I take a quick shower and straighten up the apartment. It doesn't take me long. After, I prepare meatloaf and put that in the oven on low for dinner. Left with nothing else to do, I decide to check my e-mail and Facebook. Afterward, I end up on the couch reading for a bit. It takes a good thirty minutes for me to force myself to forget about what's happening tonight. I know if I don't find something to keep my mind occupied, I'm going to drive myself crazy.

The buzzing of the oven timer is what pulls me from my book. I look at the clock and realize three hours have passed. I turn the oven off but leave the meatloaf inside to keep warm. Nick is due to be here in less than ten minutes.

The thought hasn't left my head when I hear a knock on the door. He's early. Maybe he's just as anxious to see me? I smooth my hands down my knee-length black skirt, nervous energy moving through me. Taking a deep breath, I open the door to see Nick in all his hot glory. He's wearing an old pair of jeans with one hole in the knee on one leg and another where the pocket is. His black button-up shirt with the top couple of buttons undone and the sleeves rolled up to his elbows fits perfectly over his muscular torso. His dark brown hair looks like he's been running his fingers through it. The scruff on his face is longer than the last time I saw him, but it looks well-trimmed.

My heart does a pitter-patter at the sight of him. I eat him up with my eyes and a shiver runs down my back. I've missed him so damn much.

His hooded eyes run up and down my body, making it feel like a soft caress. When they meet mine, I suck in a breath at the heat I see there.

Forcing my feet backwards, I open the door wider so he can enter.

"Come in."

He doesn't say anything as he steps inside. I close the door and turn back to him. He's a lot closer than what I thought he would be.

"I have dinner in the oven keeping warm. Would you like—"

Before I'm able to finish, he reaches out, snags me around the waist, and the next thing I know, I'm against his chest. I squeal at the sudden movement, but it's quickly replaced by a moan when his lips meet mine.

My back hits the wall, my arms circle his neck, and my fingers delve into his hair. He palms my ass through the thin material of my shirt. I want to rip the material away and feel his fingers against my skin. Our tongues tangle and our moans mingle. He nips at my lips and moves to my neck. I tilt my head back so he can reach his target better.

"Fuck, I've missed this," he groans in my neck.

My breath hitches, and I let out a throaty, "Me too. So much."

When his hands start lifting the hem of my shirt, I drop mine on top of his to stop him, knowing I need to tell him about the baby first.

"Wait," I say breathlessly. "We need to talk first."

"Fuck first, talk later. I can't wait." He grunts and starts pulling my shirt up again, effectively dislodging my hands. The tips of his fingers graze my sides and send shivers all throughout my body.

"Nick—"

His lips cut off my protest, and I lose the ability to think when his fingers brush the underside of my breasts. He pulls the cups of my bra down and pinches my nipples. All thought of protesting flies out the window. I know I need to stop this, but it feels too damn good.

God, he's going to hate me.

I tug at his shirt and he pulls back just long enough to shed both his and mine. Our bodies mold back together and it's never felt so good. We fit perfectly against each other.

His hands move back to my skirt to pull it up. Dipping his fingers beneath the waistband of my panties, he gives them a tug downward and they fall to the floor. Cool air hits my ass and it feels good against my heated skin. I want to crawl up his body, wrap myself in his essence, and never let go of him.

I almost come out of my skin when I feel his fingers at my core. He slides a digit through my folds and stops at my entrance. A cry leaves my lips when he plunges two fingers inside. Unconsciously, I grip his hair tighter and he snarls. I reach down for his pants, impatient to release the part of him I need.

I must move too slow because he knocks my hands away and yanks at the button and fly. He springs free and my mouth waters at the sight. I remember the taste of him in my mouth, and I want that again. Not right now though. Right now I need him inside me like I need my next breath.

"Nick, please," I beg him with a needy voice.

"Fuck," he hisses. "I know, Sugar. Me too."

Once his jeans drop to the floor, his hands move to my ass and lift me. My legs automatically wrap around his waist and my back hits the cool wall behind me.

"I'm sorry," he mutters against my lips.

His words confuse me. I pull back to look at him.

"What for?"

"Because this is going to be rough and fast," he says, and slams his hips forward, impaling me on his hardness.

I cry out at the sudden pleasure-pain of being filled by him. I dig my heels in his ass as I tighten my legs around him. Having him in me again feels like coming home after being gone for years. There is no better feeling.

I lean my head back against the wall and hold on as he slams into me over and over again. He buries his face in my neck, and his lips latch on to the skin there. I know it'll leave a mark. Having his mark on me sounds heavenly and makes me even wetter. His hips pump up while I grind down; my clit rubbing against his pelvic bone sends vibrations through my stomach. There is no way I could ever get enough of this man.

"Fuck, woman. You feel so good," he groans. "I won't last much longer. Please tell me you're close."

"Yes!" I hiss. "Oh God, Nick."

One hand tightens on my ass, while the other goes to my hair. Gripping it tight, he pulls my head back so I'm forced to look at him.

He leans forward and rests his forehead against mine. "I want to see your face when you come. Keep your eyes on mine."

I hold his stare, biting my lip when his thrusts become stronger, deeper. My walls start clenching him and a growl erupts from the back of his throat.

Flutters start forming in my stomach and move throughout my body. I feel weightless and the same time my limbs go numb. Starbursts start flashing in my eyes, sending sparks over my skin. The building orgasm leaves me gasping for breath, but unable to pull in enough air.

Nick lets go of my hair, but I keep my eyes on him as he watches me. The intensity and emotion in his gaze is so overwhelming I almost look away. I know he sees my own feelings in mine. There's no way I could hide them from him in that moment and there's no way I can look away. My heart and body belong to him and he has to see that, which scares me.

His hands move between our bodies and he pinches my clit. I scream his name as an explosion of sensations rushes through me. I feel like I'm flying. It takes me higher than I've ever been before. I clamp down on him as my release slams into me, sending me soaring and exploding into a million tiny pieces.

My back slides up and down the wall as he aggressively fucks me. He grunts and growls with each thrust forward. A moment later he throws his head back and lets out a low groan as he finds his own release.

He hunches his weight against me, pinning me against the wall. But I don't care. Knowing I was able to do this to him sends immense pleasure through me. I'll gladly take his weight anytime he needs.

After several seconds, he pulls back to look at me. "You okay?"

I give him a soft smile. "Yeah." I smooth my fingers over his face. "Just please don't let me down. My legs are jelly, and I don't think I can stand."

He chuckles. "Wanna shower? I can hold you while we do it."

"Can't," I tell him tiredly. The stress of the last week is getting to me, and I'm suddenly exhausted. "Just want my bed."

He leans forward and places a soft kiss to my lips.

"You got it," he says, and with him still inside me, turns to walk to the bedroom. I bury my face in his neck.

"Shit," I mutter. "Forgot the food."

I feel him stop and turn. I look up as he heads to the kitchen. Without setting me down, he grabs an oven mitt, opens the even door, and pulls the food from it.

"You can put me down now," I say with a giggle.

"Nope. Where's the tinfoil?"

Holding me while he puts the food away is completely ridiculous, but I can't find the wherewithal to care though. It's certainly interesting to feel, because he's still inside of me. I can't help the couple of moans that slip free as he moves around. I point to the shelf beside the stove. He grabs the box of tinfoil, tears off a piece, and covers the pan. After, he places it in the fridge. He flips the light off and we leave the kitchen.

Entering the bedroom, he puts me down on the bed, dislodging himself from me. I whimper at the sudden loss.

He smirks at me and says, "Be back."

A minute later, he comes out holding a rag, just as I knew he would, just as he has every time we have sex. After he cleans his release from me, he tosses the rag aside and climbs into bed beside me.

Guilt starts eating at me when I remember I still haven't told him about the baby. I shouldn't have let what happened happen. I should have told him first. I feel his arms come around my waist. Tears appear in my eyes, but I blink them away. I want one more night with him. Just one more night, before I destroy the one thing I want most in the world.

twenty

Nick

MY HEAD TILTS BACK, and I feel the sun shining down on my face. Opening my eyes, I see the leaves blowing in the wind and the sunlight filtering through the canopy of trees.

A giggle off to my left grabs my attention, and I look that way. I take a few steps closer when I see a little girl on the tire swing in my yard. I'm standing to the side of her, about fifty yards away. She has beautiful long brown hair. She's too far away to see her eyes. The yellow dress she's wearing sways back and forth with each forward and backward motion of the swing. She looks to be about five years old. She's absolutely gorgeous and when she laughs, her whole face lights up.

"Hi, Daddy!" she yells. I stumble back a step in shock. My throat clogs up when I realize this precious little girl is mine. A big smile breaks across my face and the instant love I feel for this amazing child is so fierce it's indescribable. I just saw her for the first time, but she already owns my heart.

She continues to laugh as she swings her legs, making the swing go higher. All I can do is stand there and watch, completely mesmerized by the sight before me.

"She's beautiful, isn't she?" comes a quiet voice beside me. I look over, not surprised when I see Anna standing there looking at the little girl. After all, if this little girl is mine, then she has to be Anna's as well.

I look from her to my daughter, then back to Anna.

"She is. But I always knew our kids would be."

Anna brings her eyes to me and they hold sadness, but beneath that sadness lies what looks like a glimpse of hope. She takes a step toward me and lays her hand on my chest, right over my heart. I want to pull her into my arms, but I stop myself, not liking the sorrow in her eyes. What is there to be sad about?

"She's not ours, Nick," she whispers softly.

Her words confuse me. How can she not be ours? She called me daddy, so that mean she has to be mine, and there's no other woman who would bear my child. I would never allow that. Anna is mine and I'm hers. How can she say that the little girl isn't ours? It's not fucking possible.

Anna looks away from me and back toward the girl on the swing. I follow her line of sight and my breath catches. My brows pull down into a frown when I see a lone figure off in the distance. Her red hair blows in the wind and her black dress whispers across her legs. Her head is bent as she looks at her clasped hands. When she looks back up, her green eyes land on the girl on the swing. Even from this far away, I see tears sliding down her cheeks. Seeing the anguish on Chris's face sends a sharp pain straight to my heart.

"This can be your future, Nick," Anna says gently, gesturing to the girl.

I whip my head around to face her. Her stunning blue eyes capture mine.

"What? No! This is our *future, Anna!" I implore, then feel a pinch in my stomach when I realize that can't be true. Anna is no longer here.*

"Be happy for me, before it's too late. Don't give up on love," she says, ignoring me.

"Anna—" I start, but don't finish. I want to repeat to her what I said the night she died. I want to tell her I could never be happy without her,

could never love another. That she is my one and only and my world is dark without her in it. But the way she's looking at me, pleading with her eyes, stops me.

"Please don't leave me," I beg her instead with a broken whisper. "Please stay with me."

She smiles sadly. "You know I can't. But you can be happy if only you'll let yourself. This can be your future, if only you'll grab on to it."

I look back at the little girl on the swing and then to Chris beyond her. Something shifts in my stomach and my chest feels tight. I want to run to Chris and take away her pain. Panic sets in, and I swing my eyes back to Anna.

"I don't want a future if you can't be in it. I want only you, Anna."

"Let me go, Nick," she says in a voice that sounds faraway. My breaths come faster when I realize she's starting to fade.

"Anna!" I yell and run to her, only to have my fingers slide through her. "Please, don't leave! Anna!"

"Let go, Nick, before it's too late," she says again, her voice carried away in the wind.

I drop to my knees and scream to the sky...

I JACKNIFE UP IN bed and clutch my pounding head, pulling at my hair. My stomach flips at the dream I just had. There's no fucking way that will come true. No way Chris and I are ever having kids. Even as I think it, I hear Anna's voice in my head telling me to be happy. The image of the little girl comes to mind and pain slashes through me. And ache forms deep inside.

You do *want that dream to come true*, my own voice says in my head. *You want it so much you ache for it.*

"Nick?" Chris says from behind me.

When her fingers graze my back, I jerk away and jump out of bed. I stumble in my haste to get my clothes on. I've got to get out of here. I can't be near her right now.

"Nick, what's going on?" Chris says, her voice laced with panic.

I pull my jeans up my legs, and without looking at her, I tell her, "I've got to go."

My shirt comes on next, when I sense her getting out of bed. She comes to stand beside me.

"Tell me what happened. What is it? Another dream?" She lays a hand on my arm, but I snatch it away.

"I just need to leave. I can't be here right now." I go for my boots next. Sitting on the side of the bed, I yank them on.

"I can't do this anymore," Chris says, her voice cracking. I look at her and see the same pain I saw in my dream. My stomach plummets at the sight. I yank my hands through my hair. "I can't, Nick. I thought I could, but it hurts too much."

I walk to her on numb legs. I know this is it. I knew from the beginning it would end. I also knew I would end up hurting her. The one woman who could give me everything, and all I've ever given her is pain. I'm a bastard, and I hate myself for every bastard thing I've done to her.

She doesn't look at me as I stand in front of her. Needing to see her eyes, I put my hands on her cheeks and bring her face up to mine. Resting my forehead against hers, I watch as silent tears fall down her face.

"I'm so sorry, Chris," I tell her with a thick voice. "I'm sorry for everything I've ever done to you. For every pain I've caused you. I wish so much I could be different, that I could be the man you deserve. The man who could give you every part of himself. I can't be him. I don't possess all the pieces of me to give. You deserve someone whole, and I'll never be whole again. I'll never be brave enough to take that chance on love again. It broke me last time. This time, with you, it would destroy me."

A sob escapes her throat. She brings her hands to my stomach and clenches her fists into my shirt. I lean down to kiss her lips softly one more time. Pulling back, I look at her face and see the heartache I've caused.

I let her go and walk away. I'm at the door when she stops me with her words, making my heart pound rapidly inside my chest and my lungs freeze.

"I love you," she says on a sob.

I squeeze my eyes shut, so fucking scared of her words. I drop my head and keep my back to her.

"I just wanted you to know. I love you, Nick. I have for a long time. And I know if you had let me in your heart I could have made you happy. I know you think you don't have any love left to give. But what you don't get is, love is endless. There're no measurements or an end to love. The heart can hold any amount. It can be scary and frightening, and it can be hard, but it can also be beautiful. The beauty comes after all the scary and hard stuff. You just have to work through it and earn it. I may not be what you want, but I could have given that to you. We could have given it to each other. I hope one day you can find your happiness, even that isn't with me."

Her words destroy me. They're uttered with so much pain. Pain that I've caused. I ball my hands into fists, fighting the urge to go to her. To get down on my knees and beg and plead with her to forgive me for everything I've done. To tell her I want exactly what she said she can give me. I want her love. I want the happiness she promises. But I'm a coward. I'm a coward and a bastard for not allowing myself to let go of a dream I can no longer have, and for realizing I could have another dream that could be just as good, if not better, and not grabbing a hold of it.

On laden feet, I walk away without looking back, knowing that I'm breaking the one woman who means more to me than anything else in this world.

I PULL UP TO MY darkened house with a heavy heart. I get out of my truck and head toward the porch, but at the last minute make a detour to the barn. Flipping the light on, I walk to the work bench and the cabinets above it. I open the door and immediately see what I'm looking for and grab it off the shelf. Cracking open the cheap bottle of liquor, I take two hefty swallows. I wince as the harsh liquor burns its way down my throat and into my gut. I stashed the bottle here months ago and forgot about it until now. I've missed the taste, but at the same time, I hate it. It shows my weakness.

With bottle in hand, I walk back to the house and head straight to the basement door with one destination in mind.

Pushing the door open to Anna's room, I'm met with a heavy wave of her scent. A chill runs down my spine, but I ignore it. I pick an open box and sit next to it on the floor. After taking another couple swallows of my liquor, I slide the box closer and tip it over until the contents spill out in front of me. Hundreds of pictures spread out across the floor. All of me and Anna, ranging from when we were kids to adults. I sift through and look at each of them. The pain of seeing Anna happy and carefree hurts, but the breathless pain I'm used to feeling isn't there. I love Anna and I'll always love her, but I need to let her go. I can't keep doing this. It's literally destroying my life. I'm terrified to let her go, but I know I need to.

I know what I have to do, but gathering the courage to do it is something I have to work on. I haven't been back to her gravesite since the day we buried her. I don't know if it's because I was in denial or if the thought of going to the place where her body is, is just too painful, but I've never been able to bring myself back to that place. I'm ashamed of that fact.

"I'm sorry, Anna," I murmur into the quiet room.

I pick the pictures up and put them back in the box. Grabbing a roll of tape off another box, I slide a piece across the top, sealing it shut. I do that to every box that's open, and each one I close, pain lances my heart. Once they are all closed, I grab my bottle of cheap liquor by the neck and carry it with me to the open doorway. I don't want the shit, so I'm going to pour it down the drain.

I turn and take one last look at the room.

"I'll always love you," I whisper, then turn and close the door behind me.

Chris

A COUPLE OF NIGHTS LATER, I'm sitting at the bar at Jaxon's with Bailey and Mia beside me. They came by earlier and demanded I come out with them, saying it's been too long since I've been away from the apartment. It's true. Besides going to Jase's house the other day, going to work, and then to Jaxon's for my shifts, I've been huddled up in my apartment. I just have no desire to deal with people. I miss hanging out with my friends, but I also need the time alone.

Bailey doesn't know what happened between me and Nick two nights ago and Mia still doesn't know about the baby. I feel terrible for not telling her. My reasoning is I still haven't told Nick, and he deserves to know before even more people do. As soon as I opened the door to the two women, Mia knew right away something was wrong. Before she got a chance to ask me about it, Bailey dragged me from my apartment, saying we were going to play pool. I've avoided Mia's questioning gaze all night. I've also avoided being alone with her, because I know she'll ask me what's going on as soon as we are. When she tried ordering us shots, I turned mine down with the excuse of a headache coming on and not wanting to make it worse.

I've tried showing that I'm enjoying myself, but I know I fall short. Jase is here as well and he keeps giving me worried glances. I know he's wondering if I've told Nick yet. I've avoided his phone calls the last couple of days, not wanting to deal with telling him I haven't. Having built the courage to tell Nick a couple days ago, I found I lost it again after what happened that night. I know keeping it from him is wrong, and I'm sure Jase thinks badly of me for it. I plan on stopping by Nick's house tomorrow after work to tell him. It's been kept a secret long enough.

Speaking of Nick, my breath whooshes out when I see him walking through the door. His eyes immediately catch mine and he stops in the doorway, like he's going to turn back around. He looks like he hasn't slept much, and I wonder if his dreams are keeping him up again. He obviously had a bad one that night in my apartment and that's what had him so spooked.

After standing in the doorway for several seconds, he lets the door close behind him and walks over to take a seat on the other side of Bailey.

I turn back to face the bar and eat the rest of my burger.

"So," Bailey says. "Thanksgiving is coming up soon and Jaxon's mom wants everyone at her and Levi's house for dinner. That includes your mom, Andrew."

Andrew leans on the bar, grabs a length of Bailey's hair, and gives it a gentle tug. "I'll talk to her about it."

She nods and adds, "She also invited Ally, Becky, and Brent."

"I'll talk to them, too. I'm not sure of their plans yet. They may be going to one of their parents' houses."

"Okay. Let me know when you do, so I can give her a head count." She turns to Nick and asks, "You'll be in town, right?"

It's loud in the bar, so I don't hear his reply, but obviously it is a yes, because Bailey looks happy with his answer.

"Hey!" all of a sudden Andrew shouts across the room. "Keep your damn eyes off my man's ass before I pluck them out."

We all turn to see Jase standing by the pool tables looking back at Andrew with a smirk on his face. Jesse and Mac are there with another guy. The poor unknown guy looks frightened by Andrew's shouted words and immediately walks to the other side of the pool table, far from Jase.

A few chuckles are heard as we turn back to face Andrew.

"Can't take the damn man anywhere without someone ogling him," Andrew says, taking away my empty plate and wiping the counter. "No lie. We were in town the other day and some fool ran off the road because he was eyeing him instead of watching the fucking road."

"I think maybe you're embellishing that tale a little bit, Andrew," Jaxon says, walking up beside Andrew and catching the conversation.

"The hell I am!" he replies incredulously. "The guy damn near took out a telephone pole. Luckily, he missed and hit a mailbox instead. Besides, have you looked at Jase lately? He's better looking than me, and that's saying something, because, you know...." He trails off and sweeps his hands down his body.

"Yeah, yeah, we know. You're one hot mofo," Mia says on the other side of me, rolling her eyes.

He throws her a wink. "You said it."

We all laugh, because, well... that's what we do when we're around Andrew. He's conceited, but he's also one of the most loyal and nicest guys anyone could ever know. I look down at his shirt and smirk. It's black with white letters that read Cocks Wanted above a rainbow-colored rooster. He sees me looking and grins cockily at me.

Mac walks behind Mia and puts his arms around her and places his hands on the bar. She snuggles back against him. My stomach rumbles and hunger pangs hit me. I just had a burger and fries but it feels like I haven't eaten in a week. You'd think I was eight months pregnant with all the food I'm scarfing down lately. The nausea and headaches haven't been back since that day I took the test. I'm grateful for that, but I'm going to be as big as a house before I have this baby.

"Hey, Andrew," I call before he can walk away. "Can you get Hoot to cook me another burger?"

His eyes widen at my request. "Damn, woman. You just had one, and fries on top of that. You eat like you're pregnant or something."

I hear several laughs but they sound distant. His words have me freezing on my stool and all the air in my lungs whooshing out. There's music playing from the jukebox, but I swear the place just went dead silent. I see spots float across my eyes and sound is muffled.

All I can do is stare at Andrew. When he sees my reaction to his words, his lips form the words "Oh shit" before his eyes leave mine to look at, I assume, Nick. No one moves around me, but I can feel all their eyes on me. I draw in a large lungful of air and let it back out, trying to relieve some of the pressure in my chest.

"Oh my God, you're pregnant," Mia says softly beside me.

I don't move my eyes off Andrew. All I can do is hope and pray that Nick didn't hear him. I don't want him to find out this way. I need to be the one to tell him.

My hopes are dashed when I feel a hand clamp down painfully on my arm. I know who the hand belongs to, but I don't want to look. I'm terrified of what I'll see.

"Is what he said true?" Nick demands. My hearing comes back tenfold. It sounds like the question was shouted in my ear.

I squeeze my eyes shut to push the tears away, and turn to face him. The look in his eyes when I open mine again has me shrinking back in my chair. I've never seen them look so hard and filled with hatred. He doesn't look like any Nick I've ever seen.

"Nick, man, careful," Mac warns him.

Nick ignores him and brings his face closer to mine. "Is it true?" he asks harshly through gritted teeth.

I move my eyes over his shoulder to see Bailey looking at me with sympathy and concern. She has tears brimming in her eyes. I look next at Andrew and Jaxon. Andrew still looks shocked, but also apologetic. Jaxon has his narrowed eyes pinned on Nick.

Nick grabs my chin and jerks my head back to him. "Look at me, damn it!"

"Hey, asshole!" I hear a shout from across the room. "Get your fucking hand off my sister!" Jase storms up beside Nick and yanks his hand away.

It happens so fast there's no way anyone could have stopped it. I cry out when Nick whips around to Jase and slams his fist into his jaw, causing him to stumble back a few steps and bump into a table. Both Andrew and Jaxon jump over the bar. Andrew heads to Jase, who's rubbing his jaw, and Jaxon goes to Nick, who has turned back to me. I watch in horror as Jase pushes Andrew off him and charges toward Nick.

"You motherfucker!" Jase roars as he plows into his back, pushing him forward. I screech as Mac pulls me out of the way and they ram into the bar right where I was standing, before falling to the floor in a tangled mass of muscle.

"Stop!" I scream at the top of my lungs, fisting my hands in my hair. "Please, just stop!"

They both hear me and come to a stop. Nick's on top of Jase on the floor, with his fist reared back, ready to lay into him. When he looks up at me, I see a red mark forming above his eye. Jase doesn't look much better, a purple bruise on his jaw already forming. I hate seeing them like this. I hate knowing it's because of me they are fighting. I feel a twinge of pain in my stomach at being the cause of the two men I love the most wanting to hurt each other.

"Please stop fighting," I yell hoarsely.

I look at Nick, who's crawled off Jase and is now standing facing me. Andrew's trying to help Jase up, but he looks too pissed to want the help. Andrew brings his piercing eyes at Nick. He looks like he wants to take a swing at Nick himself as he glares at his back. "Yes, I'm pregnant. Okay? I'm sorry I haven't told you yet. I was still trying to come to grips with it myself."

I see him trying to calm himself down. He takes a couple of deep breaths and squeezes his eyes shut. When he opens them again, they look wild and crazy. His hands clench and unclench at his side.

"Let's go," he says, and takes a step toward me.

"She's not going anywhere with you, fucker," Jase growls, trying to throw Andrew off, who now has his arms around his middle.

"Back the hell off, Jase. This isn't your concern," Nick tells Jase, keeping his blazing blue eyes pinned on me.

"The fuck it's not, you bastard. It was my sister you were grabbing."

"Nick, maybe you should calm down first," Mac says, coming up beside him.

"Fuck you, Mac!" he snarls. "Chris and I need to talk and we're going to do it alone."

"The fuck you—"

"Both of you stop! Now!" I shout. I walk over to Jase and give him a hug. Pulling back, I beg him with my eyes for him to understand.

"He's right," I tell him softly. "We need to talk in private. I shouldn't have waited to tell him."

"Chris—"

I cut him off.

"I'll be fine, Jase. You need to trust me. Please."

He yanks me forward and we wrap our arms around each other. Tears clog my throat when I think of the pain I've not only caused Nick, but Jase as well. I know this has to be hard on him. I'm his sister, and in his eyes, he's supposed to take all my pain away. But with this, there's nothing he can do. I've brought this on myself and only I can fix it. I pull back and can tell it's taking everything in him to let me go. His jaw ticks as he grinds his molars together. His eyes flicker over me and the look he sends Nick's way would bring most men to the knees.

I walk back over to Nick, who's watching me with his dark brown eyes. I don't look at the others as we turn and make our way to the exit down the hallway. Nick doesn't say anything and neither do I. I feel like I'm walking to my doom. I knew Nick would be pissed I kept this from him, but the way he looked in the bar was beyond livid. Yet, underlying that emotion was another. He tried to hide it, but I saw the deep-seated fear in his eyes. My heart cracked seeing that fear.

I lead Nick through the back door and up the stairs that lead to my apartment. Unlocking my door, we step through and walk to the living room. When I turn to face him, the anger on his face has me taking a step back. I've never been afraid of Nick, never feared he would physically harm me, but if there ever was a time for that, now would be it.

"How long have you known?" he asks, his voice deceptively quiet.

I pull in a deep breath and answer him. "A little over a week."

I wince at the look that crosses his face. If eyes could shoot laser beams, I have no doubt Nick's would be burning holes in me right now.

"Is it mine?"

His question leaves me feeling like I was punched in the gut, and I almost double over from the pain of it. My breath leaves my lungs with a loud hiss. My chest gets tight and my stomach muscles spasm.

"Did you really just ask me that?" I whisper.

"Yes, I did," he growls, and takes a step back from me. "Now answer the fucking question!"

"Of course the baby's yours," I cry. "I haven't been with anyone except you for almost a year!"

"How in the fuck am I supposed to believe you!" he shouts. "You've kept this baby from me for almost a week!" He stops and turns, roughly raking his fingers through his hair. He whips back around and pins me with his intense gaze. "You knew that day I came by your place. The day you were sick. And then again, the night you asked me over. Why didn't you tell me then?" he demands to know.

I hold my hands tightly together in front of me and tell him the truth.

"I found out the day you found me sick. It was actually Bailey and Karyn who figured it out. The possibility of being pregnant hadn't even crossed my mind until they mentioned it could be the reason for my migraines. And I had you over that next time to tell you, but... we got sidetracked. Then you bolted in the middle of the night."

"Bailey and Karyn know? But you didn't tell me? Who in the hell else knows?"

"Just them and Jase."

"Fuck!" he roars to the ceiling, making me jump.

I watch him pace back and forth, wearing a hole in my brown carpet.

"I'm sorry, Nick," I tell him croakily. "I was going to tell you. It was a shock for me, too. But I swear I was going to tell you."

He looks at me scathingly as he passes by. All I can do is stand there helplessly, my heart breaking with each pass he makes.

"Did you fucking plan this?" he asks, whipping around to face me.

"What?" I screech, appalled, hurt, and pissed beyond belief he would think I would do something like that. I ball my hands into fists. "How can you ask me that, Nick?"

"You said you were on the pill. For all I know, you lied. You've been after me for over a year. Who's to say you weren't desperate and thought you could trap me by getting pregnant?"

"Nick," I plead, tears gathering in my eyes. "I would never do something like that. Yes, I love you, but I would never even think about doing something like that. You know me better than that."

He stops across the room from me. "I don't know you at all, Chris."

"And whose fault is that?" I ask, my voice rising. I don't give him time to answer. "You've never tried getting to know me."

"Because I didn't want to!" he says, his voice rising. "I didn't want to know you! I wanted you to leave me alone! You kept pushing and pushing until I finally gave in! And now you're pregnant with a child I don't want!" He stops and lets his head drop forward.

I've known from the beginning that he wasn't going to want this baby, but hearing him confirm it makes the pain of that knowledge so much worse.

I wince when I feel a small twinge of pain in my lower back, but I ignore it.

"Nick, please." I take a step toward him. He whips his head up at my movement and takes a step back, putting more distance between us. I forge ahead anyway. "I know this is a shock to you. I didn't want to have a baby this way either. But we are, and we need to try to work something out for the baby."

The look he sends my way has me stopping in my tracks. I hold my breath at the pure venom in his eyes. Never has he looked at me with eyes that carried so much disgust. Another niggling pain hits my lower back, but again, I push it away.

"I said I don't want the baby." His words are calm, almost lifeless. "You did this; you need to fix it. Get rid of it, I don't care. I'm leaving town. When I get back, I don't want to see your face. Just stay the fuck away from me."

"What... what do you mean?" I gasp, not believing I'm hearing what he's saying. "You can't be saying what I think you are." There's no way he's telling me to destroy the small life I carry in my womb. There's no way he could be so heartless.

"I don't care what you do with it. I just don't want anything to do with you or the baby. I refuse to let you or *it* force me into a situation I don't want."

"Get out!" I cry through a thick throat. "Get out of my apartment!"

"Chris—"

"No!" I scream. "Get the fuck out of my apartment." I run over and shove him hard in the chest. He stumbles back a couple of feet with my harsh push. "Leave!" I demand and push him again. I can't look at him anymore. Just the sight of him makes me sick to my stomach. Never in a million years did I think Nick would be so heartless. He didn't outright say kill our baby, but I know that's what he meant.

"You're not the man I thought you were, and you're certainly not the man your friends claim you are!" I yell hysterically. He grabs my hands, trying to keep me from pushing him, but I'm past being rational and push his hands aside. "That man would never demand I kill an innocent baby! I hate you! I hate you for everything you've ever done to me! I hate you for asking me to kill my baby!"

"I fucking told you I could never be the person you thought I was!" he snarls at me.

I roll up on my toes, get in his face, and scream, "Get the fuck out!"

"Fucking gladly!" he roars back and turns to the door. He stops and faces me again when he has it open, like he's going to say something, but I don't give him a chance before I slam it in his face. I need him out of my sight now. I can't believe I ever thought he was a good man. I can't believe I let myself fall for a man who could be so cruel.

I frantically reach for the deadbolt and twist the lock. My chest heaves with adrenaline as I slump back against the door. I hear the thump-thump of Nick's feet taking him down the stairs. The sound sends shards to my soul.

A searing pain hits my stomach and back, and I bend over double with it. I gasp for breath and stumble back to the living room in search of my phone. I feel wetness between my thighs and fear strikes me.

"No," I moan. "No, no, no."

I search wildly for my phone before I realize I left it sitting on the bar.

"Oh, God," I gasp as the pain doubles, then triples. "Please, no. Please don't take my baby," I cry.

Hunched over, I wobble to the door, clutching my stomach. Looking down, I see blood soaking through my jeans. Nausea rolls in my stomach. I manage to get the door open and stumble out into the hallway. I try, I try so damn hard to make it to the stairs, but the pain is just too unbearable. Falling on my side at the top of the stairs, I huddle into a ball and wrap my arms around my stomach, desperately trying to protect the precious life I carry, but already knowing that it's too late.

twenty-one

Nick

I PUSH THROUGH THE back door from Chris's apartment and slam it behind me. Storming around the building to my truck, I whip out my phone and send a text to Jaxon to tell him I'm leaving and that someone needs to check on Chris, before yanking my door open, climbing in, and peeling out of the driveway. I may be beyond pissed at Chris, but I recognize hysteria when I see it, and Chris was damn near hysterical when I walked out.

I can't believe that fucking bitch kept something like this from me.

A fucking baby!

My hands grip the steering wheel until my knuckles hurt. My fucking dream is here to haunt me. I don't want a damn baby with Chris. I never thought I would have a child with anyone other than Anna, and the thought of someone else taking her place twists my stomach into knots.

I head toward home, intent on grabbing my shit and heading out of town. I hadn't planned on leaving for West Virginia until tomorrow, but I've got to get out of here tonight. Seeing the pain on Chris's face sent a searing pain in my chest. Never, after everything I've done to her, have I seen such pain in her eyes. She looked ruined, and seeing that look broke something inside me. But I just can't....

I slam my hand down on the wheel as I drive the dark curvy roads. I was a complete bastard to ask her if I was the father. I know she's not the type of person to sleep with random guys. She's wholesome and sweet. But what did it, what put the nail in my coffin, was when I told her I wanted her to take care of the situation, to get rid of it. Like a baby was some garbage that could be taken out and dumped. As soon as the words left my mouth, I knew that's not what I wanted. The thought of Chris ending the precious life we created together wraps a band around my lungs so tight I can't draw in breath. But I'm scared as fuck and hurt, and I wanted to hurt her just as much. Telling her to get rid of the baby definitely accomplished that. I know she would never do anything to harm our child, and I hate knowing she thinks I would.

My phone rings on the seat beside me. I don't pick it up or look at the screen. I'm sure it's either Jaxon or Andrew calling to rip me a new one. I deserve it for what I've put Chris through. She was pretty upset when I left. Instead, I ignore it and put more pressure on the gas pedal. The faster I get my shit, the sooner I can get the hell out of here. I need time to think and come to grips with the fact I'm going to be a dad. The vision of the little brown-haired girl from my dream pops in my head. I give my head a shake to make it go away, the pain of it too great.

I reach over and grab my phone when it starts ringing again. Without looking at the screen, I turn it off. I can't deal with someone bitching in my ear right now. I know I was a total asshole, and I've got a lot of apologizing I have to do when I get back to town, but right now I need to be left alone with my thoughts.

An hour and a half later, I pull into a rest stop to get gas and something to eat. I decide to shoot an e-mail to my client to let him know I'll be in town early tomorrow and see if he wants to move our appointment up. Even being a hundred miles away, I'm going to need to stay busy.

When I power up my phone, I see I have twelve missed calls and five missed texts. Most are from Jaxon, but a few are from Andrew, Mia, and Bailey. A sense of foreboding hits as I pull up the first text message.

Jaxon: *Where in the fuck are you? Call me.*

Something's wrong. I can feel it. I pull up the next one, this time from Andrew.

Andrew: *Wherever in the hell you are, you need to get back here. Now.*

The next text has my heart in my throat and undeniable fear spiking through me.

Jaxon: *Chris is in the hospital. Fucking call me you bastard!*

My fucking heart drops to my stomach and sweat starts to bead on my forehead. My hands shake so bad I can barely scroll though my call log to call Jaxon.

Please, God, don't let it be what I think it is. Please let her and the baby be okay. The stark pain on Chris's face comes to mind. I fucking left her there. I was a bastard to her and then I left her. I told her I wanted her to kill our baby and then walked out the fucking door. What kind of man does that?

"You're not the man I thought you were, and you're certainly not the man your friends claim you are!"

"That man would never demand I kill an innocent baby! I hate you!"

She's right. I'm nowhere near the man she thought I was. But I want to be. I want to be the man worthy of her and of our baby. I want the opportunity to have a life with her. I want to let go of the pain and be whole again. I want to be there for her and cherish her. I want to be brave and grab hold of what having her promises. And I want to be a father to our baby. I just don't know if I can be brave enough to do those things. Will I be a good dad? Will I be good enough for Chris? Can I let go of something I've held on to for so long? I've got to at least try. For her, for me, and for our baby.

Jaxon answers on the first ring, bringing me out of my thoughts.

"Where in the fuck are you?" he growls in my ear.

"What happened?" I demand my own question.

"Tell me where you are first," he asks in a hard voice.

"South Ohio. Now tell me what the fuck happened. Is Chris okay? The baby?" My questions are frantic. I need to know if they are okay.

"Why weren't you answering your phone?" He fucking asks another question.

"Jaxon," I growl, my impatience wearing then.

I hear his sigh over the phone and it does nothing to help my pounding heart

"You need to come home," he says quietly, so unlike the angry man I heard a few seconds ago. What he says next steals all my breath and leaves me feeling crippled. "They're monitoring Chris. The baby... they think she lost the baby."

I drop my head to the steering wheel. A pain enters my chest, so sharp it feels like a blade is slashing me open from the inside out. It hurts to breathe, so I let the air out of my lungs and just sit there.

"Nick?" I hear Jaxon say.

"I'm here," I say numbly. I can't feel anything right now, except for the pain that's centered right over my heart.

"Come home."

"I'm on my way."

We hang up, but I just sit there for several minutes.

"Let go, Nick, before it's too late."

Anna's words come back to me. She knew, in my dream, Anna warned me. And I ignored it because of my fear of the unknown. And because I wasn't ready to let go of her. Instead, I walked away from a dream that I now know I desperately want.

"Please don't leave me," I beg her instead with a broken whisper. "Please stay with me."

She smiles sadly. "You know I can't. But you can be happy if only you'll let yourself. This can be your future, if only you'll grab on to it."

That dream will haunt me for the rest of my life. I had a chance to find something I never thought I could have again because the woman I wanted it with was taken away from me. I destroyed that chance. It's my fault Chris is currently in the hospital, more than likely having or already had a miscarriage. It was my reaction to the news that upset Chris. And then I ran and wasn't there for her. She'll never forgive me for that. And I don't blame her. But I won't run again, no matter the outcome. Whether she lost the baby or not, I'll be by her side and we'll both get through it together. I won't let her push me away.

I don't know when my feelings for Chris changed. Maybe they were there the whole time. Maybe knowing that I've probably already lost her, I realized how much I really wanted her. Maybe I didn't want to acknowledge them because my grief was in the way. Or maybe it was her tenacious behavior and her unwillingness to give up and to always see the good in me. It doesn't matter though. Chris has become a vital part of my life, and I refuse to live it without her. It took a tragedy to realize this, but it won't be in vain.

I pick my head up, turn the key to start my truck, and head home, knowing I have a fight ahead of me, but also finally knowing what I want. And that I'm willing to fight for it, no matter what it takes.

A COUPLE OF HOURS LATER, I pull into the main entrance to the hospital and find a parking spot. I barely turn off my truck before I'm opening the door and jumping out. I run straight for the front desk and give them Chris's name. I'm told she's up in Maternity, and I run over to the bank of elevators. My finger pushes impatiently on the button, but the fucking doors won't open. I'm just about to turn around and find the stairs when the doors slip apart. I wait with gritted teeth as several people get off. I find the number three and punch it, and then the Close button when the doors don't slide shut fast enough. I'm nearly bouncing on my heels as I watch the number two light up, then the number three. What feels like ten minutes later, but in reality was only a few seconds, the elevator doors slide open again. I rush over to the nurses' station.

"Christabelle Matthews. She was brought in a few hours ago," I tell the blonde nurse, my fingers tapping the counter impatiently. My nerves are shot with not knowing what's going on.

"And your name, Sir?" she asks.

"Nick Daniels. Chris's fiancé and the father of the baby." The lie rolls off my tongue easily as I look at the nurse.

She turns back to her computer and is typing something when I hear my name called.

"Nick!"

I turn to see Jaxon coming my way. I leave the desk and walk quickly over to him.

"How is she? The baby?"

"Let's move somewhere more private."

He turns on his heel before I can say anything. I follow him to a corner with a few chairs. Karyn, Ethan, Mac, and Mia are there. All three are looking at me with sympathy oozing from their eyes. The look in Jaxon's when he turns to face me, mixed with their expressions, has alarm spiking though me.

"Jaxon—"

"She lost the baby," he says quietly, sadness lacing his voice.

My legs, no longer able to hold my weight, give out, and I fall back in the chair that is thankfully behind me. I slump forward and rest my head in my hands. The dull ache in my chest robs me of breath. My hands shake and tears brim in my eyes.

Jaxon sits quietly beside me.

"How is she?" I ask through a tight throat.

"Not good. Bailey, Andrew, and Jase are in there now."

I nod and we sit in silence for a few minutes. I try to wrap my head around the fact that in less than three hours I found out I was going to be a dad and it was cruelly ripped away from me. I can't help but feel responsible. It was my reaction that upset Chris.

"I need to see her," I tell Jaxon as I lift my head and get up on unsteady legs.

I turn toward the nurses' station to ask what room she's in, but Jaxon's hard grip on my arm stops me.

"You need to give her time."

I spin around to face him, not believing he's telling me that. Chris needs me right now, and I refuse to be anywhere else but beside her.

"What?" I growl. "No! I need to go to her. She needs me."

"Nick, you need to give her time," he says more firmly.

I rip my arm from his hold and step closer to him.

"No," I bark at him. "I'm going—"

"She doesn't want to see you right now." He cuts me off. "Like I said, give her time."

Out the corner of my eye, I see Mac and Mia get up from their chairs and make their way toward us.

Jaxon's words are gentle, but the meaning behind them is anything but. I feel like I've been punched in the gut a hundred times with serrated-edged brass knuckles. My heart feels like it's been shredded into a million tiny pieces and then ran over by a Mack truck over and over again.

I look at Jaxon. He's watching me with empathy. He knows how much this hurts me. He's known all along there was something between me and Chris. I was too stupid to see it and now it might be too late. The single time Chris needed me, I wasn't there. I was running away, licking my own wounds, thinking only of myself. Chris didn't ask to become pregnant. I wince at the reminder that I accused her of doing just that. And now that she needs me again, she doesn't want me there with her.

"You bastard." We turn at the snarled words to see red-eyed Jase standing next to a weeping Bailey. Andrew has his arms wrapped around her, but he lets her go to stand in front of Jase. Jase walks around Andrew and charges toward me with determined steps.

He's five feet away when Mac steps in his path. "Jase, you need to calm down."

Jase doesn't take his hate-filled eyes off me when he leans to the side and hisses, "This is your fault. You don't belong here. Get the fuck out."

"I'm not going anywhere," I growl at him through the hurt his words cause.

He has every right to be pissed. What he said is true. This is my fault. I did this to Chris. I was the bastard who left her. I'm the asshole who's treated her like complete shit. I'm the one who allowed our fucked-up relationship to start, knowing it would end in heartache. But I won't be the one who leaves her now, no matter what Jase says or how much Chris doesn't want me here.

"Do you know how I found her?" Jase asks quietly, pain etching his voice. When I don't say anything, he continues, slashing my already battered heart into smithereens. "At the top of her fucking stairs, lying in a ball, clutching her belly, moaning and begging God to not take her baby. Her pants soaked with blood and her face pale. That's how I found her. Were you there for her?" He doesn't give me time to answer. "Fuck no, you weren't. You were off God knows where, while my sister was left on the floor losing her baby. Your baby." His voice breaks at the end.

I fist my hands to keep from raking them across my ears, the pain from Jase's tortured words shooting daggers into them. I look around the room and see all eyes are focused on me, filled with despair.

"I'm not leaving," I tell him in a low voice. "I won't see her, because it's not what she wants right now, but I'm staying here."

Andrew steps up to him when he opens his mouth to argue. Whatever Andrew says to him has him changing his argument to a simple, "Just stay the fuck away from her." Then with a look of utter revulsion, he turns, goes to the other side of the waiting room, takes a seat, and bows his head. Andrew looks at me sadly before following Jase and pulling him into his arms.

I wipe my hands down my face and squeeze my eyes shut. Feeling a soft hand on my back, I turn and open my eyes to find Bailey standing there, tears sliding down her face. Seeing pain in her eyes only makes my own pain worse. Without thought, I snatch her in my arms and hold on for dear life. I bury my face in her thick hair. Her arms wrap around my middle and squeeze me just as tight.

I have no idea how I'm going to get through this. And Chris. My pain is bad enough, but knowing hers is probably ten times worse decimates me.

I feel drained by the time I pull back from the comfort of Bailey's arms. I feel so damn exhausted and drained. My arms hang limply by my side and my head feels too heavy to hold up. I take a seat in one of the chairs and Bailey sits beside me with Jaxon on her other side. Mia takes the remaining seat to my right and grabs my hand. I look over at her, expecting to see disgust or disdain in her features, but it's not there. Her expression is filled with sadness and compassion. Why the anger isn't there, I have no idea. Everyone here should be mad at me. But then again, these people are my friends. No, they're closer than friends. They are my family. And as much as they should, they won't hold my mistakes against me. They aren't the type to do that.

"She's gonna be okay," she says quietly.

Physically, I'm sure she will be. Women have miscarriages every day. It's the emotional damage I'm worried about.

I nod, but don't say anything. Anything I have to say needs to be said to Chris. There's so much I need to tell her. I just hope she gives me the chance.

"Do they know how long they're keeping her here?" I ask whomever knows the answer.

It's Bailey who answers, using a gentle voice. "Just for tonight. She was only eight weeks, so they aren't doing a dilation and curettage because they think she'll pass everything on her own, but they want to make sure there's no complications."

Eight weeks. Our baby was eight weeks. Two months. Fifty-six days. I knew of her only one of those days and I already loved her.

"Why isn't anyone back with her? She shouldn't be alone right now."

"She wanted us to leave. She doesn't want anyone back there with her right now. She became upset when we refused to leave, so we decided to give her some space for a little while."

"Fuck," I mutter, fisting my hair with trembling hands. I don't like the thought of her being alone. No one should be alone during a time like this. It's not good for them. I, of all people, know this. I realize now that I shouldn't have pushed my friends aside like I did after I lost Anna. I should have let them in. Just like Chris needs to let us in now.

We all sit in silence for a while. Ethan took Karyn home about an hour ago. She's heavily pregnant and needs as much rest as she can get. Hours pass quietly. With the exception of Ethan and Karyn, we all stay vigilant in the waiting room. Jase and Mia went back a while ago to check on Chris, but came back a few minutes later saying she was sleeping.

Andrew and Jase get up from their chairs. Andrew stops to tell me they are going to the cafeteria for some coffee and ask if Jaxon or I want one. We both nod. Mia and Bailey are both curled up in their chairs fast asleep. Mac is over by the bank of windows, seemingly looking out into nothing.

Jaxon's mom calls for an update, so he gets up and walks across the room to speak with her without disturbing the women. The opportunity and need to see if Chris is okay are too great. I look over at the nurses' station and see she's on the phone with her back to me.

I take one last look at the women, then at Mac and Jaxon, and carefully get up from my seat. I don't know what room Chris is in, but I'll peek in every damn one I come across until I find hers. I just need a glimpse of her, something to reassure me that she's safe and sound.

I walk down the hall and look in several open doors before I come across the one I want. I see her deep red hair first. She's on her side facing away from me, huddled up into a ball. She looks so small and childlike lying there like she is. I stand in the doorway, contemplating going in. I know she doesn't want to see me, with good reason, and I don't want to upset her, but I need to see her green eyes.

I must make a noise, because she slowly straightens her legs and turns on her back. When her face comes into view, my gut drops down to my toes. Her eyes are red rimmed and slightly swollen, like she's been crying. Her already fair skin is even more pale. It's only been a several hours since I last saw her, but I'd swear she's lost weight in those short hours. Her once beautiful bright green eyes now look dull and lifeless.

She only glances at me for a second, and in that second I see a bottomless pit of pain before she turns so her back is facing me again.

"Leave," she says in a voice void of all emotion.

Instead of heeding her demand, I take a few steps closer to her. I know I should leave. The last thing I want to do is upset her, but the need to make sure she's truly okay is too much to ignore.

I stop by the bed and just look down at her. She's looking sightlessly forward. Her arms are around her stomach with her knees drawn up to them, like she's trying to protect a baby that's no longer there. Her pillow looks to be soaked from her tears. The sight of her defeated form shreds my insides.

"Chris," I say on a croak and reach out to place my hand on her shoulder. "Please, sugar—"

She violently flinches away from me. "Don't"—she turns menacing eyes to me—"fucking touch me. You got what you wanted. She's gone." She ends with a broken sob.

"No, baby, no," I whisper brokenly. Her words send jagged pains through my stomach.

Not able to bear her cries, I reach out again, intent on taking her in my arms. I only get as far as rolling her on her back before she starts bucking on the bed, shoving with her small arms to push me away.

"No!" she screams. "Leave me alone! Don't touch me! I don't want to see you." She slams her fists against my arms.

I take a step back, shocked at her hysterical behavior. She curls back into a ball and crushes my heart all over again when she starts crying uncontrollably. She tucks her head in her arms and weeps so hard her body is shaking.

There's a sound behind me, but I can't take my eyes off the sight of Chris coming undone in front of me. Never have I seen grief so great before. A nurse rushes past me and goes to Chris's side, gently consoling her.

"Sir, you need to leave," comes a firm voice behind me.

Tearing my eyes off the crumpled female in bed, I turn to see a nurse standing two feet from me. Her eyes are filled with regret and compassion. I turn back to Chris, who has quieted down some but is still sobbing. The nurse by her side is soothingly running her hand down her hair and back.

I don't want to leave. I want to stay here and witness Chris break. This is my punishment for everything I've done to her. Every cruel word I've said or action I've taken. But I know I need to leave for her sake. She's already going through so much right now as it is, I won't add any more stress to her. I won't be far though. I'll never stray far from her again. I'll wait however long it takes.

Taking one last look at the woman who's come to mean more to me than anything else in the world, I turn on my heel and walk out of her room, leaving every part of me I once told her I didn't possess to give anymore.

twenty-two

Chris

EVEN THROUGH MY inconsolable crying I hear Nick leave. As soon as he's out the door, my sobs become worse. When I heard the noise behind me a few minutes ago, he was the last person I expected to see. I told everyone I didn't want to see him. I just can't handle it right now. After what he said to me in my apartment, the way he acted, there's no way I can see him. I don't know if what he said was how he really felt or not, but knowing the thought even crossed his mind ruined something inside me.

I pull back from the nurse a few minutes later and wipe my face. My head is pounding from all the crying I've done the last few hours. I'm exhausted, but I'm scared to go to sleep. The couple times I have, I relive the scene in my apartment. Then I forget I've lost the precious life that was inside me, and I wake again to the crushing pain of the loss. Is this how Nick feels when he wakes from his dreams? Does he relive Anna dying night after night?

The thought is depressing and terrifies me.

The nurse injects something in my IV to help me sleep before leaving. I told her I didn't want anything, but she's insistent.

"Your body needs rest to recuperate," she tells me gently. "To do that, you need to sleep. You'll feel better in the morning." She pats my hand in sympathy and walks out of the room.

I wanted to laugh in her face. There's no way I'll feel better in the morning. I don't know if I'll ever feel better again. With the loss of the baby, I feel empty inside. As if when my body passed the baby, it took all the vital parts of me with it.

I roll to my side and clutch my now babyless stomach. The doctor told me it was nothing I did that caused me to lose the baby; that sometimes there's just something wrong with the fetus and nature takes over to dispel it. When I told him about my argument with Nick, he said the body is more than capable of handling stress and that I shouldn't think that was the cause either. I know he's right, but I still can't help but think I could have done something to prevent it.

I wonder if Nick's secretly glad she's gone. I also can't help but feel anger and resentment toward him for suggesting I get rid of her. I hate him at this moment. It's wrong of me to think that way, but I do. Maybe over time I can forgive him, but right now it's just not possible.

Whatever the nurse gave me is making my head feel fuzzy. I close my eyes to help with the spinning. I'm being released tomorrow. I hate hospitals. I should be excited I get to go home, but the thought of being there again is daunting. I'm worried I'll hear Nick's words echoing off the walls. I've only known about the baby for a little over a week, and I hadn't planned on being in the apartment for long after she was born, but I already pictured her there. Of getting up for late-night feedings and diaper changes or seeing her sleeping in a bassinet. Of giving her baths in the claw-foot tub in the bathroom and sitting beside her on the floor on a blanket and tickling her toes. My mind was making so many plans and they were cruelly snatched away from me. I have no idea how or if things will go back to normal.

I just know the thought of walking in that apartment again scares me.

THE HOUSE IS FINALLY QUIET. I'm in my bed, where I've been for the last couple days. I haven't gotten up much, except to use the bathroom. Not because I'm in pain, although I have been having some mild cramps. No, I don't get up because I just don't feel like it. My desire to face the world is nonexistent. With the loss of the baby and Nick, I've lost the need to do anything except lie in my bed.

Bailey and Jase have been here since I got out of the hospital. Sometimes the others stop by to check up on things, but I can't find the energy to go out there to be social. I just want to be left alone. Jase and Bailey have tried forcing me out of the room, but when I glare, they relent and leave me alone.

I feel terrible that Bailey's here all the time. Jaxon's brought Amari by a couple times to see her mom. I could hear her in the other room, and every time I do it pierces my heart, but I think they know it hurts too much to be around another baby, so he doesn't stay long. I've told Bailey she needs to go home to her own family, but she insists she's staying for a few days to make sure I'm alright. She says Amari and Jaxon are fine by themselves for a few days and on the nights he works, Amari is with his mom. She's tried getting me to talk to her, but I won't. If anyone knows the pain I'm going through, it's her. But I'm not ready to talk about it yet.

Even though I didn't want to, I spoke with my parents briefly. My mom was hysterical, and my dad was his usual calm self. It's sad to think he really only shows emotion when he's berating Jase for whatever reason. However—and it could have just been my imagination—I thought I could hear a hint of concern in his voice. Mom wanted to come immediately, but I flatly refused. I can't deal with seeing them on top of losing the baby and Nick.

Jase came in about an hour ago to bring me something to eat. It's still sitting on the nightstand untouched. I have no desire to eat, and even just the thought of it makes me nauseous. I haven't really eaten much since the day I lost the baby. I know I need to, but I just can't stomach much right now.

Although I force myself out of bed every day to shower, I stay in my nightclothes. I torture myself by wearing a t-shirt of Nick's he left behind. I miss him so damn much, but I still feel loathing toward him. It hurts to think about him, but he and the baby are all I think about. I know I'm in a self-induced pity party, but I can't find it in myself to give two shits.

Even through my closed door, I can tell that isn't Bailey or Jase talking. The walls are thin, so I know it's Andrew and Mac. I listen.

"I've told him to leave, but he won't," Andrew says to someone.

"I'll get him to fucking leave," comes Jase's growly tone. "She doesn't want to fucking see him. What doesn't he get about that?"

"Leave him be, Jase," Mac says next. "He's not hurting anything."

"Whatever. He just better stay on the other side of that fucking door." Jase again.

"He looks like shit. He needs to at least go home and sleep, eat, and shower," comes from Andrew.

"He says he's staying as long as it takes. I've been taking him food," Bailey pipes in. "I told him to come inside." Even through the walls, I hear Jase's growl. Bailey cuts him off when she continues firmly, "No, Jase. Have you see how he looks? He looks awful. I don't know what happened between them that night, but whatever it was, he's paying for it."

They turn quiet for several minutes. I've known Nick's been out there since the day I got home. He just sits out in the hallway across from my door. He never tries to come in. I don't know why he's here; maybe out of guilt. Part of me wants to go to him and beg for comfort, for him to tell me everything will be okay, while another part wants to go out and scream at him and tell him I never want to see him again. And yet another part just wants to forget he exists. I want to forget every moment I've spent with him. Which also means forgetting I was ever pregnant. Maybe I'm wrong for wanting that, but I feel like it's the only thing that will help. Nick and this baby have been a part of my life for such a small amount of time, but the impact of them both has been monumental.

Mac's next question pulls me from my thoughts.

"How is she?"

I hate when they talk about me. I know they are concerned and only want to help, but I just wish they would all go away for a while. Is this how Nick felt when everyone was hounding him all the time? No wonder he was always in such a rotten mood.

"The same," says Bailey. I can hear the pain in her voice. "I don't know what to do. She won't eat, and she sleeps all the time. I've tried getting her to talk to me, but she won't. She just lies in there and stares off into space."

God! Don't they realize I can hear them?

"She'll come around. Just give her a bit more time."

Someone else says something, but it's so low I can't understand them. Sick of hearing them talk about me behind my back, I drag my tired body from the bed and decide to make myself known. Contrary to their belief, I don't sleep all the time. Actually, I barely sleep at all, because I'm still plagued by dreams. I just pretend I'm asleep when they come in the room so I don't have to deal with them. I'm being a selfish bitch, but I don't have it in me.

The creak of my door opening has everyone quieting. I walk down the hall on bare feet and go straight to the kitchen without looking at them. I can feel their eyes on me. I probably look like shit in my ratty sleep pants and Nick's wrinkled shirt that almost comes to midthigh. I haven't brushed my hair since I've been home, so I'm sure it looks like a rat's nest.

I walk to the cabinet by the fridge and get a glass and fill it with water from the tap. I guzzle it down, then refill it. I feel someone come up behind me.

"Chris?"

I don't answer Bailey, just stare at the wall in front of me.

"How are you feeling?" she asks timidly.

"Like I just lost a baby," I tell her dully. How else am I supposed to feel?

I hear Bailey's sharp inhale at my blunt reply. I need to tone it down. I don't want to hurt Bailey. She's the last person I want to hurt. She knows what I'm going through, and we've always been there for each other. All she's doing, all everyone is doing, is being there for me. I'm know she's hurting too. I'm sure watching me go through what she went through multiple times is killing her inside.

I set the glass down on the counter and turn to face Bailey. I'm not surprised when I see them all standing there watching me with sorrowful expressions. I focus solely on Bailey.

"I'm sorry. I shouldn't have said that," I tell her.

She takes a few steps toward me, but stops, like she's unsure of my reaction to her closeness. "No," she says softly. "It was a stupid question. I shouldn't have asked it."

Tears prick my eyes for the thousandth time. I look down at my bare feet and try my hardest to push them away. I'm so tired of crying all the time. I only knew I had my baby in my belly for nine days, while some woman go through months of knowing about their babies, only to end up losing them. My situation could have been so much worse, but knowing that doesn't make me feel any better.

I just want her back! I silently cry in my head.

"Oh sweetie," Bailey says mournfully. Seconds later, her arms wrap around me, drawing my body into hers. I sag against her with my head on her shoulder and let the tears fall once again. I don't sob uncontrollably like I have been. This is more of a hollow cry, where I just let the tears flow, feeling almost detached from them.

I pull back from her, wipe my face, and look over her shoulder at the others. Jase looks like he's about to break down himself. His eyes are red and look tired. I'm sure seeing his sister like this is hard on him. Andrew is standing behind him but off to the side with his hand on Jase's waist. He doesn't look much better. Neither does Mac.

"I can hear you all," I tell them quietly. They look confused, so I enlighten them. I can't deal with hearing them talk about me like I'm some child that's been abused. "When you talk out here, I can hear it. The walls are pretty thin."

Guilt washes over their faces. Jase moves to stand in front of me. I hate the sympathy I see in his eyes.

He places both palms on my cheeks and says in a low voice, "We're just worried about you. You won't talk to any of us. You need to talk to someone."

"I'm not ready for that, Jase. It's only been a few days. Give me some time and space."

His look of understanding sends a wave of relief through me. I hope what I said is right. I hope one day I can open up and be able to talk without it crushing me so much.

He nods and bends to place a kiss on my forehead before letting me go.

"I want you all to go home. You need to get back to your lives. I'll be okay here by myself."

"Chris—" Jase and Bailey begin to object.

"No, Jase." I start with him. "You have a shop to run. You need to get back to it. Joe's counting on you. I won't let you jeopardize that." I turn to Bailey. "And you need to get back to your family. Until now, you hated leaving Amari even for just a few hours. I know it's killing you leaving her like you have. I'll be fine. And if it makes you feel better, you can come check on me. But I need time alone and knowing you are a room away isn't giving me that."

They both look like they want to argue again. I look from one to the other, showing them with my expression that I'm not backing down on this.

"Okay." Although I see the reluctance in his eyes, Jase agrees first. "But promise me if you need anything, you'll call one of us."

"I will."

"And you have to eat," Bailey adds. "And please don't stay in bed all day. It's not good for you. You need to move around."

"I'll do my best," I reply. That's the most I can give her.

"That's not good enough, Chris," she says firmly. "I'll bring by something to eat each evening and check on you to see if you need anything."

"I'm not an invalid. I can make my own food," I tell her. This is ridiculous.

"It'll make me feel better," she says softly.

Giving in, I nod.

"I'm going to lie back down for a bit."

Jase and Bailey hug me one more time before I walk to the doorway of the kitchen where Andrew and Mac are.

Andrew pulls me into a tight hug. When he pulls back, he wipes away the few tears that are still lingering on my cheeks.

"I hate seeing you like this," he says, his deep voice rough.

"I know. I'll be okay." I try to give him a reassuring smile, but it falls flat.

"I know you will be." Leaning forward, his kisses my lips lightly and lets me go.

Mac steps forward next for his own hug. As much as all these hugs are starting to annoy me, I also love them. I'm so blessed to have so many friends.

At my ear, Mac whispers, "I'm so sorry, Chris. Please know we're here if you need anything."

I nod and pull back from him. I'm so damn tired, I just want to crawl back in my bed and pretend to sleep again.

Leaving the kitchen, I turn to face them one more time.

"Please leave Nick alone," I tell them, but my gaze locks on Jase.

His jaw goes hard, but eventually he nods.

Satisfied, I leave them and go back to my room and slide beneath my covers. I don't sleep though. Instead, I just continue my vigilant stare at nothing.

A COUPLE OF DAYS LATER, after getting a measly few hours of sleep, I wake to something hot and hard pressed against my back. It feels and smells incredibly good. I snuggle deeper into my blanket and bask in the glory of it. I haven't felt this comfortable in days. I'm don't want to open my eyes because I'm scared the feeling will go away. The arm around my waist tightens. I know who it is. I want to push away from him, and I will in a minute, but I want to give myself this one moment before I do. I've missed seeing, feeling, and smelling Nick so much that I ache all the time. I want to reach out to him and have him hold me just like he is now, but I'm afraid that if I do, I'll be hurt by him again. I'm not under the illusion that he miraculously is over Anna and can now move on. I'm not important enough for him to be able to do that. I'll never be that for him.

Judging by his behavior he feels guilt for what happened, but that still doesn't tell me he's not secretly glad he's no longer stuck being a father to a child he never wanted.

After having a couple days to think, my resentment toward him has lessened. I can't blame him any longer for not wanting something he never asked for. Yes, it still hurts that he reacted the way he did and then left me afterwards, but it was a big shock for him. Many men in his situation would have acted the same way. I'll never know if his feelings would have changed.

That thought brings on another bout of anguish.

The head that's pressed into my hair shifts. Time to end this now, before I let the feeling get to me and decide to never let him go.

I'm gently lifting his arm to move away from him when he whispers hoarsely, "Please don't."

I tense and ask despondently, "How did you get in here?"

"I still have the key Jaxon gave me the night of your migraine," he mumbles into my hair.

"Why are you here?" I've been wondering this since the first time I realized he was staying out in my hallway.

It takes him a minute to answer, and when he does, his voice is thick with emotion.

"Because I need to be. I need to be here with you. I left you alone, Chris, and I'll regret that for the rest of my life."

I don't know exactly what he's saying, and I don't ask him to clarify because I'm terrified of his answer not being what I want it to be.

We stay silent for several minutes, me lying stiffly and him with his face buried in my hair, until I can't take him touching me any longer. It's too agonizing.

"You need to let me go and leave, Nick. I can't be around you right now."

It was barely noticeable, but I felt the slight jerk of Nick's body at my words. I harden my heart against his obvious pain. Nick's already ripped me apart with his actions. I don't know how much more I can take before he completely obliterates me. I refuse to wait for the impending backlash from him. And it *will* come. It *always* comes.

Instead of letting me go like I desperately need him to, he strengthens his grip. "I'm so damn sorry, Chris," he says gruffly, nearly breaking my resolve.

"Let me go." I harden and wipe all emotion from my voice.

He finally releases me, and I scurry to the other side of the bed. When I turn to face him, I'm shocked at the state he's in. His hair doesn't look like it's been brushed in days and the hair on his cheeks is longer and looks unkempt. Before when he had the scruff it looked trimmed and well cared for. That's not the case now. His eyes are red and sunken, like he's gotten little to no sleep, and his clothes are way past wrinkled. But it's the expression in his eyes that catches my breath. He looks devastated, like he just lost everything he cares about.

My fingers itch to reach out to him. I curl them into fists instead to hold off the need. Without a word, I get up on unsteady legs and walk to the bathroom to get away from him. I take my time, hoping he'll leave. My hopes are dashed when I go back to the bedroom and see him sitting on the side of the bed with his head bowed. I opt to stay standing in the doorway.

"I understand you want me to leave. I also understand you probably hate me right now. But I'm not leaving you alone." He looks up at me, and I'm struck again at the immense regret I see in his eyes. "I'll stay out in the living room, but I'm not leaving this apartment. The last thing you need right now is to be left alone."

It pisses me off that he's being so forceful, especially in light of how he treated me when I tried doing the same thing. What gives him the right to insert himself when he essentially said he wanted nothing to do with me? Why the change of heart? And why in the fuck is he making this so damn hard on me? Haven't I been through enough? Haven't I given enough?

"I don't need or want you here, Nick. I'll be fine on my own. And if I do need anything, I'll call Bailey or Jase. There's no sense in you being here when you really don't want to."

Pain flashes through his eyes before he wipes it away. "None of that matters. I'm not going anywhere. And this *is* where I want to be."

I laugh harshly. "Are you kidding me? Why on earth would you want to be around someone you've tried so hard to push away? Why now, Nick? Because I lost a baby you never wanted? I'm not stupid. I know you're privately jumping for joy because you no longer have to deal with it. Are you here out of guilt because you feel responsible? Don't, because I don't blame you. I did at first, but I know now that it just wasn't meant to be and God knew it. He saved my baby a lifetime of pain of either not having a father or having one that resented her mother." I take in a shaky breath, my own words tearing me up inside. "Just leave, please. I'll get through this on my own."

He watches me while I talk, the hurt in his eyes deepening and his body flinching with each word I say. He's quiet for several seconds, then gets up from the bed and at first I think I finally got through to him. For those seconds, my chest gets tight. I want him to leave, but then again, I want him to fight me on it and not leave.

I am so fucked-up in the head.

Instead of walking past me out the door, he stops in front of me about a foot away.

I'm shocked speechless when he drops to his knees on the floor at my feet. He sits back on his feet with his hands on his thighs. Staring up at me with so much anguish, he says, "I hate myself for saying those things to you, Sugar." I close my eyes at the nickname. He continues when I open them again. "I swear I didn't mean them. There's no way I could ever wish harm on our baby. I regretted them as soon as I said them. But I was just so scared. No, I didn't ask or want you to get pregnant, but five minutes after I left you, the fear disappeared, and a fierce need took hold. I would have never resented you, Chris. *Never*! Because I wanted the baby, too." He finishes by grabbing my thighs and placing his cheek on my stomach, right where the baby would have been.

I don't know how to react to his confession. I'm not ready to believe him yet. I'm not ready to let go of the pain he's caused me.

I swallow the lump in my throat before telling him, "I need time."

He nods and looks up at me. "I can do that. But I'm staying here while you have it. I'm not leaving you alone through this, but I'll back away and give you space."

I don't know if I want to scream at him or drop to my knees and throw my arms around his neck. He has me so confused right now.

I do neither. I nod and back up a step until he's forced to let my legs go. I hate seeing the dejected look on his face. He climbs to his feet and runs both hands down his tired-looking face.

"You should get some sleep," I tell him.

"I will. After I make you something to eat," he responds.

The thought of food turns my stomach. I shake my head. "Thank you, but I'm not hungry."

"You have to eat, Chris," he says, walking out the door, essentially dismissing me. Gritting my teeth, I follow him.

"I don't want to eat, Nick. I'll get something later," I reply firmly.

He stops and turns to me once he reaches the living room. "I'm making you a sandwich. Can you at least eat half of it? Please."

Ready for this conversation to end so I can go back to bed and wallow some more, I give in. Besides, I don't remember the last time I ate, and I'm starting to feel the effects of it. As much as I want to wither away, I know I need to keep my strength up. Bailey called the school for me to let them know what's going on. They gave me two weeks off, which is more time than I would have asked for. I'm already not looking forward to going back out in to the world again.

Relief flashes in Nick's eyes when I nod. He goes to the kitchen, while I go back to my safe haven. I crawl back in bed and hug my pillow. I'm lying so I'm facing the pillow that Nick used. I reach out and lay my hand on it. It still feels warm. His smell fills my nose and it brings tears to my eyes. I squeeze them closed to push the tears away. I'm so tired of crying. There can't be much liquid left in my body, because all I've done lately is lie in my bed and cry. It's pathetic, but the heart feels what it wants. And right now it wants the baby it lost and the man who will likely destroy it.

twenty-three

Nick

I QUIETLY PUSH OPEN Chris's bedroom door with my foot and carry the plate of bacon, eggs, and toast over to her nightstand and set it down. I put the coffee beside it. I look down at the sleeping form on the bed and my chest tightens. Watching her sleep has become one of my favorite things to do. I almost enjoy it as much as watching her when she's awake. Right now she looks peaceful, like she didn't just have her world ripped apart a week and a half ago.

I hate to wake her up; she doesn't get enough sleep as it is, I think because of her dreams, but she needs to eat. She only eats when I force her to. I've been here for a week and all she does it sit in her room. I've done what I told her I would and left her alone, except when I make her eat. I'm wondering if I shouldn't, though. Sitting by herself with her thoughts can't be good. The others still come by daily, but she won't come out to visit them. And when they go to her room, she feigns sleep. I know she's faking because her eyes always look tired and swollen from lack of sleep. I know the symptoms intimately.

Everyone else is just as worried as I am. We all expected for her to go into a depressive state, but this goes beyond that. It's like she has no will to try and move past it. It's only been a little over a week, but she's made no progress, except for the unacknowledged shaky truce between us.

Jase came by with Bailey and Andrew the day after I snuck my way into Chris's apartment. To say he was livid when he saw me on the couch watching TV is putting it mildly. It was only Andrew that stopped him from rushing me. I wouldn't have. I deserve everything he wants to throw at me. I hurt his sister in a way that nearly destroyed her. I can't imagine anything would have stopped me from pummeling the guy's face had it been my sister. He still hates me; I can see it in his eyes every time he looks at me, but he knows I'm the only one Chris hasn't made leave, and he knows I'm the one who needs to be here. I've been in Chris's shoes. I've lost someone I loved with all my heart. I know what's running through Chris's mind, and I know how to get her out of her funk. It's the same thing she did for me. Persistence, and letting her know she's not alone. He despises it, but holds his tongue for Chris's sake. I would have stayed regardless, but it makes things much easier with him not trying to force me to go.

I'm still not sure how deep my feelings are for her, but I do know it physically hurts to see her in so much pain and withdrawn. I don't know why Chris hasn't kicked me out. I'm just grateful she hasn't. It wouldn't have mattered, though. I would have just ended up back in the hallway across from her door.

I gently sit on the side of the bed. She's facing me. Her hair is fanned out behind her, except for a few strands that've fallen on her face, over her lips. I run my finger along her cheek and push the strands away. She licks her lips in her sleep, and I feel it in my groin. One hand is tucked beneath her cheek while the other clutches a pillow to her chest. I wish so hard I could lie down and gather her in my arms. Every night I sleep on the couch is torture. I just want to hold her and give her the comfort she needs to make it through this.

And if I'm honest with myself, I want the comfort of her arms around me too.

Her brows pucker and she moans in her sleep. There've been a couple times I've caught her in the middle of a dream. It splinters my heart every time. She shouldn't have nightmares. Her life should always be easy and carefree. It's not logical, but she should never have to worry about anything. Chris deserves and should have a worry-free life.

She shifts on the bed and a second later her eyes slowly open. They look soft at the moment, and I want to push Pause and keep that look on her face always. I wish she always looked at me that way. She gives me a small smile in her half sleeping state before she snatches that little glimpse of heaven away from me.

Before she can tell me to leave, I get up off the bed and gesture to the plate and coffee mug.

"I've brought you breakfast."

She looks from me to the plate on her nightstand, then back to me. She's stopped fighting me on the whole eating issue. Once she realized it wasn't something I was going to back down on, she finally gave up. She pushes herself up until her back is against the headboard. Her hair is a tangled mess and she has dark rings around her eyes, but to me, she's still breathtaking.

I grab the plate once she's situated and set it on her lap. "I'll come back for it later. Get dressed when you get done. We're going out."

I turn to walk out and hope she doesn't protest. It was a futile hope. She mutters, "I don't want to go anywhere."

I close my eyes and sigh deeply. Chris hasn't been very cooperative lately. She's actually been outright stubborn. She's usually easygoing and doesn't care much about what's going on as long as we're all having fun. This person is a grouch. I miss the old Chris.

She has a piece of bacon at her lips when I turn to face her. It's no surprise to see her still wearing my shirt. It was at first, but every day I've been here, she's had one. I had Jaxon stop by my place to grab me some clothes the other day. She must have gone through my bag and grabbed one. I don't know why she wears them, but it gives me hope. And if it helps her in some way, then she can have all my shirts. I haven't asked her about it and she hasn't brought it up.

"You need to get out of the house, Sugar." She winces at the nick-name I gave her. She does every time I use it now. It hurts knowing that it bothers her, when before when I said it, her eyes would go soft. "It's not good to stay in all the time. You need the fresh air."

"I don't want the fresh air. I just want to be left alone," she mumbles over her cup.

"Well, that's not happening," I tell her sternly. "I'm not going to let you wither away in your bed. When you get done eating, get dressed into something warm. It's snowing outside."

I see interest light her eyes. Chris is from the south where they don't get snow. She was here last winter, but unfortunately it was a mild one and we got hardly any. The interest falls flat a moment later and she just glares at me. I hold her stare until she's forced to look away. I don't care if she's mad. I'm done being cautious around her. She needs a firm hand, and I'm the one to give it to her.

Chris doesn't say anything else, just picks up another slice of bacon and crunches down on it. She's dropped her eyes from mine and is instead looking at the wall beside me.

Sighing, I walk out of her room and to the kitchen to eat my own breakfast. I wish she would come out here to eat with me, but anytime I suggest it, she shuts it down immediately, insisting she wants to stay in her room. If I force the issue, she throws a fit.

Finishing my now cold bacon and eggs, I wash the dirty dishes and wipe down the counters. After, I make a couple phone calls to Kevin, my foreman. I pulled him from the site in Kentucky and put him with the West Virginia project so I wouldn't need to cancel with the client. It's a big job and I didn't want to miss the opportunity to put my bid in, but there was no way I was leaving Chris. Kevin has been handling things. So far it looks promising, but we won't find out for sure for another couple days.

It's been forty-five minutes and Chris hasn't shown her face. It shouldn't take her that long to eat and dress. Worried she may be being ornery; I decide to go check on her.

As I pass the bathroom, I catch sight of Chris inside through the gap left by the slightly ajar door. She has a towel wrapped around her with the end tucked between her breasts. Her dry hair is piled on top of her head with a few loose wet curls fallen free from the hair tie. Her creamy white shoulders are on display. Her face, which hasn't had much color lately, has a stunning flush to it from her shower. I can't help the twitch my dick gives.

She's leaning on the sink, looking at her reflection. I stand there and watch, desperately waiting. I forgot about her silly mirror behavior until just now. The need to see something normal from her is overwhelming.

She stands there for several moments, just looking at herself. I frown when she pulls back and turns away from the mirror without making a face. I push open the door and she yelps at my sudden intrusion.

"What are you doing?" I ask.

She looks at me with confusion. "I took a shower."

"Why didn't you do it?" I take a step toward her.

"Do what?" she asks with bewilderment.

"Make a face at yourself. You said you've done it since you were little. Why didn't you do it just now?"

Understanding dawns on her face before she shrugs. "I just don't feel the need anymore."

I don't like her answer. It's like she's giving up all the joys life has to offer. As if life will only ever be about the seriousness of situations and not the pleasures it can give as well.

Her eyes go wide when she sees me come up behind her. I grab her shoulders and turn her to face the mirror. She stiffens with my touch, and I ignore the pain that causes.

"What are you doing?" she asks over her shoulder.

Instead of answering her, I gesture to the mirror with my chin. "Do it."

She turns and looks at me through the mirror.

"No," she says, and breaks our stare.

"Come on, Chris. I'll do it with you," I cajole her, and give her shoulders a slight shake.

She looks up again and watches me. "I really don't want to, Nick. What's the point anymore?"

I disregard the kick in the gut her soft words cause me.

"Just because life sucker punched you doesn't mean it has to all be serious. Life can still be silly and fun, Sugar. You taught me that. Now come on. Make a face with me."

At first, she doesn't do anything except look at me through the mirror. After several seconds, she brings her gaze to her own face. She briefly sticks out her tongue, before tucking it back in her mouth.

"You can do better than that," I scold her. "Look, like this." I twist my lips so the top is pushed to the right and my bottom is to the left. Then I cross my eyes.

When I bring my eyes back into focus, Chris's lips are twitching at me in the mirror. Just that small glimpse has my heart soaring.

"Your turn."

She does better this time by puffing out her cheeks and scrunching up her whole face. I rest my chin on her bare shoulder and move my hands to her hips. She brings her face back to normal. We both look at each other's reflection. I've missed her so much. We've been together nonstop for over a week, but she couldn't have been further away from me if she was across the globe.

My arms snake around her waist until my chest is flush against her back. My cheek rests against hers. Her hands are on the sink in front of her. I feel the flutter of her pulse in her neck. Neither of us says anything, just opting to stand quietly for a couple minutes.

"I've missed you," I whisper.

Pain flashes in her eyes. "Nick—"

"I know it doesn't seem that way now, but it gets easier."

She drops her eyes from mine, and I feel the loss. I want to snatch it back. I carry my own pain of losing Anna, and then of losing a baby I thought I didn't want, and also of losing Chris, but I'd take on her pain as well in a heartbeat. I'd do anything to have back the woman that forced her way into my life, whether I wanted it or not.

A wave of her delicious vanilla scent hits me, and I dip my head to kiss her shoulder, still watching her face in the mirror. Her eyes flutter closed, and she inhales sharply. I skim my lips up the smooth skin of her neck until I reach her ear. "I miss you," I repeat again.

When she opens her eyes again, there's undisguised lust in their depths, as well as a hint of longing and remorse. I pull back from her. I want nothing more than to take her back to bed and leisurely explore her body, but she's not ready yet. Not to mention, her body isn't physically ready for it. She sags against the sink as I see both disappointment and relief at my retreat.

"Get dressed and meet me in the living room," I tell her and walk out.

I blow out a harsh breath when I make it to the living room. Adjusting my hardening cock, I sit and put on my boots. I'm pulling on my jacket when she walks in a few minutes later. It's amazing at how the tables have turned for us. For so long it was me pushing her away, wanting nothing to do with her attempts at pulling me out of my depressed and destructive state. It's now she who needs my help, and I'm determined to do whatever I have to do to bring back my Chris.

I grab her jacket off the couch and walk to her. After she puts it on, I hold her gloves up for her to slip her hands inside, then I wrap her scarf around her neck and put her hat on her head. Bending down, I lift her feet to put them in her boots and then tie them.

"I'm not an invalid, you know," she says, as I zip up her jacket.

I smile at her. "I know. I just like helping you."

"Where are we going anyway?"

Grabbing her hand, I lead her to the door, throwing over my shoulder, "You'll see."

She huffs and puffs behind me, and I have to force back my laugh.

When we walk out the back door, the snow is coming down in huge flakes. It dumped quite a bit of snow overnight, which isn't too common this early in the year. There's almost a foot on the ground. I came down fifteen minutes ago to turn my truck on to warm up and to brush off the thick layer of white fluff on the windshield.

I'm forced to stop when Chris suddenly halts in her tracks. When I look back, she has her head tipped back, letting snow fall on her face. She looks mesmerizing and I can't help but watch her in awe.

"Why didn't you tell me we got this much snow?" she asks, when she brings her head back down.

"Because I wanted it to be a surprise. Let's go," I tell her and give her hand a tug. She follows reluctantly, still carrying a look of yearning.

I open the passenger door and help her inside the warm truck. I walk around and climb in behind the wheel. Chris has her hands tucked between her legs and her shoulders hunched over. I turn the heater up more.

"Warm enough?" I ask.

She doesn't look at me when she nods. I pull out of the back parking lot of Jaxon's. It doesn't take us long to get where we're going. Yesterday when Jase and Bailey were here, Jase mentioned Chris has always wanted to play in the snow, but hasn't been able to because they never got snow where they grew up. It's about time she's given that opportunity.

I turn down a road that leads to Mac's property, but instead of taking a left at the fork that would take us to his house, I turn right. I ignore Chris's questioning look.

A few minutes later when I turn the truck off, she turns to me.

"What are we doing here?" she asks.

I get out of the truck and walk around to her side and open the door. She still hasn't unbuckled her seat belt, so I do it for her.

"We're playing in the snow," I tell her and grab her by the hips to pull her from the truck.

She can't hide her excitement. It makes me feel like the king of the fucking world when she smiles the first real smile I've seen in what seems like forever.

I walk to the back of the truck and flip back the tarp covering the two plastic sleds. Chris doesn't pay attention to what I'm doing. She's currently bending down and fingering the snow with gloved-covered hands. She scoops some up and lets it fall through her fingers.

I drag the two sleds out of my truck and drop them to the ground. I grab the ropes that're attached to them and walk over to Chris, who's still hunched over.

"You ready to do this?" I ask her.

She stands, brushes the snow off her hands, and nods eagerly. "Yes. I've never done this before though."

I lead her to the perfect hill to sleigh down. As kids, we used to always gather at Mac's place to use his hill for sledding.

"It's a piece of cake. You're going to love it."

It takes us a few minutes to reach the top because it's so steep and walking through thick snow is tough. I drop the ropes when we reach where we need to be.

"Okay." I turn to face her. "Want me to go first to show you how it's done, or do you want to wing it? Or we can go together."

She chews her lip for a second, before she answers with, "Together."

"That's my girl." I smile at her. "Grab your sled and put it next to mine." She does so. "Just make sure you don't put it too close to the edge or it'll go before you're ready."

I climb on my own sled and gesture for her to do the same.

"You ready?"

She graces me with a big smile and says excitedly, "Yes!"

She looks adorable with her white winter hat over her bright red hair and her white scarf tucked into her mint-green coat. She looks cheerful and carefree. The empty look that's hidden her pain over the last week is currently gone, something I'm thankful for. I just hope it lasts longer than just our snow play.

"Okay, just hang on to the edges and have—"

Before I get a chance to finish, she pushes herself over the edge of the hill and off she goes. I don't follow her, too captivated by her joyful scream as she slides down the hill. She jumps on the uneven ground and bounces around. Right before she hits the bottom, the sled tips over, spilling her onto the ground. She just lies there. I can't be sure, but it looks like she has huge smile on her face.

I push my own sled over the edge and slide down the hill. I steer it so it misses her, and tip it over so I land close to her. She turns her head and what I see has my chest tightening. Her green eyes shine so bright it almost takes my breath away.

"Was that fun?" I ask.

If it's even possible, her smile gets bigger.

"So much fun. Let's do it again!" she says, laughing.

She scrambles to her feet, grabs the rope, and tries her best to run up the hill. I laugh at her as she slips and slides in the snow. At a slower pace, I get up and go after her. She already has her sled on the ground and is sitting on it by the time I make it to her.

"Together this time?" I ask, with a quirk of my lips.

"Maybe," she says, with her own smirk.

"On the count of three. One... two..." I reach over and grab her rope to hold her in place when I see mischief in her eyes. She sticks her tongue out at me, causing me to chuckle. "Three!" I yell, and let go of her rope at the same time we both push ourselves over the edge.

I laugh as she screams again. Hearing and seeing her having fun makes my heart expand. I don't think I've ever seen her laugh so much. A pang hits me square in the gut when I think of all the time I've missed and all the times I was a dick to her.

We make it down the hill at the same time and both fall off our sleds because we're laughing so hard. After we're able to catch our breath, we get up and race back up the hill. We do this over and over again, always landing at the bottom of the hill in a fit of laughter. I don't think *I've* laughed this hard in a long time. It feels good to let loose, especially with Chris by my side.

I roll to my side and see Chris on her side as well. She has the biggest smile I've ever seen on her face. Her cheeks are pink from the cold and the hair that's sticking out of her hat is a damp mess. She has snow on every inch of her body. I reach over with my gloved hand and tuck a piece of hair behind her ear. My finger lingers on her cheek. My eyes drop to her lips when she licks them.

I slide over in the snow until I'm right beside her. Unable to help myself, I lean forward slowly, just in case she wants me to stop, and place my lips on hers. She doesn't protest, so I apply more pressure, until she opens up to me. Finally having her vanilla taste against my tongue again after almost two weeks is like entering heaven. I want to bottle the addicting taste so I can drink from it anytime I want.

I feel her hands at my sides and even through my clothes, it sends shivers over my body. I fit my body more over hers and brush my tongue over her lips. She moans, and I bask in the sound. Setting my hand on the other side of her head, I lean down until my chest meets hers. I don't want to push her too far, but the taste of her is getting to me. My body is primed and ready for hers, even knowing we can't take it any further.

I groan into her mouth when her body stiffens beneath mine. Before she has a chance to push me away, I pull back and rest my forehead against hers. Our breathing is heavy, and it makes me hot knowing I can still affect her so much.

Her eyes flutter open to look up at me. The sadness is back in their depths and an ache forms in my chest.

Not ready to lose the jovial attitude of a few minutes ago, I get up on my knees, make a snowball, and launch it at her. It hits her square in the chest. Her look of shock has me busting out laughing.

"Did you really just throw a snowball at me?" she asks incredulously.

Ginning, I say, "I did, Sugar. What are you going to do about it?"

Sitting up, she looks at me with what I'm sure she's hoping is disdain, but she doesn't quite pull it off when I see a twinkle in her eye.

"Oh, you're going to get it now, buster," she says, getting to her knees.

"Buster, huh?" I taunt, getting on my own knees and backing up. I gather more snow in my hands, making sure it's not packed too tight.

"Yes. You are so going to pay for that."

She grabs a bunch of snow, packs it into a ball, and brings her arm back to throw it.

I drop the snowball to the ground and pick up more to make another. Casually, I tell her, "Just so you know, I was the snowball champion around these parts."

She drops her snowball on the ground as she bends over laughing. I watch, but don't stop making my cold weapons.

Once she's got control of her laughter, she asks me with merriment still in her eyes, "Does that really exist? How can you become a snowball champion?"

"It most certainly does exist," I tell her, readying the snowball in my hand. "To become a champion of snowballing, you have to have good aim." As soon as the words leave my mouth, I launch a snowball at her and hit right on target, the center of her chest right between her boobs.

She narrows her eyes at me. "You're asking for it."

I ignore her and pick up my next snowball. "You also have to be quick with making snowballs. The quicker you are, the more you can hit your target, and the more distracted they become from making their own snowballs because they are too busy trying to avoid yours."

My next snowball hits her on the upper stomach. I laugh when she glares at me. I bend down to grab another snowball and get hit on the top of my head. I look up at Chris's expression of triumph. I slowly get back on my knees with three snowballs in my hands. When she sees them, the gloating look disappears. Her lips form an O and her brows rise with worry. I grin cheekily at her and throw my next snowball. It smacks her right in the pelvic area. She looks down at the white spot on her pants, then back up at me, determination glittering in her eyes.

"That's it!" she cries and starts rapidly packing snowballs and throwing them my way. She's doing it so fast she doesn't have enough time to pack them tight enough, and most either miss me or fall apart before they make it to me. Being an expert, I make my snowballs fast and tight, and launch them at her one after the other.

We're both back to laughing and having a good time. She's got a ton of white spots on her where my snowballs have hit her. I only have a few. She turns her back to me to avoid getting hit in the front, but that's okay, I just tag her ass over and over again.

Out of breath, we both fall back in the snow and look up at the gray sky. The snow is still coming down, but not as hard.

"It's so beautiful out here. You see white everywhere you look."

"Want to know a secret?" I ask her.

"What?" she says.

I look over at her when I say, "I hate the snow."

"What?" she screeches and sits up quickly. "How can you hate the snow?"

I chuckle at her reaction.

"Because I've been around it my whole life. It sucks to drive in; because of it we have to salt the roads, which rusts cars; when it's plowed it leaves behind dirty snow, and the plows also knock over mailboxes; it's hard to walk in; and it leaves the ground nasty and soggy when it melts. Oh, and it's cold as shit."

"Well," she huffs. "I love the snow."

I chuckle at her. "You'll learn to hate it too if you're around it enough."

She looks at me like I've lost my mind. "I'm never going to hate the snow."

I shrug and look back up at the sky. "If you say so."

"I do."

She lies back down. We stay like that for a while before we get up and sled down the hill a few more times. We spend the rest of the afternoon making snow angels, snowmen, having snowball fights, and sledding down the hill. Overall, I'd say it was a damn productive day. It took her mind off things for a while and that's what she needed. I'm not under the illusion that she'll be miraculously better, but I hope she now realizes there is joy still to be had in life.

We pack up the sleds in the back of my truck and then climb inside. We sit for several minutes, waiting for the truck to warm up.

"Thank you for today," she says quietly.

I look over and see her staring out the window, her breath puffing out white clouds.

"Anything for you, sugar."

She looks at me oddly, like she's not sure if she wants to believe my words or not. I put that doubt on her face, and that's another thing I hate myself for. The loss of Anna is still buried deep in my heart. I'll always hurt over that loss. I'm not exactly sure what I'm feeling for Chris right now. I don't know if my feelings run deeper or if I just have this need to get her through the loss of our baby. What I do know though is if she ever needs me for anything, I'll always be there. I don't know if we can ever be more than what we were before the baby, but I refuse to go back to the unpredictable and heartless prick I was.

I lift the middle console, reach over, grab her hand, and tug her to the middle of the seat. I pull the middle seat belt across her and buckle her in. After putting her hand that I'm still holding on my thigh, I put the truck in gear and pull away from our play spot.

Chris may not believe now that she can count on me, but over time she will. It may take me a while, but I'll make it my life's mission to ensure she does.

twenty-four

Chris

I DROP THE PHONE on the bed and scramble up to get dressed, worry and anxiety making my attempts clumsy. I ignore the pain in my stomach as I slip my jeans up my legs. Noah, my troubled student from school, just called. He wouldn't tell me what was going on, but asked me to please come to his house quickly to get him and his little sister. His voice sounded muffled and frantic, like he was trying to be quiet so no one would hear him talking to me. I gave him my number a couple months ago and told him to call me if ever needed anything or to talk.

I look at the clock on the nightstand. Nick has only been gone thirty minutes. He had to go to the next town over because, ironically, a pipe burst in the kitchen. The memory of Jaxon's and my fib to Nick about a false burst pipe in my bathroom comes to mind and it almost makes me chuckle.

I'm out of food here, so he was going to pick up some groceries while he got the things he needed to fix the pipe as well. I was supposed to go with him, but I woke up this morning not feeling well and running a slight fever. Cramps still plague me, and the bleeding hasn't stopped. I have an appointment tomorrow with my doctor for a follow-up. I'm secretly glad I wasn't able to go with him to town. I'm still not quite ready to face the world. Going out with Nick a couple days ago helped some, but I'm just not there yet. It's already bad enough I'm going back to work Monday. I'm not looking forward to pitying glances and whispered words. The pain of losing the baby is still too fresh and leaves me gasping for air at times.

There's no way I can wait until he gets back so he can go with me. I promised him I wouldn't go alone, but sometimes you have to do what you have to do. The urgency in Noah's voice says he can't wait.

So I don't totally go against his wishes, I pick up my phone once I'm dressed and call Jase to see if he can go with me. It rings until it hits voice mail, and I throw the phone back on the bed with a growl.

"Damn it!"

I bite my nail, deciding on what I should do. The longer I wait, the longer Noah and his sister are at home with God only knows what going on. I can't just leave them there. Picking up my phone again, I try Mac. Something tells me he may be needed. Again, I get voice mail. I leave him a message to let him know where I'm going. Hopefully he'll get it fairly soon and will be right behind me. I don't want to call the sheriff's office until I know what's going on.

I sit on the edge of the bed and slip on my boots. The snow has mostly melted outside already. That's living in Ohio for you. One day you have a foot of snow and will be below freezing and the next day it's in the fifties.

I get up too fast from the bed and have to steady myself for a minute until the wave of dizziness passes. I regret not eating like I should have over the past two weeks. It's made me weak.

I dig through my purse to make sure I still have my pepper spray that Jase gave me after Damien held me at gunpoint. I don't really think I'll need it, but I'd like to have it just in case. With all the shit that happened with Bailey, Anna, then Mac and Mia, and what happened with Jase and me, I've learned you can never be too careful.

I find my pepper spray and throw my phone in beside it. Grabbing my keys from the table and with my purse over my shoulder, I bolt for the door.

Noah lives on the outskirts of Jaded Hollow. It doesn't take me long to get there. The place doesn't look to be in bad shape. It's a one-story brick house on a large piece of land. I spot a blue Corolla in the yard with a red Ford truck beside it. I park and take a deep breath before grabbing the pepper spray out of my purse, slipping it into my jacket pocket, and getting out of my car.

There's no noise coming from inside the house. I don't know if that's good or bad. I walk up the porch steps, open the screen door, and knock. It takes several minutes for someone to answer.

I've never seen the scowling man in front of me. First impressions more often correct and the vibe I get off this guy is not a good one. He eyes me up and down with his nearly black eyes before settling on my face. He's not a bad looking guy, except for the nasty look he's currently giving me. His dark blond hair is neatly trimmed with not a piece out of place. His face is clean of any scruff and his white dress shirt with the sleeves rolled up and creased slacks are in impeccable shape.

His deep rough voice startles me when he asks, "Who the fuck are you?"

I grip the pepper spray in my jacket pocket and reply shakily, "I'm Chris, Noah's teacher from school. I'm looking for him."

His lip curls up in disgust, making him look more sinister. Something isn't right here and now I'm wondering if I shouldn't have waited for Nick after all. I wipe the thought away. It doesn't matter. I couldn't just ignore Noah's call.

"He's busy right now. You can see him at school tomorrow," he growls at me, before trying to close the door.

I hold my hand up to keep the door from closing in my face. "That's just it, Mr..." I wait for him to supply his name. When he doesn't, I continue. "He hasn't been to school in almost a week. I came by to make sure everything was okay. If I could just speak with him for a moment, or maybe his mother, I will be on my way."

I spoke with Mary, the receptionist at school, a couple days ago. I called to confirm I would be back on Monday and she updated me on Noah not being in school lately. It worried me and I had plans to talk with Nick this afternoon about making a visit out here, before Noah called.

When the man sees my hand on the door, the menacing look morphs into rage. Inconspicuously, I pull out the pepper spray and hold it to my side.

"Look, bitch," he snarls, taking a step towards me. "I already told you he's busy. And so is his mother. You need to leave, before I fucking make you."

I try to look around him into the house to see if I can spot Noah, his sister, or mother, but he steps to block me. If it's even possible, the look in his eyes turns even more sinister.

I'm just about to turn around to leave and call the sheriff office when a slender hand lands on the man's arm. A second later a small blonde woman appears at his side. Except for her short frame, Noah is the spitting image of her. I barely hold back my cry of alarm when my eyes flicker over her face. Her lip is cut and her eye is starting to swell and bruise. Her white button-up shirt is torn on one side and there're blood splatters on the front.

"Danny? What's going on?" she asks when she sees me standing there.

Against my better judgment, I take a step toward her. "Ms. Taylor, my name is Chris. I'm Noah's teacher. Can I speak with you for just a moment?"

She tries to smile at me and winces, presumably from the pain of her split lip. "Hi, Chris. We're busy at the moment. I'll give you a call tomorrow."

I can tell she's just trying to get me to leave. There will be no phone call tomorrow. She's scared and wants me gone. There is no way I can leave her and the kids here. There's no telling what this man will do, especially since I've seen her in the condition she's in. I need to get them out of here. I need to make a call to the sheriff's office.

I try to stall for time and hope Mac has already gotten my message and is on his way. "Are Noah and your daughter in there? Can I see them please?"

I guess the man named Danny has tired of my interference. He slings Ms. Taylor's hand off his arm and snarls, "Get back to what you were doing, woman! I told you I'll take care of this." He then turns to me and grits out between pristine white teeth, "This is your last warning, lady. Get off this property now before I do something you'll regret."

I hear a whimpering inside and my head jerks to the side once again to try to look around him. The blow comes before I even realize Danny moved. I stagger back from the backhanded hit and bump into the porch railing porch. The pepper spray in my hand flies through the air and lands on the ground. I shake my head, trying to clear away the dizziness and pain from the hit. My lips throbs and I run my tongue over it and taste blood. The asshole busted my lip. Danny stalks my way.

"I fucking told you, bitch," he growls, and slaps me again. This one is harder than the last, and I fall to my knees. I bring my hand to my stinging cheek and feel heat radiating off it.

I cry out when I watch him bring his booted foot back to kick me. He's not given the chance to make contact though. I hear a roar from behind him and see a blur of movement. Noah launches himself at Danny and tackles him off the porch and onto the ground. Through my fuzzy head, I watch as Noah lands on top of Danny and starts whaling on him. His blond hair is sweaty from exertion. At closer inspection his jaw looks red and he has a cut on his upper cheek. Noah isn't a small boy, so the punches he's landing on Danny are doing damage fast.

"Noah!" Ms. Taylor's scream pulls me from my frozen state.

I scramble to my feet and fight the lightheadedness. My stomach cramps, nearly bringing me back down, but I push through it. I rush past Ms. Taylor, who's holding a small crying girl in her arms. Noah's still on top of Danny, sending punch after punch to his face. Danny is no longer moving, having already, hopefully, passed out.

"Noah, stop!" I yell and reach for his arm. He looks up at me with frenzied eyes. His nostrils flare and his chest heaves with his heavy breathing. He has a drop of blood running down from the cut on his cheek and sweat dribbles down his face. "He's out, Noah. You can stop now." I try to soothe him.

He looks around frantically until he sees his mom and sister off to the side. He stumbles off Danny and runs over to them. I hear a loud single blare of a siren and look over just as Mac's car skids to a stop. He gets out and hurries over to us.

"What the hell is going on here?" he asks. When he catches sight of my busted lip, he curses. "Fuck!" He walks to me and gently grabs my chin and turns my head both ways to check the injuries on my face. "What the fuck happened? Are you okay?"

"I'm fine," I tell him, and pull out of his grip. I'm out of breath. I reach up and finger my lip and cheek and wince at the sting. "Go see to them first." I gesture to Noah and his family.

He bends down and checks Danny's pulse before getting back up. He looks over at Noah, who's standing with his mom and sister in his arms, then back to me. "Where's Nick?"

"In town picking up a few things."

"Isn't he supposed to be with you?" he asks with narrowed eyes.

"I'm not child that needs to be babysat, Mac," I bark at him. "I can take care of myself." He lifts his brows at me. "I had no way of knowing this would happen," I mutter. "Just go check on them, please."

Instead of leaving, he asks, "What happened?"

I give him a quick rundown of what happened when I got here.

"I'll be back," he says, and walks over to Noah and his family. He talks quietly with them for a few minutes, making sure to keep an eye on Danny on the ground as he does so, then pulls his phone out to make a quick call. I watch as Noah leads his mom and sister over to the porch to sit on the steps. My face is really starting to ache, and I know I'm going to have a nasty bruise. Nick is going to be so pissed

I came here by myself. This was the very reason he wanted to come with me. He's just going to have to get over it, though.

"They're okay," Mac says, walking back to me. "But I called an ambulance for him," he gestures to Danny with his chin, who still hasn't moved. His chest is moving, so I know he's going to be okay, which is good for Noah. He'll just have a killer headache when he wakes up.

"I called Nick. He's on his way back."

I nod. "Okay." My chest tightens at the thought of Nick's reaction.

The jerk on the ground moans and Mac bends, rolls him to his stomach, and puts handcuffs on him.

When Mac stands back up, he looks at me with a frown. He takes my chin again and takes a better look. "Are you sure you're okay? You don't look so good."

"I just got slapped twice, Mac. What do you expect?" I ask him dryly.

"No, it's more than that," he lifts the back of his hand to my forehead. "You're warm. Are you feeling unwell?"

I throw off his concern with a shrug. "I woke up this morning not feeling too good. I'm sure I'm just getting a cold or something."

He looks at me with concern. Having seen enough pity to last me a lifetime, I turn from him and walk over to Noah.

"Hey, are y'all okay?" I ask the three.

Noah gets up from the steps. The look in his eyes as he sees my face shows remorse.

"I'm so sorry, Ms. Matthews. I shouldn't have called you," he says, looking down at his feet.

I cup his cheek and lift his face. "Don't ever apologize, Noah. You probably would have done better calling the cops, but I understand. You needed help. I just wish I could have helped sooner. Who is that man?"

"My dad." He sighs, still looking contrite.

"But I thought your dad left when you were little?" I ask, confused. He hasn't told me much about his home life, but he did divulge one day that his dad left when he was five years old, right after his sister was born.

"He did, but he came back during the summer break."

If I remember correctly, Noah and his family moved to Jaded Hollow about five years ago. It makes me wonder something.

"Has your mom been running from him?" I ask him gently.

He looks back his mom before turning back to face me. "Yeah," he says softly. "As you can see, he's not a nice person. It wasn't him that left. It was her."

I pull him to me for a hug. Surprisingly, he hugs me back. I look at Ms. Taylor over his shoulder to see her watching us with desolate eyes. I release Noah and walk to her. The little girl in her lap looks up at me, and I smile at her. I'm relieved to see she doesn't have a mark on her. I just hope she doesn't have them in places I can't see.

Ms. Taylor stands and shockingly pulls me forward into a hug. I hear her sniffling at my ear. "I'm so sorry for what happened to you. But thank you for helping us."

When she pulls back, anguish is clear on her face. I push back the hair that's stuck on her cheek.

"I'm glad I was able to help." I give her a sad smile. "Mac will get everything taken care of."

She grabs my arm before I can turn away. "I'm sorry for your loss," she says quietly.

Her words steal my breath and leave me feeling empty again. I'm not surprised that she knows. I'm sure the everyone in Jaded Hollow does. That's part of living in a small community. I hate when people bring it up, though. I'm trying to forget, and when people bring it up, it makes it harder. It's not her fault, just like it's not the others' fault. The only thing I can do is nod.

As I leave, I stop by Noah and squeeze his arm. "I'll see you at school next week, right?"

"Yeah," he says. I pull him in for another quick hug before I walk back to Mac, who's in a squat talking to a now awake Danny. The look on Mac's face would make anyone shrink.

When he sees me coming over, he gets up and walks the rest of the way to me.

"Is it okay for me to go home?" I ask, a wave of tiredness hitting me, almost making me dizzy.

"I'm not sure. Are you okay to drive?" he asks, uncertain.

"I'll be fine, Mac. It's just a few miles," I reassure him. "I'd like to be there before Nick gets back."

After several seconds of contemplating, he relents. "Okay. But call or text me when you get there. If I don't hear from you, I'm coming over," he says sternly.

I promise, then get in my car and head home to the confrontation I know is coming.

TWENTY MINUTES LATER, I'm sitting on my bed when I hear the loud crash of my apartment door slamming shut. In seconds, the sound of Nick's boots coming down the hallway can be heard. The look in his eyes when he appears in my doorway can be called none other than wild and feral. I brace myself when he strides toward me. I'm sitting in the center of the bed, so when he makes it to me, he gets on his knees until he's inches from my face. I saw the damage and know what he sees. It looks worse than it feels.

He puts his hands on the sides of my neck and uses his thumbs to tilt my head first one way, then the other. He doesn't say anything as he examines my cut lip and the bruise on my cheek, but I can see the barely hidden wrath in his eyes. I just don't know if it's directed at me or the person who did it.

I get my answer when he wrenches himself off the bed and snarls at me, "What the fuck did I tell you?" He doesn't wait for me to answer before he continues. "I fucking told you to not go out there by yourself!"

I ignore his outburst and say quietly, "I'm fine, by the way."

He whirls around, and I flinch at the scarcely contained rage. "I fucking know you're okay! I don't know because you called me, but because Mac did. Goddamn it, Chris, what the fuck were you thinking?"

He drags his fingers roughly through his hair and starts stalking back and forth in my small bedroom, muttering curses. I clench the covers at my sides.

"I couldn't leave them there, Nick. Noah called me, and I knew something was wrong. I couldn't wait until you got back. I tried calling Jase, but he didn't answer. And I left a message on Mac's phone. I knew he would be right behind me."

I'm hoping that pacifies him and lets him know I tried. It doesn't work.

He leans over the bed and gets in my face. "Obviously he didn't get there fast enough, did he?" he sneers. "Shit!" He snaps back to standing. "How can you be so fucking stupid?"

I wince. I see the old Nick is making an appearance. The thought brings a sharp pain to my stomach. I thought we were moving forward. He's been so kind lately. I've almost gotten used to it, but deep down, I've been wary, knowing it wouldn't last. This is what I've been afraid of, what I've been waiting for.

"Do you have any goddamn clue what could have happened? How much worse this could have ended?"

"Yes!" I shout, slamming my fists down on the bed. I feel like crap and I'm tired of him snapping at me. I was the one who was assaulted today. Not him. I get that he's upset because I didn't wait for him. And I'm sure he's worried, but that doesn't give him the right to be an asshole. "Stop fucking yelling at me! I should have waited! I know that now! I didn't, and I paid for it! Now back the hell off, Nick!"

"Fuck!" he roars to the ceiling. When he looks back to me, the old pain I used to see in his eyes is back and it almost knocks me on my ass. "You know what? I can't fucking do this shit again. I just can't." He grabs his hair furiously and gives it a tug.

"What does that mean?" I ask, needing to know his answer as much as I fear it.

He lifts his head and I know, I *know*, what he's saying without him even saying it. The pain of that realization has me desperately trying to pull air into lungs that feel like they are rapidly deflating. Tears prick my eyes and one trickles down my cheek before I can stop it. I knew this was going to happen. I knew it, but I still let him back in against my better judgment.

His eyes have emptied of all emotion. The dead look is back. A hurt like no other slams into my chest when he says quietly, "I'm sorry, but I'm done. I have to go. I just... can't," he repeats.

With one last look at me, he turns on his heel. He's at the door when I stop him with a question. There are things I need to know before he leaves. I need to know if the pain I'm feeling was ever worth it.

"Do I have any of your love, Nick?" I ask tearfully.

He drops his head and keeps his back to me when he answers, ripping my world apart piece by piece.

"No," he replies gruffly.

"Do you care about me even a little bit?" I ask hoarsely.

"No," he says again, taking another chunk out of my heart with his words.

"Do I mean anything to you?" I choke out.

"No," he mutters roughly, making the wound on my heart fester.

The tears are now pouring down my cheeks. I throw my hand up to my mouth when a sob escapes. I turn away from him and lie down on my side, the agony in my heart making it impossible to stay upright. All I want to do is curl into a ball and let out all the hurt he's caused me. I don't want to feel the pain anymore. I'm so tired of living in misery. I'm just tired, period. I just want to sleep and hopefully wake up numb.

"Chris—"

"Please leave." I cut him off, my voice sounding dead even to my own ears. There's nothing left to say. His three one-syllable words said enough. I'm done. I can't bear to hear his voice anymore. It's too painful.

"Chris—" He tries again.

"Leave!" I cry loudly and put my hands over my ears. I draw my knees to my chest and tuck my head into them. I feel like I'm going crazy. Insane from losing my baby and now Nick once again. He's the one who was helping me get through the loss. It was he who dragged me out of the depths of my despair. And now he's the one who's plunging me back inside, only this time it's much deeper and darker.

I don't know how long I keep my huddled position. I listen intently when I pull my hands from my ears. Nick's gone and the apartment is silent. I bring my hands up and put them both under my cheek. My head pounds from crying and my throat is dry. Even lying down, I feel the vertigo as my world turns fuzzy. My mind blanks of everything as I lie there and stare vacantly at my wall.

twenty-five

Nick

I LEAVE CHRIS'S APARTMENT with several feelings rushing through me. Pure rage at the guy that dared to lay a hand on her. Anger at her for being so damn foolish for going to the kid's house alone. Fear, because what happened to her could have been so much worse. Fear at what it would have done to me if it *had* been worse. And finally, brokenhearted at the damaged woman I left behind. The utter devastation in Chris's voice gutted me.

I lied to every single question she asked me before I walked out. I couldn't tell her the truth. I'm too afraid to admit it to myself, let alone her. When Mac called me earlier and told me what happened, I nearly lost my shit. I was in the middle of the grocery store with a cart full of food. I left the cart behind and rushed back home. Seeing Chris on the bed with her face busted up and knowing the outcome of her little trip could have been worse made me realize I wouldn't survive if something happened to her. I wouldn't be able to deal with it. The pain of losing Anna damn near killed me. If something happened to Chris, I know I wouldn't be able to live through that.

And that thought right there had me panicking. I had to get out of there. I can't do it again. I can't love someone so deeply and completely that I lose myself. I can't afford to give my heart away like that again.

I think this even knowing it's already done. Chris has already claimed my heart and now has it in her clutches.

That thought has me pulling over to the side of the road and resting my head on the steering wheel. I don't know which is worse: Giving myself to her wholly, only to have her snatched away; or willingly walking away from her, knowing I'm leaving my heart behind. Either way, my heart no longer belongs to me. I thought for a long time it was just a dead organ in my chest, no longer functioning. Chris has brought it back to life and made it her own. It no longer beats for me, but for her.

I ride around the dark streets of Jaded Hollow for a while. Not even realizing it, I find myself outside the iron gates of the Jaded Hollow Cemetery. My hands shake as I pull one open. Even though I've only ever been here once since Anna died, I know exactly where Anna's grave is. With laden feet, I walk toward the grave that will forever hold a piece of my heart. It's dark, but there are small solar lights along the path. The gray headstone comes into view, and I have to force my feet forward. My abdomen clenches with each step I take.

When I'm standing in front of it, the pain of not coming here sooner has me dropping to my knees. I rest my forehead against the cold stone.

"I'm so sorry, Anna," I tell her grave with tears gathering in my eyes. I try to force them away, but a few manage to slip free and fall to the ground. "I'm so sorry for not saving you. I'm sorry for lying to you. I tried so hard to be what you wanted me to be, but was just so scared." I whisper the last.

The freezing wind rustles around me as I kneel on the cold ground, hunched over. I pull back and gaze at headstone. I run my fingers over the words.

Anna Walker

DOB 03-26-1985

DOD 08-21-2014

Beloved daughter and friend. You will forever live in our hearts.

"I'll always love you, Anna Banana. But I'm going to try to do what you wanted. If she'll still have me. You'd like her, Anna. I think you would have picked her for me if you could. I promise not to wait so long to come see you next time."

I rub the smooth stone one more time before getting to my feet. I swipe the wetness from my face and tip my head back to the dark sky. I feel good, different, like the huge weight I've been carrying around on my chest for so long has finally lifted.

I walk away with determined footsteps, but I'll be back. Next time I'll bring Chris with me. I'm finally ready to open up to her and tell her all about Anna. Talking about Anna with Chris, letting her understand what Anna and I had together, will help me let her go. And will help me move forward with Chris. I want that more than anything, to finally let myself have a life with Chris. I just hope I'm not too late and that Chris will give me a final chance to prove to her I'm ready.

FIFTEEN MINUTES LATER, I'm opening the door to Chris's apartment. There're no lights on, so it's dark inside. Knowing she's probably asleep, I walk down the hallway on silent feet. I don't want to wake her, she's still not sleeping like she should, but the need to talk to her, to explain things and beg her to take me back is just too great to ignore. I can't wait until tomorrow.

When I walk into her room, she's on her side facing away from me. It's dark in her room as well. She looks sweet and childlike with her hands tucked beneath her cheek. I noticed she sleeps like that a lot.

I get down on my knees by her head and reach out to touch her on the shoulder. "Chris," I whisper, not wanting to startle her. She doesn't stir.

She has on a long-sleeved shirt, and even through the thin material I can feel the heat radiating off her body. Concerned, I flip on the light on her nightstand. Worry slams through me when I see her flushed face. When I pull the covers down her body, a wave of heat hits me in the face. I touch her cheek.

She's fucking hot to the touch.

"Chris," I say more loudly. She still doesn't move.

Panic starts to set in, and I roll her. She just flops to her back. With fear eating at me, I lean my ear over her lips and feel her warm breath hit my skin. My fingers desperately try to find her pulse in her wrist. When I do, a flash of relief hits me for a second before stark terror takes over. I sit on the side of the bed and give her a shake. My heart slams in my chest when she still doesn't respond.

What the fuck is wrong with her? my mind screams. *Why won't she wake up?*

I shake her more. "Sugar! Come on, baby! Wake up!"

Frantically grabbing my phone from my pocket, I dial 911 with shaky hands. I watch her as the phone rings, scared to take my eyes off her.

"911. Please state your emergency," comes a calm female voice over the line.

Pushing past the lump in my throat, I tell the operator how I found Chris. I explain the altercation from this afternoon and how she woke up not feeling well. I also explain she had a miscarriage a couple weeks ago.

"Sir, I need you to calm down," the lady says smoothly. That shit's easy for her to say. The person she loves isn't currently lying beside her, comatose.

She asks for my name, the number I'm calling from, and the address. I give her the information and explain we're in the apartment above Jaxon's Pub.

"We have someone on the way. They'll be there in ten minutes. I need you to tell me if she's breathing and has a pulse?"

I haven't removed my eyes from her and my hand is still on her pulse, I see her chest still rising and falling and I can still feel the pulse in her wrist.

"She has both," I tell her hoarsely. "Please tell them to hurry," I beg her.

"They'll be there as soon as they can, sir. I want you to stay on the line with me until they get there, okay?"

I nod, then tell her, "Okay."

It feels like it's forever before I hear the blare of the ambulance, and I swear every second we wait, the lump in my throat gets thicker and the sharp pain in my heart gets deeper. When I left earlier, she looked fine, except for a slight redness to her cheeks and the split lip and bruise. She didn't feel well when she woke up this morning, but we both thought it was just a cold coming on.

Why in the fuck did I leave her?

Again!

I fucking left her again when she needed me. Regret, shame, and a pain so piercing it snatches my breath grab me, suffocating me. What the fuck is wrong with me? It seems like every time I'm needed the most, I'm not there.

I swear to myself with everything I am I'll never leave Chris's side again. She's stuck with me. I'll handcuff her to my wrist if I have to.

I fucking finally hear the sirens. I don't want to leave her, but I rush from the room to the front door, pull it open at the same time I hear the bottom door open, and yell, "Up here!"

Not waiting for a response, I rush back to Chris. Seconds later, two paramedics enter the room carrying medical bags and a back-board. They rush to the bed.

"Sir, we need you to give us room."

It takes everything in me to let her hand go. Only knowing they need to do their work makes me let go.

I take a few steps back and watch helplessly as they huddle over her, taking her blood pressure, checking her temperature, and placing a breathing mask over her face.

"Is she going to be okay?" I choke out.

One of the paramedic looks at me with pity and my stomach drops to my damn toes.

"We can't answer that, sir. Once they assess her at the hospital, they can give you the answers you need."

His answer doesn't make me feel better at all. It only causes the ache in my chest to intensify.

I'm not surprised when Jaxon comes into the room, followed closely by Mia and Andrew. I'm sure they heard the sirens in the bar. I don't pay them any attention as I keep my damp eyes on Chris. They have her shirt open and are placing electrodes on her chest. That alarms me.

"What's wrong with her?" Jaxon asks, walking up to me.

"I don't know," I tell him gruffly. "She wouldn't wake up."

"What do you mean she wouldn't wake up?" Mia asks, watching the paramedics work.

"I don't fucking know," I tell her, my voice breaking. "We had an argument, and I left. I was only gone a couple hours and when I came back, I tried waking her up to talk, but she wouldn't. I shook her and called her name, but she wouldn't move. *Why the fuck isn't she waking up*?" A tear slides down my cheek.

Jaxon places his hand on my shoulder. "Breathe, Nick. They'll figure it out and take care of her. She'll be okay."

I take in a lungful of air, not realizing I was holding my breath. I pray he's right.

"Someone needs to call Jase."

"Already taken care of," Andrew says roughly behind me.

Once Chris is hooked up to all their medical shit, they lift her onto the backboard. I follow them when they lift her and walk out the room.

Jaxon stops me at the door. "We'll meet you there. You need to stay positive, Nick."

I nod numbly at him and walk away. I hold my breath as they carefully maneuver Chris down the stairs. The door at the bottom is still open and they carry her outside to the waiting ambulance. The lights flashing are almost blinding but I don't see them as I climb inside the back of the ambulance after one of the paramedics.

We sit for several minutes without moving. I want to scream at them to drive. The woman I love is lying unconscious. Why in the fuck haven't we left yet? I reach over and grab Chris's hand from on her stomach. It's hot. I keep my eyes on her face. She's wearing a breathing mask. Her face still looks flushed and she has a sheen of sweat on her forehead.

I bring her hand to my lips and hold it there. I stay that way the entire ride to the hospital, keeping her hand in mine and my eyes on her face, begging and pleading with anyone who will listen for her to be okay.

I SIT IN THE CHAIR by the hospital bed Chris is now lying on. I'm bent over with my head resting by her hips. I'm gripping her hand tight in mine. The bed beneath my head is soaked from my tears. I don't give a shit though. Jase and Andrew are on the other side of the bed. I don't know where Bailey, Jaxon, Mac, and Mia are, but I know they're in here somewhere.

The doctor just left after telling us what was wrong with Chris. His words completely shattered my world. I'm broken inside and the only way I can be put back together is when Chris wakes up.

If she wakes up. The thought brings a new wave of despair.

According to the tests, Chris has sepsis, an infection in her blood caused by not passing all of the placenta and fetus from the miscarriage. She's in a coma right now. They are running tests to see what the damage to her body is. They've also started her on a round of antibiotics to stop the infection. It's a waiting game right now until the results come back in.

My heart felt like it was ripped out of my chest, stomped on a few hundred times, and then set on fire when the doctor said the survival rate for severe sepsis is only 50 to 70 percent. I can't lose Chris. I thought I already found the one woman I was meant to give my life to, but I was wrong. Chris is that woman. She's the one I live and breathe for. She's the one my heart beats for. She's the one I'm meant to make a family with. And she's the one I'm meant to grow old with and die beside.

I squeeze my eyes shut and clutch her hand tighter when I remember how I walked out on her. I left with her believing I didn't love her, that I didn't care for her. The sound of her broken voice plays over and over in my heart. The questions she asked me and my stupid answers. Answers she believed, but answers that were far from the truth. And I may not ever be able to tell her how stupid and scared I was. How much I love her. She's only ever said she loved me once. I want to hear her say it again and again for a lifetime.

The others talk quietly around me, but I don't listen to them. The only sound I hear is the beeping of Chris's heartbeat from the machines they have her hooked up to. The doctor said her heart rate was low due to the infection. Hearing the steady beeping sound soothes me. When they first brought her in, her temperature was 104.1, which is dangerously high for an adult. Her hand is still warmer than it should be, but they've managed to bring it down some.

I feel a hand at my shoulder and look up to see Bailey standing beside me. She has on a pair of scrubs and gloves cover her hands, just as everyone else in the room does, except for me and Jase. Although the chances are low, there is a chance that the infection can be passed on to others. The nurses required everyone to wear the scrubs and gloves for protection. Jase and I refused. There's no way I'm putting something between Chris and me. If I become infected, then so be it. I wouldn't want to live without her anyway.

"Why don't you go grab some coffee?" she suggests softly.

I shake my head. "I'm fine." There's no way I'm leaving. I'll sit here until Chris shows me her beautiful eyes.

"Nick—"

"I'm not leaving her, Bailey," I tell her and turn back to Chris.

Her mouth is open around the breathing tube they have down her throat. They gave her one to take the stress off her breathing on her own. Her hair surrounds her head on the pillow. She's only been here for a few hours, but she looks like she's been here weeks. The red in her cheeks isn't as deep as before, but it's still present. She has several IVs hooked to her arms and she still has the electrodes on her chest so they can monitor her heartbeat and pulse.

"Okay," Bailey relents when she realizes I'm not going anywhere. "We'll bring something back for you."

I nod, not really caring. After she and Jaxon gets everyone's orders, they walk out of the room. I briefly notice Jase standing next to the bed, holding on to Chris's other hand. He also has tears in his eyes. Andrew stands beside him with one of his hands in one of Jase's back pockets. Down at the end of the bed are Mac and Mia. She's standing in front of Mac and he has one arm thrown over her shoulder. The look on both their faces is worry.

I lay my head back down and continue watching her.

FOUR DAYS LATER, I'm still in the same spot. The tests came back showing no damage to Chris's internal organs. Luckily, they caught the infection before it had a chance to do harm. They did emergency surgery to remove any remains of the fetus and placenta. The antibiotics and fluids the doctors have running through her body are healing her, but she's still not waking up. The doctors aren't sure why not. They removed the breathing tube yesterday, saying she no longer needs it. Their only real concern now is her heart. Although there was no damage found and they can't find any reason for it, her heart rate continues to be low.

I feel a presence at my side. I keep my eyes on Chris.

"Nick, you need to go get some rest," Mia says. "You've been here for days. Why don't you go home, take a shower, and get a few hours of sleep? We'll call you if there's any change."

I don't even consider her ridiculous suggestion. It's the same thing every day. They try to talk me into sleeping, or eating, or just going out to get some fresh air. And I always refuse. The blazes of hell couldn't pull me away. I already have to force myself to get up to use the bathroom and shower. I sleep and eat right here beside Chris. An orderly brought me a rollaway bed the first night, but I still haven't used it. My back's killing me from leaning over the bed and resting my head beside Chris to sleep, but I'll take the pain over being even across the room from her.

The only comfort I get is from the steady beat of her heart on the monitor. Only when I can't hold it anymore do I use the restroom, and my showers are the quickest I've ever taken. When I leave the room to do those things and can't hear the beep of the monitor, my heart pounds triple time in my chest, and I start to freak out. I become panicky and sweaty and have to rush back until I hear the sound. It's not lost on me that Chris is fighting to pick up her heart rate and when I leave the room mine beats too fast.

"Dude, you need to get up and move around some. At least go take a walk down the hall." This comes from Jase, who is standing leaning against the wall a few feet away.

Aside from me, Jase has been here the most. He's almost as bad as I am. But he at least leaves at night. I can see the wear and tear on his face and what this is doing to him. I was surprised when he didn't try to kick me out of the room when she was first brought in. I think some of it had to do with Andrew. He threw me dirty looks the first night, but since then his attitude toward me has changed. I don't know if it's because he sees how much this is tearing me up or he's just tired and too worried about Chris. Either way, I don't care. I would have laid his ass out if he even attempted to move me from my spot.

I look at him with bleak eyes. "Would you leave if it was Andrew?"

He drops his eyes from me, and I turn to Mia, "What if it was Mac? Would you leave to go sleep somewhere away from him?"

Her eyes, which are already sad, turn even more sorrowful. With a shake of her head, she utters, "No."

"I can't leave her. I'm scared something will happen if I'm not here," I whisper brokenly my deep-seated fear.

"She's gonna beat this," Jase says, his own voice rough. "She has to. She's too damn stubborn not to."

I pick up her limp hand and bring it to my mouth. I do this a lot. Having her as close as I can helps. I'd lie in bed with her if I could, but it's so damn small and I don't want to jar her.

"I'm going to go down to the cafeteria to grab something to eat," Mia says, getting up from the chair down at the end of the bed. "Do you want me to bring you something?"

"No," I say, without looking at her. I only eat when I have to and when I do, it turns my stomach.

"Nick, you need to eat something. You need to keep your strength up for Chris."

She's right. I've lost weight. I can see it in the mirror. My cheeks are narrower and my jeans hang loose on my hips. But I can't seem to care. If Chris doesn't live, I don't see a point anyway. I won't want to live if she doesn't. As soon as she opens her eyes, I'll start taking better care of myself. Until then, I'll only eat when I have to.

"Just go. I'll get something later," I tell her, knowing it's a lie.

She looks at me doubtfully, know it's a lie herself. Thankfully she doesn't call me out on it.

"I'll go with you," Jase says.

"Wait," I tell him, and he halts in his tracks. "There's something I need to tell you first."

He stays quiet as he waits for me to continue. This is something I need him to know because next to Chris, he's been the most affected by my actions. They're very close, and I know the pain I've put Chris through is something that was hard for him to witness.

"I know," I start, but stop to clear the dryness from my throat. "I know I'll never be what she deserves, I'll never be able to make up for the pain I've caused her, but I swear on my life, Jase, on everything I've ever held dear, that I will *never* hurt her again. I'll *never* leave her again. If she wakes up, *when* she wakes up," I reiterate because I refuse to think otherwise. "I will cherish her and love her for the rest of my life. And I'll do everything in my power to make her happy. I need you to understand that. I waited too fucking long to realize that

Chris is my life. I have a lot to make up for, and I know nothing I do *will* make up for it, but you need to know I'm sorry. So fucking sorry for everything I've done and all the shit I've put her through. You're her brother and you love her too. I know you've hurt as well because you had to watch her pain from my asshole behavior, and I'm sorry for that too."

He watches me while I talk, and I hold his stare. He needs to see in my eyes that I speak the truth. The rift between us made by my behavior needs to be closed. I want him to know that he never has to worry about Chris again. I'd rather cut off all four limbs than see even a smidgeon of hurt cross Chris's face.

After several tense seconds, with an unreadable expression, Jase walks to my side of the bed. I stand up from the chair I'm in and Jase places his hand on my shoulder.

"You have no idea how many times I wanted to kill you for what you've put her through," he says roughly, squeezing my shoulder tightly. "The kind of pain I saw on her face was one of the hardest things I've ever had to see. I hated seeing the love shine in her eyes when she looked at you, and then watching it be replaced by pain. You're right, she's my sister and I love her. And with that and because I've watched the pain you've been in these last few days, I realize now that only someone who loves deeply would hurt as much as you have been. I can't imagine the pain you went through when you lost Anna, but I'm glad you finally realized that my sister should be loved just as fiercely."

His words bring an ache to my chest. Love is nowhere near a strong enough word for what I feel for Chris. There's no way to describe the feeling I have in my heart for her. But it feels good to know he recognizes that I'll do anything to keep from hurting her again.

"Thank you." I push the words out through my tight throat.

Jase pulls me forward for a hug, surprising the shit out of me. What's even more surprising is when I hug him back. We cling to each other as we both grieve the woman lying in the bed beside us.

We pull back a few seconds later. I look over and see Mia standing by the door with tears rolling down her face.

Jase backs away from me. "We'll be back in just a bit," he says roughly.

I nob, sit back down, and grab Chris's hand again.

I'm glad Jase is leaving with Mia. It's just me and the two of them here at the moment. Mac's working and Jaxon's at the bar, Andrew is on his way here, and Bailey's at home with Amari. It's not often I get alone time with Chris. I know they'll all be by later though. They always stop by at least once a day. Karyn, Ethan, Jaxon and Mia's mom, Lily, her fiancé, Levi, their aunt and uncle, Maggie, Mac's mom, Nitra, even Jake and Jack, they've all come by. Chris's room is filled to bursting with flowers, teddy bears, and Get Well Soon balloons. She's become such a huge part of the community and they all love her.

I swallow back the tears that are threatening to spill over as I look at Chris. Bailey braided her hair the other day to keep it out of the way and so it won't get tangled. Her face is tilted toward me. Her thick lashes rest on her cheek. Her features are relaxed, as if in slumber. How much I wish that were true.

I reach up and run my finger down the soft skin of her cheek.

"Chris, baby, please come back to me," I whisper.

I lay my head on her stomach and feel the rise and fall. It gives me some comfort.

"I'm so sorry, Sugar. I'm sorry for being too fucking scared to realize what I had in you. And I'm sorry for lying to you."

I put her hand on my cheek as I stare up at her, tears leaking on her green-checkered nightgown.

I whisper the words I should have told her when she asked me those questions in her room four days ago.

"You don't mean anything to me, Chris, because you mean everything to me. I don't care for you a little bit, because I love you with everything I have in me. And you don't have just some of my love, you have every single ounce I have to give."

Keeping Chris's hand in mine, I lift my head, lean my elbows on the bed, bow my head for several seconds, and then lift it again.

"You once told me that love was endless, that we all have enough to give it to anyone we choose. You were right, Sugar. But you were also wrong. I'll always love Anna. The love we had was special. But my love for you is different than the love I have for her. My love for you is so much more. And it will only ever be yours. It runs all the way to my soul and fills every fiber of my being. It fills every gap and crevice until I'm completely consumed by it."

I take a deep breath, trying to pull air into my suddenly empty lungs. They fill with Chris's vanilla and sugar scent. It's hard to talk past the lump in my throat, but I need her to know how I feel. I don't know if she can even hear me, but I hope she can. I hope my words reach wherever she is right now in her mind. It tears me up thinking she may think I don't love her. That she lay in that bed in her apartment after I left thinking I didn't want her.

"Don't you see, Sugar," I say, my voice cracking. "You have to come back to me, because I'll be nothing without you. You hold my heart in your hands. Please don't crush it. Please don't leave me."

I drop my head back to the bed and let the pain wash over me. I jerk my head up when the steady beeping on the monitor turns to one long beep. I look at Chris and then to the monitor beside me and see the straight line across the screen.

"No, no, no! Jesus, no!" I yell. "Chris!"

I shoot up from the chair and hit the nurse call button. I lean over her and shout, "Help! Someone help!"

Unashamed tears pour down my face. Clutching her hand, I bend down until my forehead meets hers.

"Please, Chris," I cry. "Please, baby. You can't leave. I can't do this without you. Please, God. You have to fight, Chris. You have to come back to me." I beg and plead with her, trying everything to convince her that this is where she belongs. "Don't you fucking dare do this!" I shout the last.

A couple of nurses and a doctor come rushing in. A nurse shoves me out of the way. I barely stop the snarl and the fight to get back to her. I watch helplessly as the doctor barks orders to the nurses. They move quickly.

I bring my hands to the top of my head and lace my fingers together. My chest pumps heavily as the doctor starts compressions on Chris's chest. He does this several times, before one of the nurses places a bag valve mask over her mouth and pushes air into her lungs. They do this over and over again.

My knees become weak at the constant long beep that says her heart still isn't working. I fall back against the wall and sink down to my ass with my knees drawn to my chest. My elbows are on my knees, and I grab handfuls of hair and yank at the strands. The long beep pierces my ears, driving me out of my goddamn head. I want to block the noise, but I don't want to miss it if it starts a rhythm.

I barely register Mia, Jase, and Andrew rushing into the room. Mia comes to my side and gets down on her knees beside me. She tries to bring my head to her chest, but I don't let her, worried it'll block out the noise. She settles for wrapping her arms around my shoulders. She's crying, but I can't comfort her. All of my concentration is on the fucking constant beep that's not changing.

twenty-six

Chris

I'M LYING BACK IN a beautiful field filled with yellow flowers. The sun shines on my face, but it doesn't blind me. I look down at the silky green strapless dress I'm wearing. It feels good against my skin. Closing my eyes, I let the warmth of the sun wash over me and breathe in the sweet floral smell. Birds chirp in the distance, and I smile at the relaxing sound. I grab one of the flowers and feel the soft petals between my fingers.

A noise off to my left brings me out of my blissful state. I look over and see the silhouette of someone walking toward me. The sun is behind the person so I can't tell who it is. I sit up and slowly get to my feet as the person gets closer. I can tell it's a woman from the way she gracefully walks and the dress that floats behind her in soft waves.

For some reason I'm not surprised when I realize the woman is Anna. I've only seen her in pictures, but they don't do her justice. She's stunning. Her thick blonde hair falls over her shoulders and lies right above her chest. Her tanned skin is flawless. She has high cheekbones. Her gorgeous blue eyes watch me as she stops a few feet away. She smiles prettily, and I can't help but smile back at her.

"Hello, Chris. I'm so glad to meet you." Her voice is soft and innocent.

"Hello, Anna."

She shows no reaction to me knowing who she is.

"It's beautiful here. What is this place?" I ask and look around again at the gorgeous field.

"This is where you'll stay if you decide to not go back," she says.

I look back at her in confusion. "What do you mean? Go back where?"

I don't want to leave this place. It's perfect here. It's warm and safe.

"You know where, Chris."

I shake my head. "I don't—" I start, but then stop when I hear murmurs.

I look around trying to find the voice. It's familiar and it sounds sad. I don't like that it sounds sad. It causes my chest to hurt. Anna follows me as I look for the voice. I have this uncontrollable need to find it. The murmurs get louder so I know I'm getting closer. All of a sudden, my surroundings change. My field of flowers doesn't disappear, just dims some, almost like it fades a little. I'm still in the field, but I'm also in what looks like a hospital room.

The voice is stronger, and I whirl around.

"...you mean everything to me. I don't care for you a little bit, because I love you with everything I have in me. And you don't have just some of my love, you have every single ounce I have to give."

My brows pull down into a frown when I see Nick sitting in a chair, hunched over a figure in a bed. I step closer to see who it is, and suck in a shocked breath when I see me lying there.

Memories slam into me, and I stagger back a step. Anna lays her hand on my arm to steady me. I turn to look at her and see she's watching the scene in front of us unfold with tears in her eyes. I look back as Nick professes his love for me.

"You once told me that love was endless, that we all had enough to give it to anyone we choose. You were right, Sugar. But you were also wrong. I'll always love Anna. The love we had was special. But my love for you is different than the love I have for her. My love for you is so much more. And it will only ever be yours. It runs all the way to my soul and fills every fiber of my being. It fills every gap and crevice until I'm completely consumed by it."

I'm shocked at his words. The pain of our last moments together rob me of breath. He walked out after telling me he didn't care for me.

Why is he saying he loves me when he told me he didn't? And why is he crying over my still form?

"Because he does love you, Chris. And he's scared," Anna says. I don't know if I spoke out loud or if she's able to read my mind in this place.

"The question was written all over your face," she says, confirming she can read my mind.

She laughs softly before her face sobers.

"Do you see it, Chris?"

"See what?" I ask, still confused by everything that's going on.

I look back as people rush into the hospital room. Nick is shoved back. He stumbles back into a wall and slides down, clutching his hair as the people work on me. The utter devastation on his face has my hands going to my chest to try to relieve the searing pain stabbing at my heart. Tears drip freely from his eyes as he watches the doctor pump on my chest.

"Do you see how much he needs you?" Anna whispers at my side. "Do you see how you're meant to be back there with him and not in this place?"

I shake my head morosely and turn away from Nick, unable to watch anymore, not daring to believe the words he's saying or what I'm witnessing. "He'll never get over losing you. He'll never love me like he loves you. It hurts too much, knowing I'll never be good enough for him."

She takes my hand into hers. It's soft and warm.

"You're right. He'll never love you like he loved me. He'll love you more fiercely." I shake my head again, ready to protest. I desperately wish that could be true, but I know it can't be.

"He already does. It's you, Chris. It's you who's meant to be with him, not me. He wasn't broken when I left, merely damaged. You healed him because you're the only one who could. He needs you to breathe. He needs you to keep his heart beating. And he needs you to live. If you leave, he'll break and never recover. It's only you who can bring him back and make him whole again."

Her words send such a fierce hope through me. I want to believe Anna so much. I look back at Nick and see Mia with her arms around his shoulders rocking him gently. His pain-filled eyes are still locked on the bed where my body is. Could it be true? Can I take the chance of getting hurt again? I've been hurt by him so many times. I wouldn't survive it again.

"Trust me. Go back to him. Give him the life and love he deserves. You both deserve," Anna says gently.

"I'm scared," I whisper.

"It's okay to be scared," she responds tenderly. "But don't let fear take something away that could be spectacular and wondrous. If given the chance, Nick will love you beyond anything you've ever imagined."

I turn back to Anna, stunned again at her beauty. Her eyes plead with me to take a chance. I look back at Nick again. He looks broken, like his life is coming to an end. His eyes stay trained on me, desperate, like he's begging anyone and everyone who'll listen to bring me back. As scared as I am at the thought of being hurt again, there's no way I can't take that risk. I need Nick as much as he needs me. Hearing his words and watching him cry violently over the thought of losing me, the ruined look in his eyes, prove he does love me.

The realization of that gives me an intense feeling of euphoria. I give Anna a smile so big my cheeks hurt.

"I want to go back!" I tell her impatiently. Now that I understand where I need to be, with Nick, by his side, I'm anxious. I want to tell him I love him and hear him say it back to me. I want to feel his arms wrapped around me as he holds me. I want to breathe in his scent and taste his skin. I want to hear his laughter and see his eyes light up with mirth.

Anna's own smile is big, her eyes watery with tears. I know they're happy tears.

I hug her and whisper in her ear, "I'm so sorry for what happened to you, but thank you for giving him to me."

She pulls back. A tear trickles down her face as she cups my cheek.

"Thank you as well. For taking care of him. Love him hard for me."

"I will. Always."

twenty-seven

Nick

I JERK UPRIGHT WHEN the constant beep on the monitor changes. It stops, then seconds later it beeps again, and then again, and again. I furiously wipe my eyes and quickly climb to my feet, but have to put my hands on my knees when a wave of dizziness hits me. My eyes stayed glued on Chris though.

"We have a heartbeat!" The doctor says loudly.

Relief like I've never felt before hits me. My legs become weak, and I have to lean back against the wall so I don't fall back on my ass.

"Thank God," I hear Mia whisper beside me.

I look over at her and grab her in my arms. Over her shoulder I see Andrew has his arms wrapped around Jase from behind. He has tears falling from his eyes, but there's a look of hope on his face as well. I look back at Chris while the doctors check her over. They stay huddled around her for several minutes, making sure her heart stays pumping.

I watch in amazement as Chris's hand starts to move. My heart fucking soars with that small movement.

"Chris," the doctor calls, leaning over her. "Can you hear me?"

I get as close to the bed as I can. I don't know when so many people came in here, but it's now crowded.

The doctor turns his head and puts his ear close to Chris's mouth, like she's whispering something. I can't see her that well because people keep getting in my way. I want to knock the shit out of them, but that probably would end with me out in the hallway. There's no way that's happening. I still haven't seen her eyes and it's killing me. The only thing keeping me sane is the rhythmic sound coming from the monitor.

The doctor's eyes meet mine and he gives me a small smile.

"He's right here," he says and brings his eyes back to her. "Let me check a couple things first and then you can see him, okay?" He pulls his head back and for the first time since I left her four nights ago, I see her beautiful green eyes. I release a painful breath of air when they meet mine. Another tear falls down my face.

Her gaze holds mine as the doctor asks her a few questions. Her voice is a scratchy whisper as she answers. I wait impatiently at the end of the bed for him to finish, only just suppressing the urge to push him out of my way.

Fucking finally, he turns to me. "Don't keep her up. She needs to rest," he says sternly and then turns back to Chris. "I'll be back in a little bit to explain a few things."

He pats her hand and then turns and walks away, taking a few of the nurses with him. One stays behind and continues writing notes on Chris's chart.

I can barely contain my excitement as I walk around the bed. I feel like a kid who's gotten everything he's ever asked for at Christmas all at one time. I immediately grab on to Chris's hand and bring it to my lips. She looks rough. The hair that was in a braid has pieces falling out all over the place. She looks paler than normal. Her eyes have shadows under them, despite her being in a coma for days. And her face looks leaner, even though she was constantly being given nutrients through her IV. Even through all this, she's absolutely beautiful.

A tear slides out the corner of her eye. I lean down and kiss it away.

"Hi," I whisper with my forehead resting on hers. We both have our eyes open. This close I see the little black specks in the green.

"Hi," she whispers, her voice sounding weak. "What—" She croaks.

"Shit!" I reach over and pour some water in a Styrofoam cup. After putting a bendy straw in the cup, I help her sit up a little and bring the straw to her lips. There's a pinch in my heart when she winces from moving. She takes a few sips before lying back down, out of breath just from that movement alone. She wiggles her fingers by my hand and I know she wants me to grab it again. I lace our fingers together, kiss the back of hers, and bring her hand up to lie over my heart.

"What happened?" Her voice sounds clearer, but still weak.

"You were in a coma for four days. The placenta didn't pass all the way, so you developed an infection," I tell her and watch helplessly as pain flashes in her eyes, making my chest ache.

"I'm sorry—" I start. but her squeezing my hand stops me.

"Don't," she croaks out. "I love you."

I squeeze my eyes shut with her words. Another tear falls from me, landing on her cheek. I feel like a damn fountain. I've never cried so much in my life.

I open my eyes, stare deeply into hers, and tell her what I've should have told her a long time, but was too afraid to.

"I love you, Chris. So goddamn much."

Her eyes light up brighter than any firework I've ever seen.

"There's something I have to tell you, Sugar. And you need to let me say it, okay?"

She wants to protest, I can see it in her eyes, but after several seconds, she gives me a single weak nod.

"I am so sorry for what I said that night. I'm sorry for leaving you. I'm sorry for walking away from you when you told me about the baby. I'm so fucking sorry for every single pain I've caused you." I stop and close my eyes for a moment, the reminder of every shitty thing I've done to her momentarily robbing me of breath.

"I was so scared," I whisper hoarsely. I open my eyes and bring my face away from hers a few inches. I want a clear view of her face. "I'm still terrified that I'll lose you somehow, but there's no way I can stay away. It's just not something I have in my power. You should hate me and never want to see my face again, but I swear, Chris, on everything I am, I'll never let you down again. I'll never walk away from you again. I'll always be where you need me to be. And I'll always love you with every piece of myself."

The smile that comes across her face is one that I want to see a hundred times a day, and I'll make it my mission to give her something to smile at like that for the rest of my life.

Her smile dims some and with it my world darkens.

"I love you, Nick," she says shakily, her words bringing my world back to burning bright. "And I know you love me." Something flashes across her eyes that has my heart skipping a beat. "I saw you." She halts for a minute to take in an unsteady breath. I'm about to tell her stop, that she can talk later after she rests, but she stops me. "No, I need to say this." After a second, I nod. "Anna was with me. We saw you when you thought I was dying on this bed. I never want to see that look on your face again. It torn me to shreds. It was Anna that made me realize I had to come back. It was she who gave me to you."

Her words shock me to my core, but at the same time don't surprise me. I always knew Anna was watching over me. As clichéd as it sounds, I've felt her presence with me from the beginning. I think that's why I've held on to her for so long. It never really felt like she was gone. After my visit to the gravesite, the presence was no longer there.

It would be just like Anna to send someone for me. There's no way she could have picked someone better than Chris. She's perfect. More fucking tears appear in my eyes, but this time I blink them away.

Thank you, Anna, I send up silently to her.

A throat clearing has me and Chris turning to Jase, who is now standing on the other side of the bed. His eyes are red rimmed from crying. The look on his face is a mixture of astounding relief, happiness, and worry.

"Chris," he whispers brokenly.

As much as I don't want to, I let go of her hand and step back to give them privacy. Chris notices and immediately turns her head my way.

"Stay. Please don't go anywhere."

Her pleading words and the panic in her eyes have me stepping forward again.

"I'm not going anywhere. Ever again."

Content with my words, she turns back to Jase, who picks up her hand.

"Thank fucking God you're okay," he breathes, and bends down to kiss her cheek. "You can't ever do that again, Chris. I can't watch that shit again," he finishes, his voice cracking.

She smiles tenderly at him and whispers roughly, "I'm sorry."

"Don't apologize. Just promise me you won't ever do that shit again."

Her smile widens when she whispers, "I promise."

"Welcome back." Jase smiles back at her. "Come here." He bends and carefully gives her a hug. His shoulders shake silently as he buries his face in her hair. When he pulls back, it's Chris who wipes his tears away with a quivering hand.

"I love you, big brother."

"Love you, too, little sister."

Andrew steps up to the bed next. Jase moves to the side to give him room.

"Hey beautiful," Andrew's deep voice rumbles.

"Hey."

"You had us scared for a bit there."

"Yeah," Chris replies with a frown.

One good thing about Andrew is that he can make anyone laugh in any situation with his warped sense of humor. And right now he doesn't disappoint when he says, "Now that you're back, maybe I can finally get the Jase lovin' I've been missing for days. Poor boy's been too worried to fuck."

"Oh, God, Andrew." Chris groans, turning her head to the side and sputtering out a strained laugh. "I don't need to know that."

Even though I don't need that visual in my head, I can't help the laugh that slips out.

Jase slaps Andrew's ass and scowls at him. "Dude, that's my sister."

Andrew turns to him and winks. "So, she knows we fuck. Hell, she's practically seen us humping on the dance floor at Jaxon's."

Chris groans again and rolls her eyes, but there's mirth there. The sight sends a shot of joy straight to my chest and damn near slams me backwards.

"Yeah, but she doesn't need to hear about it," Jase retorts.

Andrew just grunts, leans down, and places a soft kiss to her lips. The move should make me jealous, but doesn't. I know that this is one of Andrew's ways of showing affection and that he doesn't mean anything sexual by it.

Mia, who's been standing beside me, steps closer to the bed. No words are spoken as her hip pushes me out of the way so she can lean over to give Chris a hug. When the two girls pull back, Mia has tears silently streaming down her cheeks as she brushes back some of Chris's hair that's fallen on her face.

"I'm so glad you're okay," Mia chokes out. She's not the type to get emotional, so witnessing it now is hard to see.

"Thank you," Chris says in a low voice, a small smile tipping her lips up.

Chris turns her head once Andrew pulls back, and I'm glad to have her eyes back on me. Eyes that have black rings around them and look like they can barely stay open. Fear shoots through me with the thought of her going back to sleep. What if she doesn't wake up again? I know it's irrational and something I'll need to get over, but I can't help the fear. She needs to rest as much as possible so her body can heal, just like the doctor said.

I push the stabbing fear away.

Sitting on the side of the bed, I grab her hand. "You need to get some rest."

Her eyes begin to droop and her body sags back on the bed. She smiles tiredly. "You look like shit, Nick. You need to sleep too." Her voice still sounds scratchy.

I chuckle. "I will."

It's going to be a long time before I'm able to sleep again. I'm too scared to have my eyes off her long enough to close them to get any sleep.

"You'll be here when I wake up, right?" she slurs, unable to hide the fear in her voice. Her eyes start drifting shut.

I kiss the palm of her hand and tell her quietly, "Go to sleep, Sugar. I wouldn't be anywhere else. I'm never leaving your side again."

Relief flashes in her gorgeous green eyes when she opens them one last time. I shove the fear away when they close. She looks just like she did when she was in her coma.

"Lie with me," she whispers.

Although the bed is small and I'm sure half my ass will be hanging off, there's no way I can tell her no. To have Chris fall asleep lying beside me is something too great to pass up. I was so scared I wouldn't have this again.

Appearing too weak to move, I gently scoop Chris up and shift her over a couple inches. She slits her eyes open as I lie down beside her. I hear a shuffling sound and look over to see Andrew, Jase, and Mia standing in the hallway talking to Bailey and Jaxon. All of them look over, and I can't help the smile that comes across my face. My girl came back to me. To all of us, but especially to me.

"Love you," she mumbles sleepily.

I bring my eyes back to her and take in her beautiful face. I lean over, kiss her soft lips, and whisper, "Love you, too, Sugar. More than you'll ever know."

epilogue

Chris
Six months later…

I WAKE TO FEEL the sheet on my back slowly move down my body until it's at my knees. Then a rough hand starts where the sheet stops and barely grazes up my leg, over my butt cheek, then my side. I moan and arch my back because it feels good, but also tickles. Warm breath caresses my ear as I'm kissed on the back of my neck. I'm on my stomach, naked, with my face turned away and one of my legs bent. The hand reaches my shoulder, slides across it, and then travels down along my spine until it meets my ass. I hold my breath with anticipation as just the fingertips travel down the crack of my ass and find my wet center. Instead of sliding between my lips like I desperately need them to, two of the fingers separate and scissor on either side.

"Nick, please," I moan into my pillow.

"Hush, Sugar," he whispers against my ear. "Let me play."

I want to protest and demand he touch me where I need him the most, but I hold it in and let him play like he wants.

The fingers run back and forth several times, tormenting me, before he pinches my clit between them. Fireworks shoot behind my eyes, and I cry out.

"Oh, God!"

Lips meet my neck once again. Nick latches his teeth there and sucks greedily with a groan. He works my pussy as he lays open-mouthed kisses along my neck and shoulders. My hands fist in the covers while I fight the urge to roll over, climb on top of him, and take his cock deep inside me.

The bed shifts and a second later, Nick's weight is on me as he straddles my upper legs. His chest meets my back and his cock nudges my butt.

"Spread your legs for me, baby," he says, nipping at my ear.

I do as he says, but I can only spread them a few inches because he has both of his legs on the outside of mine.

He reaches between us and a second later his hardness meets my soaked pussy. I whimper with the explicit sensations it sends through me. I will never, for as long as I live, get tired of the feeling of having Nick touch me. Every time he does, it feels like the first time.

He doesn't enter me like I expected him to. Instead he pushes his cock down until it lies flat against my pussy, and slides it longways between my folds. When it nudges my clit, I see a thousand starbursts behind my eyes.

He lifts his hips slightly, sliding against me over and over again. He has one arm underneath one of mine. With it, he grabs a handful of hair and tips my head up. I can't go far because of the way I'm lying with his weight on me. But it's far enough for him to reach my lips. He slips his tongue inside and tangles it with mine. His taste is another thing I will never get tired of.

"Fuck, baby, you drive me fucking insane," he says against my lips.

He plays with my pussy with his cock, and I lie there and enjoy every second. I start lifting my hips to meet his short thrusts. I'm so close to falling over the edge; I just need a few more strokes. When he senses my impending orgasm, he stops pumping and settles his weight on me. I yank at the sheets in my hand and groan in frustration.

"Do you want my cock in you, Chris?" he asks huskily.

"You know I do, Nick. Please!" I whimper.

When I try to lift my hips to get him to move, he chuckles.

Fucking chuckles.

"I want to hear you say it. Tell me what you want, Sugar."

For some reason he likes for me to tell him when I want him inside me. I love hearing him talk dirty, but I don't do it often. It's not that I don't want to, I just feel weird doing it.

"Please fuck me, Nick. I want to feel your cock sliding inside me. I *need* it."

"Yeah, baby, I know you need it," he groans. "I do too."

Finally, he pulls his hips back, notches the tip at my opening, and slowly slides inside me. He doesn't stop until he's in as far as he can go.

"Ahhh!" I cry out.

"Shit," he grunts. "You feel *so fucking good*."

He holds still and doesn't move. Frustrated, I tighten my walls around him. He has to move before I explode into a ball of burning need.

"Oh, fuck, baby," he hisses. "You can't do that."

"Then move, damn you!" I growl at him over my shoulder and buck my hips upward.

"If I move, then it's all over." He grabs my hair again and tilts my head back, exposing my throat. Leaning forward, he plants his lips there and licks against the skin.

"Nick, please," I beg him and clench around him again.

With a snarl, he gets up, grabs my hips, lifts me so we're both on our knees, and slams his hips forward. He groans, while I shout.

"Yes!"

This is what I need, what I crave. Him losing control until he has no choice but to take me the way I want.

He pulls back until just the tip is inside and pounds forward again. And again, bringing my hips back to meet his forceful thrusts.

He hits something inside me that has me screaming his name in pleasure.

"This good enough for you, Sugar?" he growls.

"Ah, God, yes," I sob. This is just what I wanted.

All of a sudden, he stops, and I want to cry. He pulls out, and before I know it, I'm flipped over to my back. Grabbing my hips, he lifts them until my legs are over his. Next, he reaches down and picks me up under my arms and I'm lifted so I'm straddling him with my arms around his neck. He sits back on his legs.

"Your turn. Work my cock, baby."

I take the tip of him and place it at my pussy and slide all the way down until my pelvis meets his. I throw back my head and moan deeply. He slides his arms around my back, pulling me forward until my chest meets his. His face lands in the crook of my neck, where he starts sucking and nipping. I ride him up and down. With each downward motion, I grind my clit down on him, sending shock waves all over my body. His hands grab my butt, and he helps lift me so I'm moving faster.

Bursts of electricity burn all over my body. When I get close, I open my eyes and lock on to his. He's looking at me with such love and wonderment. I lean forward and kiss him. I love it when he looks at me like that. I have no doubt that I'm the happiest woman alive. There's no way anyone could ever be happier than me. Nick gives me that. He makes my world perfect.

Our movements become frantic. I rock up and down as he continues to lift me. The sensations running through my body are almost too much. I feel the first wave of my orgasm in my limbs. They go limp and tingly. Next is my lower stomach, as it clenches. Then my head goes fuzzy. It completely takes over my body.

I keep my eyes on him as my body ignites, sending me over the edge of bliss.

"Chris," he whispers. His body tenses and he brings his arms tighter around me as he finds his own release.

I rest my head on his shoulder and breathe in deeply, trying to pull in much-needed air. His chest rises and falls as he tries to catch his own breath.

Keeping us connected, he leans forward until we're lying side by side with one of one my legs still wrapped around his hip. He cups my cheek and gets closer for a kiss.

"I love you," he says softly when he pulls back.

And again, that's another thing I'll never tire of. He says it all the time, and I know each time he means it because it reflects in his eyes.

"I love you, too."

A cold draft overcomes me when he pulls away, dislodging us. He doesn't go far though, just reaches over and grabs something from the drawer in the nightstand. My breath catches when I see what he's holding. It's something I've secretly wanted, but was too scared to hope for.

He watches me closely as he holds the small black box in his hand. I roll to my back when he hovers over me. He opens the box and places it on my chest right below my boobs. I look down at it. It's stunning. It's a silver band with a sapphire surrounded by smaller trilliant-cut diamonds. I look back at him with tears in my eyes.

"I wanted to plan this big gesture, but nothing I thought of was good enough. There's no way I could ever do or say anything that will show you how much I love you. If I lived a thousand lifetimes, it wouldn't be long enough. I'm here, living and breathing, because you bring me those things. You give me life, and the air I breathe. You make my heart beat and hold my soul in place."

He grabs my hand, kisses the palm, and brings it to his heart.

"Will you marry me, Chris, and continue to be my reason for living?"

With tears streaming down my face and my heart filled with so much love, I launch myself at him and wrap my arms around his neck. I force him to fall back with me and seal our lips in a crushing kiss.

"Yes! Yes! Yes," I cry against his lips. "A thousand times yes, Nick! There's nothing that could keep me from marrying you."

His lips steal my breath as he crashes them down on mine. He frames my face when he pulls back.

"Thank you for not giving up on saving me," he says quietly. "Thank you for bringing me back."

I reach up and put my hands over his.

"Thank you for letting me."

Nick
One year later...

I WATCH AS THE STUNNING vision appears at the end of the aisle. She takes my breath away every time, but seeing her now in her pure white silk gown that hangs over her milky white shoulders, and knowing she's about to become Mrs. Daniels, makes me dizzy. Her hair is up off her shoulders with a few curled tendrils floating down. Small white flowers here and there stand out against her red hair. Even from across the distance separating us, I can see the bright green in her eyes as she looks at me. Her smile stretches across her face, making her already beautiful face gorgeous.

We're at Jaxon's lake because Chris said she always wanted to get married outside with the sun shining down on her. It's a small gathering of just our family and close friends. Her parents are here as well. They started coming around when they heard what happened to her. I could tell Chris was upset when they showed up, but she lost her ire when she saw the devastation on her mom's face. Their relationship is still strained, especially between Chris and Jase and their dad, but it's getting better. Jase hasn't forgiven him yet, but he's not as hostile toward him as when they first arrived in town. I've seen the way their dad looks at them both. I still don't like the man because of how he treated Chris and Jase, but I can see the remorse and regret in his eyes. I'm still reserving judgement. He just better watch himself.

I keep my eyes focused on Chris as the "Wedding March" starts.

Instead of her dad beside her, she opted to have Jase walk her down the aisle. I saw the pain on Ben's face when she announced this, but I think he understood.

Chris has her arm through Jase's as they slowly walk down the aisle.

Too fucking slowly.

I've been waiting for this moment since Chris opened her eyes over a year and a half ago. I knew in that second I was going to marry and spend the rest of my life with her.

I smile as I lose patience and start walking down the aisle to meet them. There're murmurs as I walk by people, but I pay them no attention. Her eyes widen when I'm standing in front of her.

"What are you doing?" she whispers and flicks eyes to the left, right, and then back to me.

Jase's lips quirk up as he gives me her hand. I bend down and scoop her up into my arms. She squeals and laughs as I turn back to the minister. People laugh and clap as I walk down the aisle.

"You were taking too long," I tell her as I eat up the space between us and the man who's going to make Chris mine forever.

She kisses my cheek and laughs, her eyes crinkling at the corners. "You're crazy, you know that?"

I look down at her and smile. "Only about you, Sugar. You make me crazy."

We reach the minister and I reluctantly put her down. If it were up to me, we'd get married with her still in my arms, but I don't think Chris would go for that.

Not caring that I'm not supposed to yet, I lean down and kiss her sweet lips. She tastes just like she always does, vanilla and sugar. It's my favorite flavor.

I pull back and lean forward again to kiss the tip of her nose. She scrunches it up at me, making me chuckle.

"Dude, you're supposed to wait until *after* you get married to kiss her," Andrew says at my side.

Without taking my eyes off Chris, who's quietly snickering, I remind him, "Like you waited with Jase?"

"Touché," he responds dryly, then chuckles.

"It's get married time. You ready?" I ask Chris.

I know she is, but I want to hear her say it.

"I've never been more ready."

Her answer and smile have my own lips tipping up into a big-ass grin as we both turn toward to the minister to start the rest of our life.

Six years later...

CHRIS AND I SIT on the porch swing I installed several years ago, enjoying the warm spring weather. She's curled up to my side with her feet drawn up beside her on the swing, her cup of coffee clutched between her hands. My arm is slung over her shoulders as I push us back and forth. I bring my cup of coffee to my lips for a swallow and set it back down on the table.

"Momma and Daddy, look how high I can go!" comes a sweet high-pitched voice.

We both look over at our daughter, Grace, and watch as she pumps her little legs as hard as she can. Her long brown hair flies around her face. Her yellow dress billows back and forth. She's not able to go very high with her short five-year-old legs, but she seems to think she's almost reaching the sky. Whatever brings a smile to her beautiful face is fine with me. She tips her head back and laughs loudly. Chris and I laugh with her.

She turns back to us with Chris's green eyes.

"Did you see?" she yells, eagerly awaiting our approval.

Chris moves away from me and we both get up and walk hand in hand off the porch toward our daughter.

"We did see," Chris says, grinning. "You're getting higher and higher every day. Pretty soon you'll be able to reach heaven."

I move behind Chris, wrap my arms around her middle, and rest my chin on her head.

"Maybe one day I'll be able to reach Anna," Grace says innocently as she kicks her legs back and forth.

At the mention of Anna's name, it's not pain I feel, but immense gratitude. It's because of her I have Chris and our precious Grace. I would never wish what happened to her, and I still regret I wasn't there to save her from that pain, but I realized a long time ago that things are the way they are because they are meant to be that way. Anna will always be my first love, but Chris is the person I'm meant to love for the rest of my life.

"You'll get to meet Anna one day, sweetie. I promise," I tell her.

She smiles her gorgeous smile at me. "I know I will, Daddy."

Grace knows all about Anna. It's not just Chris and I who have told her about Anna. Everyone talks about her. The room in the basement is cleared of all of Anna's things. I kept some pictures, but gave a lot of them to Lily, Jaxon, and Mia. We have a couple on the shelf in our living room and the painting Anna painted that hung in the living room is now in Grace's room. Grace loves it. Chris and I have both caught her just lying there staring at it. When we asked her about it, she just shrugged her little shoulders and said she likes looking at it. I think it's more than that. I think she feels a connection to the painting, like she's somehow connected to Anna in some spiritual way, as crazy as that sounds.

I think back to the dream I had all those years ago of me and Anna watching the little girl on the tire swing, while a distraught Chris looked on. Anna told me the little girl could be my future if I wasn't too late. After that dream, I assumed the little girl was the baby Chris carried and lost. I was too late to have that future, just as Anna warned me. It wasn't until after Chris had Grace that I realized I was wrong. As sad as it is, the baby Chris lost was a tool to help me realize what I wanted. Chris and a future with her. I'll always mourn our unborn child, but she still had a purpose, and she fulfilled it by bringing me and Chris together. The little girl on the swing wasn't the baby we lost. She was Grace, and Anna gave her to us.

I pull Chris closer to me and kiss the side of her neck. Her vanilla and sugar scent surrounds me, and I breathe it in deep.

Grace continues to giggle as she swings higher and higher. A patch of clouds open up and sunlight shines down on her, illuminating her dark brown hair. I turn Chris in my arms and look into her green eyes. She gazes up at me with the same expression she always uses to look at me; love and adoration.

"I love you, Sugar." I speak the words I'll never be able to say enough. And she replies with words I'll never hear enough.

"I love you, Nick. Forever."

I bend and kiss the soft lips of the woman I'm lucky enough to call my own, knowing that no matter what, I'll always cherish her and everything she's ever given me.

other books by alex

JADED HOLLOW SERIES

Beautifully Broken

Wickedly Betrayed

Wildly Captivated

Perfectly Tragic

Jaded Hollow: The Complete Collection

THE CONSUMED SERIES

Mine

Sex Junkie

Shamelessly Bare

Hungry Eyes

The Consumed Series: The Complete Collection

HELL NIGHT SERIES

Retribution

Vindication

Vengeance

Wrath

The Hell Night Series: Complete Collection

WESTBRIDGE SERIES

Pitch Dark

Broad Daylight

Salvaged Pieces

BULLY ME SERIES

Treacherous

Malicious

ITTY BITTY DELIGHTS

Heels Together, Knees Apart

Teach Me Something Dirty

Filthy Little Tease

For I Have Sinned

Doing Taboo Things

Lady Boner

Lady Boss

Lady Balls

Lady Bits

Itty Bitty Delights: 1-5

Itty Bitty Delights: 6-9

STANDALONES

Whispered Prayers

Haunted

Dear Linc

Lead Player

Just the Tip

Uncocky Hero

Until Never

about the author

Alex Grayson is a USA Today bestselling author of heart pounding, emotionally gripping contemporary romances including the Jaded Series, the Consumed Series, The Hell Night Series, and several standalone novels. Her passion for books was reignited by a gift from her sister-in-law. After spending several years as a devoted reader and blogger, Alex decided to write and independently publish her first novel in 2014 (an endeavor that took a little longer than expected). The rest, as they say, is history.

Originally a southern girl, Alex now lives in Ohio with her husband, two children, two cats and dog. She loves the color blue, homemade lasagna, casually browsing real estate, and interacting with her readers. Visit her website, www.alexgraysonbooks.com, or find her on social media!

Printed in Great Britain
by Amazon

41271248R00219